THE DERAILLEURS

...vels include the National Book Award
...*at*, the *New York Times* bestseller *The*
... the international bestseller *We Need to*
... and the *Sunday Times* bestseller *Big Brother*.
... National Short Story Award in 2014. Her
...has appeared in the *Guardian* and the *New York*
...he *Wall Street Journal* and many other publications.
...s in London and Brooklyn, New York.

...se for *Checker and The Derailleurs*:

'...nny, clever, and touching . . . [Shriver's] own lyrics are terrific.
...commended'   *Library Journal*

'...hriver is a lively storyteller, and she keeps readers guessing to
...e end . . . More compelling even than the plot turns are
...hriver's insights into human nature . . . She has a keen eye for
...he archetypal characters common to human tribes everywhere.
Checker and The Derailleurs, like its beguiling protagonist, is
hard to forget'   *People*

'Shriver is a gifted, expansive writer, and her novel should be a
big hit with rock music fans, who have been so poorly served
by fiction writers in the past'   *Booklist*

'[An] engaging novel . . . Checker triumphant is the key, a boy
so radiant that his creator has fallen in love with him. And so
has the reader'   *Publishers Weekly*

D0994179

'It is a joy to find a book that both glitters and glows'
WEBR Radio, Buffalo, NY

'Passion, poetry, and insight. She gives us fiction that breathes and dances and taps out time . . . an accomplishment . . . Her talent is certain'
The Grand Rapids Press

'Brilliant and funny; Checker lives on in memory as a complex fictional creation'
The Milwaukee Journal

'Shriver exhibits a real fondness, and at times a flair, for language. She writes well when describing music an especially difficult task'
New York Newsday

'*Checker And The Derailleurs* is an unusual teen novel, mostly because Lionel Shriver, a lioness of style, has disguised her novel of 19-year-olds in a mainstream adult vehicle. . . . The author maintains a beat throughout the novel that is fast, steady, and rhythmic. She doesn't turn the volume down and her book will appeal to anyone over 14 including parents of 19-year-olds'
Santa Cruz Sentinel

'Some of the observations in this book are wrapped so tightly around my own experience of feelings, it seems I have been visited by the friend I always needed or the artist I always wanted to be. It honors the individual and reminds us all of the painful fullness of every soul'
Grace Slick, former lead singer,
Jefferson Airplane

ALSO BY LIONEL SHRIVER

CHECKER AND THE DERAILLEURS

LIONEL SHRIVER

b

THE BOROUGH PRESS

The Borough Press
An imprint of HarperCollins*Publishers*
1 London Bridge Street
London SE1 9GF

www.harpercollins.co.uk

This paperback edition 2015
1

First published in the USA by Farrar, Straus and Giroux 1988

A catalogue record for this book is
available from the British Library

ISBN: 978-0-00-756403-3

The author gratefully acknowledges permission to quote from the following published works: "Bang the Drum All Day" by Todd Rundgren, copyright © 1983 Fiction Music, Inc./Humanoid Music (BMI), all rights reserved / "Eleanor Rigby," words and music by John Lennon and Paul McCartney, copyright © 1966 Northern Songs Ltd., all rights for the U.S., Canada and Mexico controlled and administered by Blackwood Music Inc. under license from ATV Music (MACLEN), all rights reserved, international copyright secured, used by permission / "Darkness" by Stewart Copeland, copyright © 1981 Reggatta Music, Ltd., administered by Atlantic Music Corporation / "Dancing in the Dark" by Bruce Springsteen, copyright © 1984 Bruce Springsteen, all rights reserved, used with permission / "Blinded by the Light" by Bruce Springsteen copyright © 1973 Bruce Springsteen, all rights reserved, used with permission / "Save the Life of My Child" by Paul Simon, copyright © 1968 Paul Simon, used by permission / "Positively Fourth Street" by Bob Dylan, copyright © 1965 Warner Brothers, Inc., all rights reserved, used by permission / "Love over Gold" by Mark Knopfler, copyright © 1982 Chariscourt Ltd. (PRS), all rights administered in the U.S. and Canada by Almo Music Corp. (ASCAP), all rights reserved international copyright secured / "The Man's Too Strong" by Mark Knopfler, copyright © 1985 Chariscourt Limited (PRS), all rights administered by Rondor Music (London) Ltd., administered in the U.S. and Canada by Almo Music Corp (ASCAP), all rights reserved, international copyright secured.

The drawings reproduced in *Checker and The Derailleurs* are by Lionel Shriver.

Set in Adobe Garamond by Palimpsest Book Production Ltd,
Falkirk, Stirlingshire

Printed and bound in Great Britain by
Clays Ltd, St Ives plc

MIX
Paper from
responsible sources
FSC® C007454

To someone who doesn't deserve it, as he very well knows

Well I have tried to be meek
And I have tried to be mild
But I spat like a woman
And sulked like a child . . .
And I can still hear his laughter
And I can still hear his song
The man's too big
The man's too strong

DIRE STRAITS
"The Man's Too Strong,"
Brothers in Arms

Checker's favorite color is red

1 / blinded by the light

Foreboding overcame Eaton Striker well before The Derailleurs began to play. Much as Eaton would have preferred to chum obliviously with his friends, he could only stare at the stage as the drummer stepped up to those ramshackle Leedys and the damned skins began to purr.

"Who *is* that?" asked Eaton, not sure he really wanted to know. The drummer percolated on his throne, never still, *bloop, bloop*, like coffee in the morning—that color; that welcome.

"*Checker Secretti*," said Brinkley, with irritating emphasis. "Where have you been, the moon?"

"He's talking to his traps!" exclaimed Eaton, in whose disturbed imagination the instruments were answering back.

"Yeah, he did that last time," said Brinkley the Expert. "Checker's a bit touched, if you ask me."

"I didn't." Eaton slouched in his chair.

The humidity here was curiously high. A plumbing problem in the basement dripped right on the heater, so the whole club felt like a steam room—there was actually a slight fog; vapor beaded on the windowpanes. A proliferation of candles sent soft, flickering profiles against the walls. With its vastly unremarkable decor, Eaton couldn't explain the crawling effect of the place as he nestled down in the seductively comfortable chair, taking deeper, slower breaths and saying nicer things to his friends. Eaton squirmed. He tried to sit up straight. He looked suspiciously into his Johnnie Walker, thinking, *Black, hah!* since places like this bought gallons of Vat 69 and funneled it into name-brand bottles. Yet this was confoundingly good whiskey, some of the best he'd ever tasted. The waitress, though definite woof-woof material at first glance, now looked pretty. Eaton felt he was drowning and fought violently to rise to the surface, to breathe cold, hard air, to hear his own voice with its familiar steeliness, instead of the mushy, underwater murmur it had acquired since they'd sat down.

The drums sounded so eager, so excited. Checker laid a stick, once, *bip*, on the snare and it jumped; so did Eaton. Every time a quick *rat-tat* rang through the room, the audience looked up; the waitress turned brightly to the stage. When Checker nudged the bass to adjust the blanket curled inside its shell, women at tables stroked their own hair; men extended languorously into the aisles. The beater sent a shudder through the length of Eaton's body.

Eaton had been taking drum lessons from an expensive instructor in Manhattan since he was seven, and though he hardly ever heard a song that was fully to his liking, when that rare riff floated over the airways a cut above the ordinary fill, he took notice. Eaton was a snob, and would admit it to anyone, but in some ways he really *was* better than these people, rightfully not at home in provincial Astoria. He was bright; he had an uncanny sense of other people, even if it was largely for their failings; and he knew excellence. So while somewhere in the boy's mind he was aware that he didn't hear it when he himself played, he was hearing it now.

The first phrase rose and fell like a breath. Sticks rippled like muscle, and teased, tingling, resting on the edge of the ride. Again, Eaton involuntarily inhaling with them, the blond sticks curled up to the snare and spread to the toms, the crash, to *ting, ting, ting* . . . Someone laughed. Checker skimmed his tips across the supple ridges of the brass, raising the long, dark hairs on Eaton's arms. Yet Eaton could see Checker was just loosening up, ranging around the drums as if stretching at the start of a day. He kept low through the whole of "Frozen Towels." Slowly through "Fresh Batteries," though a strange blissful smile crept onto his face, and the music began to move underneath like lava with a crust on top—the cooler surface would crack in places, show red, let out steam; all at once the music would move forward, rushing into the club like a flow, veined with the sure signs of a dangerous interior. The keyboardist had to stand up, pushing his chair back; the musicians out front gradually stepped away to give the drums more space, until, there, pouring from the back of the stage, came an unrestrained surge of rhythm like a red wall of melted rock.

Yet later Checker slowed the lava, the blood, to a sly trickle. The restraint hurt to hear. The rest of the band, too, retreated to small, stingy sounds. The club grew stupendously quiet. Not a drink clinked, not a shoe scuffled. The sax thinned to a spidery thread of a note; the keyboard took to a small high chord; the bassist and lead guitarist hugged their instruments selfishly to their bodies, and no sooner struck a note than took it back. But quietest of all were the drums, pattering, the sticks like fingertips, until Checker was no longer on the heads themselves but only on the rims, ticking, rapid, but receding all the more. The audience was leaning forward, barely breathing. But the sound, meanly, left them, though it was a good five seconds before they realized that the band had ceased to play.

In the midst of this silence Checker began to laugh. "Clap, you sons of bitches!" And they did.

Eaton excused himself to go to the men's room. He leaned over the sink, bracing his hands on either side of the porcelain, panting. Looking up in the mirror, he found his usually handsome, narrow face pasty, with sweat at the hairline. Eaton leaned against the wall with his eyes closed and waited there through the entire break.

For the second set, Eaton could listen more clinically. He noted the tunes were original and several had to do with bicycling, of all things, like the name of the band: "Cotterless Cranks," "Big Bottom Bracket," "Flat without a Patchkit on the Palisades" "Cycle Killer" and "Blue Suede Brakeshoes." Or "Perpendicular Grates," to which Eaton caught most of the words:

Don't jump your red tonight,
You big yellow Checker.
I'm coming through the light
At its last yellow flicker.
Shine your bulging brights
Right into my reflectors.
Listen close and you might
Hear my freewheel ticker-ticker.
Hey, city slickers:

> *Lay perpendicular grates!*
> *Chuck those rectangular plates!*
> *One pothole on Sixth Avenue*
> *Goes all the way to China.*

> *I am a midtown*
> *Pedal pusher.*
> *I am a traffic*
> *Bushwhacker.*
> *My brakes are clogged*
> *With little children.*
> *Greasy strays*
> *Keep my gears workin'.*

Doggies, watch your tails;
Old ladies, hold your bladders.
Scarvy starlets, trim your sails
Or choke on Isadora tatters.
Better step back to the curb—

Enough women are battered.
Brave Lolitas, round the curve,
You don't want to be flatter.
Hey, hard-hatters:

Lay perpendicular grates!
Chuck those rectangular plates!
One pothole on Sixth Avenue
Goes all the way to China.

I am a midtown
Pedal-pusher.
I am a traffic
Bushwhacker.
My brakes are clogged
With little children.
Greasy strays
Keep my gears workin' . . .

Eaton told himself that songs about bicycling were silly. He even managed to turn to Brinkley between tunes and advise him, "You know, technically, the guy's a mess." True, Checker played as if he'd never had a drum lesson in his life. He held his sticks like pencils. Yet Eaton had never seen such terrific independence, for Checker's hands were like two drastically different children of the same parents—one could read in the corner while the other played football. *What was Eaton going to do?* Bitchy carping from the sidelines wouldn't improve matters. And everyone looked so happy! The band and the audience together swayed on the tide of Checker Secretti's rolling snare. How does he do it? Even the little singer, a perpetually dolorous girl by all appearances, had a quiet glow, like a night-light. Eaton actually wondered for one split second, since he knew percussion better than anyone in the club, why he wasn't the happiest person here. But that moment passed, and had such a strange quality that he didn't even retain a memory of it, until Eaton was left at the end of the last set wishing to plant Plato's and everyone in it three miles deep in the Atlantic, safely buried below schools of barracuda, in airtight drums like toxic waste.

Yet, more or less, Eaton had decided what to do.

After the applause and catcalls had died down, Eaton turned to Brinkley and said severely, "Brink, you dungwad, you told me that Secretti was okay."

"I didn't say he, like, raised the dead or anything."

"Could've been playing trash cans with chopsticks," said Gilbert. "Not like Eat here. Now, Eat's a drummer."

"Uh-huh," said Eaton, turning to Rad. "And what did you make of Secretti?"

Rad twisted a little. During the performance he'd been nodding his head and tapping the table with the heel of his beer. "Bang, bang. Another local band. They'll be gone soon. The world won't have changed much."

Eaton surveyed his compatriots in silence. All three of them were nervous and weren't sure why. "So you three"—Eaton rolled the ice around his glass—"think he sucks? Basically?"

They shuffled and nodded.

"Then you all have dicks for brains."

"*What?*" they asked in unison.

"The man is brilliant. Steve Gadd raised to a goddamned power. One fresh piece of cake in a pile of stale Astoria corn muffins and you guys don't know the difference."

"But you said technically he's a mess—"

"Unorthodox. May not have much training. All the more impressive, then. The man's a genius."

Eaton's three henchmen were staring at their friend as if he'd just announced he was giving up rock and roll for polka music.

"Yeah, well," said Brinkley. "I said he was okay, right?"

"Okay!" Eaton rolled his eyes and stood up. "With this crowd I need drink." He walked away and didn't come back.

"That was exemplary."

Plato's may never have heard the word "exemplary" before; its syllables queered against the walls.

"I was humbled," Eaton went on, bent formally at the waist, as if he'd watched too much Masterpiece Theatre. "You're a giant. And far better than *these* people know."

"I think they know us just fine," said Checker, looking disconcerted. Compliments made him queasy. Checker himself didn't think about the way he played. He didn't want to, either.

"You're better than you know," Eaton pressed. "It's time someone told you. So, please." Eaton handed Checker his card. "I know the names of some club owners in Manhattan. Or if you need anything at all, please call. Good night, all." With a quick flourish Eaton made a swift departure. After all, he wasn't sure how much longer he could keep this up.

I n the defined caste of high school, Eaton Striker had played a precise role, exactly shy of stardom. He passed that crucial test: more students knew his name than he knew theirs. He was The Drummer, and relished sitting in the cafeteria with a drumstick stuck behind his ear, ticking para-diddles on his tray with silverware. Yet while his traps and his rock bands saved him from obscurity, they didn't secure him quite the premier position he felt he deserved. There was always one more table next to his where every student yearned to sit, and they'd settle for Eaton's only when the first was full.

In every area Eaton was plagued with not-quiteness. There was a particular lancet-witted brunette, Stephanie, whose quips in his direction prickled his skin like the sting of a slap, but that was all the tribute he could win from her; on the other hand, Stephanie's slightly less attractive, slightly less sharp best friend showed up for every one of Eaton's early gigs. Now, he did finally acquiesce and take Charlotte as his girlfriend, enjoying the pleasant lopsidedness of the relationship—she typed his papers and packed his drums and ruined a perfectly good denim jacket with embroidery as a "surprise." All he had to do in return was treat her badly, for which Eaton seemed to have been born with a certain gift. But seeing Charlotte with first prize was torture. Eaton was dating the kewpie doll while someone else was wrapped around the big stuffed bear.

All second prizes are insults. Eaton believed that. When in the senior talent show his band, Nuclear War, was awarded second place, Eaton strode from the stage and in front of the whole assembly stuffed the certificate perfunctorily in a trash can. When Eaton's cronies nominated him for student council office, it was for *vice* president; he lost to a girl.

Even Eaton's grades were never perfectly straight-A. There was always one teacher who had it in for him in one of those mealy subjects—English, social studies—where the teacher's feeble judgment came into play. Eaton preferred math—his work was right or wrong, whether or not the instructor despised him. For while Eaton was never directly insolent, his sly, grimly bemused expression nagged his teachers like a persistent hangnail. Whenever they talked to him after class he turned his head to watch them out of the corners of his eyes, his responses laconic; he always seemed to indicate that a great deal was being left unsaid. On any point of conflict his teachers quickly abandoned personal appeals and fell back on brisk legalistic resolutions.

These were uneasy relationships. Eaton's intelligence would never redound to his teachers' glory. Rather, each would shine at the expense of the other. That was the stanchion of Eaton's world view, and it was contagious.

So Eaton was the hero of the B+ students, revered by the type in elementary school picked third or fourth for a kickball team of ten. Burdened by Eaton's disappointment, his following had a high turnover; his rock bands were always breaking up. At the moment, out of school over half a year now, Eaton was once more without a band, and it was harder to assemble a new one without high school; he paged through the ads in the *SoHo News* listlessly on Saturday afternoons. Eaton yearned for caliber. The idea of collecting one more second-rate rock band filled him with a precocious exhaustion.

That Eaton would end up at Plato's was inevitable. By January he had been actively avoiding the place, spending Friday nights instead at Billy's Pub, Grecian Gardens, Taverna 27, bars that never managed to persuade you they were anything more than rooms with bottles, full of bowlers and plumbers all too eager to confide the trials of the kind of life Eaton planned to transcend. Yet even Taverna 27 was better than the chromier corners, decorated like Alexander's at Christmas and cranking out Van Halen on the juke, cramped with high-school juniors constantly combing their hair. Eaton was only nineteen, but he'd said goodbye to all that.

There was always Manhattan, but Eaton hated coming back at four in the morning on the subway with all the plebes who couldn't afford a car. Eaton couldn't afford a car, either, but he was the kind of person who really should have been able to, and a pretty damned nice car at that. (Eaton's sense of justice was frequently confounded. Eaton should have X and Eaton did have Y, and the disparity didn't anger him exactly—his reaction was deeper than that. It *disturbed* him. When Eaton didn't get what he deserved, he felt the earth—move—under his feet—Carole King. Yich.) In the city, scrunched against the bar with his friends, Eaton would slip the straw of his screwdriver between a gap in his teeth, having to repeat three times over the music how these clubs were "tedious," though he privately considered them far more evil than that—the heaving, shifting mass of dancers would undulate and suck against him like some lowlife sea creature, swallowing him in anonymity, digesting him alive and spitting his remains out the door at three, forty dollars poorer.

Furthermore, Eaton was underage, and though he usually cooled his way past the bouncer by paying the cover with an unusually large bill, Eaton craved legitimation. He hated being nineteen. He remembered with humiliation the other night at Van Dam's, when the thirtyish man beside him had asked him, as a drummer, what did he think of "In-A-Gadda-Da-Vida"?

"Amusing, but finally bogus. I didn't go along with the brouhaha over the album when it first came out."

"Come on!" said the man. "It came out in '68! You were listening to Iron Butterfly when you were one?"

Eaton couldn't wait to turn thirty and do the same thing to kids sitting next to him. In the meantime, he listened to the radio with a pencil, and haunted the aisles of Tower Records like a law student in the stacks, studying jackets like torts, reading the fine print—dates, producers. He put together histories of who left what band and started this one, reading *Rolling Stone* cover to cover, determined never to be caught out by aging rock has-beens in Manhattan again.

Eaton yearned for a club where patrons knocked him on the shoulder and cleared room for him at the bar, where the waitresses knew him by name and remembered his liquor brands. Eaton liked to be recognized, and Astoria should have been the place for that; a small-towny Greek neighborhood in Queens with friendly shopkeepers and good-old-boy bars, Astoria would transplant easily to the middle of Iowa. Eaton's failure to carve a niche even here was one more of those disconcerting challenges to his stature, for if he went to the same bar several nights running, Eaton would sure enough get recognized, but no one seemed very happy to see him.

Besides, everyone said Plato's was "good," though the word had put Eaton off distinctly. They said it the way you'd say a "good woman," meaning ugly. Plato's was a "good club" the way you'd say Jerusalem was good, somewhere in the Bible.

T he following Friday night Eaton kept putting on his coat and taking it off again. He'd flounce in a chair, tap his fingers, turn up the radio—Journey. Awful. Off. Tap, tap, tap. Finally, he grabbed the cashmere once and for all and rushed out the door.

Gliding in with his crew, Eaton glanced hastily around the club; when he failed to find what he was looking for, his stomach sank, just as it had when Charlotte showed up at his gigs without Stephanie. The place suddenly felt flat. This time, Eaton wondered why he'd concerned himself with Plato's at all—low-lit and woody, with no track lighting or rippling bulbs around the bar, the club made no effort at any kind of effect. Furthermore, at almost midnight, there was no music. Maybe The Derailleurs were on a break, but if so they couldn't have bubbled anybody's hormones—the immediate feeling of the crowd was subdued, even depressed. No one was talking very loud, and everyone seemed sober.

"This place is sure different from last time," said Brinkley.

"This isn't a club, it's a morgue!" said Gilbert.

They sat in the corner, refreshingly disgusted.

"I thought there was supposed to be live music here," Eaton charged the waitress.

She sighed. "Well, it's happened again. You know. Check. Maybe next week. Maybe even tomorrow."

"You lost me."

She looked at Eaton more closely. "Oh, you're new here, aren't you?"

"I have to be a member?"

"No, it's just regulars are used to this. Checker—*disappears*." Raising her eyes enigmatically, she swished her tray to the next table.

That explained it, for the rest of The Derailleurs were all propped at the front table. Breathing in her cloying wake reminded Eaton of passing cosmetics counters, with their nauseating reek of mixed perfumes.

Standing abruptly in the middle of Brinkley and Gilbert's riveting debate over tequila-salt-lemon vs. tequila-lemon-salt, Eaton swirled his black cashmere greatcoat around his shoulders and strode to the lead guitar.

"Not playing tonight?" Eaton inquired.

"Our head man just won an all-expenses-paid trip to Florida," said the blond longhair dourly.

"That's surprising, for a band with your reputation—"

"What have you heard about The Derailleurs?" asked the straight kid, whose ears stuck out from his head.

"We don't need to hear about The Derailleurs, Howard,"

said the longhair. "We are The Derailleurs. We know all about us already."

"I was wondering," said Eaton, "since your delinquent member—"

"Nobody said he a delinquent," said the big black bassist.

"Your man in Florida, then."

"Our man," said the bassist firmly, "period."

Eaton took a breath and smiled. "Of course. It's just, I've kicked around the drums myself. I'm only so good, but if you stuck to covers I could keep a steady three-four. I wouldn't presume to equal your own stunning percussionist. But for the hell of it, maybe I could fill in?" Eaton looked gamely around the table.

"As the manager—" Howard began.

"Howard *listens*," said the guitarist.

"Would he like to listen tonight?" asked Eaton solicitously.

"No."

They turned toward the end of the table. The Middle Eastern saxophonist had folded his arms. "We *half* our drummer."

"On the contrary," said Eaton, "it seems that you don't."

"You say you not so good. Why we play with you, not-so-good?"

"Excuse me, but can he understand me? I see we have some second-language problems here."

"Rrreal fine, slime mold," said the saxophonist for himself.

"Aw, can it, Hijack," said the bassist. "Check on vacation,

pull this night out somehow. Let's play." Rolling to a stand, he led the rest of the band to the dais.

Eaton took his seat on the throne and pulled his own drumsticks out of his greatcoat. He tested the tom and it went *thwap!* What? The heads were completely loosened—and no wonder. Calf skins! There wasn't a rock drummer in this country who used calf skins. With annoyance, Eaton went through the tedious process of racheting the lugs tight and testing around the rim to get them even. Somehow they— resisted. The heads weren't interested in attaining the tautness Eaton required.

Eaton tried the tuning with a snappy run around the pieces. God, what a pile of tin cans. The hardware rattled. There was a buzz in the bass. And the whole set was ancient, big band or before, though Eaton did admire the Zildjian-K's—you hardly ever saw those nowadays, hand-hammered Armenian cymbals, exquisitely thin. Even the ride rang with a long resonant shimmer at the touch of his stick, though to Eaton's taste they were a little oversensitive; they—winced. He eyed the set; it seemed to eye him back. But Eaton knew how to discipline inanimate objects. Whenever his possessions broke, which was often, he imagined he was getting the last laugh.

"Boys and girls, you may have heard we've been caught out Checkless," the lanky guitarist began. "However, with a volunteer from our studio audience, we'll proceed. In consid- eration of our guest, only familiar favorites, please."

When they began with "Louie, Louie," the whole band had their ears cocked for Eaton's drumming, though that proved unnecessary—they could barely hear anything else.

The guitarist forced his voice; the bassist turned up his level; the keyboardist, something of a delicate touch the weekend before, torqued up his electric piano. When Hijack opened into a sax solo, Eaton bore down all the more, until the horn player was inserting the mic in his bell.

At the end of the song, the saxophonist turned to Eaton behind him. "You break Sheckair's head," he said quietly, "I break yours."

As they grated through Hard Cheese's "Two Is a Crowd" and on to "Johnny B. Good," Eaton pushed the tempo when the lead slowed down; he dragged just as the bass thrummed forward. Because drums set the standard, this left the musicians out front sounding out of sync. Further, even when the band was playing together, they all rushed toward the song's conclusion, as if to end was to win, as if the reason to play it was to get it over with. And it wasn't only Eaton, either. They all lashed their instruments, spitting the words out like projectiles they hoped would hit someone on the head. You got the feeling that after listening to a song like that Johnny would be very, very bad.

With "(I Can't Get No) Satisfaction" Plato's moist air turned acrid with evaporating sweat. The crowd, though not seemingly disappointed, was unusually rude; one patron in the back kept yelling, "Kill 'em!" waving his hands until he spilled his beer. A fight broke out by the bar; waitresses got testy and started carding; boys got grabby and girls got bitchy; customers recklessly mixed their poisons and threw up in the bathroom. Still, they were all apparently convinced they were having a wonderful time.

When the band took a break, The Derailleurs save the Middle Eastern muttered something to Eaton about "good job," but their remarks were muffled and short. Everyone but the girl went to swill down something stiff. Eaton felt the victim of a great lack of generosity. He may not have ever experienced genuine, spontaneous acclaim, but he knew this wasn't it.

When Eaton sat down for the next set the drums glared at him like prison labor.

Eaton outdid himself. The toms tippled in their brackets; the bass edged gradually from his foot; the Zildjian-K's began to tremble from the shadow of his hand. He broke five hickory drumsticks.

The guitarist suggested they do a slow song and let the girl sing. Rachel DeBruin had a sweet, mournful presence that could surely calm the band down, and maybe the crowd, now growing unruly. The band never had her sing too often, since she made audiences pensive; she recalled lost summers and first loves. On good nights she could raise a napkin to the corner of a biker's eye. Tonight, however, they would settle for quiet.

Yet when she sang "The Last Time I Saw Richard," its sweet romantic disappointment bittered; the other musicians harmonized in their heads. *Welsher*, thought Caldwell, the guitarist. His "friend" J.K. had owed him fifty dollars since July. Strumming next to Caldwell, J.K. felt his bass droop; he'd been lugging mail sacks for the post office all week, and his arms were tired. Two of his friends had left for Jamaica earlier in the week, but J.K. couldn't go, no—as usual. He had a wife and daughter to support. *What a hero*, he thought sourly. All day long postcards had spilled from his sacks, of palm trees, greased-up girls, with messages like "Water warm, rum cheap." The keyboardist, Carl Ming, kept forgetting the chords, but helplessly remembering everything else—fifth grade came at him like a submarine torpedo: four boys, a big brass spatula for a paddle, and a fence. Since his childhood was enough of a torment the first time, "Quiet Carl" wasn't the nostalgic type; memory itself was assault.

Howard glared from the front table. They thought they were so hot, prancing around on stage. All the errands he ran for those guys, their thanks jokes at his expense. *Airheads.* Howard recited to himself his very high SAT scores. Meanwhile, the Middle Eastern saxophonist glanced disdainfully down at the audience. *Self-satisfied Americans. Rich land, good weather, all those cars, completely wasted on 240 million fat sheep.*

In the song, a woman sits in a bar getting drunk, mooning over an old boyfriend; the place is about to close, and the waitress wants her to finish her drink. *That's me*, thought Rachel. *Twenty years from now, that's me. Same bar, same man. That bastard. Some days I don't know what I want more, to slit his throat or mine.*

Yet Eaton, insofar as he was capable of the emotion, was perfectly happy.

So there you have The Derailleurs—a motley or tropical crew, depending on your mood. The picture of that obscure Queens rock band, tripping over frayed cords fat with electrician's tape, could appear credibly striking, but you have to look at them right. Otherwise, especially with indigestion or maybe just an indigenously surly disposition, you might notice how Caldwell is overdrawn, like a cartoon—his nose is enormous, his arms are too long, a vein on his temple protrudes. He jitters around the stage in a panic, constantly adjusting amp settings and checking the jacks, in the grip of some terror, but only nineteen—what is there to be afraid of? Rachel, lost in her big maroon sweater half unraveled down the front, is arguably mousy. She always looks at the floor. Rachel is Bowie's original China Doll, perched on the edge of the stage—when she shatters you won't want to be around to pick up the pieces. Someone will have to take the blame for Rachel DeBruin. J.K.? One more hunky black kid, likes his beer, his rock and roll—a known quantity. Hijack, whose real name is Rahim Abdul, is too pretty for a boy. And in New York you sure get tired of foreigners. Those accents aren't quaint or exotic anymore after about week 6 here. From then on, it's just, I need a cabbage, a small one; Excuse—? *A cabbage!* Like that. Quiet Carl never says a damn thing, and who needs that. As for Howard Williams, their "manager"? Squid. Boat shoes! Oh, he isn't exactly ugly—Howard has even, regular American features with nice thick brown American hair—but to whatever degree looks are style, Howard is hideous.

However, it would be possible to execute a little turn like flicking the channel over and back again; the picture, black and white a moment before, blushes to color. Suddenly the spotlight on stage shadows Caldwell's face with the exotic expressions of a Kabuki mask. He has long, elegant fingers. His hair is bright gold. True, he's frightened, but at nineteen there's plenty to be afraid of, like the rest of your life. Rachel is no longer mousy, but delicate. If you circled your thumb and middle finger around her wrist, both end joints would overlap. J.K. is big rather than fat, comfortable and unpretentious as an overstuffed armchair. And so what if Rahim is pretty? Beautiful teeth—matched pearls, a two-string smile. Further, sometimes it's possible to recuperate that delight in foreigners you had when you first came to New York. His r's roll like water. Quiet Carl has a story, and you like stories. Howard *is* handsome, and you're dying to tell him that. You want to take him shopping and buy him some shirts with color and jeans that don't hike up like that, Hi-Tops instead of boat shoes. But you won't. And Howard will keep buying the pale plaids and jeans that are big in the waist and short in the leg, and that makes you smile, because people are astonishingly consistent, so carefully themselves. You don't mind. Why, he's the only person you know who wears boat shoes.

What if you added Checker Secretti to this picture? Well, if your mood is sour, Checker isn't very impressive. Few people seem to notice that he isn't very tall, but you would notice. His brown skin, kinky hair, and blue eyes would disturb you, for you can't quite tell what race he is, and it's stressful when people resist normal categories. You might say he's "cute," but he's no head turner. Not even as straight-out good-looking as, say, Eaton Striker. In fact, you would think this specifically: *Not as good-looking as Eaton Striker*, since, if you were eyeing

Checker Secretti with just this narrow annoyance, you would *be* Eaton Striker.

But if you feel fine? If you understand that people are attractive not just for their strengths but for their shortcomings? Then how would Checker Secretti look?

You might see the shadow of a nose, the flicker of a hand, a rolled-up sleeve of bright red cotton, but you wouldn't see the man from head to toe, and it wouldn't occur to you to wonder whether he was a head turner, because, leaning in the frame of the door, you would have to be Checker Secretti himself.

2 / blood and crystal

. . . and when you finally reappear / at the place where you came in / you've thrown your love to all the strangers / and caution to the wind—

"Sheckair!" Rahim stopped cold in the middle of "Love over Gold" and unstrapped his sax to bound from the stage. The rest of the band dribbled off; Eaton was the last to stop playing. Running to the doorway, Rahim clapped Checker's hand and turned him fully around like a square-dance figure, laughed, and planted a big, unembarrassed kiss on each of Checker's cheeks.

Between three and five, Plato's usually settled down to a small core of customers; The Derailleurs would put away their instruments and everyone put his feet up. The drinking slowed to a trickle, and even diehard rockers grew philosophical. Not tonight. They all pulled on their coats when Check walked forward, slinking out of the club hastily as if leaving the scene of a crime.

"You just get here?" asked Caldwell, fidgeting with his gig bag.

"Caught some of that last set."

"Yeah, well." A strap was caught in the zipper, and Caldwell went about solving the problem intently. "Just screwing around. *You* weren't here."

"We've been through this."

"Well, you can't expect us to be any good," Caldwell burst out, "without you."

Checker's eyes were steady, neutral. "It was interesting."

"You are toast, man," said J.K.

"I am a little tired." Checker turned. "Howard, you arranged a substitute. Good management."

Howard envied Rahim's leaping Virginia Reel, but could only swing an awkward, premeditated hug. "You look terrible!"

"Thanks, Howard."

"No, I mean—"

"You mean I look terrible. Mr. Striker?" Checker pulled a tattered paper from his pocket and read, "*Drummer Extraordinaire.*"

Eaton felt embarrassed by his own business card, and glared as if the pretentious tag was Checker's fault. Checker only looked back at him with exposing directness. Eaton felt discovered. Yet when Eaton glanced away and back again, Checker's expression no longer appeared incisive. There was a deadness or calm in the corners of his blue eyes—blind spots. If Checker were a car, it seems, Eaton Striker would be positioned perfectly behind the right back fender.

"Some drumming," said Checker.

"It's a battle, with these tubs."

"The drums are supposed to be on your side."

"These aren't very responsive."

"Calf heads are subtle."

"I don't think of drums as a subtle instrument."

"Yes. I can see you don't."

Checker smiled slightly, and Eaton felt condescended to. His chin rose in the air. "Antiques, aren't they?"

"'Forty-eight," said Check. "A good year."

"Might consider replacing them. The shells made now are smaller, tighter, sharper. These are muddy."

"Thanks for the advice. But I've had these since I was nine. If I replaced them they'd be hurt."

"And when you forget their birthday, do they cry?"

"I don't know," said Check mildly. "I've never forgotten their birthday."

Check eased into a chair and leaned his neck over the back, closing his eyes. Rahim dipped a napkin into the ice remaining in a drink and wiped across Checker's forehead. "Sheckair don sleep?"

"Not much, Hijack." No one asked him where he'd been. No one asked him why he hadn't slept.

While Check dozed, Rahim cooled the drummer's neck and patted it dry with the tail of his shirt, rearranged Checker's collar, and finally stood at attention beside him like a bodyguard, eyeing Eaton occasionally as a potential assassin. The rest of the band quietly packed up and helped the waitress clear drinks. No one talked, but gently the acid dispersed from the room, the heat clanking up from the basement with a fresh burst of steam. Shyly they found each other's picks and spare strings. Sweeping up, Caldwell decided that fifty dollars wasn't very much money, after all. J.K. realized that he'd only want to go to Jamaica if he could take Ceil and the kid with him; that people who counted on you were burdens or assets, all depending on how you looked at them. Carl helped wash the dishes and noticed how the waitress managed to talk to him in a way that didn't demand he answer back, but still made him feel like part of a conversation. Wisps of childhood memories were still trailing through his mind, but he also recalled some other classmates—the girl with buck teeth, the little boy who smelled bad—who were tormented along with him. When he smiled at the waitress while she dried, she blushed.

Howard felt liked. Rahim felt American. Rachel felt sad, but Rachel always felt sad. And in the quiet, steamy closure of the dark club, surrounded by the sound of Checker's breathing and the hollow expansion and contraction of the pipes below, Eaton Striker had to leave.

As Rahim walked him home Checker wheeled his bicycle between them, the clicking of the back hub ticking off the moments in precise, perfect points like the stars overhead, bright from cold.

Checker said, "I want to show you something."

They detoured to a run-down industrial block of Astoria Boulevard. The sidewalk shook under their feet as they approached the building, whose sign said VESUVIUS, nothing more. Directly in front, they heard a dull ominous roar. Checker put his hands gently on the front door, like cracking a safe; it trembled under his fingertips. Putting his finger to his lips, he led Rahim down an alley and pointed to a small window. Rahim climbed a trash can to see.

The pane buzzed in its frame; the glass tickled his hand. Here the sound was louder, huge and ceaseless, like a lion that never inhaled. Through the muddy window Rahim could see dimly inside, though he didn't understand what he was looking at. Fire framed a square of black like an eclipse. As he watched, the black square moved to the side, and a long stick plunged into pulsing vermilion.

Lit only by this hellish glow, an unearthly woman pulled the rod from the fire. She was tall, which always unnerved Rahim in women. She wore a long industrial apron and dark glasses that flashed yellow when they caught the light. Her hair was tied back carelessly, but most of it was escaping. Cut jaggedly in different lengths, it was the hair that made this figure so amazing. Thick and wild, it raged from her head like black flames. Rahim felt he was witnessing some satanic worship service, with a lean, terrible shaman prodding a dangerous god.

While he told himself she was only a woman, Rahim felt even at first glance that this one demanded a whole other word. Trying to rub the window cleaner, Rahim stood up on his toes and took a step closer; his foot missed and he tumbled off the can. The barrel itself fell and made a terrific crash, for it seems the whole container was filled to the brim with bits of broken glass.

Checker laughed softly and helped him up. Together they began to throw the glass back in the barrel.

"Sh-sh!" said Checker, still laughing, when Rahim tossed a piece in the can and it smashed loudly hitting bottom. It was hard to see, and grasping for hunks in the dark Check exclaimed, "Jesus!" and pulled back. Rahim didn't have a chance to ask what had happened before he looked up to find a molten glob pointed menacingly at him on the end of a metal pole.

"Move and you're fried," said a voice. "A minute ago this lump was twenty-four hundred degrees. It may be cooling fast, but it's still hot enough to turn your face into a pork chop."

Rahim froze, crouching; Checker, despite the warning, stood up.

The woman pointed a flashlight at Checker like a second weapon.

"What *is* that?" asked Checker, not sounding very frightened. "It's fantastic!"

All three of them turned to the glob, changing quickly from a rich yellow to a duller, more smoldering red. As Checker reached toward it, the woman jerked it away.

"Hot glass, toddler. And what have you done to your hand?"

In the beam of the flashlight was a second red glob, on the end of Checker's arm. There was a quiet, regular patter-patter; the woman trained the light on the ground, where Checker's blood was spattering onto the chunks of clear glass. The glass sparkled, and the red drops bounced and drizzled over its crystals like expensive rain. Strange. It was beautiful.

"Sheckair!" Quickly Rahim shed his jacket and tore off his shirt, and began to wrap Check's hand.

"Don't use your dirty shirt," she said sharply. "I have medical supplies inside. I suppose you can come in." She led them reluctantly in the door and smashed the rod against the cement floor. The glass, now black, cracked off; she tossed the rod in a barrel and went to get first aid. "Christ," Check heard her mutter on the way, "I start to run off hoodlums and end up playing Sara Barton."

"That's *Clara* Barton," he shouted after her. Unexpectedly, she laughed.

Checker didn't seem very concerned with his hand, more delighted to have weaseled his way in here. He and Rahim approached the furnace. Inside, the roar was deeper, striking a broader range of tones. Checker couldn't take his eyes off the fire though at a certain point he stood back from the heat. In fact, the whole room was sweltering, and recalled the febrile interior of Plato's Bar.

When she returned she switched on a light, to Rahim's disappointment—it ruined the satanic religiosity of the scene. As she rinsed out Checker's cut in warm water over her sink, they both stared at the glassblower, not quite as mysterious without the glow of the furnace, but no less intimidating.

Everything about her was long: her neck, her waist, her

face. Her cheeks were hollow and drawn; her expressions were conducted in the narrow range between amusement and irritation. As she tended his hand, her face sharpened in an intentness that seemed usual. Her oversized green shirt billowed under her apron with accidental style. Her jeans shone with dirt. The musty smell wafting from them suggested she'd been in these clothes for a while.

"You're filthy," Check observed joyously as his blood ran in diluted swirls down the drain.

"You're stupid," she shot back. "Why were you and your friend crawling around in a pile of broken glass at four in the morning?"

"Watching you," said Check. As she went for the antiseptic, he followed her hands. They looked older than the rest of her—fiftyish, sixtyish even—scarred and craggy, with abused nails. Her fingers were long like Caldwell's, but ancient and knuckly. They tended his cut with care but authority, like a good mechanic's.

"What are all these little scars?" she asked about his own hand, which was covered in small white lumps.

"From drumming."

A look. "Violent."

"Passionate."

She laughed.

"Why is that funny?"

"Well, how old are you?"

"What does that have to do with passion?"

"Maybe nothing," she admitted.

Her motions were jagged, like her hair. When she turned

to find the gauze, a peak of hair touched his face; Checker reached up as if to brush it away, but really to feel it—a little coarse; he noticed a few strands of gray.

"How old are you?"

"Why?"

"Cause I can usually tell. You, I can't place within ten years."

"Twenty-nine."

"I'd have guessed older."

"Real diplomatic."

"You're not insulted."

She stopped wrapping his hand and looked at Check as if seeing him for the first time. She seemed surprised by what she saw. "No?"

"It doesn't matter to you, looking young," Check explained. "Just now—I think you were flattered."

The woman sucked in her cheeks and shot him a sour, bemused little smile. "Maybe."

"You must finish wrap."

This whole time Rahim had been following the medical process suspiciously, examining the label on the antiseptic; when she stopped working on the bandage Rahim couldn't contain himself.

"*What?*"

"Wrap," said Rahim staunchly.

"You spy on my work and knock over a whole barrel of cullet and I still take you in to patch up your bloody bungling and I don't do it fast enough. So sorry."

"'Sokay," said Rahim, who had no sense of American

sarcasm. "Just finish quickly, please. Sheckair vedy tired. I take him home now."

"Well, I'm a little tired myself," she said with genuine annoyance. Disappointed, Checker watched her tie up his hand summarily and stand, hands on her hips. She was taller than both of them.

"Come." Rahim took Checker's good hand and began to pull him toward the door. The Iraqi had his proprietary side, like a severe, overly protective secretary.

Check dragged. "Can I come back?"

"What for?"

"The glass. I want to watch."

"You've been watching."

"Tomorrow!" At last Rahim succeeded in hauling Checker out the door, but not before he'd gotten one last glimpse of the glassblower, who was looking at him, he thought, terrifically hard. She had the same drastic features as Caldwell Sweets, and she certainly did look older than twenty-nine, but Checker, who had a lot of experience with looking at people right, knew full well that she was gorgeous.

3 / bad company

Astoria Park is bordered by two bridges—on its northern end by a lumbering rusted railroad bridge called Hell Gate, named for the dangerous eddies that churn below its girders. Several workers lost their lives in its construction; gruff and awkward, Hell Gate would have bid them farewell without ceremony. It has the terse, groggy, and potentially violent character of heavy drinkers; accessible only by the desperate clambering of lonely adolescents, it isn't a trellis to which you'd ordinarily appeal. Still, Hell Gate is comforting in its way, quiet, protective, and steady. Whenever it rained, the band huddled under its belly, leaning up against the rough concrete abutments to smoke.

The Triborough, on the southern end, is an entirely different animal. Constructed in 1936, she's young, for a bridge. While Hell Gate arches downward, the Triborough is a classic suspension span, with the grace and desire of a cathedral. Unlike the craggy umber of her senior upriver, the Triborough is painted a soft blue-gray; while even more enormous, she never gives the impression of weight. From that vain sally over the river, the swoop and cinch of her waist, Checker had detected her feminine nature, but she still seemed to have a boyish sense of fun. Riding the powerful rise and fall of her pedestrian ramps, he could tell she was athletic, well-toned.

Checker had respect for Hell Gate; he was glad the old man was there, and did sometimes consult the older bridge on difficult and purely masculine matters, but his heart belonged to the Triborough. In spring he bounded across her walkways in new tennis shoes; in winter, Checker and his bicycle, Zefal, scrumpled fresh squeaky tracks in her snow.

While the two bridges embrace all of Astoria Park, a lush, well-populated recreation area old as the neighborhood itself, another finger of public land extends north of Hell Gate called Ralph DeMarco, recently developed with the help of nearby Con Edison to spruce up the rather bleak city projects across the street. Like so many good deeds, Ralph DeMarco has an overplanned, overdeliberate quality that defeats it. Ralph DeMarco is a failed park. It has no intermediate vegetation, for example—only very short grass and whole young trees, sunk in lifelessly regular rows. The trees themselves are pretty but too exotic—willows, cherries, and beeches; foreigners like the Indians who live here, they don't fit in. Benches are set in optimistic semicircles, as if to encourage the kind of warm community closeness no one here feels—unwed mothers sit facing each other blankly, not talking. The railings by the river are painted a shocking shade of plum, a color some commission must have hoped would be brightening but which ended up simply peculiar.

Lately Astoria Park was thriving, overcrowded in summer, but Ralph DeMarco was nearly deserted even when it was warm, and Checker felt sorry for it. Ralph DeMarco was hanging on by a thread. He sometimes took the band here evenings just to cheer it up. The little park broke Checker's heart. It tried too hard. It reminded him of Howard.

Besides, the relative quiet of the place had advantages, like the time last summer Danno's *Late Show* was playing a Perfect Album Side from Talking Heads' *Speaking in Tongues*. Caldwell never tired of telling the story, because that night a Corvette braved the terrifying void of the land from Con Ed and parked right in front of The Derailleurs' ghetto blaster, challenging the Heads with loud, ill-tuned Judas Priest.

Checker had approached the man in leather leaning against the hood. "Can't you get NEW in that car?"

"Can. Won't. Gotta problem?"

"Actually, yes," said Checker, with that disconcerting innocence of his that made the rest of the band's skin crawl; for once it was apparent that Check was small. Still, he stared up at the tough with his odd Sicilian-blue eyes. "I'd appreciate it if you'd either tune into the same station or park a block or two away. They're coming up on my favorite song."

"And this lunk," Caldwell would recall later, "some Hulk or Bubba or Crusher, cracks his Bud with his teeth. *I don't give a livin fuck, suck-ah*. Howard here is creaming. Old J. de K. is rolling up his sleeves, so for once we're glad the man's had a few too many pancakes. Q.C. starts getting that Chinee squint, like maybe he's studied karate, though all us knowing good and well Carl hasn't even studied algebra. Rache gets this High Noon look, with hair everywhere . . . All the while the Heads bouncing through 'This Must Be the Place,' the Priest screaming, I don't know, Hate-your-sister-smush-your-mother-kill-the-whole-world—you've heard their stuff. It was tense, boy. Crusher, he steps forward from the 'vette. Check, he's had his hands behind his back the whole time, okay? And he doesn't step back. He smiles this tiny don't-fuck-with-me smile. The tunes, they break at *exactly* the same time. And for two, three seconds there's total silence, even the wind stops. In the break, behind Check's back, there's a click. Oh, God. You know that sound, man. That little blade sound, and that is *it*, man, that is the end of the old hangout-in-the-park-one-more-summer-night kind of thing and into this, oh *shit*—

"Or that's what Crusher figures, anyway, and you can see his face twist up and he reaches inside his jacket and—"

J.K. always starts laughing here.

"Shut up, man, you'll ruin the story!"

"I heard the story a hundred time, Sweets—"

"They haven't heard it! So don't—"

"It a *umbrella*."

"What?" asks the new audience.

J.K. keeps laughing. "The snap! Check don't have no blade, man! It one of these portable suckers, see—"

"Shut up, J.K., it's my story—"

"Everybody story, longhair. Real small and real sweet. Jus like a candy, that night a little candy night."

It was, small and perfect, it lay on your tongue. That's what nights with Checker were like. Before the man in leather had reached all the way into his pocket Checker brought the little umbrella out front and propped it pleasantly on his shoulder. "They say," he said, "it might rain."

His hand still in his jacket, the man released a single, unintentional guffaw.

It's funny how people will deal with you on the level you choose for them. Suddenly everything got very subtle. The smiles. The shifts of stance. The eye contact, the looking away. "Okay, Fred Astaire," said Crusher. "Hey, Bilgewater," he said to the man in the passenger's seat. "NEW.—Just for a while." Then he raised his beer with a weird sort of—suavity. The whole thing became an excruciating, delicate joke. Checker twirled the parasol gaily on his shoulder.

Checker tried to explain later: it's easier to change the station. All most Crushers need is a look in two blue eyes that say: The river is rushing black and furious tonight, the wind is whipping at the cherry trees and sweeping the branches of the willow like Rachel's High Noon hair; it will rain later, lashing the rocks and bottles below us—you see, there are enough battles already. Instead, take the lights of the

Triborough bright in my eyes, feel the cut of the air before a storm, try my station and roll onto the balls of your feet, coiling your calves and rippling the tops of your thighs. Keep the fight in your body. Besides, said the eyes, there is so much else to do—let me introduce you to the miracle of your neighborhood. *This is Ralph DeMarco.*

Later that night Checker was keeping time to the end of the Music Marathon with his drumsticks on the body of the car, trilling up and down its decals as the flames on the hood licked at their tips. But it was the snap of the umbrella that did the trick. Clear and pretty, the turn of a key in a lock. Checker changed what happened. He went in and tampered and fixed things. He tinkered with events as if nosing through the engine of a car.

As the sun set behind her, the lights of Manhattan just beginning to rise, the Triborough was in a delicate and passionate temper. The sun trembled, red like the furnace early that morning. The lines of the cables shimmered and distorted. Poignant, fleeting, something about the quality of the light transferred to Checker's sense of the evening itself, as if he knew that the Saturdays he and the band would spend in the uncomplicated flush of each other's company were painfully numbered. In the approaching darkness, each remaining ray sliced Checker's chest like a shard of glass.

"Listen," said Checker.

"What?"

"Sssh."

The band was quiet, and for a moment only heard the murmur of cars from the bridge, the whir of a helicopter doing traffic reports, the rev of a nearby Trans Am; but gradually they each heard it, a tinkling and lapping, a singing and breaking, a sad shattering tune below the embankment on which they stood.

"Beer bottles!" said Howard.

True enough, the entire shoreline didn't show an inch of sand or dirt but was covered instead with broken glass where locals had thrown their empties in summers past. Yet, rather than littering the bank, the bits of brown and green winked opulently in the sun. The wake of passing barges picked up pieces and threw them against each other with an Oriental pinging sound, dissonant and unlikely.

"I got a new job," said Check.

"I thought being a bike messenger was the most majorly up-jacking job in the whole world," said Caldwell.

"It was. Not anymore."

"You go back there," said Rahim heavily.

"Had to, Hijack."

"Did not."

"Had to."

"She is not normal lady, Sheckair."

"Sure as hell not."

"I have this—"

"I know," said Check. "So do I."

Those two talked in this way all the time.

"Do you *mind*?" asked Caldwell.

"*Syria Pyramus*," said Check, leaning into his italics.

Rahim clicked his tongue against the roof of his mouth. "That is the name."

"Of WHO?" demanded Caldwell.

"Take care, Sheckair. That furnace is hungry."

"Yeah, it wants something. Always dangerous, you want something."

"You two looped, you know that," said J.K.

"It *roars*," said Rahim in his throat, so that big J.K. stepped back.

Checker laughed. "Like a great bloody animal. I like it." Though "like it" was inaccurate. He was attracted to the furnace, an ambivalent sensation with an object that hot. Much the way great heights made him want to jump, the furnace enticed Checker to crawl in.

With both Caldwell and J.K. now glaring over the rail at a passing tugboat and pointedly asking nothing, Checker broke down and explained. "There's a glassblower up on the Boulevard. She needs somebody to clean up, shovel cullet—"

"Cullet?" asked Rahim.

"All that broken glass. Boffo word, huh?" With his good hand, Checker selected his favorite brand from among the bottles at his feet and sent the green glass careening splendidly to shore—the *cullet*-strewn shore. "Anyway, people," he announced. "We have an agenda." "Agenda," like "cullet," curled with unreasonable relish over his tongue.

"You've decided you're too good for us and you're accepting an offer from David Byrne."

The band turned away from Caldwell. No one laughed.

"Sweets," said Checker stop that."

They all knew exactly what Checker was talking about. Caldwell was terrified that these evenings, or the nights in Plato's, were the times he would remember wistfully in his middle age. He was overcome by a premonition of missing the Good Old Days, and he wasn't sure what his nostalgia drove him to do. When seasons changed, Caldwell panicked; he would refuse to wear any but the lightest jacket even through November, as if that would slow the weeks down. Caldwell had a way of looking at the band as if he were calling roll. And surely someday he would be extra nervous; he'd be a little older, and a few of those long strands of white-gold hair would fall out in his hand. One of the band members could very well have left or married; Caldwell would whip his head from side to side, the vein at his temple bulging like a son of a bitch—and it would happen. The Good Old Days would be over, right then. He would never get them back, and he would have it, what he expected—death and memory. So then he'd slow down and get a gut, hard as it was to imagine on that tall skinny kid now. He'd put his feet up and tell stories. It's strange how often you get exactly what you're afraid of.

"I'm here. You're here," Check reassured him, not for the first time. "We're all here."

"You're not always here," Caldwell shot back.

"True," Check conceded. "That's what I wanted to talk about."

"It's all right," said Rachel. "We understand."

ot," said Caldwell.

o, Rachel sweetheart, it isn't all right." Checker had a way of talking to Rachel, like crooning to a pet. He could as well have reached out and stroked her hair. "So this man Striker. Why not use him as a backup?"

"Look, just give us notice, we make other plans—"

"I can't," said Check. "Even me, I can barely—" He stopped. "You don't really want to know." He sounded regretful.

"We take your word, then," said J.K. glumly.

Checker looked around the band, amazed as he always was by their deference. They really wouldn't make him say. Supposedly they were being respectful. That was a lie. It was easier and they knew it—their deference let them off the hook; it simplified matters enormously. Checker was still tired. It had taken longer to get back this time. He hoped this wasn't a development, some kind of sign. No, it's just some times were different from others. Take care of this here. Forget about that, there's the band now. They like what they see. They choose what they see. They've created you. Be a sport.

"Okay," J.K. agreed sulkily. "Guess I play with this dude Striker 'steada watch the paint flake off my ceiling."

"Sheckair," said Rahim, with unusual softness, "this is worst idea you ever have. You don want this boy in your band. You remember I warn you later and feel vedy foolish."

"Why?" asked Checker flatly.

"I know."

"That is a load of mystical crap."

Something in Rahim's face corkscrewed. Checker was no longer playing.

"You played with him last night—"

"It was not same!" cried Rahim.

"Big deal, it doesn't have to be—"

"Something bad happen, Sheckair!"

Checker sighed. Sometimes he got tired of it. It just seemed stupid. He wanted only to lean over with J.K. and talk about strings and amp gain.

"The thing is, he said he had connections," Howard contributed. "Could be worth it, if he could even get us a toe in the door of a company, and, Check, it's times like this we should have a demonstration tape ready—"

"We don't need to make a record, Howard," said Check patiently, no longer paying much attention. Across the river, the yellow bricks of Rikers prison glowed like the color of a sandlot when your team is winning.

"Check, The Derailleurs have the sound, the style—!"

"We play in Plato's, Howard. That's fine. That's enough. We're plenty jacked there already."

Howard kicked a piece of cement in frustration; it hurt his toe. "Check, you're a great musician, but you have no ambition."

"That's right, Howard," said Checker, watching intently as the very last disk of sun slipped behind the Empire State Building. "Not a bit."

*   *   *

Eaton was convinced he came down to the river out of almost chemical perversity. How disgusted can a person get without spontaneously combusting? Evenly clustered along the rail like the trees in Ralph DeMarco, boys shivered because back home they looked better in the mirror in open jackets, the girls this year huddled in those horrific square sweaters and squat little pedal pushers, the strip of their exposed ankles red from cold. Block after block, the posed slouches and raised hoods, carburetors polished like candelabra for anniversary dinners—it was all so trite Eaton could cry. Why, this strip couldn't have changed since 1955. These kids must take Teenager Lessons, the way they used to take Cotillion. Sit-on-your-car. Toss-your-hair-from-your-face. Above all, try not to look self-conscious. These guys had read up. The whole parade was so obscenely obedient, even stiff, that it could have been an audition for a marching band.

Yet from half a mile away a single face caught the last ray of the setting sun and went gold. It shone at the end of the strip like a burn hole. From that point the plastic flatness of this canvas shrank back, as from a lit cigarette poked through cellophane. Clumps on hoods flowered open and cliques on the rail did flips, balanced on their hipbones, skipped rocks on the river, twisted to old Rolling Stones songs. Eaton knew only that he was surrounded by many children playing. And he looked down the row knowing very well that nothing had changed.

* * *

F ive ninety-five for a turkey sandwich," said Brinkley. "Like, this place thinks it's a restaurant."

While they ritually mocked the diner's naïve attempts at *haute cuisine*, snickering at the awkward murals with statuary and Corinthian columns, for some reason Eaton could hear only how often Brinkley said the word "like," Gilbert said "you know," and Rad said "I mean." Soon Eaton had lost track of what they were talking about altogether, for he could discern only a horrifying repetition of verbal tics that was slowly driving him insane.

"Eat wasted Secretti last night. I mean, compared to Eat, Checkie's like *puh, puh, puh*—"

Suddenly Eaton blanched. He coughed and rolled his eyes, but no, these doorknobs didn't get the message; the man in the entranceway turned his head to their table when he heard his own name. When their eyes met, Eaton was once more afraid, as he'd been the night before, of discovery. Nodding weakly, he shoveled a forkful of shrimp salad and looked back to Brinkley with an absorption the boy never deserved. Eaton's hands were clammy and he no longer had an appetite. When his friends had finally noticed The Derailleurs at the big round table and had therefore switched into their seeming-to-have-a-good-time mode, Eaton found their cries for more beer and their leering after the waitress embarrassing. Abruptly he stood up, said he needed to say hello to someone, and walked away.

"Well, la-di-da," said Brinkley, seeing where Eaton was headed. "Eat's got himself new little friends." For some reason it never bothered Brinkley when his emotions were transparent.

"Careful. Pond scum," Rahim warned.

"Evening." Eaton nodded. "Come here often?" Feebly, he resorted to an old pickup line.

"Yes," said Checker. "We love the murals. They're so—innocent."

"They're ugly," said Eaton automatically.

"Why would you want to look at them like that?"

"I enjoy hating them."

Checker laughed. "So you must come here often, too. For the murals." Fondly he reached for the saltcellar and stroked up and down its facets, cleaning off fingerprints. Waves of hot and cold crossed Eaton in ripples; the hair raised on his arms. Each object Checker reached for seemed to glow. "I like their saltshakers," said Check. "I like their napkin holders with the rounded sides. I like their waitresses and their garnishes and their slaw, and the little diamond shapes in the floor. And after thorough research the band has concluded they have the best home fries in all of Astoria." Check looked up; Eaton stepped back.

"Is there anything you don't like?"

"You."

"Hijack," said Checker.

"Why the bandage?" asked Eaton, ignoring Rahim.

"My hand fell in love with a piece of glass," Check explained. "It was a destructive relationship."

"So you can't play tonight? I mean, was it serious?"

"Pain is always serious, that's what makes it exciting."

"You mean you enjoyed cutting your hand?"

Checker pulled at his bandage, looking inside at the cut with contemplation. "Well, yes."

"There are words for people like that."

Checker smiled. "I like blood. I like the color."

"You also into animal sacrifice?"

Checker laughed. "Pull up a chair."

With a flicker of hesitation, Eaton did so, but when he tried to intrude between Checker and Rahim, the Iraqi wouldn't move over. Checker eyed the saxophonist until Rahim finally screeched aside, though only far enough for Eaton's chair to jam tight between them. Eaton was forced to climb into his seat with just the kind of awkwardness he particularly detested.

"We need a backup drummer," said Checker. "You game?"

Eaton's face flushed, whether from insult or flattery it was impossible to tell. "To calm the belligerent fans when the star has a headache?"

"Something like that . . ." said Check, looking Eaton up and down like a new amp, searching for the plug. "What you did last night. You were—challenging."

"He was poison."

Eaton turned on Rahim. "Where are you from that they insult people for no reason who are about to do you a favor?"

Rahim said nothing more, only sat looking calm, almost pleasant.

"Iraq," said Checker. "Where they have lots of funny feelings."

"I see. And you're in our country visiting?"

Rahim remained quiet.

"He doesn't understand your question," said Checker.

"I mean, you're not a citizen, isn't that right? This is the way you act as a guest."

"Hijack lives here," said Checker.

"Yes. But under what auspices?—I assume I can use 'auspices,' since he seems to have a translator."

"No," said Check, though Eaton had continued to look only at Rahim. "The translator doesn't know an auspice from a hole in the ground."

"He means—" Howard began.

"I mean," Eaton interrupted, "he's wet, isn't he? From head to toe."

The band squirmed. No one answered.

"Come on," said Eaton. "I'm in the band now." Eaton smiled.

"See," said Rahim.

It happened the next weekend, and was over in surprisingly short order, though that is the nature of most events—with a few gory exceptions, murders are over in seconds; the most hurtful remarks often use the fewest words; neither falling off a cliff nor running a car into a telephone pole is a lengthy enough process to require scheduling into your day.

The band hadn't taken the man seriously at first when

he clumped over to The Derailleurs on their break—with the big biker boots and shredded T and bright pink bandanna knotted at his neck; why, the costume wasn't even coherent. At the flap of his ID, they resettled in their chairs and time got very fat. The whole table was suspended in the interface between two alternate universes. Change is like that: you are no longer where you were; you are not yet where you will get; you are nowhere exactly.

Rahim answered the man's questions idly, readjusting the brim of his Astoria Concrete hat, toying with the tail of the *hattah* he routinely wore underneath it—a winter one this time, with the black Armenian stitching. He stroked the little pom-pom on one corner like a rabbit's foot not likely to do him a hell of a lot of good. If Rahim seemed a little sluggish, he was in hyperspace—journeying from the universe in which he was trying to remember if he still had a can of stew left in the room he rented above the fruit market to the universe in which he was being arrested by the U.S. Immigration and Naturalization Service and in real danger of being summarily shipped back to Iraq. It was a big trip for thirty seconds.

"Excuse me," Checker interrupted politely. "But could I consult with my friend for a moment? He's new in the States and could use a little advice."

The agent began to explain about lawyers and rights, but Checker had already raised a just-a-moment finger and ushered the Iraqi smoothly through the back door labeled RESTROOMS.

Checker's advice was fast and straightforward and supremely American. As soon as the door closed quietly behind them, he grabbed Rahim's arm and pulled him through the exit to the back hall, where they'd often helped waitresses take out the garbage. Checker dribbled Rahim down the basement stairs and curled him around the back of the dripping water heater like sinking a shot. "Stay!" was all Check took time to say; whipping off Rahim's Astoria Concrete hat and *hattah* and shoving it on his own head, he was off again, up the stairs and careening down the back hall at just about the time the INS agent had finished checking the bathrooms. When the man opened the last door he caught only the flap of an orange bill and a flurry of headdress as it flew out to the alley and past the trash cans.

As the agent rushed after him, Checker consumed Ditmars Boulevard with wider and wider strides, laughing out loud, leading the man into Ralph DeMarco. A big, sharp night, isn't it? Feels good to run, without a coat, and it must be twenty degrees. But you aren't cold, you're excited. You loved our gig, didn't you? Sure, you used to play a little guitar way back when, and you gave it up; you went to school, you kicked around and ended up working for the government, and you haven't quite digested that yet. You never expected to be on this side of things, chasing a kid for Immigration— you haven't run in a while and you're panting and he's laughing at you, he's waiting for you to catch up, he's rolling, clutching his stomach on that little knoll at the end of the park right in front of the Con Edison plant, and *That's the drummer, where is the wetback?*

"Man, how the hell you get into this line of work?" asked Checker, still laughing on the grass.

The agent shook his head and caught his breath, collapsing on the hill, noticing how brightly the lights shone from the garbage-processing plant across the river. "Jesus," he said. "That's a long story."

Which he told.

Even Eaton Striker is afraid of Syria

4 / the house of the fire queen

People had always talked to Checker, they never knew why. Even for chronic truancy, his high-school teachers preferred asking Check to stay after school to turning him in. They'd get feverish toward the end of sixth period, rushing the lesson, anxiously shredding spare mimeos after the bell, afraid he wouldn't come. But usually, in his own sweet time, Checker would appear at the door, humming, and glide to the desk, a small secret smile pointed at the floor; he'd glance up shyly, down again, back, down, then suddenly, when they least expected it, *whoom*, he'd carve straight into their pupils, coring their eyes like apples. It was terrifying. Have a seat, please. Sure. The pads of his fingers on the desk rippling. His leg jittering up and down so the floor trembled. In trouble, and perfectly happy. No matter how severely the teachers began, his eerie blue irises flashed like heat lightning, his smile, a joke, would trigger an aside, and before they knew it they were talking about their children, their wives or husbands or lovers, the problems of teaching bored people, then all about what boredom was exactly, whose fault it was, until pretty soon Checker's feet would be up on the desk and his chair tilted back on two legs; the teachers, too, would be leaning back and playing with their pencils and jabbing excitedly with the eraser to make a point. Checker would finally remind them that it was six or seven and dark, so the two of them would stroll out and stand another half hour in the parking lot, an hour if it was spring; only out of a reluctant sense of duty and decorum would the teachers pull into their dumpy cars and away from this—this—*student*. Sometimes they gave him a ride home.

Checker was not precisely rebellious; he simply had his own agenda, and if that happened to coincide with the school's, good enough; but if it diverged, he didn't let it "rattle his cage," as Check would say. He cooperated with authority but didn't recognize it; he was no more or less conciliatory with a principal than with the boy at the next desk. He was pleasant and attentive when called in, unless another matter took precedence, like a science exhibit on refraction at the IBM Building, or a variety of orchid in the Botanical Garden peaking that afternoon, in which case he might pencil a neat and polite note declining the invitation to the principal's office, ending with the genuine hope that they could reschedule sometime soon. Dazed, the principal would read it over three or four times: *Looking forward to our talk. Until our next mutual convenience, Checker Secretti.* With even more incredulity, the man would find himself courteously negotiating with Checker over the phone, trying to find an afternoon he was "free." By the time Check showed up, the principal would feel grateful and offer the boy the big armchair and a cup of tea.

After all, appealing to his mother was hopeless. Lena Secretti was illiterate; Check had been signing her name to permission slips and even money orders to Con Ed since the age of six. His mother had borne children much the way she scrounged junk from trash piles—she carted them from the hospital and placed them in the apartment and sometimes, at moments, would remember having brought something interesting home once and look around for what had happened to it. After picking up the roll of bubble wrap, checking behind the broken adding machine, and moving the big box of paint-sample strips, nubby crayons, and plastic surgical gloves, she would dig up a dirty, hungry, but contented son playing Olympics with roaches. Now, Lena Secretti was not exactly insane, and no one ever died or got permanently misplaced in her care, but she was not the kind of woman you sent curt notes about truancy.

In his obliviousness of rules and even of law, Check had been accused of being "unrealistic," but in fact his world was profoundly concrete. He understood tangibles, like, there is an agent who wants to ship your sax player back to Iraq, so you take your friend away from the man. Checker tried to explain.

"But we'll get him eventually, and you could get prosecuted yourself, bucko," said the agent the next day at Plato's.

The club was closed for The Derailleurs' rehearsal on Sunday
afternoons, which the man had interrupted with his enthusi-
astic investigation. "Aiding and abetting, harboring fugitives.
We're arresting Catholics for that shit lately, for Christ's sake.
Think we'd bat an eye at a black rock drummer?" But somehow
the agent, Gary Kaypro, didn't sound very threatening. Like
all the high-school teachers before him, he was leaning back
with Checker Secretti, waving his cigarette, trying desperately
to entertain.

"Gary," said Check affectionately, "we have a gig next
weekend. I can't find another sax player in five days."

"Play here, man, your buddy won't be around for the
encore." Gary Kaypro said "man" a lot. He'd shed the pink
bandanna from the night before, but still propped heavy
leather boots on the table. He'd managed to emphasize early
how very much guitar and saxophone he'd played in high
school. The agent was vaguely middle-aged, for from the
vantage point of nineteen anything between thirty and sixty
is simply *not young*; after sixty you are *old*. Kaypro himself
knew this, and though he kept trying to intrude the fact that
he was only thirty-six, he guessed correctly that they didn't
care.

"Well, say we toe the line," Check proposed. "How can
I get my sax man legit? You must know immigration law—how
does it work?"

Kaypro shrugged with casual expertise. "There's the
political-asylum gambit. Say they're going to flay the kid with
a potato peeler if he sets foot in Iraq."

"They would," said Check. "He's a draft evader."

"Still a bad bet," said Kaypro. "None of that shit is flying lately, see. With the Cubans, the Haitians, and now the Salvadorans, we're burned out on the but-they'll-shoot-me routine. Pretty much the U.S. says, So what? Unless you're Eastern European or Soviet. And you ever read the newspaper?"

"Only the little articles on the inside pages."

"Well, the big articles are full of Middle Eastern maniacs blowing up Americans and shoving them out of planes. Imagine how overjoyed the INS gets when they apply for asylum. We figure most of them belong in one."

"So what's another angle?"

"He could disappear. Get out of New York, or at least never show up here, or at his room on Grand."

"No good. What else?"

"He could marry an American."

"No kidding."

"Sure. Even gets you citizenship eventually. But—only if it's for real."

"What do you mean?"

"We're on to that scam, see. We do interviews now, in *intimate detail*. Ask the couple the colors of their underwear? Any moles? Form of birth control? The works. Sometimes split them up, compare their stories. I've done it. A scream, really. Catch these guys, picked up a wife for three thousand dollars, can't even remember her first name. Man, they're on the plane by sundown, bingo."

"But if Hijack got married this week, you couldn't arrest him?"

"I could. He's still illegal until he goes through channels."

"But would you?"

"What are you trying to pull here, bucko?"

"I'm shooting straight, Kaypro. If he gets married, will you leave him alone and let him go 'through channels'?"

"You have a lady in mind?"

"I might."

"Depends," said the agent, clicking his eyeteeth together. "You know the INS is famous for corruption, don't you?" He smiled.

"We don't have any money, Kaypro."

"No, no. What I want I can't buy. I—" He seemed flustered. "I'd like to play with you guys!"

"What?" said the band.

"Just a set once in a while. I used to get in my licks, see? And—you're half decent, Secretti. Three-quarters, even."

Checker laughed. "Deal's on."

"But the kid has to do the whole bit," the agent added. "Someone turned him in; I have to report. And if the marriage is a fraud, they'll skewer him and the girl both. Likewise, you don't get wedding bells to chime before I find him, the ax is gonna fall. I'll look the other way if he's got a solid claim to living in this country, but as of now he's moist, through and through. I'd like to beat out a few oldies with you kids, but I'm not a sleazebag—I do my job." With that moment of officiousness, he left the club.

"Well, that's the ticket," Check announced.

"Ticket's on the family plan," said J.K. "What about La Señorita, Jack?"

"Well . . ." Check drawled, moving to his Leedys to tune the heads for their upcoming rehearsal. "That's the one tiny hole in an otherwise flawless scheme, isn't it? Rache, why don't you run down and tell Hijack we'll get him out of that steam bath before the week's out."

"Tell him he has Super Check on his side. Mild-mannered rock drummer by day, wild-man immigration lawyer in a phone booth."

Checker turned to the door, unable to decipher Eaton's tone. Eaton kept a straight face. So many of Eaton's compliments would have this quality—balanced perfectly between admiration and mockery. Never quite sardonic, never quite sincere. "Right," said Check uncertainly. "Guys, I thought Strike should rehearse with you instead of me today, learn our tunes."

"When I talked to you last, you were all in a tizzy," said Eaton, languishing in a chair. "Now you've solved everything?"

"We just have to find him a wife."

"The Sheik doesn't have a sweetheart, does he?" asked Caldwell.

"Who needs a sweetheart," said Eaton, "when your band leader has such a pretty smile?"

Checker looked at Eaton with anthropological curiosity.

"Surely, Secretti," Eaton proceeded, "with those big broad shoulders and wide blue eyes and that impressive set of drums there, you must have quite a harem. Just point. Marry your friend? Sure. Anything for you, Checker. Whatever you say."

"Now that," said Check, ratcheting his keys, "is a laugh."

"Check don't have no harem," said J.K. "He got a death squad."

"Remember Janice?" said Checker, pointing to four faint white scars scraped parallel down his arm.

Checker remembered Janice. Sure. Last summer, right here. More than once that wiry little creature waited all night for some joker to finish his beer, methodically splintering the edge of The Derailleurs' regular table with her nail file. The way she dug into that wood and twisted as it got so damn late and the son of a bitch ordered another one. But she liked it on the table, hard and half off the edge. She said she sat here during sets and kneaded the varnish, watching Checker drum. She said she liked knowing what they did there and no one understanding why she was smiling. So she'd chip away until the waitress packed out; Checker had a key.

It was the last time he remembered, best and worst. Before, he'd always figured her a hellion, a vicious little animal survivor, with long, stringy muscles and wary eyes. He didn't worry about her. Janice was thin, but more flexible than fragile, like Rachel. That afternoon she'd been to the beach; sand still stuck to her skin. Stubble had risen on the sides of her pelvis, where she shaved for her bikini, leaving only a little black tuft in the middle, like a Mohawk. Checker needed a shave, too, so between them the grind of their bodies had a satisfying grit, a resistance. She never liked it too smooth, too perfectly, simply good. And she wouldn't let him roll her onto her back. The positions she preferred were more contorted, and she'd wrestle to stay on top. There was nail in her caress, bite to her kiss.

Sand imbedded in his pores. She was bony, without cushions; their hipbones jarred. At last she bit too deep, and reflexively he pulled her off him by her ragged wet mop, surprised to find that with the strands pulled taut he could feel her heart beating in her hair. That was when he noticed the frantic pulsing everywhere, the way her arteries exploded on the sides of her neck, at her throat, her armpits, in the shaved cups of her hips—it was amazing, this girl stripped so thin she was like a Compton transparency of the circulatory system. He stared at her veins, their rapid beat and alarming syncopation.

"Musicians," she'd whispered over him; he moaned a half step lower each inch her hand descended from his shoulder. She meant it was not all cacophonous grappling, that he understood distinctions, different notes: here not there, and no longer—sustain, cut; press, lift. She would extend her hand and then delay; she played like funk, behind the beat, the little stop, the little reluctance. Checker smiled and thought, Give this girl sticks, but she was more keyboard really, resting her hand light and relaxed like a good pianist—Checker could have balanced pennies on her wrists. Her chords down his side grew increasingly deft, his pecs, nipple, under the ribs, off, to the hip socket, off, less and less, only tickling over the hairs now, right by his balls, but refusing, because it was too obvious, to touch the genitals themselves, like lyricists who leave a line at a rhyme so inevitable that they don't sing the word at all.

Only at the end did he shrink back, from the long, scrappy fingers with the tight-in, pointed nails, black—an urchin's. The urgency went too far. She clutched his collarbone like a ledge; he could see her hanging. His hands slid from her sides, and she slipped down his thighs. Checker's prick sucked out, bent down, and sprang free of her like a perch that wouldn't bear her weight. Her knees hit the table. She fell only three inches between his legs, but far enough for Janice to see he wouldn't hold her up. She had wanted him, but getting him didn't solve anything. She would need to find later there was nothing to solve, but he refused to teach her that much. He was a man and enjoyed this. He loved her childlike clambering, her skinny athletic daring, the way she climbed and swung and gripped at his limbs like at the rungs of a jungle gym. But he was not her father or brother or rescuer, and her wide brown eyes saw that in horror and went wild, then flat. She rolled completely off him onto her back, her palms to the wood, breathing at the quick, inconceivable pace of a hamster, the tiny rib cage filling up and down, her nostrils quivering, her short black hair frayed and chopped-looking, stricken. She would look only at the ceiling. He stroked her forehead, but would not comfort her too much, because he wouldn't take back what she'd discovered.

They all thought they needed saving. They all got a surprise. And sooner or later, the nails came scraping over his arms, eyes clawing at his face. They screamed. Janice was the worst, since of course some of them were calm, pretend-cold, but he could always see the fingers opening and closing at their sides, the muscles springing in their jaws, hear the air grating through their teeth. Checker would spread his hands. He thought he'd given them what they wanted. Instead, he'd come too close—he gave them more than the others and stopped. He let them touch what they could not own. So many Alices, longing for the tiny garden, who couldn't reach the key. For the girls it must have been worse than nothing. All his memories of that table had an edge in them, like Halloween apples filled with razor blades.

Little wonder none of these lovelies sprang to mind as Rahim's bride-to-be. The last favor Janice did him was slashing her initials in the head of his snare, and Checker had known her well enough to see that the gesture cost her some restraint.

"What about your vocalist here?" Eaton proposed.

"You mean Rache?" asked Caldwell, no one looking straight at her.

Rachel immediately began to unravel her sweater, from a moth hole, with such concentration it was like knitting in reverse.

"Rache do enough for the band, man, I don't know you want to involve—"

"Checker," Rachel interrupted J.K. softly, "would you want me to?" She looked up at the drummer. "Would you like me to marry Hijack?"

Rachel's hair was loose today, and washed; it wafted out from her head, and her face was lost inside it. Looking into her eyes was like staring into a dark ball of fur which, with the slightest puff of air from the stage, would tumble away. Checker found himself actually holding his breath. He said absolutely nothing.

That was enough. A moment later the ball of fur blew out the door, caught on the breeze of its own shudder.

"You should have said no right away, man," said Caldwell.

"I know," said Checker. "I was thinking of Hijack. Back soon as I can." *They all think they need saving.* Checker pulled on his jacket and jogged out of the club.

"Are they . . . ?" asked Eaton.

"No!" the band answered at once.

"It's just, that wasn't a great suggestion, Strike," said Caldwell.

"Rachel—" Howard hesitated. "Rachel is a romantic."

"How the hell did I offend her?"

"Rache and Check—" Caldwell began.

"Sweets!" said Howard.

"Everybody know, Howard," said J.K.

"Everybody knows if you tell everybody," said Howard.

"Okay, okay."

They sat in silence.

"I've never figured out how she stands it," Caldwell remarked.

"It's very delicate," said Howard, his delight in analysis getting the better of his loyalty. "Like photosynthesis. A perfectly balanced chemical process that by all rights shouldn't work—"

"Where you get *that*?" asked J.K.

"The point is"—Howard glared—"if plants can turn air to branches, anything is possible."

"Howard's right, Big J.," said Caldwell. "There's something real incredible about those two. Like, it's a miracle little Jackless hasn't killed herself."

"Where is Checker Secretti?"

A shadow cut the length of the club.

"What you want with Check?" braved J.K., whose voice sounded strangely high for a 210-pound bass player.

"His ass in my glassworks."

She stepped into the light and the whole band subtly recoiled. Even Eaton wasn't inclined to say anything smart and private-school. Once more the woman was in her apron and earthy, ancient, unwashed clothes. She hadn't bothered with a coat, nor had she taken off her dark glasses. Her hair, askew as usual, glittered with sleet. She appeared like the Wicked Witch of the West and Cinderella's Fairy Godmother all wrapped into one enthralling but appalling creature. You did not know whose side she was on.

"He got business," said J.K.

"He has business with me," Syria boomed. "You tell him he's late. You tell him I don't have time to chase him down in his little clubhouse. You tell him he shows or I throw him in with the next load of cullet. Got that?"

"Cullet," Caldwell repeated softly.

"What?"

"Check taught us the word yesterday," he explained meekly. "Broken glass."

"My, my," said Syria. "A for the day, rock star." She stopped and looked down at him. "You're cute."

"Thank you," said Caldwell formally.

"You tell your drummer friend, one more hour, he's fired." Bang. She vanished.

"The Towering Inferno!" exclaimed Caldwell.

They marveled over the apparition until Checker returned.

When told of his employer's visit, Checker seemed pleased. Before he hurried out again, Check assured the band that Rachel was all right now—once more, air had been turned to branches.

S orry I'm late," Checker panted. "I had a problem."

"What do you know about problems?"

"Plenty."

She took off her glasses, sifting Checker up and down through a queer mesh; her eyes were green. She seemed to see him differently from other people. Checker felt exposed, and pulled his jacket closed, raising its collar around his neck.

"Sweep." She handed him a broom.

"When do I get to work with the glass?" Check shouted. All their conversation was loud. It had to be. The roar of the furnace was voracious.

She didn't answer, and from then on, apart from giving him orders, she ignored him completely. Once again she was at her own work, which soon sufficiently absorbed her that she didn't notice he'd run out of things to do. Checker settled quietly behind her to watch.

Syria gathered a lump of molten glass, then swung the pipe like a pendulum until the glob elongated; it cooled and darkened, and she returned it to the top of the furnace, propping the pipe on a stand and rolling it in quick, regular circles until the shaft was warm again. She repeated this process until the glass stretched into a rod with a knob on its end; she hung it glass down and made another form like it on a separate pipe. After reheating the first, she plunged the two shafts together, filed into the glass on one pipe, and cracked it off clean with a rap on the metal. Though working with a huge amount of material that must have been heavy, she manipulated the now three-foot-long piece like balsa wood, swinging it with grace and, he could see, pleasure, feeling its momentum, finding the fulcrum point on the pipe. All her motions were rapid and sure, without excess; they reminded him of good basketball. They reminded him of good drumming. They reminded him of anything he had ever done right.

Syria hefted the pipe over to a chair with flat arms and rolled it in front of her with her left palm, all the while shaping the middle knot with a wet wooden cup. Steam rose from the glass, hissing at her touch, a whisper of pain—cold water and hot glass don't mix, but Syria would marry them, anyway. Checker remembered how she tended his cut: this will hurt but it will heal you. She was a person who would do something terrible for your own good.

It was only when she'd cracked the shaft into the annealer that Check realized that while he'd been waiting for her to blow a vase, a bowl, she wasn't making a vessel. She was making a bone.

At last Checker noticed a dark corner room, and ducked inside to turn on the light. There they were. All over the walls, stacked shelf after shelf: glass bones. Clear, glistening femurs. Ice-blue rib cages, fragile, almost breathing. Strange assemblages of knuckles and kneecaps, like remnants of a mass grave turned mysteriously to crystal—deep sad greens and buried ambers. Some of the longer bones were distorted, curved, as if they were melting.

Checker felt dizzy. It was like walking into a glass morgue, shuddering and deadly, but beautiful, too, shimmering in the glow of the low-wattage bulb. The walls hurt to look at. Nothing should be that disturbing and that attractive. As his intestines began to gather, he closed the door tightly behind him, like shutting the top of Pandora's box.

Checker felt woozy and weaved to a nearby bench.

"So what was so funny?"

"What?"

"When I was working. You laughed."

"The way you moved," he remembered. "I played a song in my head and you danced to it."

She smiled. "Which one?"

"'Burning Down the House.'"

"Three-hun-dred-six-ty-five-de-grees. It's hotter than that."

"You know the Heads!"

"What do you think I grew up on, Frank Sinatra?"

"Sorry." Checker took a deep breath.

"You don't look well."

"Give me a second." The sensation was receding, but

not quickly enough, as if he'd woken a sleeping dragon—even if it only yawned and went back to sleep, the ground rumbled.

"So you went into the crypt."

"Yes."

"And?"

"I don't know."

"What a critic."

"That room is dangerous!" he burst out.

"Sure," she said casually. "Being alive is dangerous."

"The red ones."

"Yes?"

"The red ones," Check repeated, shaking his head. "I don't know."

Somehow she seemed pleased with his reaction, though Check had said nothing nice.

"You sell those things?"

"Not very hard. Nobody understands them. But once they're cooled they don't matter. I like *hot* glass." Her eyes glittered like the sleet that afternoon.

Checker returned the next night, on time. Rahim was on his mind, for earlier he'd visited the Iraqi in the basement, where it was hot and dank and boring, and they couldn't think of any girls. Yet it had been impossible to stay moody, with the rise coming up through his All-Stars all the way to his throat. In the park the car radios had played the right songs, marathon; at six o'clock the sky was purple; the

pavement was still icy from Sunday's sleet, radiant with orange
streetlights. The river swept the skyline into dizzy, turgid
swirls.

The broom swished around the concrete, curling dust
like whirlpools under Hell Gate, glass tinkling in its wake
like the shores of the East River; Checker could feel every
individual hair of the brush stroke the floor. Unloading the
annealer, he loved all the student pieces. Lurching off center,
bubbled and drooped, each vase and goblet charmed him,
each bowl would hold ripe fruit.

All the while he could feel Syria as heat source move from
room to room. He liked it best when he was perfectly between
the two of them, the woman and the furnace; the sweat would
pour evenly down his body. Each drop traced his spine like
the tip of a finger.

Later, the cleanup done, she showed him how to work
the furnace; Check felt on friendlier terms with the animal
once he could control it. Finally she let him thread one of
those sturdy pipes into the mass itself, and wear his own pair
of glasses. The heat stung; he wondered how she got used to
it. His face stiffened and his knuckles sung. Sweat showered
down his chest. Even with the dark glasses he couldn't focus
on the glass itself—it shifted uneasily before him, rippling
like flesh. He could tell when the pipe hit the glass only from
a tugging, a nagging when he pulled it back. Awkwardly he
withdrew a drizzling glob, like Little Jack Horner pulling a
plum from a pie.

She showed him how to blow the first bubble, putting
her mouth around the pipe. Checker stared.

"Don't just stand there. This is your piece."

When he pressed his lips to the metal he was surprised how hard it was to blow; nothing happened. The sharp taste of steel mingled with something musty. Syria.

"It's too cold now. Heat it up."

When he was finished, Check had made a tiny cup he knew was ridiculous, though that didn't keep him from being enormously proud. It was thick, with a lip that curled accidentally inward, but smooth and round, later to rest perfectly in his hand, like a small breast.

It was three in the morning; only the glow of the furnace lit the shop. Checker lay on one of the benches, exhausted, having perspired away about five pounds. Syria turned down the gas, so the furnace settled to a steady purr; it was easier to talk. She leaned up against a post and studied her new assistant. Syria herself seemed a little tired, softer; her hair had relaxed.

"So what's your story?" she asked.

Checker laughed. "I drum." His voice vibrated the bench. "I love—things."

She waited.

"I love this," he explained. "Glass and color. Heat. Work. Shapes. And shit, the sky tonight—"

"Fuchsia."

"You saw!"

"You own the sky?"

"Yes."

She was so jagged, he was surprised by the roundness of her laughter. "Well, so do I."

"I own every color," Check went on. "I own this neighborhood. Most of all I own the *Triborough*."

"I've wondered whose that was."

"Mine. Shore to shore. We're in love."

"I'm jealous."

Checker's whole body was humming; the furnace and the rhythm of their voices were both trembling in the wooden bench now, as if a good song was playing loud. He closed his eyes. "My bicycle is jealous, too. Sure, Zefal's pretty, thin, tight. But there's something about a frame so big. Like a tall woman." Hmm. At that point Checker decided to open his eyes and shut his mouth. Syria had edged away to turn down the annealer.

"And what's your story?"

"When you're twenty-nine, there isn't one anymore, there are hundreds. And I don't feel like telling any of them tonight."

"Don't," Checker chided.

"Maybe later," she said more kindly. "You said you had a problem tonight. What is it?"

Checker explained about Rahim. "So," he finished, "I need a woman."

"Common complaint. Where will you get yours?"

Lying on the bench, Checker felt a wave of nausea ripple from his feet to his throat, just as the elation had risen earlier that evening. He swallowed, the taste of his own saliva sour. He waited for the sickness to pass, and used the silence to make his next question seem to be changing the subject.

"Are you married?"

"No."

"Why not?"

"By the time most men reach thirty they're picking out their headstones already. All that's left is to fill in the dates. I'm not interested."

"Do you ever want to get married?"

"Stop it."

"Stop what?"

"Go ahead."

Check said nothing.

"I said, go ahead."

Maybe something flew into the furnace, something live. A strange smell passed over the two of them, like singed hair. His saliva was viscous from dehydration. "Syria," he said thickly, "will you marry Rahim?"

"That's better," said Syria. "Now we're there." She sat down on the bench at his feet. "Now, you explain to me why I should do such a thing." She patted his ankles.

"To do me a favor."

"Oh?" She seemed amused. "You really think I'd be doing you a favor?"

"Both Hijack's brothers were murdered in Iraq. If they send him back he'll be axed right off the plane. Even if they don't bother, he'll be drafted. And Hijack says—he says it's not a nice war."

"What's a nice war?" she asked mildly, not paying much attention. She held the toe of his tennis shoe.

Checker turned on his side away from her, resting his cheek against the warm wood of the bench as if it were a pillow. He felt like a small boy wishing he could clutch a ragged one-eyed bear. Instead, he reached down and stroked the leg of the bench, conscious of how hard it was. Checker almost never felt sorry for himself; it was a funny curled sensation, shaped like a sickle with a point on the end or like a very sharp question mark. "He's my friend and he's in trouble."

"Why should I care?" She pulled her hand away and leaned back. "I met you ten days ago spying on my shop and making a mess of my alley. You're a total stranger."

It would be different if she was really trying to give him a reason why the whole idea was ridiculous. But no, she was forcing him instead to make a good case. "I'm not a stranger," he said muddily, his cheek against the wood. "We're alike."

"That's arrogant." Yet she didn't seem offended, and expected him to go on.

He couldn't. He felt as if soon he'd have to go deeply and dreamlessly to sleep.

"Don't women usually get paid for this sort of thing?"

"About three thousand dollars."

"And how much money do you have?"

"Forty."

"Thousand?"

"Dollars." Checker sat up and pulled a scrumple of bills from his pocket. "Forty-three. But it's not all mine, it's the band's. My share would be six . . . fourteen. Plus Hijack's . . . $12.28, then."

"Well. That's at least six beers. Two apiece. A party."

"How's that?"

"For the three of us. You, me, and my husband." She let

him hear the sound of it. Checker winced. "How are you going to pay off any woman with $12.28?"

"And a lifetime's admission to Plato's?"

"Well, what's the cover?"

"Two dollars."

Syria did a quick calculation. "So, if I went every weekend, I'd start to break even after twenty-seven years."

"Want to watch me drum that long?"

"Maybe." Checker kept waiting for this to be a joke.

They both sat facing each other, leaning against opposite posts, their feet on the bench. Sensing they'd reached an impasse, Checker began to cheer up.

"You know, I've never much wanted a husband . . ." said Syria thoughtfully. "But I wouldn't mind a wife."

"What?"

"I teach all day, do bones at night. I get tired of carrots and bad Astoria pizza. My apartment looks like glacial slag. At the end of the month my clothes have gotten so filthy that I have to throw them away. I've lived this way for years. But it might be refreshing to clean up my act. Only, though, if someone else did the cleaning."

"Are you serious?"

"What else could I possibly get out of this?"

Checker tapped the bench. "What all would you want him to do?"

"Cooking, shopping, picking up. Laundry, phone bills. I would like to see out my windows again, maybe even find the floor. Fresh flowers. I have a little money, can you believe it? The stuff accumulates from neglect, like dust. I wouldn't mind having someone to spend it, which is only work to me. And once in a while he could have the afternoon off to go to the hairdresser's or the garden club or to buy a new hat." She laughed.

"There's just one person won't find this funny," said Check uneasily.

"He's Muslim, isn't he?"

"Very."

"This could be quite an education, then."

"Maybe," Checker warned, "for both of you."

"You are talking about that lean, bright-eyed, dark thing at your heels last Friday, with the pretty teeth? A puppy dog. Needs housetraining."

"If Hijack is a puppy, he bites. I don't think he does windows."

"He could learn."

"I'm trying to tell you—Hijack has some ideas about women—"

"That can be changed."

"I've never met anyone who was actually more optimistic than I was."

"Do you think he'd rather clean up the mess his head would make rolling on the runway or my living room?"

"Good point." Checker was confused. It was lucky for this to work out, wasn't it? Then why did he feel so depressed? "There's another thing," he added. "The INS is getting tougher. You'd have an interview—"

"Sounds entertaining."

"And you'd have to live together, for a while, anyway."

"How else would he fix me breakfast?"

Syria, Check was all too aware, didn't know what she was getting into. He tried to imagine Rahim rising cheerfully in the morning to stand at the stove in a little white apron, making sure to put in the toast so that it would pop up just when the eggs were still loose; maybe in the other room Syria would be ordering more oxides, to stride into the kitchen immediately angry if the coffee wasn't already dripped. He tried to see the Iraqi cringing and apologizing, slipping a spoon between the cone and the filter to make the coffee drip faster, a little trick he'd picked up from the neighbor next door—

No way.

"Your Iraqi friend, does he have a lover?"

"Only me."

"Oh?"

"Not like that. But Hijack is—around."

"He adores you."

"We're friends."

"That must mean a lot to you, then."

"I tried to explain before. Everything means a lot to me. Bridges. Water. So you can figure how I might feel about human beings."

"What about yourself?"

"What do you mean?"

"Never mind."

"So we have a deal?"

"He'd have to work. I'm not the Statue of Liberty."

Checker went to get his coat, feeling chilly, though even with the gas low it must have been ninety degrees.

They stood side by side before the furnace, staring at the eclipse around the door.

"Now, Checko," she said softly, right by his ear. "Now you may get out of it."

Checker leaned down and picked up a long glass drip he'd failed to sweep up, and held it up to the light of the fire. The bead at its end was crimson, frozen at the end of a thread of glass like a crystal tear. *Sheckair!* A wet napkin smoothed over his forehead; *r's* rolled over his ears. "No," said Check with a sigh. "I'm in."

It was over. So many dramas are decided in minutes, though the consequences may loiter in for decades, as leisurely as they are inexorable. Don't worry. Sit back. Watch the show. It's like after the polls have closed and there's nothing to do but follow the returns, staring at the screen with Scotch as the numbers change, digit by digit. Once the votes are cast, it's almost relaxing.

They shuffled on their wraps with a curious embarrassment; the evening, especially the first of it—*what is your story*, long and easy on the bench—would not return. You are my good friend's fiancée. I am the matchmaker, the go-between. The employee, too; a business relationship. Checker felt almost formal. "I'll be in at nine tomorrow night."

"Just hold on there."

"What?"

"How about my twelve dollars?"

Checker laughed and fished out the tattered bills, counting them fondly one by one into her beautiful hands, so full of scars and hard work and twenty-nine years of stories.

"Uhn-uhn." She stopped him as he started to leave. "Twelve *twenty-eight*."

The last thirteen cents of Syria's bride price were in pennies.

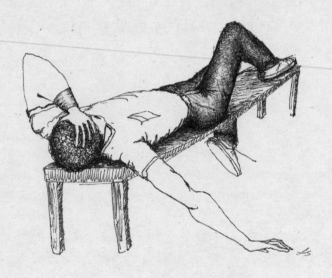

Checker is about to make a mistake

5 / bye, bye,
miss american pie

Just to play the devil's advocate," said Eaton, "don't you think this inundation of aliens has to be stopped? According to Kaypro, the U.S. is on its way to being a full third Spanish."

"Hijack isn't Spanish," said Checker.

"By the turn of the century, over half the school-age kids in this country will be Spanish."

"Hijack isn't Spanish," said Checker.

"We're being overrun by Hispanics."

"Hijack isn't—"

"Foreigners, then."

"This country is made of foreigners."

A tired point. "Granted. But while personally we all like Rahim—"

Caldwell guffawed. "Come on, Strike. That little terror

would send an army of raving Shiites after your ass in a minute. He hates your ever-loving guts. Let's not play pretty."

Eaton sat tapping his foot. It was impossible to have an intelligent discussion with these people. "I'm trying to approach this politically. While I'm not saying you're doing the wrong thing with Rahim—"

"Then why make the point?"

"There's something to be said for ideological discourse," said Howard.

"What?" asked Check.

Howard shrank, and shrugged. Howard was often paralyzed by direct questions.

"See, I'm not much of an intellectual," Check went on, "like Howard here—"

Howard beamed.

"—But ideas in the air. They're funny animals. They seem to come kind of—afterward. Like, you decide you don't like some Iraqi, or Spanish people, and then you grab one of these flying things and make it squawk."

"You're saying all abstraction is invalid?"

"Just seems like a shifty business, you know? To talk about Hijack but to say that the one thing we can't talk about when we talk about him is—Hijack." Checker raised his eyebrows innocently. "That make sense?"

"Not much," clipped Eaton.

"Let me put it this way. Hijack goes back to Iraq—"

"Thwack," said Caldwell.

"Exactly. Or at least he gets drafted, and this thing with Iran—"

"Which isn't America's problem."

"Everyone is everyone else's problem," said Checker promptly.

"That sounds—burdensome," said Eaton. "How do you take it all on and keep from killing yourself?"

Checker studied the table. "Interesting question."

Eaton took a shrewd look at the other drummer. "The point is: personal loyalty is one thing. But if you look at the big picture, our borders are being overrun. It's practically a national emergency. And you're about to engage in immigration fraud. Sure, you want to help your friend. But morally—even if you won't recognize the category—your operation is iffy."

Finally Checker responded, with unusual gravity. "I live in a little picture. It's the only picture I have. You say personal loyalty is one thing. I don't think so. I think it's everything. It's the beginning of everything, anyway, Striker. It's the bottom line."

Checker had closed his eyes; finished, he opened them and the whole band applauded. Eaton didn't know what had gone wrong.

C hecker slid down the basement rail, swung around a water pipe, and tripped into the tiny alcove by the heater where Rahim was once more dripping along with the candle. Check threw the Iraqi a beer. Keeping Rahim hydrated was a full-time project, but with his nights in the glassworks Checker was getting used to cooling his own body like a nuclear reactor and never forgot to bring the hideaway something to drink. He whisked around the cramped back room picking up gyro wrappers and soda cans, noticing how in only a minute or two the steam from the leaky heater began to condense and bead on his skin. The wide cuff he wore on his left wrist shifted; constant perspiration was making the leather slick and Checker carefully readjusted it. In the light of the candle his muscles gleamed, the veins down his forearm shone in golden branches, and water ran in runnels between his tendons. Checker stopped to admire the shine. Sweat reminded him of Syria.

"Sheckair?" Rahim whispered, sitting in a puddle on the greenish concrete floor. "Not complaining and thanking you so much for the many drinks and the books and the tapes, but—"

"It's hot here and this sucks," Checker finished quietly for him, taking Rahim's waste pail from the corner and running it unsqueamishly upstairs. "So," he announced on his return, "a deal."

"Wife?"

"Sort of, but you're not going to like it."

Rahim wilted a little further. "She is ugly?"

"No," said Check, smiling at the picture. "She's a knockout."

"So how is problem?" Rahim immediately cheered. "I marry pretty girl, stay in Amedica."

"She's no girl, believe me."

"How she is pretty, she is old dog?"

"English lesson, Hijack. Pretty is for sweet girls with

pastel sweaters and heart-shaped lockets around their necks. Pretty girls had braces. Pretty girls take a shower at least once a day and never have dishes in the sink. They keep their nails trimmed and their shoes match their pocketbooks. Or they may even wear black leather and metal studs and ride a Harley, but they still have a way of looking at you, a way of smiling, that means they'll never hurt you in a million years. They like to hold hands and they're nice, they're relaxing. But Syria Pyramus isn't a girl and she's not pretty and she's definitely not relaxing."

Rahim's eyes widened. "Fire lady?"

"Yes, but—"

Rahim leaned back and stretched out his legs as much as he was able. "Not bad, Sheckair. But she need discipline."

Checker groaned. "That's what she said about you."

"I work at my market. She make supper. Have rooms clean, flowers—"

"Hold *everything.*" Checker took the candle and placed it ritualistically between them, crossing his legs on the floor. "This is the scam, my man: *You* make the supper. *You* have the rooms clean. *You* buy the flowers."

Rahim Abdul, loyal Muslim and recent Iraqi immigrant, born and faithfully raised in the bosom of paternity, looked genuinely confused. "What you say?"

"She wants—an assistant," said Check uncomfortably. "To cook and clean and shop. She wants—"

"Slave!"

Checker shrugged. "Yeah. Take it or leave it."

"Leave it!"

As Rahim glared, Checker stood back up and stretched, pointedly knocking his arms into the pipes overhead. "Well, I guess we could get you a little lamp here, a table. And maybe a TV, though with Kaypro around all the time you couldn't use the sound . . ."

"Don make funny."

"Well, is it a joke, Hijack? That they'll shoot you for draft evasion, was that just a good story?"

"No story," said Rahim glumly. "Only—shoot if lucky."

"And we might be able to rustle you out of here, but you could never come back. You'd have to leave The Derailleurs—"

"I never leave Derailleurs!"

"Sh-sh!" There was scuffling in the upstairs hall. "All right, then," said Checker softly when the steps retreated, kneeling to his saxophone player. "This is the real thing, Hijack. Pulling this off is going to be tricky. We're going to marry you in a wet basement, real quiet, no champagne. And even when you're married, the INS is going to investigate you down to the drawer you keep your underwear in. Frankly, they don't like Iraqis. I've done the best I can and we don't have any money, the woman has to get something out of this, okay? But I don't want to see you ground into a falafel just because you're too much of a man to fix her one yourself."

The expression on Rahim's face changed, and Checker wasn't sure he liked it. "We make me Amedican," said Rahim, eyes glittering with complicity. "Then we teach this Fire Lady to make her husband falafel with warm, fresh pita and walk three steps behind him in street."

"No way, Hijack—"

Rahim raised his hand. "I do how you say."

"You do what Syria says and agree to it now or we can't go through with this."

"No problem," said Rahim mildly, who had learned this neutralizing phrase only lately and found it immensely handy.

"You mean you agree?"

"No problem," Rahim repeated.

"There'd better not be," Checker warned.

"Is one more thing." Rahim put a hand shyly on Checker's arm. "She is—clean?"

Checker guffawed. "*Syria?*"

"No, I mean—she is not used?"

Checker paused, and said carefully, "I'm sure Syria hasn't ever done anything like this before." He had the sensation with this statement of balancing on a very thin beam—he held his breath, every word a smooth, sure step, as long as he didn't look down. He knew Rahim.

"Excellent," said Rahim. "Because in my country, if she—"

"You really don't need to worry about that," said Checker hurriedly. "We have a deal? With cooking and cleaning?"

Rahim only rose and said eagerly, "I can go now?"

"Kaypro likes it here, bridegroom. You stay put." Checker left the Iraqi in the basement to stew, much like shutting a child in his room to restore his good behavior. But Checker remembered grimly that the tactic just created wilier, more rebellious children in the long run.

* * *

Sure enough, when Checker returned upstairs Gary Kaypro was back again, this time commiserating with Eaton about how the last thing you found in New York nowadays was "a real American." Kaypro was drinking Wild Turkey, bemoaning the incompetence of the INS, and Checker wondered how Rahim had gotten snagged in one of its rare moments of effectiveness. As Kaypro went on about their tiny budget and ludicrous responsibilities, though, Check did start to feel sorry for him—though he wanted to play sax with The Derailleurs, Kaypro didn't seem corrupt really, and he had a stupid, impossible job.

"But it's flattering, isn't it?" Checker intruded gently. "Immigration?"

"Yeah, how?"

"Well, we can't let everybody in. But it's nice to run a place that everybody wants into instead of out of. Nobody's beating down any doors to get into Iraq."

"God, no," and Kaypro proceeded with a string of Middle Eastern horror stories, then back to nightmare bureaucracy and fraud. "You know, for a couple hundred dollars any wet can outfit himself with birth certificate, driver's license, and social security card? They sell them in packets."

Checker restrained himself from asking. "Where?"

During the week Checker dragged a doctor down to the basement and over to Vesuvius for blood tests, and stood in line for forms at City Hall. Most of his pocket money went to buying Rahim six-packs, most of his time to finding a minister, rushing pizza slices down Plato's back stairs before the cheese congealed, and calming Syria after she inflamed at the least inconvenience this odd project cost her. But Checker didn't mind being busy—he loved all forms of motion. He ran his errands with Zefal, and in January the roads were uncluttered with other cyclists, the air slapping his skin, sharp in his throat. Winter coloration in New York has a subtle palette—the ashen crust of dried salt on macadam, the dun scrub of dead grass in the parks, the dapple of tabloid pages flapping down cracking sidewalks, the flat cardboardy bark of beeches and ginkgos, the leaden loom and pulse of the sky—all these grays, depressing to some, were tender to Checker.

Friday, Kaypro showed up at Plato's with his saxophone. He'd returned to the club every night that week, on the pretense of doing his job. Eaton, especially, seemed to like talking to the man, scattering their conversation with brands of shells and pedals and guitars, testing Kaypro's knowledge of obscure bands and backup musicians. Eaton liked to prickle these games with "Of course, at your age . . ." "You must not get to . . ." "I don't suppose you've heard of . . ." Check watched each "your age" hit Kaypro like a little dart. Eaton would casually refer to late-night recording sessions and wild impromptu coke parties by the river, full of spontaneous pranks and backslapping camaraderie. He must have enjoyed the pinched, left-out look on the officer's face, an expression not even of nostalgia but of pure deprivation—Kaypro's own youth wouldn't have been like that, because nobody's was.

While the agent didn't seem to mind Eaton, picking up

the latest jargon and memorizing the names of hot bands and clubs, he virtually leaped at Checker whenever The Derailleurs' drummer walked in the room. Yet Checker himself began to avoid the man. The carefully ripped T-shirts the agent appeared in every night embarrassed him, the same way fat people did who insisted on wearing pants three sizes too small. And Kaypro said "used to" and "I remember" far too frequently for Checker's taste. He would lean too far over the knotty pine tables, he talked too loudly, he laughed too long, and in his rare pauses Kaypro's wistfulness trailed under Checker's nose like the smell of an electrical short. Kaypro was losing his hair and weighed too much and showed up every night in a different hat, trundling into the club with a panicked expression until he found one of The Derailleurs at the bar. He was a terrible influence on Caldwell.

Later Checker wrote a song about their gig with Kaypro Friday night, though he never showed it to Gary for fear of hurting the man's feelings. To this day Check hasn't allowed his band to play "In the Pocket" publicly in case the agent might hear. For archival interest, though, this is the song, though Checker wouldn't even approve of our printing it here:

In the Pocket

Last week tooted a few tunes through—
Kids look younger than they used to.
Rapped so fast with all new lingo.
(We don't say "rapped" now, Mr. Kaypro.)

My reed kept rasping through their song;
When they stopped I still blew strong.
I missed the beat, I lost the key—
But who wants teenage sympathy?

My life's on digital delay,
Echoes the rate of my decay.
Hey, Warhol, what are we to do
When our fifteen minutes
Are through?

Extension cord
Won't reach the socket.
Can't seem to play
In the pocket.

On the charts in '69—
I'm a scratched-up 45.
Fingerprinted, grooves grown moldy,
Sunday morning Golden Oldie.

I was once a pretty boy,
Crooned a sax with purple joy.
Was it good as I recall?
Has purple haze obscured it all?

My life's on digital delay,
Echoes the rate of my decay.
Hey, Warhol, what are we to do

When our fifteen minutes
Are through?

Still on stage
But off the docket.
I used to play
In the pocket.

It was a sad song.

H e'd thought Syria would find the afternoon amusing.
She didn't. He'd thought he would find it amusing.
He didn't. Oh, the band was having a good enough time.
They'd snuck with muffled laughter down the back stairs,
with napkin bow ties twist-tied to their collars. Caldwell
buzzed the Wedding March softly on his kazoo. J.K. had
snatched up a beer-can pop-top and a radiator hose clip for
rings. Sure. Ha-ha.

But as Check had escorted the bride to their ad hoc chapel
she'd said practically nothing. "You don't seem like the sentimental type," he commented. "Are you?"

"This sucks," she said simply. Only several blocks later
did she volunteer, "When I was growing up we thought everything was a joke—the prom, graduation. We mooned princi-
pals, crashed formal dances in patched jeans. But the joke was
on us. It was a cheat."

"Why a cheat?"

"Those ceremonies were for us. We only sabotaged ourselves."

She said sabotage. She said travesty. She even said violation. All she didn't say out loud was disappointment.

The basement was in top form, a steam engine. By this time Rahim's complexion was the pasty, bloated color of some of the creatures that washed up on the rocks in the park. His hair had twisted into damp jerricurls, his fingers were pruny, and he claimed the back of his neck was beginning to mold.

Checker introduced the minister, a Quaker who saw Rahim as a persecuted political refugee and who was therefore feeling liberal and pleased with himself. He was elaborately understanding when Rahim began to carp: in a Muslim wedding, men and women should stand on opposite sides; though in the cramp of Plato's basement it was more practical to divide them into separate layers. Wasn't Syria going to sit the Seven Days, with seven different dresses, each more exquisite than the last?

"No, we'll do a variation," Syria proposed. "For a week I'll wear the same green work shirt, and every day it will get a little bit dirtier. Then finally the big night will come, just the two of us, and you can *wash* it."

Rahim didn't laugh.

As the minister began, mopping his forehead between vows, Checker didn't look at the couple but down at the pop-top in his hands; by the time he offered the ring to Rahim, he'd twisted the tab off, leaving the aluminum jagged; slipped on Syria's finger, it must have scratched. "Best man." He thought about the term. It was a role he could tire of.

Instead of "I do," Syria said, "I suppose."

Rahim had finally stopped whining. Through the ceremony he kept slipping his gaze over to Syria, rippling his eyes up and down her lanky figure, darting incredulous glances at the wild Picasso angles of her face. Little by little he was starting to smile, until his small even teeth were spread so wide and white that he had to look down at the floor. He couldn't have stopped smiling if he'd tried.

When the minister said, "You may kiss the bride," Rahim's smile spread more extravagantly than ever, and Syria paused to examine her new husband; perhaps for the first time he was real to her, an attractive, exotic boy soon to be installed in her apartment. She leaned over with exploratory care and kissed him on the cheek; but Rahim reached over to that serpentine neck and kissed his new property on the lips with victorious possessiveness.

Syria laughed, uneasily at first, but soon with real humor, and she tied her apron under her eyes like a hajab. They went upstairs to the club, closed in the afternoon, and drank beer out of plastic champagne glasses. Syria belly-danced to the refrain "Never gonna do it without the fez on" with Rahim, then to "The Sultans of Swing" with Checker, until, abruptly, she stopped in the middle of the song, untied the apron, and announced coldly that she had to get to work. She was such a strange combination of flamboyance and rigidity, Checker couldn't figure her. Rahim called forlornly after her, "Don stay with husband?" but already he was making entreaties rather than firm Muslim demands. The two of them watched Syria stride away, her hair shooting by the yard behind her like a train, her big work shirt billowing like a gown, both wondering whether any bride in white lace could be more splendid.

W hy are you so angry?"

Syria threw the punty halfway across the studio like a javelin; it landed in the barrel with a clang. "I'm not angry," she said, tossing the pieces she'd just made crashing into the trash. "I'm normal."

"Why are you normally so angry?"

"Why aren't you?"

There was more tinkling and clattering; Syria slid the door of the furnace fully aside, the gas up high; it roared so that Checker couldn't answer her question, which was fine—he didn't understand it. When she'd finished swinging her glass around the shop, wielding punties in the big turns of a baton twirler, she reluctantly rolled the door shut again. He'd never seen her motions more graceful or more dreadful, either.

"So," she turned to him. "This is my *wedding night.*" She whipped off her apron and threw it up so it looped around a pipe over the ceiling. "Tell me," she said, with the dark glasses still on, "you did everything for the license, didn't you?" Checker shrugged. "And that kid isn't going to know how to apply for a green card by himself, is he?"

"Maybe not."

"But of course you've already found out how it's done."

"Federal Plaza."

"That'll take days, you know that. All the forms?"

"Yes."

"Why?"

"I don't understand."

"Why all this? Why everything?"

"Why not?"

He'd never seen her look so disgusted. The emotion suited her. The only thing he could imagine as more flattering was full-fledged disdain. "Are you always so *good?* Because it's gross to be around. You still use that word, 'gross'?"

"Not much."

She couldn't stand still, and kept ranging around the studio, throwing her coffee cup in the sink so the last sip splotched over the counter. She drank it strong and black. "Don't know if I can stand you around here five nights a week. You annoy me."

"Sorry," said Check, and a quiver ran through him, a ripple of distortion like a wave of heat.

She turned fast enough to catch it. "Don't wilt! Say, Fuck you! You're a mess, you know that?"

Another ripple.

"Say, I am not. Say, Leave me alone. Say, I do my work and this is none of your business."

"It's your business if I annoy you."

"God!" She looked around the studio and, finding nothing to smash, turned on Checker—he would learn not to clean up so well. "Those friends of yours," she said. "They're sickening."

"Why?"

"The way they coo and prate over you. Really, it makes

me want to puke. But they ever do anything for *you*, mister?"

"They're good musicians. They make me laugh—"

"I'm not impressed." She cut him off. "And what's this about your being so happy all the time?"

"I get pretty—worked up. They like it."

"You don't seem that happy to me."

"At the moment I'm having trouble."

Checker was sitting on a bench; she glared down at him. "Why don't you tell me to cram it? Why don't you say, Leave my friends out of this?"

Checker was frantically sifting through everything he'd done in the last few hours for what could possibly have offended her. "I'm sorry I got you involved with Hijack—"

"You damned well better be. And sorry now? Just you wait."

"I'll do what I can to make it easy—"

Syria pushed the bench with her boot and it toppled over, Check with it. He picked himself up and dusted his hands of glass slivers. "You'll do what you can! Tell me, You said you'd marry him, no one forced you! Say, You accepted, it's not my problem!"

"You did say yes," Check conceded.

"Oh, that's powerful," she taunted him. "And do you have anything to say about being thrown on the floor just now? That was fine, you just pick yourself up and clear your throat?"

Checker decided that doing anything she told him to do, saying anything she told him to say, would drive her all the more into a rage from his sheer obedience. He stood, then, quietly. She breathed at him, and if there had been fire shooting from her nostrils, not hard to imagine, it would have been in the ensuing silence gradually reduced to smoke.

"Do you," said Check with perfect gentleness, "ever do anything else at night? Anything but glass?"

"Why?"

"Answer me."

". . . No."

"Do you ever wish you did something else, once in a while?"

"Like what?"

"Just go to a bar. To a movie. Go dancing."

"I've done those things before," she said warily. "I need glass now."

"Every night?"

"Yes."

"It's just I was wondering," Check proposed carefully, "if you'd take one night off. You see, the band would like to celebrate. And it would help Hijack's case with the INS if we had a real reception. You're supposed to bring wedding pictures to the interview—"

"You're kidding."

"No, and maybe a reception would do. I was wondering, even though it's not a real wedding exactly, if we had a party, would you come?"

"Is that right." She seemed disarmed.

"I'd like you to hear me play," Check admitted.

"That's the most egocentric thing I've ever heard you say. It's a relief."

"Would you?"

She smiled, a little. "Where?"

"Plato's, I guess."

"No," she said, her eyes shining. "The Olympic Pavilion."

Check laughed. "Money—"

"I told you, I have money."

Once the Pavilion was mentioned, nothing else would do.

6 / simply red

Astoria Boulevard stretches through the least fetching part of the neighborhood, lined with the sorts of stores facing so many small-town American streets, tiny miracles of capitalism: the kind that open promptly every morning and no one goes in. The Pasta-Mat shelves four big cans of tomato puree and a few boxes of yellowed ziti. Bakeries will keep one crusty box of anisettes under the counter and three or four loaves of overbrowned semolina bread in the window—one sometimes suspects, the same bread. The shoe store solves the problem of keeping up with changing styles by displaying pumps that have never been in style, and so can't go out, and never will be in style, either, barring the fall of Western civilization. In abundant pizza parlors on each corner, whole pies stiffen under ineffectual heat lamps, recipes with so little sauce, even less cheese, and such thin crusts that it's a wonder the slices exist at all.

Yet there is something encouraging about this array, made impervious to the whims of the national economy by generating a permanent depression of its own. These heroic entrepreneurs are the urban equivalent of hocked Midwestern farmers still sowing their crops or tiny drought-withered African villagers carving little wooden animals every morning and refusing to die. Astoria Boulevard is a monument to Faulknerian endurance, real Southern perversity flourishing in the Northeast. Meanwhile, the Athenaiki Pitta Company bathes the western end with the smell of warm bread like a blessing, an infusion of life. And shining smack in the middle of this commercial wasteland, across from Black Jack's Coffee Shop and the Cephalonian Association, down from Dominick's Buy-Rite and the United Cyprians of America, sandwiched between Louise and Ralph's Sweet Shoppee and Terry's Beauty Cage, and catty-corner to the New York Greek-American Athletic Club, attracting incongruous fleets of silver limousines and packing in enormous shipments of liquor like an actual business, the Olympic Pavilion casts its rejuvenating light down the whole street.

Slatted with ten-foot mirrors over its façade, the Pavilion catches the late-afternoon sun and throws gold over the drying semolina loaves as they drop their sesame seeds one by one across the way, multiplying the overweight plaster statuettes under its cursive marquee. Blowsy and bloated with a bit too much cannelloni, the castings lift their skirts to expose thighs like Corinthian columns, with the blurred, vacantly affable expressions of lonely aunts at the end of a party with an open bar. Often enough Checker had padded up to the window to peer between a crack in the drapes, watching live versions of these statues fork roast beef in a room where every single appointment was miraculously the same dusty powder blue.

The afternoon Mr. Diamond showed him around inside, even Checker realized that from a sophisticated point of view the Olympic Pavilion, with its gold-and-white trim, huge brass cigarette urns, and loud floral carpeting, was a gaudy, even ridiculous place. But good taste denies certain forms of magnificence. Mr. Diamond was serious and quietly proud; Checker admired his "life of celebration."

The manager liked that way of looking at his job, which he often found tedious, with gobs of icing hardened on the parquet dance floors and grisly edges of prime rib wedged into seat cushions; he tired of drunks and garter belts and withered pink bouquets. Mr. Diamond often spoke of marriage as "an industry"; he and the maître d' placed bets on couples, how long they'd last. Divorce, of course, was good for the Pavilion since clients might return here three or four times. But a "life of celebration"—that was refreshing.

A massive converted movie theater, the Pavilion had ten different halls, each a different color, reminding Checker of fairy tales in which castled princesses wandered dolefully from the "green room" to the "pink room," waiting for a spell to break or a man to appear. Princesses in those stories were never happy.

Checker purred at each new room, with its scrupulously coordinated colors, but when Mr. Diamond opened the last door Check said, "We'll take this one."

It was red. Not just any red, but a voluptuous, violent

red, ignited by three nine-foot chandeliers. It was in this room more than any other that the sincere quality of the Olympic Pavilion shone through. However condescending you might feel toward the chintz of a catering palace, this one was older than most, and surprisingly solid, even heartfelt. Its ceilings were high, floors hardwood, cushions real velvet. The three chandeliers were genuine crystal and clattered softly as Checker circled in the shatter of their light—glass and this color followed him everywhere.

"I'm so glad we've found what you wanted!"

And it was the strangest thing. How many times had Mr. Diamond given this tour? How many times had he said he was glad? How entirely sick was he, after thirty years, of the Olympic Pavilion? And how suspicious had he been of a black kid in sneakers wanting to rent out a hall? But watching Checker do a turn on the well-waxed dance floor, Diamond beamed at the boy as if he were his own son.

"And you'll have steak and baby carrots and cake!" Check exclaimed, echoing through the hall.

"Yes, and exquisite new potatoes, with paprika!" cried Mr. Diamond, almost wishing he could attend.

Checker turned quickly. "Would you come?"

"Oh no, policy—"

"I won't tell. We'll cover your plate. And you can hear me drum."

"But surely you'll be seated at the head table—?"

"No, I'll be in the band."

"Aren't you the bridegroom?"

"No," said Check, and he stopped dancing.

The conclusion of the deal became oddly funereal; Mr. Diamond spoke in hushed tones, as if to the bereaved. "I'm so sorry," Mr. Diamond felt compelled to add, though he had no idea for what.

"That's all right," said Checker, bucking up. "And you have to come. I'll put you on the list."

"Perhaps," said Mr. Diamond, and as he watched Checker bound off down Astoria Boulevard he decided that, for the Pyramus affair, he would lower the price a tad.

S yria had been in no mood for the arrival of her new roommate the day of the ceremony, leaving her husband angry and confused. Why on his wedding night had he once again slept above the fruit stand on his bunchy mattress and mildewed pillow, to wake damp and sour, boil his own Turkish coffee, and gnaw on an old crust of pita, too tired and depressed to buy fresh only across the street? This was better than Plato's basement, but only barely. What about bringing the stained sheet out to the old women for inspection (what old women, Hijack?); when were The Derailleurs going to pile into cars and blow horns around New York, while passersby would *halahal?*

While Rahim did not actually expect these rituals in America, still he and Syria were in accord: a great day had been defiled. When Checker pressed Rahim to choose between prime ribs and stuffed flounder, the Iraqi could only reminisce about whole slaughtered sheep, trays of rice with almonds and raisins, parallelograms of baklava and piles of doughy *zlabia* glistening with grease and powdered sugar.

Yet as the party drew near, Rahim had to admit that even in his hometown of Almahtani they could not have drawn a finer crowd to a feast. Checker invited all of Plato's regulars and more: the waitresses at the Neptune, the foot patrolmen from Astoria Park, all the commissioners and councilmen listed on the sign in Ralph DeMarco, including, by mistake, Donald Manes, who had gutted himself with a kitchen knife the year before. Check invited the doctor who did the blood tests and the Quaker minister, Howard's boss at Baskin-Robbins, Caldwell's whole karate class, and the salesman at Drum World who was always trying to buy Checker's Leedys for his percussion museum. Checker remembered the girl at Terry's Beauty Cage who trimmed the band for free; the postman who delivered the invitations without stamps; Claude, who read the gas meters in Checker's apartment; Al, who repaired Lena's hunching old Crosley Shelvador twice a year and charged only for parts; and certainly Gus, from Astoria Bicycle, where Check had often discussed the merits of oval chain wheels while he helped adjust brakes and change kids' flat tires. Checker invited all the djs from WNEW—Maxanne Sartori, Donna Fiducia, Scott Muni, Dave Herman, Mr. Marty-Hale-and-Hearty-Never-Tardy-Rock-and-Roll-Smarty, and of course from the *Late Show* the great Danno himself. He invited Mrs. Carlton, Mr. Diamond, Gary Kaypro, and, last but not least, a whole slew of his old girlfriends, just to give them the pleasure of turning him down.

The band rented tuxedos. Rachel dress-shopped for a week. The bride blew glass.

"Are you going to wear Levi's?" asked Check one evening.

"You don't trust me."

"No, I love you in Levi's. Wear them if you want."

"What do you look like in a tuxedo?"

Checker just smiled.

While you might expect a tuxedo to divide its tenants by class—those who do and don't look at home in it—this is not the case. All men look at home in tuxedos if they've been measured right. The Derailleurs turned up at the door of the Olympic Pavilion, then, looking passably like members of the White House staff. As always, before the first creases have cut behind the knee, before anyone has loosened a bow tie or cummerbund, the costume produced astonishing changes in bearing. Postures rose. Chests expanded. Strides lengthened and straightened, and all kinds of behavioral tics disappeared.

Taking up a whole lane of Astoria Boulevard, a fleet of carriers from Sprint arrived astride beaten, high-seated ten speeds, Zefal's old friends. Gravely the leggy black legion dismounted, releasing the right ankles of their tuxedo trousers, carefully clipped from the viscous chains, unstrapping bouquets bungee-corded to back racks, and locking up with enormous thick-shanked Kryptonites on parking signs for blocks around. As the messengers filed in, they shot Checker wry little salutes and delivered slightly greasy wedding presents from purple canvas bags.

"So tacky!" Eaton exclaimed as he strolled through the lobby with Howard. "More Parthenon murals. This neighborhood destroys me."

Milling through the red room bolting hot hors d'oeuvres, Plato's patrons turned suddenly shy with each other, embarrassed. Girls held glistening fingers out from their clothes, in horror of ruining two-hundred-dollar dresses before the main course. Yet when Check Secretti purled into the heart of the crowd, everyone eased up, laughed, and took long drafts of their drinks. In his wake they felt suave and attractive. *You have looked forward to this and now it is happening*, the bright black shoes tapped out their way. *You've posted my invitation on your billboards for weeks, Hijack's curling Arabic script hypnotizing from across the room; or it's rested on your dresser, been your bookmark for that novel you never seem to finish. You've mentioned this date on the phone, though you've never confessed to anyone just how many times you changed your mind about what to wear—which shoes, which flowers, whether to buy a boutonniere. But I know and I enjoy your anxiety; I relish when you care about anything. But I'm also here to tell you that today is February 21. It's possible that this whole evening could pass in a blur and you'd later say, When was that party I was looking forward to? You'd look at the calendar with sad surprise—why, it was yesterday, it was last week, it was years and years ago and you can no longer remember what happened. But I will save you: you are here.* That's what Checker Secretti was for, actually. He told people simple, obvious things: You enjoy your job, or: This is the party.

Syria had advanced him his pay for the shoes, and he loved the way they rolled on the floor, wax against wax, coasters on his toes.

Girls kept Checker in the corners of their eyes and smiled

and said nothing to each other. Only later, rearranging disheveled necklines in the bathroom mirror, would one of them finally sigh, "Checker," and the whole roomful of girls would burst out laughing—a mutual confession, though they all had boyfriends of their own. Then at last it would be out, and they'd trail from the women's room looking at each other with complicity for the rest of the evening. All, that is, but the one in the last stall, who would remain there for longer than the rest, because none of this was funny to her; so she'd stay curled on the toilet, letting her big gauzy formal wrinkle up around her waist, her head on her knees. She wouldn't stay indefinitely, though she might have, had they not been waiting for her—Rachel DeBruin was in the band.

Checker had instructed all the guests to wear only black and white, though he himself had cheated with a crimson tie and cummerbund, and tiny red studs. The rest of the party had complied more strictly, anxious to please him, and the perfect checkerboard of the room was worthy of the ballroom scenes in *War and Peace*. Even Rahim had cooperated, waltzing in with traditional Muslim dasha; the white material fluttering around his delicate face suggested a role reversal the Iraqi himself wouldn't have appreciated.

Checker had told everyone to wear black or white except Syria, whom no one told to do anything. Besides, whatever she turned up in was bound to be interesting.

Her gown was better than interesting. The neckline streaked to the waist, where the material gathered and draped over her narrow hips, snuggling down those long legs, laying claim—and Checker could hardly blame the dress. It had a good thing going. It was a dress that would want to stay on. With padded shoulders and long tight sleeves, it glared protectively at Checker from across the room, hugging her figure, possibly regretting the way her entire leg could so easily escape its clutches—the slit sliced all the way up her thigh. While he was intrigued to see her finally without the Levi's and big green shirt, that she'd done nothing with her hair delighted him—it was alive, and pinning it up would have been as offensive as caging wild predators in a zoo.

"I knew you'd wear red."

"I almost didn't. You said the room was red. I don't like to blend in."

"You couldn't if you tried."

"Listen, later we're going to have to talk. Your friend—did you explain?"

"Yes, but—"

"He *married* me, do you understand?"

"You'll have to make yourself clear."

"You can count on that, kiddo. But he's very sweet and very young, and I don't want to hurt his feelings."

Check said nothing.

"Those robes, they're sincere, Checker. This is his *wedding* reception. We have a communication problem here."

"Uh-huh."

"You fucked up."

"I tried, but—I think he likes you."

"Great." Syria shook her head. "I've done some weird shit, but this one takes it." She watched Rahim billow through the crowd; he waved to her, his delectable teeth gleaming in the light of the chandelier. "You know, he's actually kind of cute."

"Yes." Checker swallowed. "Maybe you could get to like him, too."

"I already do," said Syria distractedly, still following the flapping robes as they wafted ebulliently across the room. "He's a raving lunatic, isn't he? I like that."

When she turned back to talk to Checker, he was gone.

"You'd think the two of them were getting married," Eaton snickered. Rahim had swaddled his garment around Checker like a cocoon. "Those two aren't, uh, close?"

"Check's no fag," said Caldwell sternly.

"Sure," said Eaton, trying not to roll his eyes. The Derailleurs seemed so good-timey, but they had a humorless streak a mile wide.

Checker escorted Mr. Diamond through the throng and introduced him to everyone. Mr. Diamond hadn't actually attended one of his own affairs for many years. He made a mental note that the phyllo around the spinach pie was soggy. But besides that, why, it really was a grand thing he did for people, wasn't it? And he hadn't felt so clever in his life.

After dinner, The Derailleurs took over from the dj and the event began in earnest. Checker sat down at his traps, and at the first rat-tat, *zing*, the velvet chairs slid back; it was hard to wait out the first dance while the peculiar bride and groom took the floor. But it was worth watching, anyway: Rahim swirling in those robes of his, already a little drunk, doing full rippling turns and running the length of the hall like Lawrence of Arabia leaping down the cars of a captured train, his arms extended, flapping his headdress behind him from the head table to the bandstand. As for Syria (who, according to Rahim later, unsuitably made a show of herself), she danced with the same precision and economy with which she blew glass, centering her body on its axis like a vessel. She was a craftsman. She understood material in motion; you got the feeling flesh and glass weren't that different to her, that she believed all matter operated basically by the same rules.

Yet after "Baby, You Convenient," written for the occasion, Checker hit the splash and rolled into "Cotterless Cranks," their fastest song. In three measures not a guest was still mashing the heavy white icing around his plate, and the floor churned like an ant colony someone had just stepped on.

Even Mr. Diamond liked the music. It was louder than he preferred, but bounced him on the balls of his feet. Though portly, he'd eaten sparingly tonight, and for once his chin didn't fold and sweat in its creases. He felt broad rather than fat. Though it was now late enough that he could disperse this party, he decided to allow the band to play a third set.

The Derailleurs were cranking, that's why it was queer. Everyone agreed, too, that Checker had been "majorly jacked" even "ultra-jacked" Rahim observed quietly, "Too jacked," but no one heard him. Only Rahim noticed the trace of hysteria that laced the drummer's second set. The pulse that Checker ordinarily gave off was heavy and uneven, like a heart that is overstrained. He was somehow dangerously happy, with a flush under his coffee complexion: too much blood, too much sweat, cuts and blisters on his hands. He was shaking.

H e's gone." Syria sat back summarily in her chair at the head table.

"Sheckair!"

It was time for the third set. All was cleared with Diamond, and they'd even routed Rachel from the bathroom. But Checker Secretti had disappeared.

C aldwell was ready to announce an early retirement when J.K. remembered Eaton Striker, and the party went on. But funny things started happening. The dance floor, though thinned, felt crowded, and couples elbowed one another out of the way. Guests eyed the head table, making surly remarks about immigration. "What's in it for her?" carped a girl, loudly enough for Syria to hear. "I bet she's making a mint on this. Marry for money, you'd think a woman that old would have more pride."

The wrong boys asked the wrong girls to dance. Two best friends fought over a date and knocked down a table; she watched blankly from the sidelines as glasses skittered and smashed across the floor. Eaton kept playing.

"*What?*" Syria rose over her new husband.

Rahim burst into raging Arabic. He'd drunk too much and could no longer scream in English. He was communicating, anyway, and Syria threw the red wine in her glass all over her husband's white wedding robes.

"Out!" shouted Mr. Diamond. "Every one of you out this minute!"

But the music was too loud and no one heard him. More

fights broke out, and the Olympic Pavilion lost considerably more crockery before he finally grabbed the mic from Caldwell; after a screech of feedback, the drums petered out and the hall stopped.

"Get out," said Mr. Diamond in an ugly voice.

Sheepishly the crowd wiped the wedding cake off their faces. Many of the girls' dresses were irrevocably splattered with beef gravy and grenadine; some of the boys would have to purchase their tuxedos, after all—bloodstains were the living bitch, their mothers had taught them at least that. Spilled champagne spread and flattened over the dance floor, its bubbles popping, pip, pip. The musicians packed up their instruments as fast as possible.

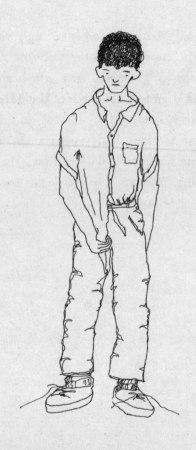

Howard in one of his yellow shirts

7 / my love is chemical

An Inquiry into the Ecstatic State
~~By Howard Williams~~
~~By H. Williams~~
By H. ("The Head") Williams

*O*ur *studies have discovered an extraordinary case. Subject displays an unusual aptitude for heightened emotional and sensory experience. Proposal: To pin down the source of this capacity, and whether it can supplant the costly pursuit of a "high" state through alcohol, marijuana, hallucinogens, and opiates.*

(Besides, beer makes me tired. Drugs make me nervous.)

From examining and interviewing our subject, little or no evidence surfaces of consistent substance abuse. This observer's first hypothesis, however, is that our subject's state is still chemical in nature. We draw the reader's attention, for example, to the recent discovery of "endorphins"—chemicals produced by the brain that create a sensation of "jack." Endorphins can be excited by rigorous physical exercise.

"Howard?"

Howard jumped, and stuffed the notebook quickly in a drawer. "Yes, Mother?"

"I got that shirt you asked for. Only they didn't have the style you wanted in red. So I got yellow. I hope that's all right."

Howard took the shirt. "Great," he said faintly. "Just great."

He inspected it when she left his room. Yellow! And pale at that, tinged with ocher, as if washed in the wrong load.

Rot. This always happened. Like the cuff? Howard loved that bracelet—heavy plain leather, well oiled from long wear, darker by the year. It laced at the inside, and the end of the tie whipped the drummer's wrist when he threw licks from tom to snare. It was neat. Why should Checker Secretti be the only guy who wore neat stuff?

But the only cuffs Howard ever found were either covered in cheesy tooling, horses, paisley, or with bulky macho studs. The only plain one he ever found was brass, and that week everyone stared at him and his skin turned green.

In a little surge of optimism, Howard tried on the new shirt and looked in the mirror. Yep. There was Howard, all right. Howard in one of his yellow shirts. Howard pulled it off and flopped on the bed in despair.

*   *   *

Where have you been?" Syria leveled the smoldering blowpipe at the door. "It's been over a week. You figured I was sleeping late at Niagara Falls so you wouldn't need to come to work?"

Checker's mouth twitched in a half smile.

"You always so talkative when you come back from a vacation?"

Checker took a deep breath and sat on the bench, leaning up against a pole and gazing into the furnace.

"According to your little friends, you're off smelling the flowers somewhere. Is that right? You're just too bloody high on life to visit the mortals for weeks at a time?"

"Your glass." Check nodded. "It's getting cold."

Syria slung the blowpipe to the yoke and turned it abruptly in circles until the glass sagged, and whipped it over to her bench to blow.

"A vase?"

"Goblets. SoHo."

For a while Checker watched her work in silence.

"I should fire you."

"Maybe." Checker raised his hand in front of him before the flames; it trembled slightly. "I shouldn't have come back for another day, I think."

"The surly helpmate in my apartment claims you pull this disappearing act all the time."

"Mmm."

"It's bullshit. I don't see why I should have to put up with it."

"Don't, then."

"You want to quit?"

Checker raised his eyebrows, smiled, shrugged, and drifted toward the door.

"Come back here."

Checker obediently stopped and turned.

"Where did this idiot complacency come from?"

Checker looked around the studio with interest, as if he'd never been there before. "What?"

She looked at him hard. "Are you all right?"

"Yes."

"You seem different."

Checker looked up and down and patted the cinder block beside him like a friend. The wall was cool, porous, and musty. "I'm good." Checker smiled.

Syria put her pipe in a barrel, taking unusual care it didn't clatter. "Come here." She took his hands, studying his face. Gently she reached up and touched his hair.

"Sheckair!"

Checker sprang back from the woman and turned on his heel. The Iraqi looked confused, even apologetic. "You are back. Is good." He looked back and forth between them. Ordinarily he would have flung his arm around Checker's shoulders; instead, he smiled weakly. "Rehearsal tomorrow?"

First time I seen a tugboat on land," said J.K. From far off down the park a small figure chugged turgidly toward them, raising a poof of dust like a spray of river water, gray sweats billowing in the breeze.

"You don't look like you're enjoying yourself, Howard," shouted Caldwell.

As Howard puffed past, a stolid purple, Caldwell and J.K. began to lope effortlessly beside him.

"Now, don't you think Howie looks unjacked?"

"Lack of jack, that what I see."

"There's more to life than having a good time," said Howard with difficulty. "There's discipline. There's suffering." No matter how reasonable Howard's assertions, somehow they never rang true.

All three of them suddenly slowed at a long, high whistle from up the hill. Leaping the sidewalk between the columns of Hell Gate, a figure streaked down the slope. As he came up from behind, his wake pushed them faster, until all four, even Howard, were ripping down the walkway by the river, jumping cracks and puddles, passing sports cars. They accelerated into Ralph DeMarco, vaulting its queer plum-colored railings to the rocks by the water. At last their leader reached the edge of Con Ed, assaulting a neat knoll where children played King of the Mountain. He turned and tackled the three of them as a group; they rolled on the grass and laughed. It was early March; the grass was cold.

"Oh, man," said Caldwell. "You're back."

"Yeah, the manager flipping out," said J.K. "He into suffering, man. It serious."

But Howard wasn't suffering anymore. He lay panting, looking up at the sky, an amazing cloudless cerulean, with the unreal intensity of cheap postcards. His vision was awhirl with tiny points that curled the sky. Though he knew this was called "seeing stars," to Howard these comma-shaped distortions were each tiny endorphins, creeing to each other ecstatically like faraway birds returning north in spring.

A bicycle?"
          "So? I've thought about getting one for a long time."
     "I bet." Caldwell walked around the new purchase, shooting looks at J.K. "Must do at least five miles an hour. That is, if you hold on to a bus."

     "Don't make fun of him," said Howard, clutching the big rubber grips. "You'll hurt his feelings."

     "Your bicycle has a personality, too?"

     "Checker says everything does."

     "Yeah," said Caldwell. "Checker says."

     "Check doesn't have a monopoly on bicycles!"

     "He right, Sweets. So the man bought a bike. Nothing wrong with that."

     "I'll just be curious what Check has to say," Caldwell said, quietly off away from Howard, who was proudly pumping the heavy treaded tires.

     "Think he be pissed off?" asked J.K.

     "I'd be, wouldn't you? Jesus—the red shirt, the bracelet. And did you notice the tennis shoes?"

     "No, why?"

     "Same brand. Converse All-Star low-tops, white canvas. I wouldn't be surprised if he bought the same size."

     "How much you get it for?" asked Eaton.

     "Thirty dollars," said Howard briskly, oiling his chain

with a drop in each link. "It must be, oh, twenty years old."

"Why not get a new one?" asked Eaton. "Because the bicycles they're making now—"

"You say *they* too much," Howard observed severely. "There's no they. Check says."

"All the same," said Eaton coldly, "bicycles are much lighter now."

"But when a bicycle gets old," said a voice behind them, "it has scars. Stories. And it gets real cool, you know? You can't mess it over anymore." Checker leaned Zefal against the park railing. Once copper with black trim, her finish was evenly scraped, the scratches filled with grease. The black handlebar tape, washed by rain and snow, was now tattered and gray; the rubber brake hoods had lost their pigment; the once-suede seat had bits of fur only on its tip, like a stuffed animal loved bald. The whole machine, packed in with the dregs of a harsh New York winter, eaten by salt on its underside, was an even gray-brown. Nothing gleamed but a muted inner warmth. Zefal didn't demand a lot of attention, never asked for or expected praise. She was good at waiting at parking signs without complaint. She was nine years old, as aged for a bicycle as for a dog. Her treads were worn and brake shoes nubby, her derailleur clogged, but you could tell she was a loyal vehicle all the same, and surprisingly fleet for such an enfeebled creature. Checker suspected Zefal was starting to go blind, for she didn't spot pedestrians lately until they were practically under the front wheel, but you didn't replace a bicycle casually. He would clean and grease her, repack her bearings, and ease her fondly through another year.

"Better than people, anyway," said Eaton. "They get old, they look like sun-dried tomatoes."

"See if you say the same thing when you're seventy-five." Check suddenly pulled up short, and blanched. "It's funny, I—"

"What?"

Checker hesitated. "Sometimes I can see people, old. How they'll look. I saw you, that's all."

"And what did I look like?" asked Eaton tolerantly.

"Nothing," said Checker with an involuntary shudder. "Never mind."

Checker rapidly put the image away, like shuttering a bad snapshot to the bottom of the stack.

"Howard, your bicycle is perfect!" Check exclaimed. "It's exactly the bicycle you would have."

"Yeah?" Howard felt tentatively insulted. The bike had upright handlebars and only three speeds. It was red all right, but less red like a Corvette than red like a wagon.

"Let's go for a ride, Howard," said Check, sweeping over Zefal. "The ramps on the Triborough are still slagged, but the snow's melted now, and if we go to Manhattan we've got the wind downtown. Then I'll show you how to get on the Queensboro—a real no-nonsense bridge, serious. Fifty-seventh still has big chunks of the street mysteriously missing, so watch your rims . . ." Still rabbiting away, Checker led off, with Howard pumping eagerly behind him.

"Didn't shake his tree one bit," said Caldwell. "In fact, he seemed pretty jacked about it."

"Think he notice?" asked J.K. "About Howard?"

"Sure. But he doesn't care." They shrugged. "Let's go, old man." They motioned to Eaton.

Eaton started. He'd been thinking. Eaton had decided he wanted a motorcycle.

H ave you scoped out this furnace deal Check's got going?" asked Howard.

"Yeah, so?"

"Well, doesn't it seem terrif?"

"Check likes it."

"Geez, I think—that furnace. Terrif. How does he do it?"

"Do what?"

"Well, first there was that job at Tower Records—with the discount, and rock and roll all day? Then the messenger job, riding around skipping potholes, and he'd come back—"

"Jacked out of his ever-loving mind." Caldwell laughed.

"Yeah. And now this, this tops it. Sweets, all I can find is that Baskin-Robbins late shift, and if I see one more scoop of Oreo ice cream, I'm going to lose my own cookies—"

"Howard," said Caldwell patiently, "it's not the job, dummy."

"What do you mean?"

"If you worked for Sprint you'd come back saying how dirty it was, how wiped you got, how it was dangerous; at Tower you'd complain about the pay; the furnace would be hot. What do you think Check would be like at B-R? It's not the job."

Caldwell shrugged and walked off, leaving Howard to imagine Checker Secretti scooping ice cream. Checker would wear his paper hat at a jaunty angle and never spill Rocky Road all over his apron. He'd take the apron home every night, washing and pressing it with real affection. He'd memorize all the flavors and recommend his favorites; he'd never make the mistake of eating too much ice cream for dinner and feeling sick the rest of the night. By the end of a week he'd know all the regulars' names and the ages of their children. He'd give away a lot of tastes and a few free scoops and make jokes with fat people that for some reason they didn't find offensive from Checker. Business would pick up during his shift, and Brockton would notice. He'd let Checker decorate cakes, and pretty soon Check would abandon the Snoopy and Big Bird patterns to do his own designs, caricatures of children in pink and yellow icing. They'd sit for him as for a photographer and giggle, and he'd give them icing mustaches if they promised not to tell. Customers would start requesting that Checker do their cakes. In the meantime, the band and a lot of other hangers-on would start congregating in the parlor, loitering on the curb, waiting for Check to get off, and when business was slow Check would drum with tiny pink plastic tasting spoons on the glass counter, ticka-ticka. He'd learn to balance five scoops at a time and develop theories that matched flavors to types of people. The rising office types in their thirties now moving into Astoria from Manhattan would listen to Check talk sometimes and linger and ask him if he planned on going to college. People were always asking Check that—Howard wouldn't be surprised if someday this whole neighborhood took up a collection.

Howard trudged down Ditmars to work, and tied on his messy apron. The freezer wasn't working well, and several chocolates were soft. People would complain. Howard would feel helpless. It seemed a long way to ten o'clock.

Y ou're kidding. Howard!"
          "I wanted to see if you were right. If it was the job or not. And it'll get me in shape."

"What's this campaign of yours lately? All the exercise?"

"A little experiment."

Howard had applied for Checker's old job at Sprint, walking into it with surprising ease. Since Checker Secretti had been one, it had never struck Howard that messengers did low-prestige work. He found out in short order.

Messengers are at the very bottom of the corporate ladder, even under secretaries' sharp, resentful heels. In elevators, having marked the purple canvas bag, executives stared straight through him to the numbers overhead. Howard had looked forward to the exotic film studios Check had described, and he did often find himself aimlessly ambling over high-ceilinged sets scattered with cold cups of coffee; but tripping over wires and dodging cameras wheeling by, Howard might lose half an hour locating "M. Rayson." Paid on commission, Howard found this costly entertainment.

Furthermore, he never seemed to get much exercise. Terrified by taxis and buses cutting him off just when he got the heavy red bicycle going, Howard poked through midtown, disdainfully passed by other messengers, who weaved casually through clogged avenues as if running a maze in a video game. Policemen made him nervous, and he wouldn't run lights. At least the job alerted Howard to the value of his life. He refused to take rush jobs. Under his breath he would lecture cyclists that whipped by him, clipped the heels of old ladies in crosswalks, and brought whole lines of cars signaling right screeching to a halt: "There are only two kinds of cyclists, careful—and dead." Yet watching his less responsible colleagues careen through midtown, he was forced to add a third kind: lucky.

Howard developed a cough. By the time he dragged home at five o'clock, the hairs on his skin had collected a delicate dusting of exhaust that turned his limbs gray. He found he could actually write his name in the soot on his arm. Nostalgically Howard remembered the nights when rocky-road stains were made of ice cream.

"What happened to that cute black guy?" secretaries would ask him. "With the blue eyes and light skin?"

Sometimes Howard pretended not to know whom they were talking about.

"You know," a pretty girl once pressed, "he's got dimples right here. And he always seems so—" She couldn't find the word.

"Jacked," said Howard.

"What?"

"Happy?"

"Yeah!" She seemed pleased the word was simple. For an ordinary adjective, "happy" gets curiously little use.

"He's helping run a glass furnace."

"No kidding! Well, there wasn't much chance that kid would stay a bike messenger, I guess . . ."

"Actually—he's not very ambitious."

"How do you know?"

"He's my best friend," said Howard shyly.

"Well, you tell him Wanda says get off his butt, then. He's got the stuff. Tell him Glenda had a girl, and that he was right about my kid. That it worked."

"What worked?"

"Just tell him. He'll understand."

It was like that, all the time. Where's Check? Where's that sweetheart who could never stand still? Even on the street when other messengers would pass and recognize his company's bag, tall terrifying black boys would stop and ask, "How that maniac you got at Sprint doing?"

"Who?"

"The drummer. Lean back on that seat like he sipping a martini. An he play traffic like music, man. Tell him Race says hey." And in no time Race would be ten blocks away.

Howard had been working for Sprint two weeks when he called in for his last job of the day. He had to go through five pay phones—a record—to find one that worked.

"2 West 178th—?"

"Don't make me say it again, we busy here."

The pickup was surprisingly far away for so late in the day, and Howard was exhausted. Yet dutifully he pulled the red bicycle off its parking sign. The machine seemed beleaguered, and increasingly more like a tricycle than a bike—ungainly and awkward, it didn't fit in here. At Checker's suggestion, Howard had named it Charlie, and lately he related to it as if it were a retarded younger brother he was compelled to baby-sit. The two of them alone got along all right, but socially Howard was ashamed. Charlie was slow. If Charlie could talk, he would stutter.

When Howard finally got up to Washington Heights he couldn't find the address. Men in cars kept signaling him over. "Nickels and dimes." Howard was in the middle of the cocaine district, but Howard wasn't the sort of person who noticed that kind of thing, though he was the sort of person who would later pretend to have known all along if you mentioned it.

Howard called into his service to discover that the address was wrong and he'd gone a hundred blocks out of his way.

"*Don't make me say it again,*" Howard grumbled, strad-dling Charlie. "*We're busy here.* Ten extra seconds for him, ten miles for me."

Back down on the West Side, Howard found the right address; it was getting dark. No one answered the buzzer.

So: one of those days. As he cranked back to Fifty-ninth Street, Charlie's fender began to rub on the tire; the wind picked up, and trees bent ominously on Riverside Drive. It started to rain. His brakes worked badly and taxis sprayed his left side. Pedestrians looked Howard straight in the eye and then proceeded to walk right in front of his bicycle. Pedestrians are like that.

By the time Howard reached the bridge he was soaked, and in no mood to marvel at the view. A miracle he had noted before: he went from a head wind going south in Manhattan to a head wind going north in Queens. Little wonder, then, that plodding up Twenty-first Street, his tennis shoes sloshing squisha-squusha, it took him several blocks to notice he had a flat tire.

H oward!" Checker quickly necked his vase and cracked off into the annealer.

Covered in the grim black sand distinctive to New York City pavement, Howard dripped in the doorway of the glass-works, his chest lurching. "Doesn't anything ever go wrong for you?"

Check pulled Howard into the studio, prying the handle-bars from Howard's clammy, white-knuckled hands. He glanced at the flapping back tire, but decided against a caution on the dangers of bare rims. "What happened?"

"Everything!" While Howard recounted his woes, Checker peeled off the boy's clothes and retrieved one of Syria's over-sized button-downs, pausing as he slipped Howard's arms through the sleeves to smell the sweet rise of old sweat coming off the shirt like perfume. He rested Howard's jeans on a yoke near the furnace; steam rose from the denim. The sneakers slowly curled as their canvas tightened. Howard himself was not so easily warmed. Even two feet from the furnace he still shivered; his lips were purple. Howard refused Check's jeans, and wrapped the dark shirt around his body, the sleeves draping beyond his hands; for all that bicycling, the pale hairless legs dangling under the tails were still scrawny.

"You have to make them give you the address slow and clear," Checker sympathized. "They're bored is the trouble, and they're inside on the phone and don't have the least comprehension that you're out on the street in the cold."

Howard wiped his nose on a sleeve and sat in the chair Check brought him, pulling his knees to his chest. "You didn't warn me. You'd come home and rave about carrying films from Jason Robards and how you got all the way across Fifty-ninth Street without missing one light. That's all you'd say. How the sunset from the bridge was amazing." Howard turned on Checker with uncharacteristic ferocity. "Didn't you ever get a flat, or two, or three? Didn't you ever miss every light on Fifty-ninth Street? Didn't it ever rain?"

"Of course, Howard. There are just ways—"

"You mean it's my fault I'm not all *jacked* now? That today could have been a peach if I only had the right attitude?"

"No, no. I mean for me, Howard. Sometimes I just—have good shocks. And sometimes so much goes wrong that it's funny. So I laugh."

"When you're cold it's not very amusing, Check. I don't buy it."

"Well, *cold*. That's a whole—thing."

"A thing."

"Like, when I can't feel my feet anymore? And pains are shooting up my arms from my fingers? I think about Arctic explorers."

"You're joking."

"I know it sounds dorky. But when I watch movies about

the Eiger, or see bums sleeping over vents in December, I think, *I know that*. I know what it's like to be incredibly, incredibly cold. I'm glad I know that feeling."

"Later. But at the time it's horrible."

"No," Check responded evenly. "Inconvenience, discomfort—that's not what's horrible."

"Then what is?"

Checker didn't answer.

Gradually both Howard's body and demeanor thawed. It was hard to stay angry at Checker, and Howard didn't really enjoy it, anyway. They commiserated as it got later over people who opened their doors on you, and about buses—Checker said the only way he stayed cool around buses was to imagine what it must be like to drive one and how annoying bicycles must be late in the day, swerving in front of you, so small, like flies around a cow. They compared favorite routes, delis, and dispatchers. Checker asked about Glenda and said that she'd wanted a girl. Finally Howard's jeans were dry; though stiff and gritty, the fabric burned pleasantly from the heat. Checker fixed Charlie's tire—claiming he enjoyed it—wiped the frame down, oiled the chain, and adjusted the brakes until Charlie didn't seem so goofy anymore. Howard stepped out to discover it had stopped raining and there was an unusually warm breeze coming up, for once, in the direction of Howard's house. As Howard would later document, Checker attracted tail winds.

Toward midnight the drummer was unusually quiet, puttering around the bicycle, and when he was finished, wiping the grease pensively from his hands, he said, "Howard?" as if he was going to say something, but then he didn't. When Howard wheeled out and said goodbye, Checker did add, "Listen," and put a hand on Howard's shoulder, "I do have bad days."

They looked each other in the eye, and Howard said, "Really?" Checker nodded and smiled weakly.

"Thanks, Check," said Howard, sweeping his leg over the frame and pushing off, feeling, perhaps for the first time in his life, graceful, to ride newly paved roads on fully inflated tires, toasty now but very clear on what it felt like to be cold.

Y ou quit!"

"That's right," said Howard calmly. "You have to pick your spots."

"Check says?"

"That's right," said Howard, not embarrassed. "And my spot is definitely not midtown Manhattan on a bike. Check says."

"So what's next?" asked Caldwell. "Tower Records?"

"Nope. B-R said they'll take me back. Some kids've been asking for me. Stop by if you want. The new coconut fudge is top-notch." Howard raised his eyebrows. "Free sprinkles." And smiling, he pedaled away to work.

Caldwell laughed. "Howard—"

"What say?" asked J.K.

"He's all right." Caldwell shook his head. "Sometimes he's all-fuckin'-right."

8 / hot rocks, or: the igneous apartment

The first time Checker stopped by the Carver Arms he was reminded of fierce dogs that girls had somehow managed to dress up in doll clothes. Rahim met him at the door with an apron and a scrub brush and something very close to a snarl.

Each step across the living room crunched. Winking in a variety of colors, broken glass covered the floor. In one corner was a tiny clean spot and a broom.

"Is it always like this?" Checker ventured.

"No, no," Rahim assured him, throwing the scrub brush at a shard of plate and breaking it in half. "Sometimes much worse." He brushed the chips off a chair and spread his apron on the seat for Checker. Slumping into an armchair opposite, Rahim picked slivers one by one off his jeans and pitched them sulkily into the wreckage.

"So this isn't the first time."

"First time?" Rahim laughed dejectedly. "Every day, like in border trenches back home. Why I bother run from army? At least there I kick-ass Khomeini crazy with roaches in his head. Here, fight all day wonky lady, like old man stuck in village, too weak for war." He kicked at the carpet and it tinkled. "Syria say I don crawl on hands and knees, she turn me in. Send me back to my country. Is not possible, no?"

"She could. Besides, you have that interview coming up for your green card. You better stay on her good side."

"This woman don have no good side!"

They heard a key in the lock. Whether to please her or to protect himself, Rahim shot out of his seat and grabbed the broom. When Syria walked in, he held its handle like a stave. She glared. "Haven't gotten very far, darling. And I see we have a guest for dinner. Hope you've got something special planned." She sauntered to the kitchen. "Like our new decor?" she asked, tossing Check a beer and taking Rahim's cleaned-off chair. "We've done the living room over in Early Divorce."

"Throwing plates. Very Greek."

She toasted. "*Opa.*" Syria looked at Rahim with complicitous affection. "Teaching your buddy to scrub porcelain is like getting Helen Keller to fold her napkin."

Rahim swept ineffectually at the glass, unamused.

"How about a beer for Hijack?"

"You're just the sort of softie who'd let Helen eat off other people's plates, aren't you? No, this kid's been on a break all day. I'm tired and I want some dinner, and look what I come home to. Besides, this is all your fault to begin with, so don't interfere."

Checker looked around the room, studying Syria's walls. They were covered with volcanoes. In some pictures steam trailed over lazy, crusting flows; in others the craters spewed luminescent lava, the color of molten glass. Her volcanoes reduced the furnace, with its small square door and dull contained roar, to the infant child of a race of fire giants, a tiny glowing ember from a worldwide inferno. Checker felt intrigued but uneasy. The photos were hung edge to edge, walling the whole room with a volatile, incendiary light. In the corner hot orange globs bobbed in the liquid of a lava lamp, whose glow infused the photos with immanent eruption. Broken shattered femurs and disjointed hip sockets at his feet flashed red. As the sun set luridly outside, the whole room took on a sinister crimson. Once more his intestines turned, rumbled; the dragon yawned in its sleep.

For distraction he reached for one of the funny black lumps on the table beside him. Frothy and porous, glinting with purple highlights, the rock was labeled *Etna—'84*. Next to it was a white one, with a crumbly texture like dried bread, labeled *Krakatoa—'79*.

"I go on pilgrimages," Syria explained. "Hawaii, Italy, Japan, Costa Rica. Alaska is next."

"Pretty cold for you."

"Never gets too cold around me." She smiled. "Mount Saint Helens erupted on my birthday." She said this as if taking credit. "I think that's how I'd like to die, actually. Like in Pompeii. Fried in rock. Quietly rotting away to leave a perfect hollow half a mile down. Wouldn't that be wild?" She looked around at her own posters, and Checker sensed she never tired of studying the steam, the crags, the splurts of red earth; he knew she came home at two, three, even four in the morning, and he could see her sprawling out on the couch with only the lava lamp on, images of bright bones and trailing drips of glass still burned on her retinas, and in her tiredness the whole room surging under her, all red and afloat and melting, steam coming off her sweaty shirt, her hair black and strangled like something charred.

"I might have been a volcanologist," she supposed, "but I hated school. So I kick around flows when I take vacations. The smell of sulfur; a rumble under my feet—that's my idea of a good time."

Rahim had been pinging the debris toward them until he swept a wave of variegated cullet right over Syria's boot. She sprayed the glass against his jeans; Rahim kicked it back. Syria swung up from the chair and slapped him across the face; Rahim slapped Syria; she hit him back even harder, and then they froze. All this happened in a matter of seconds, the three volleys of glass, the three slaps—right-left-right, left-right-left, like drum exercises.

"It's time for supper now," said Syria.

Rahim marched coolly to the kitchen. Syria sat back down as if nothing had happened.

Soon smoke billowed across the volcanic posters like a Sensurround disaster movie. Regularly the smoke alarm in the adjoining bedroom would emit a piercing screech, and Rahim would hurry out to wave a newspaper under the sensor to cut it off. At last he announced that dinner was ready, and Syria, who'd been sniffing the air suspiciously since he began to cook, strode warily into the kitchen. She picked the lid off a pot and slammed it down again. "I said spaghetti."

"For Sheckair," said Rahim defiantly, "Netional Deesh."

"Netional Deesh," said Syria between her teeth, "tastes like Dinty Moore beef stew."

"I make food from my country," said Rahim, rolling his r's majestically.

"Your country," said Syria, her voice ominously level, "is a squalid little sandbox where wizened old men sit around a fire with meat on a stick. It is the last place in the world I would go for recipes."

Meanwhile, Checker diffidently looked into the pot himself, finding a few gristly chunks of meat with potatoes and heavily cooked vegetables.

"All Amedican know is pizza," Rahim muttered, serving up the stew. "I make real food."

"I was hungry!" Syria scooped the entire helping in her hand and flung it at the sink, *thwap*. Rahim catapulted the mound of Netional Deesh on his spoon at Syria's shirt; Syria commandeered the pot and flung a wad of stew smack in the boy's face. Checker found himself looking down at what was not long ago a dubious dinner, now turned scarce and valuable ammunition. Hijack looked enviously over at Checker's serving. Once again, this whole interchange had taken no time at all, and was executed with a bizarre, almost mechanical immediacy—splat, splat, splat—they seemed stoic, or at least normal.

Syria turned the pot upside down, and its contents lumped reluctantly off the bottom to thunk on the floor. "Now, is that the sound of something you would eat? I'm going out for a slice and back to work. Ta-ta, darling." With one finger she raised Rahim's chin and kissed his gravied lips with a surprising tenderness. "Tastes terrible," she said softly, and strolled out of the apartment, glass shattering in her wake.

Checker and Rahim sat at the table and didn't say anything. Rahim dabbed gravy from his nose. They looked around, at the globs on the floor, the smoke still drifting through the air, the bits of carrot in Rahim's hair.

Finally Rahim looked at Checker and asked, "How you make—spaghetti?"

They spent the next two hours cleaning the kitchen, then sautéing onions, pressing garlic, tossing in basil and oregano. Rahim seemed intrigued by the concept of *al dente*, and leaned over the pot as Checker spiced the sauce. They sat down to eat, and Rahim twirled the pasta on his fork, debating whether another splash of red wine would have given the tomatoes more body. When Checker described a variation with sweet Italian sausage, the Iraqi asked where to buy it.

As Check pulled on his jacket to go clean Syria's studio, Rahim surveyed the disheveled apartment with a shy, incongruous pleasure. "She is vedy beautiful, no?"

"Your wife," said Checker with effort, "is very beautiful, no." While the whole evening might have been a drain, it was that one word which fatigued him; Checker left the Carver Arms noticeably pale.

*   *   *

S o you and Hijack are getting along—smashingly."

      "I haven't enjoyed myself more in years."

"Then you like him."

"I adore him."

Checker washed out Syria's mugs at the sink, pensively scraping the dried black rims of coffee. "Have you always been such a terror?"

"As a child. But later . . ." She slipped a bone into the furnace and twirled. "At your age, or a bit older, I was quite contained."

"That's hard to imagine."

"My father died."

There was a long silence; Syria inspected the joint on her bone; Checker dried the dishes, though he hardly had to in this heat.

". . . Are you over it?"

"I'll never be over it. A funeral isn't like a lousy party and then you go home. It's not a bum movie that's over and the lights go up. When people are dead they're dead for the rest of your life."

She talked so little about herself, Checker didn't want to say the wrong thing and so said nothing.

"With a father," she said, "your world has a top. It's like sleeping with enough blankets."

"I don't know," said Checker. "I don't think about mine much."

"You don't have to. He's alive."

He was so pleased she was talking. He loved it so much when she was talking.

"See, it doesn't matter, the thinking," she continued. "You don't have to talk to the guy. Visit. My father drilled wells for loaded film types with out-of-the-way ranch houses near the Mojave. We could both talk about heat, but besides that, he didn't understand about glass. Then all that stuff, profession—it's overrated, isn't it? Just keeping busy . . . Point is, months, even years went by; lived on different coasts, didn't phone much, write. Fact, practically, my life hasn't changed much. But all that time I knew he was somewhere. Know that feeling in a house when there's someone reading in the next room? You can't even see them and they don't say a word? Know the difference between that and being there by yourself? That's what I mean. The day my mother told me, it was like hearing the door open, and close. A little cold breeze. Nothing else, except that everything suddenly felt totally different. The next room was empty. Pages of the book were flapping in the wind."

She was quiet for a long time.

"You know, ordinary people have a reputation for leading dumb little lives," she went on after a while. "Aluminum siding, plastic seat covers, *TV Guide*. But it knocks me out what just about everyone goes through. Did you know that every schmo's father dies? That didn't occur to me until years later. For a long time I thought it was only me."

"'Ordinary' is a dangerous word. I avoid it."

"Well, yes. Did you know—" She turned to him, startlingly sincere, straight; rage seemed to clear her out, for her air had the clean, crisp quality of after a thunderstorm. "Did you know that everyone was born from a woman's body? That everyone dreams? Makes up stories every night and thinks they're real?"

Checker nodded. "If you tried to describe a dream to someone who'd never had one, they'd think you were crazy."

"Everyone gets old. Dies—"

"Has kids—"

"Some days I'm not disgusted, I'm blown away. So that who makes headlines and who has Jaguars and who's a movie star seems so—"

"Beside the point."

"Yes! Because it's tempting to condescend, isn't it? Toward *those* people. But what's really hard, and really good, everyone does."

As the drummer and the glassblower finished their work, Astoria twisted in its sleep, astir with quixotic and demanding lives. A retired schoolteacher with a son in jail wrung her sheet. A two-week-old child who had no names for any separate object opened her eyes to a benevolent pastel blur, their only neighbor who saw the universe tonight as a coherent bubble. A carpenter with uterine cancer hunched on a toilet in Astoria General, bravely preparing for a life of leaky yellow bags. An accountant was dreaming he could fly. And just across the street a young man and woman wrestled with each other, in love, then not, in love again, all under a bedspread the most alarming color of blue.

W hat about your father?" Syria asked the next night. "He's Italian?"

"Black. Secretti's my mother's name."

"What does he look like?"

"Good, I guess."

"Come on. Talk."

"D.C."

"Divorced?"

"And married. Divorced. Married. My mother was an early mistake. She says he used to be real different."

"How?"

"Kind of a wild man. Impulsive. It was even weirder back then for him to marry a poor white girl. His family's pretty well off. But he worshipped her. Even took her last name. More musical than Jones, he said. His parents were furious. So's his new wife, actually."

"Why?"

"'Secretti' is his souvenir. See, my mother was a riot. Still is."

"You like her?"

"Oh yeah. She's like a little kid. My father sends her enough money to get by on, and she—plays. All day. Makes things, for no reason. Lately it's pillows. She's just coming out of a quilting phase. The quilt on my bed is a retrospective of my favorite shirts through the ages. I wake up, and there's the corduroy from fifth grade, the velour from third. It's nice. The mobile thing was a pain, though. She hung them too low."

"You've managed to change the subject from your father."

"You bet."

"You don't get along."

"I bug him."

"Why?"

"He wants me to be something. Go to school, all that. He thinks I'm happy-go-lucky, and later I'll be sorry."

"You don't like him."

"I think he was probably terrific when he was my age. But then he—decided something."

"What does he do?"

Checker shrugged. "Government."

"You can't have that dumb an idea of your father's job."

"An appointed position," Checker dodged.

"Covers anything from attorney general to janitor."

Check flickered a smile. "It's just—Syria, I'd rather the band didn't know. They treat me—"

"They idolize you."

"Whatever. It's bad enough. So I'd rather keep my father out of it."

"He's a big shot."

"You could say that."

"If he's so connected, why couldn't he help you with my wife?"

"I tried," Check groaned. "He said he wished the United States would deport *all* the riffraff I hang around with. And my father had something to do with Carter, so he's not so hot on Middle Easterners."

"You see him much?"

"Three, four times a year. I sit in big poofy chairs in a nice sweater and meet his new wife. He lectures me. I look around the room, play with the flower arrangement. By the time he's finished, there are petals scattered all over the carpet. I measure how bad it was by whether there are any roses left in one piece at the end of the night. I think he's just about given up. He says my mother's ruined me. And he's right." Checker smiled. "I think he misses her. He asks about her when the wife goes to the bathroom. I tell him about the mobiles and he rolls his eyes, but I bet later he thinks about it and smiles a little and looks around his own living room and feels tired. They're always stiff, those places, like hotels— nothing kills the character of a room faster than money. I feel sorry for him. He feels sorry for me. We've got it worked out.

"I have a theory, though. I think if I walked in there one day and said, Dad, I'm going to Yale. And, Dad, I'm going to make something of myself. Music is a crapshoot and Mom's a crackpot and I've got to stop daydreaming over the Triborough and tackle some long-range goals. If I came in and said, Dad, bike's gotta go, I want a subcompact for my birthday, with great gas mileage—God, Syr, I think he'd burst into tears. Because he pushes me hard as he can, and then when I don't budge I can see he's relieved. Sometimes it gets real late and the wife goes to bed and it's just us over a bottle of vodka, and he asks me about Plato's and my friends and how I feel and—the look on his face. I don't know."

Check roused himself. "Sorry, I don't usually talk about my father."

"He's one of your secrets, isn't he?"

"He's a shortcut."

"How?"

"It's easier to decide you don't want a swimming pool if

there's a bulldozer in the back yard about to dig the hole."

"What?"

"A lot of people get so hung up on what they can't have that they don't think for a second about whether they really want it. They have to win the lottery to find out they like to work, after all; that they like their little houses. You know, what we were talking about last night, ordinariness, that it's crap. Well, I know I can have Yale and D.C., so I know I like my mother and the quilt on my bed and Plato's and Howard and Hijack and Caldwell. Like I said, Dad's a shortcut."

"And you walk around knowing that your father's important, like having a hundred-dollar bill in your back pocket."

"Oh no. My mother is my hundred-dollar bill."

Before they finally got down to work, Syria asked, "Could you get into Yale? If you wanted?"

Check laughed. "I have no idea. I never checked my test scores. Threw out most of my report cards. I used one of them, unopened, as a coaster for a month. It got rings on the envelope—coffee, beer, Coke. Collected dust and bugs, and the address blurred. Interesting experiment."

"Did you ever open it?"

"Finally Romaine did, my brother. He was furious. 'How you get a A in English if you never went?' So I know one grade. Not surprising, though. Ms. Carlton was—well, we had a good time." Checker smiled and seemed to be keeping a great deal to himself.

"Did you ever have affairs with your teachers?"

"Affairs!" Check exclaimed, not answering. "We talked. We talked a lot."

Later that night he asked her, "Would you like it if I went to Yale? Would I seem better?"

"I like the idea of your being able to go and not going."

"Yeah, I can see that. But if it really doesn't matter, then it doesn't even matter if I could get in, either. You can't give these people any credit at all."

"Which is why you wouldn't open your report cards."

"Right. Even if they were straight A's, you can't believe the A's any more than the D's, Syr. You just don't pay any attention, period."

Syria shook her head and took a pipe, continuing to stare at Checker, when he wasn't looking, for the rest of the night.

I talked to one of your students today. He said you terrify him."

"And what did you say?"

"I said you terrified me, too."

She smiled. "What are you afraid of?"

"That you won't like me."

"I like you, kiddo," she said, a little too casually. "Relax."

"Bullshit. You don't want me to relax. Or your students. You scare people on purpose. Why?"

"Keeps them out of my way," she said cryptically, with exactly the same edge he was talking about.

"Keeps them in the next state. Why, Syr?"

She sighed, concentrating on her work. "Teaching? I used to fall in love with every one of them, even the girls. I couldn't afford that after a while. It was killing me.—Listen, this glass is getting cordy and the tank's about blown out. You're going to have to drag after I finish."

"What's wrong with liking your students?"

"I didn't say 'like,'" she said sharply, hefting her piece to the bench. "You get so 'jacked,' mister? Let me advise you, stay in love with that bridge of yours. Iron and concrete. Color."

"Glass."

She nodded. "I've traveled a lot. But if I hear another guy tell me hiking up a mountain that 'it's not the place, it's the people,' I'll throw him off the ridge. There's plenty else— texture, temperature, the sky. Ask me? Keep people out of it."

"That doesn't seem possible."

"It's not."

"I think it's bad advice."

"You'll pay for not taking it."

"I'll pay, then."

"You don't know what you're doing. You're too young."

"I can't help that."

"Your age," Syria pondered more gently. "It's like a test. Like a ring of fire."

"What happens on the other side?"

"Sometimes you come out a shrunken-up old cinder. Burned and burned out. Smoking a little, resentfully. And you get meaner and harder, and then they bury you. Thank God."

"I don't see myself turning into a briquette."

"No, maybe not. See, sometimes you come out harder, but that's good. You shine. Not like soot, but like steel. You temper."

"That's what happened to you?" Checker smiled. "Some temper."

"Yes," said Syria. "But, kiddo, there's one more thing that can happen. Some nineteen-year-olds go into the fire and—"

"What happens?"

"Something sad," she warned him. "They don't burn out or temper, they melt. Like throwing a piece of cullet in the furnace and closing the door and never coming back." She said, "Watch out," and handed him a punty to drag the tank; the discussion was over.

9 / in defense of subjective reality

I've found a studio, Check, that's fantastically cheap, and—"

"What do we need a studio for, Howard?"

"To make a demo . . ."

"Why do we need a demo, Howard?"

"To send to clubs? To record companies . . . ?"

The drummer sighed. "You know what a one-hit band is, don't you?"

"Yeah."

"Well, just about every band that ever got anywhere is a one-hit band. And they're bitter, Howard. They want something and they think they've got it and they spend a lot of money on nice clothes and maybe a car, and then it turns out they didn't get it, after all. It's like *Let's Make a Deal*, when you think the Caddy is behind Curtain #3 and you jump up and down on camera and it turns out there's been a mistake—Curtain #3 is just a pile of dog food. But nothing's the same after that. They can still play and write songs, but it's all ruined. They end up hating rock and roll and selling insurance."

"We wouldn't have to be a one-hitter, Check, that's defeatist—"

"Even if we weren't. Even if we made it or, if we were lucky, only kept trying and got nowhere, it would mean we'd started doing the right things for the wrong reasons. There's really no difference between that and just doing the wrong things."

"Why is trying to get somewhere a bad reason?"

"What if you send that tape to CBGB's and they tell us we aren't any good? What then?"

"You're just afraid of rejection, then."

"The point is, Howard, do we believe them? Or if they tell us we're good, do we believe them? What does CB's have to do with us, Howard?"

"I don't understand."

"You don't ask people questions unless you're interested in what they tell you. I'm not interested, Howard. If CB's likes The Derailleurs, does that mean we play better?"

"It might make us feel better—"

"I feel very good, Howard. It's dangerous, this tape business, don't you see?"

"NO!" Howard screamed in frustration. "What's wrong with a little ambition?"

"Everything. You drag other people into something that's not their business. You make it their business. It's not your business anymore. You let them say what you are and you're lost, Howard. You've sold your soul."

* * *

Later, in Plato's, Checker went so far as to suppose, "Maybe it doesn't matter if we're 'good.' I don't even know what that means."

"Are you honestly claiming you don't care about excellence?" asked Eaton.

"I care about feeling excellent. I tend to think that's the same thing."

"But if I walked in and said, 'You suck and your band sucks,' you'd blow it off?"

"I'm not perfect—"

"Can I quote you?"

"What?" A lot of things Eaton said, Checker literally didn't hear.

"Go on."

"Of course that would be a drag. But if I were perfect, it wouldn't matter. And it also wouldn't matter if you came in and said, 'You're—exemplary.'"

Eaton smiled. "You remembered."

That weekend the band took one of its traditional rambles through Manhattan. Caldwell picked up a little plastic dinosaur in a gutter; they came across a store that sold thousands of different light bulbs, where Checker bought a Mickey Mouse night-light for his mother. Toward the end of their walk they serendipitously happened upon the Washington Square Art Exhibit, which burgeoned beyond the park for blocks, the sidewalks crammed with booth after booth of notoriously bad art. The artists sat on stools, gnawing sandwiches.

"Somebody should suggest that these people move on to Sheetrock."

"No, Eat, I'm proud of them. Of their kitty cats. Their spirograph sailboats. Their seascapes with the moon on the water." Checker held a crystal unicorn up to the late-afternoon sun.

"You like this stuff?"

"I like that they do it."

"Don't you have any standards, man? Look at that tiger, with the disjointed nose. You're going to tell me that isn't atrocious?"

Checker didn't look at the picture, though, but at the artist. A brassy woman in her late fifties, she stared back at Check with a clang. Her name was Lydia Myers, and she was a jewelry polisher from New Jersey. She owned a small split-level in Paterson, with walnut paneling and wall-to-wall beige carpeting that didn't show dirt; she had a large pantry; it wasn't a bad life. She was a woman who knew what she liked: lasagna; Sunday afternoons; acrylics. Inside her head was weirder than anyone knew, and it wasn't her fault if that never came out on canvas.

Checker couldn't quite fill all of this in, but he got a start on it. Most of all he could see Lydia Myers at her kitchen table passing the hours tracing stripes, stirring gesso, mixing oranges, the refrigerator humming on and off, a cat at her feet. He was sure she didn't watch television, and Check very much preferred to picture Lydia Myers wrestling with that difficult big black nose to watching one more *Donahue*. He bought the tiger.

10 / howard and the
flow state

CONCENTRATION IS LIKENED TO
EUPHORIC STATES OF MIND

The seemingly simple act of being fully absorbed in a challenging task is now being seen as akin to some of the extravagantly euphoric states such as those sought in drugs or sex or through "the runner's high."

New research is leading to the conclusion that these instances of absorption are, in effect, altered states in which the mind functions at its peak, time is often distorted and a sense of happiness seems to pervade the moment.

Such states, the new research suggests, are accompanied by mental efficiency experienced as a feeling of effortlessness.

One team of researchers describes these moments of absorption as "flow states."

According to Mike Csikszenmihalyi, a psychologist at the University of Chicago, "flow" refers to "those times when things seem to go just right, when you feel alive and fully attentive to what you're doing."*

Howard finished taping the article carefully into his notebook and wrote beneath it:

Hypothesis #2: Subject has achieved a nearly permanent "flow state," by acts of sustained concentration, "including a rapturous joy, a sense of some profound meaningfulness, vivid imagery, and an altered sense of time . . . Such people . . . may go through much of the day lost in a pleasant, reverie-like state."

Researchers agree that "flow" can be learned.

Howard tucked his notebook under the cushion of his bedroom chair and leaped outside.

The Secretti apartment was a sprawling, timeless place, junk from the family's different eras littering the rooms like stray memories. All events were spontaneous, like the incidental bombardment of molecules—occasionally foods

---

* "Concentration Is Likened to Euphoric States of Mind," by Daniel Goleman, *New York Times*, Mar. 4, 1986 (pp. C1, C3).

collided in the middle of the living room, and hands in bags, bread on newspaper, the family would eat together; but for the most part it was fistfuls of corned beef, crumples of chips. The debris of this grazing scuttered over the stuffed gorilla, the Matchbox cars, the hook and ladder like tumbleweed.

When Howard burst in that afternoon, Checker was nested in the living room at his piano. Magnificent for a toy, ludicrous for an instrument, Checker's baby-blue grand was a present from his father for his fifth birthday. He sat cross-legged before it, plinking out a tune with one finger. Leaning on the wind-up bear a few feet away, a personal stereo buzzed at high volume, a tinny chirp wheedling from its earphones. While Check had bought the machine for cycling, he didn't use it much. Checker was already afraid he was the only one who heard the music.

Howard cleared a space on the floor. The drummer grabbed two pickup sticks from under Howard's leg to drum on top of the piano while he sang:

Eeensie, weensie sound of Walkman,
Meensy-teensy.
Tiny, whiny sound of Walkman,
Rinky-dinky.
Mincey, wincey sound of Walkman,
Shrimpy-wimpy.
The squeal from your earphones,
Like Alvin's chipmunks—
Don't tell me this is rock and roll.

Give me a bandstand,
Crank up those tall amps,
I play my traps with two-by-fours.
We make your table shake,
We make your glasses break,
We make your drink fall on the floor.
We make your stomach sink,
We make your scalp shrink,
We drive your mother out the door.

Hunky-chunky we Derailleurs,
Funky-thunky.
Hunky-dory we Derailleurs,
More-and-morey.
Rowdy-crowdy big Derailleurs,
Loudy-shouty.
Who needs your microtapes,
You high-tech jackanapes,
Don't tell me you know rock and roll.

Got bad reception?
We take exception.
We snip your wires and pull your jack.
We rip your shirt silk,
We scorch your baby's milk,
We knot the tie around your neck.
We sound your smoke alarms,
We shave your underarms,
We shake your engine block until it cracks.

Grab the extension cords,
This is an encore.
Toss out your tiny double A's.
We make your roof leak,
We make your hinges squeak,
We break your lease and strip your paint.
We make your car stall,
We make your cake fall,
We blister polyurethane.

Got bad reception?
We take exception.
Go find a shovel, dig a hole.
Grab the extension,
Toss your invention—
No way it's big enough for rock and roll.

"That's great!" said Howard, and asked, without skipping a beat, "Do you think I could write rock songs?"

S top it. I'm focusing. I'm almost in a flow state. I can feel it."

"A *flow state*—?"

"It's too complicated for you to understand."

Caldwell read over Howard's shoulder, "Rock-n-out, late at night, pock-a-pock-a?"

"This is private!"

"How, don't tell me you're—"

"Check said why not, that's what he said."

"Know what else Check says? Never write a lyric with 'hey, hey' or 'yeah, yeah' or 'all night long.'"

"Bull. Checker never says never. Now look what you've done. You've ruined my flow state. I was almost euphoric, and now I'm just ordinary."

"No! Howard Williams feel ordinary?"

"Sweets."

"Check, How here—"

"Don't worry. Lay off. There's no problem."

But there was a problem. Howard wanted The Derailleurs to play his song at their next rehearsal. The band squirmed.

"Got a tune?" asked Check.

Howard hummed something bouncy and indistinct. "I can't sing, but—you know. Like a rock song."

"A rock song," said Caldwell.

"It's not quite ready, Howard," said Check gently. "Give me a copy, we'll see what we can do."

They went on to learn "Walkmans Make Creepy Squealy Sounds," but Howard folded his arms and didn't say "Great!" when it was over. After the rehearsal dispersed, Eaton slid beside the manager, who was slumped in his chair smoothing and creasing and resmoothing his lyrics.

"You've got a real classic sensibility," said Eaton.

"What?"

"The song. Good solid rock. Bedrock."

"Yeah?"

"Does he always dismiss other people's tunes like that?"

Howard shrugged. "Nobody's ever tried before."

"So the others are afraid of him."

"Come on. Of Check?"

"Sure. And just now you obviously threatened the guy."

"Yeah?"

Eaton sighed and put his feet up. "I think our friend Secretti has a hard time with competition."

"Well, why shouldn't someone else write songs!"

"Of course. But when you're running your own little empire—" There was a look in Howard's eyes; Eaton pulled up short.

"Check is a friend of mine," said Howard warily.

"And of mine, of course. Though I don't know him well, I'm sure he's a fine person. An excellent drummer. He just strikes me as a little insecure, that's all."

"Yeah?"

"Just a little. It's hardly even a criticism. That's so common, at his age."

"Aren't you nineteen, too?"

Eaton shrugged. "Why don't you give me those lyrics? I'll work on the arrangement."

With a slightly funny feeling, Howard handed Eaton the words.

I don't see what the trouble is. You just say, Little boy, you can't write music, go home."

"I can't either, Syr."

"You don't understand anything that's not *nice*, do you? If it's not one big Fourth of July picnic, you panic. You get all confused."

"I don't."

"You're pathetic."

"And you're no help."

When Checker showed up at rehearsal the next week, he wanted to start immediately on Howard's song. Checker coached the band on the rhythm, got Rachel to croon in the background, and sang the lyrics himself. The tune had been retitled "No Frills."

By the end, Caldwell and J.K. were doubled over laughing. "Perfecto!"

"You changed it," said Howard.

"I thought you'd get a kick out of it, Howard. Don't you like the tune?"

"Sure, but. My song, it was serious."

"What happened to the line about the moon?" Eaton interjected. "I thought that was especially good."

"It was good. It didn't fit my concept, though."

"So your concept was that Howard's song wasn't good."

Checker shifted on the throne uncomfortably and tapped the base, bu-bu-bu-bum. "This is just The Derailleurs, right? Plato's? Rehearsal?"

"Just Howard. Just Howard's song."

"And just my songs."

"Only your songs aren't jokes—"

"Most of them are, too—"

"They're not parodies." Eaton licked his lips. "I did some work on 'All Night Long' myself. But I gave it a little more of a break—"

"Strike, come on," said Caldwell.

"Any lyric has potential." Eaton looked at Caldwell with an inside smile. "So may I?"

"Go ahead," said Check, stepping down.

As Eaton approached the Leedys, the sticks clattered away from him. When he picked them up, the beater fell over.

"You have to wire—"

"I *know*." Eaton glared at the shoddy traps. He retuned the snare until it was taut, nervous, like a horse on short rein.

Eaton coached the band on their parts, until, *wham*: Howard's song. Whether the lyrics were weak didn't matter, since you couldn't hear them. All the same, Howard was proud. It sounded like a real rock song.

"So which do you like better, Howard?" asked Check heavily.

"No offense, Check. But Eat's does make you tap your foot."

W hat's the trouble? I think the demo's going well. The songs have a lot of drive."

"Yeah, they sure do." Caldwell mopped his forehead and unstrapped his guitar. "I don't know. This isn't the same."

"It's not supposed to be the same," said Eaton coldly.

"I guess I'm feeling a little sleazy, creeping around behind Check's back and all. Lying."

"You're not lying. You're just not telling the truth."

"But what happens when we finish the demo?" asked Caldwell. "If we get a gig, or especially a contract?"

"Check find out way before that," said J.K.

"Well. Check's pretty naïve."

Eaton smiled. "Or we are."

"How's that?"

"You assume Secretti's life is one big Care Bears movie, don't you?"

"What are you getting at?"

"I know something about the industry, okay? In recording it's easier to get somewhere as an independent. You sign as a single musician, you're flexible. A whole band is an albatross. And especially with a motley crew like this one—"

"Who you calling 'motley'?"

"Not you, J.K., obviously I—we—selected the cream of The Derailleurs; that was the whole idea of this project—"

"Not by me, it wasn't," J.K. interrupted. "I just want to play more, check out recording. I never said I's better—"

"But you are," Eaton dismissed. "You and Sweets are real musicians. But for once let's be frank with each other. Rachel's voice is thin, and Carl has no stage presence. Rahim's style isn't nearly commercial enough for mainstream rock. And poor Howard thinks he's a manager, when all he can do is clap. Now that he's decided he can write songs, he's an even bigger liability. Let's face it, we salvaged those lyrics for him by playing over them, but—"

"You stuck up for Howard song," said J.K.

"I didn't happen to think Secretti's joke was considerate

of Howard's feelings. But you're missing my point: why do you think Secretti hasn't noticed all these weaknesses in the band himself? Who would want that kind of baggage in an ambitious career?"

"Check, ambitious? What are you on?"

"A good dose of savvy, and I suggest you take two. When he disappears, what do you think he does, really?"

"It a female, Sweets. Gotta be."

"But why hide a girl?"

"Maybe he likes his privacy," said Caldwell. "And maybe he wants to protect Rache."

"Or himself."

"Why, what do you think he does?"

"I can't say for sure, of course. But as you can see, cutting demos can be time-consuming."

"No way! You don't know Check, then."

"I wonder if you do."

"He's not an asshole!"

"Sweets, I'm giving him far more credit than you are. What kind of dimwit with a talent like that would keep playing in a run-down nightclub in Astoria?"

"So you think Check is good?" asked Caldwell, leaning forward. "I mean really good?"

"I think," said Eaton carefully, "that you'd better enjoy playing with your friend Secretti while he's still around."

Caldwell sat back in his chair and snapped a string on his guitar, *thwack*, against its neck. "That's what I was afraid of."

Eaton almost said, "I know," but held his tongue.

Syria did not dress up to go to the INS

11 / the newlywed game

Big J., what do you make of Striker?"

"Seems okay. Drums good. I guess."

"But not like Check."

"Nah." They both seemed uneasy, hands in their pockets as they strolled through the park.

"He's a little—" Caldwell stopped.

"What?"

"Well, do you think he's something of a scow?"

"Some." J.K. leaned over the railing and studied a parking meter down on the rocks. "He got a lot on the ball, though, that so?"

"Yeah, I think he's massively smart. See, the thing is—"

"Spit it out."

"Well, damn it, J.K., I like the whole band, I do. And I

said he's a scow, but it's almost a relief, isn't it? I mean, Rachel's voice *is* thin."

They breathed deeper, more relaxed breaths. "Yeah," said J.K. slowly. "It thin."

O n a bench in Syria's studio, Checker and Rahim held their hands under a light. The Iraqi's fingers were still black from fingerprinting at Federal Plaza; the swirls of their prints were dizzying and mysterious, the tiny triangles, the slurping concentric designs.

Checker couldn't match his prints to the FBI's three standard categories of "loop," "whorl," or "arch." The form's small print noted, *Other patterns occur infrequently and are not shown here.* That must be it, for Checker's prints expanded and exploded off the sides of his fingers. Circles were never closed. The current of the ridges took sudden curves, unpredictable diversions, like the whirlpools under Hell Gate churning at the turn of the East River tide. A fortune of sorts, he supposed.

"Okay, kiddo. Immigration forms, right? Let's get this over with."

Checker started at her voice. There was nothing like it. Nearly always she spoke briskly and with a sarcastic twang, like now, though once in a while that broke into a sudden gentleness, even sweetness, that struck Checker as thoroughly inexplicable. Where did that come from? It was like knocking along a smooth steel wall, bang, bang, bang, *bong*—suddenly the sound went low and hollow; you'd found the door. Checker listened for it deliberately now. He wanted in.

Syria put her boots up on a bench and paged through her Petition for Alien Relative, sucking on her pen. She tapped the page. "This is going to take some creativity."

"Lying," said Checker. "Though Kaypro says you guys should stick as close to the truth as possible. Still, you're going to have to come up with a version of your meeting that's a little more romantic."

"Old Muslim tradition," said Syria. "Arranged marriage."

"But it was romantic," said Rahim softly, who had of late grown curiously shy around his wife, almost diffident. "Sheckair." Rahim pointed to a word. "How this say?"

"Consummated."

Rahim looked blank.

"It means you're supposed to have . . ."

"Fucked," Syria intruded flippantly.

"They *tell*—? They *ask*—!"

"Yeah," said Check. "Maybe. They can be pretty rude about it, too. Be prepared."

Rahim flapped the triplicates with agitation. "Is not their business!"

"They think it is. Just chill, Hijack. Tell them what you have to . . . or make up what you have to . . ." Checker reached for the papers and burrowed into the instructions. "Just get through the interview, okay?"

Checker led Rahim through the form; when he came to memberships in U.S. organizations, Rahim proudly had

Check list THE DERAILLEURS in big block letters.

"Have you ever knowingly committed a crime for which you haven't been arrested?"

"Right," said Syria. "Now's your chance to get arrested."

Murdered my grandmother, Check started to enter.

"NO!" screeched Rahim.

"Have you been treated for mental disorder, drug addiction, or alcoholism? Have you engaged in, or do you intend to engage in, any commercialized sexual activity?"

Syria, impatient with the tamer inquiry into the life of an American, pulled the Application for Permanent Residence from Checker's hands and read down the page. "Jesus, who's going to say yes to these questions? 'Hello, my name is Rahim Abdul, and I want into your country. I am mentally retarded, insane, and psychopathic. Yes, I am an anarchistic Nazi saboteur, and I advocate the assaulting or killing of government officials. In addition to being a sexual deviant and chronic alcoholic, I am riddled with the following contagious diseases. Yes, I am a professional beggar, and likely to become a public charge. In spite of my severe retardation, I have somehow managed to try to overthrow your government and to perpetrate visa fraud. It is true that I deal illegal narcotics across international borders, and the only reason I haven't been caught before now is that no one ever asked me on a form if I sold drugs so I could say yes. Otherwise I am a model citizen.' I mean, why isn't there a box here to check 'Yes, I have married only to stay in this country and hope to hoodwink the INS in my upcoming interview'?"

Checker laughed. "It's a test! If you really do check yes to any of this shit, then they do know you're retarded!"

"Don marry only to stay in country," said Rahim quietly, but they were having too good a time and didn't hear him.

Checker took the forms back. "See, it works! 'Are you insane or have you suffered one or more attacks of insanity?' And if you say yes, you're insane!"

"'Have you committed or have you been convicted of a crime involving moral turpitude?'" Syria read.

"That's gorgeous. What's turpitude?"

Syria raised her eyebrows. "Come back later tonight, I'll teach you all about it."

"How is turpitude?" asked Rahim severely. "No later tonight."

Syria looked over at her husband queerly. "Any number of acts of savagery and depravity that free Americans are welcome to indulge in."

"Syria is not free. Syria is married."

The couple looked each other squarely in the eye, and Syria seemed to be contemplating a variety of statements, but made none of them.

"Here's one for you, Hijack." Check proceeded in the uncomfortable silence. "Are you a polygamist, or do you advocate polygamy? That is, do you want more than one wife?"

"One," said Rahim, still looking Syria in the eye, "is enough. This one."

* * *

The three of them waited a sufficient number of hours in the reception room of the INS Investigation Branch to memorize the patterns of handprints on the walls, to discover a range of animals in the water spots on the ceiling tiles, to dislodge several wads of gum from the beige linoleum with the toes of their shoes. It was one of those places of almost sadistic blandness, since there was so little to see and so much time to look at it.

Yet amid the faded red panels behind the desk, the rows of weak yellow plastic chairs, the guard swatting flies, major dramas played. Pregnant women walked up to that desk trembling, and came out half an hour later leaning on someone's shoulder, the men patiently explaining, throwing up their hands. Couples conferred in whispers while children asked to go to the bathroom loudly in several languages. "Hush." Forms fluttered, photocopies of forms; sweat blurred the ink. It was such a queer combination of boredom and terror—Rahim listened to the dull blare of the air conditioning drone behind the beat of his heart.

Everyone spoke quietly except Syria Pyramus. "You know what a joke this is?" she said clearly. "All these documents and sneaky questions, while during the time we've sat here a thousand Mexicans have waded over the Rio Grande."

"Syria!" Rahim censured her.

"Chick-pea, the whole garment district in this town is sewn up with illegals. It's like you were on an interstate where the entire flow of traffic was going 75 and you were the only one they pulled over."

Everyone else in the waiting room was nicely, even

primly, dressed, with women in high lacy collars, heels, stockings, and little silver pins. Syria had at best conceded to a fresh shirt. Her jeans were only dirty but not shiny yet—her clothes were a little cleaner now that Rahim did her laundry. But she'd blown glass early that morning; grit lined her neck and crooked at her elbow. Never one to waste time, she'd brought the set of goblets she was delivering to SoHo when this was through, and while they waited for their names to be called, she pulled out a battery-powered engraver to sign each glass on the bottom. The engraver buzzed like hair clippers, and as she ground her spidery signature, wiry and wicked like the trails of her hair, nervous families searched the room for the source of the sound that so perfectly articulated their state of mind—the grating of the burr, the growl of the motor like unsettled intestines, the horrible little shrieks when she changed direction: a sound track.

The goblets themselves were insanely tall and narrow; you would fill them only with grappa or hundred-proof vodka, something clear and dangerous. The glasses looked fragile, but their master handled them casually, rolling them in her long, filthy fingers, with their crumbled black nails, wormy scars, and latest burn blisters.

"So, Checkers," she asked while she worked. "Is this interview the end of the bullshit?"

"They can decide to investigate you further if it seems suspicious. Or turn you down flat."

"This one joker can say no? You hear that, Chick-pea?"

"I do how Sheckair say." Rahim looked pasty. He'd spent

a long time dressing, having borrowed ties and shirts from
the rest of the band to put together a suitable outfit, but by
now his clothes had wilted. He was no longer thinking what
a fine handsome boy he was in the mirror, or even what a
magnificent wife he'd scarfed up. He was sitting in a plastic
chair with his wool trousers sticking to his thighs and he was
thinking about Iraq.

"Rahim and Syria Abdul."

Syria switched off the engraver with a jolt and stood up.
"Abdul?"

"I thought it looked better," Check whispered.

"My name is not Abdul." The entire room was apprised
of this fact. Syria strode up to the desk. "Pyramus," she
announced. "This is Abdul. Heel, Chick-pea." She walked
down the hall, with Rahim scuttering nervously after her. As
Checker watched them go, he held a goblet to his cheek to
feel its cool comfort, sensing in this material the certainty,
the clarity, the edge of Syria herself, and trusting her.

Their interviewer had a thirty-year-old face, a forty-year-
old paunch, and a fifty-year-old leer. The only part of
him that was well groomed was his hair, carefully combed
over his bald spot. The nameplate on his desk said DAVID
REESE, and he greeted Syria, looking her up and down with
a "Well, how do you *do*?" that was not a question. When he
shook her hand, he held it too far up the wrist and for a beat
too long; when he let go, he trailed his fingers over her palm.
Syria wiped her hand on her jeans.

"Just have a seat, honey, I've got to look over your papers first."

"All right, lambikins." She shot him a sour smile and sat on the frayed couch, crossing her long legs and glancing around the office, looking bored. Rahim, dead white now, perched on the edge of the couch and held his knees.

"Quite a place you've got here," Syria intruded. "They don't even give you a door?"

Mr. Reese glanced up, and went back to tapping importantly at his terminal. Syria coolly appraised the cubicle, the dog-eared manila folders stacked on every side, the crumpled candy-bar wrappers, the button on the phone that had been blinking on hold since they'd come in. Phones rang unanswered in adjoining rooms in a regular refrain; outside, two officials strolled languidly past, slurping coffee and clutching fried foods. One said, "Salvador!" the other laughed. Syria reached over to a big dusty mailbag by the couch and picked an unopened letter off the top. Its cancellation date was almost a year old.

"Getting a little behind on the correspondence?"

"Mrs. Abdul, if you would leave that—"

"Pyramus. Please."

"You didn't change your name?"

"A point of contention. Hubbie here is from the old country."

"And you won the fight?"

Syria smiled. "I win most fights. You'll see."

The official started taking ominous little notes as he scrolled through their file. He tapped his pencil, keeping them waiting. At last he looked up. "It says here someone turned your husband in as illegal two weeks before you married him. That we even sent an agent after him, and he eluded arrest."

"You were about to deport the kid. Our timing seemed opportune."

Reese tapped some more, pressed some keys, and worked his eyebrows theatrically. Finally he leaned back in his chair, sprang the tips of his fingers against each other, and sighed. "This looks ridiculous, you know that."

"Yes," said Syria pleasantly.

"I'm tempted to save us all a lot of time here and skip this whole thing—send what's-his-face back to his sand pit and you can give him his money back if you're a nice girl, or you can keep it and—"

"Split it with you."

"Maybe. For keeping my mouth shut. You could be in big trouble. The wet here just gets to take a free ride. Your ass I could fry."

"You can't do anything with my ass without proceeding with this interview."

He smiled. "That's downright inspiring." Reese leaned forward. "Let's start with the obvious question, then. What are *you* doing with *him*?"

"Why not?" asked Rahim hotly.

Reese turned to Rahim as if noticing him for the first time. "Son, that's a lot of woman you've got there. Let's be honest—"

"Oh, let's not," said Syria.

"You don't want to be honest?"

"I don't want you to berate my husband."

"Syria!" Rahim reprimanded her. He turned to Reese and declared, "You insult her, I mess your face."

"You guys are going to make me nail you, aren't you? Okay, Mr. Immigré, out in the waiting room. I'm going to ask the little woman a few questions."

"Syria? I stay if—"

"Go on, Chick-pea," she said, with that rare softness of hers. "I'll be okay. It's part of the deal."

Rahim looked uncertainly from Reese to Syria, then bent down and carefully kissed his wife on the mouth. She smiled.

Reese saw Rahim to the front desk, and returned to the cubicle with a gesture that would have been closing the door collusively behind him, but of course there was no door. "So let's talk about your marriage, Mrs. Pyramus. How much money was involved?"

"Twelve dollars and twenty-eight cents." She paused. "And this, the application fee. I wouldn't pay it."

"Twelve dollars. Pretty cheap for a whole country."

"No, marrying me has cost him enormously."

Reese licked his lips. "Tell me about it."

"Not in detail." She uncrossed her legs, left off right, and crossed them back, right on left. "A little Middle Eastern therapy. I should run workshops."

"Can I come?"

"As long as you can scrub linoleum."

Reese was beginning to feel a little over his head. He

brought the interview back in line. "He's nineteen? You're"—he checked—"twenty-nine."

"I like young boys," said Syria readily.

"Mmm. Why is that?"

"They're still alive. You don't find many of those anymore."

"Live people?"

"That's right."

"I suppose boys do have a reputation for stamina."

"Yes."

Reese couldn't understand why this seedy line of questioning was proceeding with so much dignity.

"Though no control," she went on. "They don't know what they have. They don't know how important it is, how rare. They take it for granted, and left to their own devices, they'll burn it up, or even throw it away."

"But you're going to make sure this little Arab doesn't waste his talents." He smirked.

"I'm a teacher and a protector. That's one of the responsibilities of getting older."

"You married the kid to protect him? Say, from the INS?"

She shrugged. "Among others. There was a time not long ago when I was quite difficult. I caused people a lot of trouble—"

"If you want an amateur opinion—"

"Which I don't."

"You're still difficult."

"I cause different people trouble now." She smiled. "I was

a drain, and now I'm a resource. I'll be around when the time comes. I have things that boys need."

"I bet." But he could say anything! It didn't matter. Syria sat sweetly on his couch, her neck arched back with her Adam's apple out, unusually distinct for a woman's. She kept her arms spread expansively on the back of the couch, claiming a good proportion of his office's territory. Her fingers rippled, her top boot nodded up and down, as if keeping time to music only she could hear.

"You get tired of looking at that thing?" she asked conversationally.

"The American flag?"

"I've always thought the design was a little busy.—You're supposed to ask me if I'm a Communist now, aren't you? Or is it a Nazi?"

David Reese had been studying the woman in front of him. "You're planning to play this straight," he determined incredulously. "You're going to tell me you're in love."

"I am in love." The expression on her face was of gliding through water. Breaststroke.

"All right." Reese came around to sit on the front of his desk, with one thigh raised so the crotch of his pants pulled taut. He spoke more quietly. "I don't know what's in this for you, but you obviously want to keep it. So maybe you and I can work out a deal to make us both happy."

"I'm already happy. What's *your* problem?"

"I get a little tense."

"Is that so."

"It's a hard job."

"Which seems to have its compensations."

"I do like to relieve that tension."

"Oh, spell it out," said Syria, rubbing her hands down her thighs and raising the nap of her jeans. "I'm enjoying this."

"I know I'm a little old for you. But I thought we could investigate what kind of a wife you really are."

"You do want to scrub linoleum."

"This investigation would be in depth."

"Mr. Reese," she said with mock surprise, "you want to fuck me."

Reese shrugged with gentlemanly embarrassment.

Syria leaned forward. "And we could stay up all night? And we could get all slick and sweaty with your saliva all over me until it was light out, then you'd let Rahim have his green card?"

Reese's breathing had increased.

"Getting tense, Mr. Reese?" Syria stood up and towered over him. "Getting jammed up under the band of your underwear?"

He nodded. "You're good at this."

"Isn't it too bad you don't have a door, Mr. Reese, or you could take me down on your big, messy, disorganized desktop—"

Reese had risen toward her, and rocked slightly. "Keep going. Keep talking." He reached for her hand.

She slipped away. "No, I'm finished, *honey*. Because I'd rather sleep with nineteen-year-old wetbacks than with your pudgy American ass. Dark, foreign, funny-smelling Muslim boys." Syria sat back down and crossed her legs again and looked him straight in the eye.

Reese snapped into a somewhat different person. "You're not just a bitch, lady, you're a stupid bitch. That's the worst kind."

"Aren't you supposed to ask me the color of our shower curtain, Mr. Reese? It's blue, and Chick-pea finally got all the mildew off the bottom. Go ahead. Ask me the kind of tooth-brush I use. It's a big black-and-white check. Rahim's is a tiny Oral B. Ask me what's on the walls of our living room."

"All right," said Reese through his teeth, "what's on the halls?"

"Walls. Volcanoes. Next?"

"You want to be grilled? Fine, I'll hang you both. I can have that wet on a plane before this office closes."

"Not without reasonable suspicion, Mr. Reese. Please proceed."

He pitched questions one after the other like fastballs; she hit them back, easy. What was in the refrigerator? Spoiled things. Another disagreeable Netional Deesh. Cold pizza. Half a surprisingly decent pan of moussaka. Rahim took out the garbage. She went to bed at four in the morning. They met through a mutual friend.

"Who?"

"A boy. A disaster."

"How often do you sleep with your husband?"

"Often as I like."

"And what positions do you use?"

"Don't you think we've had enough dirty talk for one afternoon?"

"I'm only doing my job, Mrs. Pyramus."

"We've already explored the extent of your professionalism."

"Go get your 'husband,' Mrs. Pyramus. Let's get this fiasco over with."

Syria rose smoothly and retrieved Rahim, who had now lost all his Middle Eastern pigmentation and could readily pass for an albino who took a lot of baths. His tie straggled from his neck, and his shoes were untied. It had recently occurred to him, the way it does when we say something to other people over and over again until finally we hear it ourselves, that Iraqis really do execute draft evaders. He clutched Syria's hand down the hall.

"He do anything, Syria?" Rahim rasped. "He touch you?"

"He can't touch either of us, Chick-pea."

"He touch you, I kill him." Syria smiled. Rahim could barely talk.

Syria waited out in the hall. She could see part of Rahim's face on the couch, staring down into the floor, curling gradually over as the questions beat down on him from the desk: Who markets? Who does the laundry? Who mends? Who does the dishes? *What kind of Arab are you?*

"And what's one of your best dinners?" asked Reese sardonically.

"Spaghetti."

"You're kidding."

"I make with sweet sausage," said Rahim, bravely raising

his chin up. "Last time, add green pepper. Sheckair, he don have to tell me. Syria, she say vedy good."

"And do you shop for curtains for your love nest?"

"Have trouble," said Rahim, his chin still up, getting the feel: play it straight, that was the deal. "Kitchen strange yellow. Hard to match. I keep looking."

"And do you clip coupons, too?"

Rahim looked confused.

"So how much are you getting off her? She strikes me as a little stingy."

Rahim didn't move.

"Come on, how much does she come across? The lady claims to be a regular pedophile. She all talk, or what?"

Rahim's face clouded, and he sat up straighter. "You say anything about her—"

"Buddy, you're supposed to be banging her, or you can't stay in the States, understand?"

Rahim looked from pile to pile of paper in a panic. (*Don't get angry, Hijack. Swallow it, Hijack. Just get through, Hijack. You keep cool, that's what will make me proud of you.*) "In my country we don talk such things."

Once more Reese walked around to the front of his desk, looking down on Rahim's head. "I bet she's a tease, isn't she? I bet she makes your life hell. I bet she waltzes past you in those tight Levi's of hers and closes the door in your face."

Two tears splashed on the linoleum. "Syria my wife," said Rahim quietly. "We live together. I work hard for her, take care of her. For this, I need green card."

Syria had seen enough, and walked back into the cubicle;

Rahim rose and buried his face in the folds of her shirt. She put her arm around him and arranged a stray wet curl. "He's only nineteen."

"I have reason to press, Mrs. Pyramus. He was reported as an illegal. We send an agent after him, he disappears. Two weeks later he shows up, married. Everyone in the INS isn't an idiot."

"Just some of you. Reese, you have ample evidence we live together, no evidence the marriage isn't consummated. Why I'm doing this isn't your problem. Even if I married for money, this is America. There's no law against being a sleazebag."

"You're such a canny girl," observed Reese. "What on earth makes you think this department has anything to do with justice or due process or even the law? You had your chance at the game the way it's really played. You lost."

"No, I'm still in the game. You know the name Secretti, Mr. Reese? D.C."

Reese paused. "It's vaguely familiar."

"Well, Secretti is a good friend of mine. I could tell him about that deal you proposed, and he might not find it so reasonable. So, if you turn down this petition, you may find yourself having to explain why in an office that actually has a door."

She started to leave, and Reese called after her, "All right, Pyramus. But I'm keeping your file open, understand? This smells, and you know it. Okay, you married Baba Ganoosh here; well, you're gonna stay married for a while, hon. Because we're going to investigate up your ass."

"Investigate anywhere else you like, buttercup, but not up there. That's the point." She swept Rahim off down the hall, and when they met Check in the waiting room, Rahim stared at his friend Secretti with new awe.

Walking down the corridor of the Investigation Branch, Rahim holds Syria's hand

12 / don't be cruel

Rahim was proud of her, but being proud of anyone else is a sensation quite distinct from being proud of yourself. Leaving Federal Plaza, he was quiet.

"I'm telling you, we went about it all wrong," Checker explained exuberantly down Broadway. "While you were in there I talked to this Indian who'd overstayed his student visa. He wanted to go home but didn't have the money; he'd come to turn himself in. He went up to the desk, they didn't want to hear about it. He started screaming, 'I'm illegal, I want to be deported!' and they called some guards and hauled him away. He shouted to me as they dragged him out the door, 'No matter what you want, they'll do the opposite!' Hijack, we missed a trick. You could have come in there and begged to be deported and they'd have folded their arms and said, 'Not on your life, wetback. Stay and suffer.'"

Syria laughed. "Just don't throw me into the briar patch."

But Rahim barely smiled, missing her allusion with uncharacteristic apathy. A glutton for small cultural reference points, the Iraqi loyally watched *Star Trek* reruns at midnight, just so he'd understand when Caldwell exclaimed, "Beam me up, Scotty!" yet Brer Rabbit he passed by. Too bad. It was a gambit Captain Kirk used all the time.

At Plato's The Derailleurs had prepared for either a celebration or a wake. Still, after Checker delivered what seemed to be good news—though the file was still open, Rahim was not on an airplane—the Iraqi's demeanor made it difficult to be festive. When Check read the song he'd scribbled in the waiting room, "I Bared My Breast to the INS," Rahim chewed a seed between his teeth and kicked at Caldwell's effect box. When the rest of the band chowed down pizza, Rahim wasn't hungry.

Eaton injected with a jaundiced sigh, "Well, Kaypro says immigration control in this country is a farce. I figure any day now airlines are going to come out with a new gimmick, free U.S. citizenship with all one-way tickets from squalid countries."

"Fix the balance of payments by selling off passports," Caldwell suggested. "Better bet than tractors, that's for sure."

"Syria says we do that already," said Check. "Not just black market, but INS people."

"Why does that bother you, and your own scam doesn't?" asked Eaton.

"My marriage is no scam," Rahim intruded.

"Yeah, Hijack's pretty legit now, Eat. They've got a regular home sweet home over there," said Caldwell.

"From the look of those Levi's, real sweet," said J.K.

"You hear how these poor foreign sons of bitches crawl over here and sweat in lettuce fields? Man, I'm not impressed, Hijack. That's not suffering, not with that woman, no way."

"Come on, Sweets, our boy sweat plenty. You seen that tall order he live with. How many buckets every night it take to put out that fire?"

"He is looking a little peaked," Caldwell observed.

"This wet on overtime!"

Rahim smiled shyly. "Can complain."

"Can't complain!" J.K. exclaimed. "That girl scare me brain dead!"

"Is this at all serious to you?" Eaton asked Checker.

"Yes," said Check pensively, who hadn't been joining in the fun.

"Because, nothing personal, Rahim—"

The Iraqi blew Eaton a kiss.

"—but aliens bring down wages and take American jobs."

"You want Hijack's job making pyramids of peaches, Eat?" asked Caldwell. "And some little old lady takes one from the bottom and the whole thing falls on the floor? Bet you ask him on the right day, he'd give it to you, apron and all."

"I know the job our man give Striker easy: scrubbing Pyro's bathtub. Just stop by some Saturday and say, Hijack, you taking that work away from a American. You gimme that sponge."

"Bet there's one job Hijack's not giving up," Caldwell

leered. It was nice to have a theme so early in the evening.

"Well, Strike," said Checker thoughtfully, "if you knew there was somewhere you could make in a day what you made in a week where you were, you'd try to get to that place, don't you think?"

"All right," Eaton conceded. "But why only identify with hard-up people? Why not identify with yourself? As someone with a bicycle, an apartment, and a job, don't you want to keep them?"

"Sure, but I don't blame other people for trying to get them, either. Okay, there's only so much room in this country, but it's like musical chairs—when the music stops everyone scrambles and somebody's left out of the game. But like musical chairs, it doesn't have much to do with morality. Everyone wants a place to sit down and everyone probably deserves a place and everyone isn't going to get one. It's just kind of a drag."

"'It's just kind of a drag' doesn't strike me as a statement of terrific political acuity."

Checker shrugged. "I just don't see getting all huffy about aliens. We've got a popular club, it's called the United States. We were born members; we didn't do anything special."

"But you don't fault Americans who want to keep their country from being overrun."

"No, but I wouldn't mail them merit badges, either. You need to know the difference between when you're fighting for something because it's so great and when you're fighting for your own self-interest. People have to fight for their own interests, and I'm not saying that's wrong. But I'm also saying it's not right. When Americans defend their borders, they're being selfish. It's important to know the difference between selfishness and heroism, that's all."

"And defending Rahim is heroic."

"No, selfish," Checker corrected.

"But he's an alien. Not in the club."

"Plato's is a club. My club."

"Somehow by your definition I don't see how anyone does anything heroic, ever. If defending the people on your side is selfish, then the only thing that's heroic is betrayal."

Checker laughed. "I like that!" Checker's laughter could glitter with something nearly evil, like Carl Perkins on *Tug of War* or that immortalized studio janitor on *Dark Side of the Moon*. Sometimes it made his friends nervous, like now. He never cared about losing arguments so long as he enjoyed them.

"I don like," said Rahim. "All twisted up."

Checker stopped and took a long, hard look at Rahim. "I need to run a broom around the studio. Syr's still in SoHo, you come with me?"

"Yes!"

"I know it's Thursday, but maybe I'll come back, we'll play a set. I feel—" Slipping his sticks from his back pocket, Checker played a riff on their glasses. With a last ping on Caldwell's empty bottle and a fond tap on Carl's quiet head, he set out the door. Why couldn't they all make exits like that? Why was it always Checker?

* * *

As they detoured down by the river once more, it was coming up through the Converse All-Stars, that turgid carbonation with which different people might feel sick. The wind in the ginkgo leaves overhead fizzed like a head of beer; single drops of rain hit Checker's cheek like bubbles popping. The sky was bruised over midtown and lightning flashed behind the bridge. A yacht steamed by against the tide, its sound system blasting: *I don't want to work! I just want to bang on the drum all day!* Checker jumped sidewalk cracks and spattered water off the railing, until the drumsticks were in his hands as if they'd leaped there; he trilled along the pipe in time to Todd Rundgren, one of his favorites, his very favorite, since that's what he heard—Checker had so many favorite songs that the only way to keep track of which was on top was to tell what was playing now.

The colors were an even gray and green. The yacht plowed perfectly down the middle of the East River, its wake the regular V of migratory birds; the tips of this letter hit either shore at precisely the same time. Hell Gate held steady overhead, a protector; Checker was relieved to find an object in his life so large and reliable. It was hard to resist the urge to embrace the huge concrete stanchions, parents the way they should be, staunch, immovable, brave. Graffiti on these supports read like homage today, offerings, prayer—*The Last K; Don't go; Ellen!*—their meanings obscure, yearning.

The lights of the Triborough switched on as Checker walked under her span.

But Rahim surprised himself, feeling left out, lagging behind, too much watching. Ticka-ticka, the pearly tips of

Checker's drumsticks hit the hollow piping of the passing rail. Rahim followed the red rim of the All-Stars exalting ahead of him, as Checker had a hard time not running now. The yacht teemed past, its music drifting away, and just in time a Trans Am radio came into earshot, *Every breath you take*—With a curious perversity Hijack refused to walk in time to The Police. Of course Checker was bounding in perfect four-four. Of course Checker—*What makes you so happy?* Thrown by this unlikely blackness, the Iraqi faltered into the mud. As he pulled his shoe out, the thick wet earth sucked at his sole.

Though in June the furnace had become a source of suffering rather than solace, with the storm coming up, the air was unusually cool, and when Check unlocked the door, the dull roar met him with the eagerness of a dog whose master has returned home. The big room was refreshingly dry, and after the damp chill of the walk over, the studio achieved its womb-like winter allure.

Checker swept, unloaded the annealer, and washed a load of dirty cullet. Rahim sat, his head bowed to the concrete.

At last Checker folded his arms. "All right, what is it?"

"You know what is it. You know months what is it."

"Maybe," Checker admitted reluctantly.

Rahim took a breath and said, "Syria," as if that explained everything.

Check felt a little nervousness start up, like an itch somewhere he couldn't reach to scratch.

Rahim twisted and got up from the bench. "Syria married to me!" he cried. "But not—married married."

Checker nodded slowly. His mouth felt funny. It had an inappropriate tension at each corner, and he had to force the curls of his lips back down. "That wasn't the setup."

Rahim paced before the furnace, his hands at the back of his neck as he stared bleakly up at the gas pipes crisscrossing the ceiling. "Every night I unroll my mat in living room. Syria come in late, step over me. I watch her boots, see them go bedroom, door shut. 'Syria,' I say sometime, 'Syria, you my wife. Why I don sleep in there?' She don give no reason. Just say no. I put foot down. I say, 'Wife do with husband—'"

"Hijack, she did you a big favor already—"

"Don want favor! Want real wife! Now, back in my country, some woman take time. She frighten. Here also, yes?"

"Have you ever seen Syria Pyramus frightened?"

"In my country we no put up! So last week I force her. I say, 'You do, you learn—'"

"Jesus," said Check quietly. "What happened?"

Rahim put his hands over his face. "Syria throw my arm behind back. Syria say she hit me, I do that again."

"She would, and she'd deck you. Be careful."

"Sheckair, I love her! I love her smell and her taste and her dirty clothes. Even love she put gravy on my face. I lie on floor at night, awake until she come home. Even then I listen and listen to her breathe behind door. You know she laugh in her sleep?"

"No kidding."

"But is torture now! I want—"

"Yeah, I know what you want, Hijack."

"Sheckair, what I do? Cannot propose! Already married!"

"I don't know that there's anything to do," said Checker, wanting to slap himself in the face. All his advice was coming out wrong. His eyes kept darting oddly around the studio, and his mouth was twitching again. He wanted to turn on the radio, leap up on the bench, dance, run the broom in figure eights. "Does she touch you at all?"

"She kiss me. Hold hands. Put arm around shoulder. You think I have chance?"

"Really, I am the wrong person to ask."

"No, you are best friend I have. So tell me truth, yes?"

Checker advised uncontrollably, "Maybe it's just not a good idea!" He couldn't stop himself! He tried, and it was no good! Checker looked wildly around the room, wanting to rush to the bathroom and lock the door just to shut himself up. "I mean, she's ten years older than you, she's a real hell-raiser and you're a Muslim, you expect a woman who's obedient—" Checker turned away. When he spotted the heat-proof gloves, he had to resist the urge to stuff them in his mouth.

"Don care! I be slave, just, please, talk to her? Syria respect you. She like how you say—"

"How do you know that?"

"She say she like you—"

"Yeah?"

"So maybe she listen? You find out, maybe she change her mind sometime? You tell her how much your friend Hijack be good husband? Gentle and kind?"

"I'd leave off the gentle and kind to pitch for that woman," said Checker, feeling wretched, feeling wonderful, feeling wretched for feeling wonderful. "But sure, I'll talk to her," he said. "No problem."

Increasingly the most misused phrase of the season.

It was three in the morning; Checker rode quietly up to the side entrance of Vesuvius. As he locked Zefal, he could tell by tone the gas was up—she was working. He slipped gently in the door, stealing a glimpse of the glassblower before she felt watched. Syria jabbed the punty in and out of the furnace as if having a conversation. She stopped in the middle of a marver and said, "Jerk!" later, "Unbelievable!"

At last Checker deliberately scuffled; she noticed him. "Have you been swimming?"

Checker looked down at his shirt, a full shade darker now and plastered to his chest. "Drumming."

He stretched; his muscles ached. Syria cracked off and dropped the bone in the annealer. There was that distinct feeling in the room of two people who'd been doing what they loved to do more than anything in the world and were through.

"They like the goblets?"

"Sure. They like the new songs?"

"Sure." Checker enjoyed knowing where she was today; her knowing about the songs. "That guy at the gallery. He make a pass at you again?"

She shrugged. "Ron? After a fashion. It's gotten to be a

joke, or I've made it one. Truth is, if I ever laid a hand on him he'd shoot through the roof."

"You ever lay a hand on anybody?"

"Once in a while," she said warily.

"You seeing anybody now?"

"How could I? I'm married."

"Sort of."

"Prying today."

"Yeah." Checker smiled. "So you have seen guys sometimes? Had—things?"

"I'm twenty-nine!"

"So."

They had a seat, both still soaked in sweat, feet up, tired. "You know what it looks like when there's been a forest fire? That's what's behind me. A few stumps. Smoking cinders. A wasteland of disaster." Syria leaned her head back and laughed. One too many buttons were undone on her big green shirt, and Checker tried not to stare.

"Pretty picture. But mighty abstract."

"All right, last time the arson was Nathan Anderson. Satisfied?"

"Not yet."

"Oh, he was after me. No one ever pursued me with such determination. Came by the shop every night. He was absolutely hilarious. And so extravagant. Went on for months. Until finally . . ." She stopped.

"Why is it so hard for you to tell me anything?"

"I fell for him." She shrugged. "End of story."

"Sounds like you skipped something."

"No, I really didn't. It was like he chased me down the street calling, 'Syria! Syria!' and finally I turned around and said, 'What?' and he squealed and hightailed it around the corner."

"Couldn't take the heat."

"No, sir. Regardless of how much Scotch they swill, inside most men are filled with milk of magnesia."

"So you've had it?"

"Oh no. You can't stop. And I don't mind pain. I've even gotten to like it."

"I don't like it."

"I know."

Checker fiddled with a drip of glass intently. "So when are you planning to divorce Hijack?"

"What's the hurry?" she said slyly. "Maybe I should stay married."

"Yeah?"

"Why not? And you could come over and visit. Chick-pea could fix you dinner. Wouldn't that be nice? Ten years from now you could sit at the table and tell us about your new songs."

"Uh-huh," said Checker grimly. "And what about kids?"

"Why not?"

"I think you'd make a weird mother."

"Do you mean bad?" she asked quickly, sounding surprisingly hurt.

Checker only grunted.

"So do you think I should do that?" Syria pressed. "He's

gorgeous. And he'll grow up. Smart, good on the sax. Why not? Tell me."

"Well, sure. Go ahead."

Check got up from the bench and stood before the furnace.

"Why'd you come by here tonight, anyway?"

Checker shrugged. "It was on the way home."

"Not really."

"To dry my shirt," he said with an edge.

She got up and eyed him, fingering his sleeve for a moment. "Right."

"I'm outta here, I think." He tucked the right leg of his jeans in his sock and scudded to the door. Just before leaving, though, he paused in the darkness. "Hey, I didn't mean that about the kids, Syr," he said quietly. "I think you'd make a dynamite mother." Softly he let himself out.

*For once Eaton feels he could not have
written better lyrics himself*

13 / too much information

R achel is sad."
    "How do you know what it's like to be sad, ever?"
"Trust me."

"Trust you," said Eaton, leaning back in his chair and flicking an ash. "Like everyone else does."

"Shouldn't they?"

"You tell me."

Checker ran his thumb over those unusual fingerprints. "Listen, Eat. I need some advice."

Eaton could have been purring. "This is a switch. You don't ask for advice much."

"I spend too much time dishing it out."

"Which makes you tired."

"Very." Checker looked at Eaton with real gratitude. "I've written a song. I'm not sure I should show it to the band."

Checker handed over a sheet of verse. "Fast. The Clash, that kind of thing."

Eaton read the song, stopping to snuff out his cigarette meditatively on the nightclub table and light up another between verses—he wanted to make this last as long as possible:

You Think I'm So Great I'm Not

You think I'm so great I'm not.
You all think I'm so great I'm not.
You're very nice, guys,
But not so wise, guys,
Take some advice, guys:
You think I'm so great I'm not.

   I don't need your admiration.
   I don't need your expectations.
   I don't need your imitation, either.
   Please take your immigration,
   Girlfriend problems, bad vacations—
   This is abdication fever.

You think I can help I can't.
You all think I can help I can't.
I'm much too wrecked, boys,
To pay the check, boys,
You're double-decked, boys—
You think I can help I can't.

I don't need your approbation,
Grasping after my elation.
Put me on medication, please.
Maybe you see it now:
I am a garbage scow.
I'm not a hero, I'm a sleaze.

You think I'm so great I'm not.
You think I'm so great I'm not.
My heart is overloaded,
My battery's corroded.
Please get it through your thick heads:
Your friend's a secret shithead.
You think I'm so great I'm not.
You think I'm so great I'm not.
You think I'm so great I'm not.

"Well, what do you think?"

"It's a good song," Eaton observed professionally. "But if you show it to The Derailleurs, you're crazy."

"I was afraid of that," said Checker glumly.

"Can I keep this?"

"I guess. I've got a copy. Why?"

"It's good. I might want to do something with it." Eaton looked down at the paper, reminded of scenes in movies where the sheriff says, "Give me that gun," and the lunatic with the loaded pistol actually hands it over.

"I don't like keeping things back from the band, but—"

"Total honesty can be destructive."

"Though you get yourself into a weird area awfully fast, don't you think?"

"We are in a weird area. The existence of other people is essentially awkward."

Checker smiled. "You're smart, aren't you?"

Eaton was astonished how extraordinarily this pleased him. "Sure," he conceded. "And you're smarter than you let on."

"No." Check nodded at the paper still in Eaton's hands. "You think I'm so great I'm not."

"I didn't say I thought you were great," said Eaton coolly. "Just smart, that's all."

There was a noticeable recoil on the other side of the table. Eaton found this interesting. It was like poking at a foreign object to see how soft it was, if it had any holes. (Pretty soft. Lots of holes.)

"But we were talking about Rachel," said Eaton. "You said she was sad."

"Yes, but for Rachel her sadness is—comforting. It's not so bad."

Surely Eaton could see his point: Rachel DeBruin was like an overcast summer day that made you want to stay inside and read. As a color, she was mute blue-gray, salmon, a touch of ocher. She made you want to drink pots and pots of weak, milky tea.

"So why is Rachel sad?"

"No reason."

"Come on. Isn't she hot for you?"

Checker said carefully, "She likes me."

"Oh, but everyone *likes* you, Secretti, isn't that right?"

"Not everyone."

"Who? Who doesn't like Check Secretti?" Eaton leaned forward. "Think of one person."

"My brother," said Checker. "Romaine hates me."

"But he hates you because he adores you, isn't that right?"

Checker squirmed. He'd never been precisely accused of being likable before. "I guess."

Eaton leaned back again, easing off. "But liking, that's not what we're talking about. She's hung up on you like meat on a hook, why deny it? You should be flattered. She's pretty. Besides, isn't it a relief to talk about it square for once?"

It was. "We have a problem."

"And what do you do about it?"

"Not much."

"Is she out of the question?"

"I've thought about it. In a way she makes perfect sense. And it would make the band happy, or almost."

"Almost?"

"They'd be a little disappointed. They expect me to pull in a bigger catch. Going for Rachel is like fishing a stocked pond."

"And catching the size you throw back."

". . . Yeah. I'm supposed to troll deep-sea."

"Supposed to."

". . . Want to."

"Who are you interested in?"

Checker froze. There was a silence like a defect in the tape; this part of the conversation was missing.

"For being so keen on honesty, you're a pretty private guy."

". . . Yeah."

"You ever told Rachel straight it's no go?"

"Of course not."

"Isn't stringing her along a little cruel?"

"No, I don't lie. But she doesn't force the issue, and I don't slam any doors in her face. It keeps her on this side of a—brink. And someday she'll get older and find somebody else and it'll go away."

"Don't you believe in tragedies?"

"I avoid them."

"Sometimes you don't have any choice." Eaton said this with a certain satisfaction.

I t's true that something seemed to short out in Checker when the structure of things was fundamentally unfortunate. Take Howard, for example: Howard kept trying to write songs, and Howard wrote bad songs. This was confusing. For Check writing songs and writing good songs were the same thing.

"I thought it didn't matter, being good," Howard recalled as they strode down Twenty-first Street. "I thought it was so terrif when anyone did anything. You said."

"I think I said what matters isn't excellence, but feeling excellent. But when we play your songs, Howard, we don't feel excellent. In fact, we feel downright under the weather."

"But why?"

"Because they're lousy!"

"Says you."

"Says the whole band, Howard, don't make me say this anymore. I don't enjoy it." Checker flopped down on a bench.

"I thought you enjoyed everything."

"I'm not a sadist."

Howard looked at Checker with new interest for a moment. The drummer did look less than ebullient. The weather was hot, overcast, and oppressive; they'd stopped under the bridge, where it was rubbly; there were rats. Checker's shirt hung off him with uncharacteristic limpness, and Howard noticed for the first time that the bandleader had lost weight— his arms had narrowed; his jeans rode down his hips. It was a little irritating. Checker didn't need to lose weight, but Howard did. Howard had a weakness for local gyros; between them and the ice cream he lackadaisically shoveled at work, when he bent down the snap of his jeans would sometimes burst open.

"You should eat more," said Howard.

"I know. I've been drinking Weight Gain in the morning, but it doesn't seem to help."

The last thing someone who needs to drop a few pounds wants to hear is that you're drinking Weight Gain.

"But you've always liked to eat."

"I don't care lately."

"Check, you care about everything!" Buck up, now. People were supposed to be a certain way, and they damn well better stay that way. Howard scuffed his shoe against the dirt and kicked Checker's leg.

"Hey!"

"Sorry."

But at least Check was sitting up straighter now. "Listen. When you write a song, do you feel—" Checker leaned forward and brought his thumb and middle finger together in the air, as if holding something infinitely small, like a perfect geometric point.

"No," Howard admitted.

"Why do you have to write rock songs, Howard?"

"You—" Howard was about to explain, but he'd already explained. It was a positively elegant moment of brevity.

Checker sighed. "Howard." Well, they'd arrived. "You know how sometimes a yacht torques down the East River, and there're all these people on deck drinking top shelf, the music cranked so loud you can sing along in the park? They've got white leather shoes, and stainless flannel slacks, and shirts with little anchors on the pocket, and they wave?"

"Uh-huh."

"What do you feel when that boat passes by?"

"I guess I wish I was on board."

"You are on board, understand? Those suckers should be looking at you, wishing they were hanging out in the park with all your great friends. *You are the party.*"

"What does this have to do with writing rock songs?"

"When you watch us play at Plato's, how do you feel?"

"I guess sometimes I wish I could play, too. I hear all that applause and stuff. You know." Howard had the most bizarre tendency to tell the truth.

"You have a good time those nights?"

"No."

"Do you think you're a natural musician? Do you think you could be up there, too, if we only let you?"

Howard grubbed his sneaker in the dirt and mumbled, "I tried the clarinet in high school. I was last chair."

"How do you feel other times?"

"Well. Once in a while, people come up to me and ask if I know you. I say yeah. They're impressed. I say I'm the band manager. They ask me my name. I like that."

"And?"

"I sing along on your sets. I know all the words. You guys come and sit with me on your breaks. I get a little wasted. You know. It's neat."

Checker smiled and put his hand on Howard's shoulder. "See? You know exactly what I'm talking about."

They started walking again.

"It just seems," Howard confessed shyly, "that the party is where you are."

"Of course it is. For me."

"But don't you think it's better to be some people than others?"

"Sure. If you think that way, it's better to be anyone but you."

"I don't get it."

"If you think it's better to be somebody else, then it is better. You've lost the ball game. Besides," said Checker, a little flustered, "what's the point, you *are* Howard. You can't be anyone but Howard, it's not your job!"

"But I don't want to be Howard!"

"Don't be delinquent," Checker chided. "Somebody's gotta do it. Because I'm glad you're Howard, old man."

The air packed around them like protective cotton. It was Sunday, before rehearsal; traffic wheeled lazily by, and the neighborhood scurried pleasantly with ten-year-old girls. Howard was flattered that Checker Secretti was spending the afternoon with him, though he hadn't been listening carefully enough to think that Checker should be flattered, too.

"I've been figuring, though," said Howard, hands in his pockets jauntily, hoping that someone would see him with Check. *Check and I were talking the other day, and we decided, you know, those yachts down by the river . . . ?* "I was hoping you could help me out here. I need a nickname."

"Why?"

"Even Quiet Carl has one, and nobody ever talks to him, he doesn't need it! Everybody's got one but me!"

"Caldwell doesn't—"

"Who needs a nickname when your name is Caldwell Sweets? You need a nickname when your name is Howard Williams."

"But you look like a Howard. You are Howard."

"What about H.W.? The H. Big H.!"

"I think *H* is a problem letter."

"Check, I hate my name! A name," he theorized sternly, "has power. It's not just a label—it calls up an image, it makes people! Can you imagine if Sweets were called George or Wimpy or something? Why, if I weren't called Howard I might not *be* a Howard. Check, let's come up with something here! You know, Spike or Rap or Banger; I mean, if I were called Spike I might start acting like a Spike—"

"You want me to call you *Spike*?"

"No, Spike's not right," Howard moaned. "Something—brainy, but not stilted. Mysterious, but not creepy. Interesting, but not too fussy."

"I don't think this is the way people get a nickname, Howard."

"Come on, we could try it! You could start using it, and I could say at Plato's, Hi, I'm Ripper, and then everyone—"

"Ripper!" Checker burst out laughing.

"Well, that was just—"

"It sounds like a dog!"

Howard stamped his foot. "See! It has to be the right one! I just want a neat name, and maybe then I'd think my life was a party. I could be a great guy, but only as Zap or Crack or Wrecker. I want something like—" Howard stopped.

"I don't think I can," said Check, reaching out and tousling Howard's thick brown American hair, "but if I could I would, How baby. I'd be glad to give you my name if that would make you happy."

"Thanks, Check. But I wouldn't take it, buddy. You can keep your name."

"Thanks."

So Checker, still Checker, and Howard, still Howard, walked down Hoyt Avenue South arm in arm. As they headed for Plato's, Check looked over at his friend in wonder, thinking the boy really was doing a grand job of being Howard Williams, for Howardness had to do with yearning.

*   *   *

Checker perked into Plato's, drumsticks on everything that tinkled or sounded hollow. "Howard's shopping for a nickname. Keep your eyes peeled."

"We've got a few names for Howard," said Caldwell, with a sly smile at Eaton.

Checker stopped drumming down the bar and looked at the band. They were arranged differently today—curded in funny cohesive clumps.

"Checker," said Eaton, "you born in a cab or something?"

"No, in my mother's playroom, why?"

"So is Checker your real name?"

"It's real." Check shrugged. "Use it, I turn around."

"But what's on your birth certificate?"

"My mother wanted to call me Tonka."

"Like the truck?"

"Yeah. It's what she was leaning on when I was born. She says she got a bruise on her back from the crane. But Dad—he hadn't skipped out yet, but he was already tired of my mother and her playroom. He was already—"

"What?" asked Howard, who loved stories of Checker's parents.

"My father grew up," said Check. "She never forgave him."

"The name," said Eaton, unentranced.

"Dad nabbed the birth certificate. No way he was going to call his firstborn after a toy tow truck. When Mom found out, she was furious. She never used the name, either. I was Tonka until five or six. Then my friends started calling me

Checker, and she liked that okay. She used to hang out with us, let us play with her toys. She always liked my friends, except now they're a little old for her. My mother liked ten, I think."

"Yo momma is ten," said J.K.

"Yeah, well. Sometimes I think my father's seventy-nine. Anyway, they were at war at the time. Dad got in a good shot with my name—solid, conservative, *normal*. But when she had Romaine he'd cut out and she could name her kids after lettuce if she liked."

"So what did your father name you?" asked Eaton, one more time.

"After his bank." Checker licked his lips. "Irving."

Eaton hit the table and laughed, though the air through his teeth was a little forced. "Irving puts a whole new light on you, Secretti."

"Sheckair is no Irving!"

"No shit, bro," said J.K. "Irving, like, sell wholesale paper towel, know what I mean?"

"Yeah," said Checker. "Irving's afraid to piss in the shower."

"Irving folds his underwear," said Caldwell.

"What's wrong with folding your underwear?" asked Howard.

J.K. and Caldwell looked over at Howard in unison, and Howard shrank. "I mean, Irving," said Howard shakily, "eats strained peas and riced potatoes."

"Lima beans," said Checker.

"Irving thirty-seven years old and still get zits!"

"Irving uses toilet bowl freshener."

"Irving goes to bed at nine o'clock," said Check, "and calls the police when The Derailleurs play too loud next door."

"Irving's allergic to dust," said Caldwell. "And you're not allergic to dust, are you, Check?"

"Ain't no doubt about it," said J.K., "Irving never see a drum in his damn life. He find a snare, he use it for a TV table."

"Irving watch reruns of *Partridge Family!*"

"Can't be Check," said J.K., laying the dispute to rest. "No offense, honkies, but Irving a *white* boy."

As they set to rehearsing, Eaton noted how slyly Check had headed off derision by joining in the game himself. But a weapon as powerful as Irving didn't dismantle that easily, and Eaton slipped it in his back pocket next to Checker's last song.

For all the jocularity of Irving and the Lima Beans, the rehearsal quietly soured. Eaton suggested several times from the sidelines that he couldn't hear Caldwell's guitar over the drums, until Checker was playing so softly that the songs began to steer aimlessly around the club like cars without drivers. They couldn't agree on which songs to do, and gradually the band—clumped again. J.K.-Caldwell-Eaton. Rachel-Carl-Howard. Rahim with Checker, who was thinking, Well, why should I expect every rehearsal to be a Bing Crosby Christmas? Wasn't the party metaphor overextended? Still, it had never been like this before. Checker couldn't help but wonder: Before what?

Near the end Caldwell confessed with agitation that he'd written a song and would like the band to try it; Checker said, "Great!" but not after he read the lyrics:

Fine

Don't think I care.
I'll work, die, remember.
I guess it's fair—
had May, I'll take December.

Give it up,
it's over,
we're older—
fine, fine.
Hang it up,
give it over,
we'll molder—
fine, fine.

My life's a pill.
I'll swallow, put my feet up.
A lousy swill—
I'll gargle, turn the heat up.

Give it up,
it's over,
we're older—
fine, fine.
Hang it up,
give it over,

we'll molder,
fine, fine,
don't think I care—
fine, fine,
don't think I care—
fine, fine,
don't think I care—

"Pick it up!" shouted Caldwell in exasperation the third time through. "It's supposed to be fast!"

Checker closed his eyes. "I know," he said softly, caressing the rim of his tom. "But it's depressing."

"It's sure depressing the way we're playing it."

Checker rubbed his temples with the tips of his sticks. The nightclub seemed to shimmer, tremble, blink out. He stood abruptly from the throne. "I have to go." Checker hurried off the dais and stumbled out the door.

"Jesus," said Caldwell, kicking over his guitar stand. "What'd I say?"

The band dispersed in a desultory fashion. Out of sheer entropy, perhaps, Rachel DeBruin stayed longer than the rest, propped before the stage as the thin Sunday-night crowd threaded in and out again. Eaton eyed her, left, and caught Brinkley and Gilbert by the river; they acted hurt now and a little aloof when Eaton appeared. "Not spending the night with your little Derailleur friends?" was the way Brinkley greeted him. But Eaton didn't care and was distracted and returned to Plato's later to find Rachel still there.

She was playing with a candle, smearing hot drips around

the table. When Eaton swung next to her, the girl's fingers were covered with dried wax up to the second knuckle, peeling off like the scales of a dread disease. She started guiltily, and tried to hide them with each other.

"So what's a pretty girl doing all alone in a dank nightclub looking like Madame Tussaud's?"

Rachel looked overcome with that particular terror of simply not having anything witty to say. "I—Just thinking—"

The wax, the stutter, made Eaton feel pleasantly urbane by comparison. "Can I stand you a drink?"

She shrugged. "Seltzer with a twist."

"I think we can do better than that." He ordered her a kir instead, tooling up to the bar and checking out his reflection in the mirror there: dastardly good looks. He'd finally found a shirt whose collar would stay upturned.

Eaton returned to hold her kir to the light of the candle; bloody cassis swirled seductively into the pale wine.

"It's beautiful," said Rachel, having managed to scrape some of the wax off her hands while he was gone.

"Suits you, then."

Rachel began compulsively to paw the candle again.

"Irving not back yet?"

She winced. "I wish you wouldn't call him that."

"It's his name."

"It is not."

Eaton nodded. "Check said you were loyal."

"Oh?" Rachel's eyes momentarily focused.

"Too bad he's not as protective of you."

Eaton expected her to ask, "What do you mean?" but

instead Rachel's long dark hair seemed to frizz around her, rising about her face like a black fog. She twisted it in her fingers, and flakes of wax stuck to the strands.

"You have an exquisite voice," said Eaton, backing off from the bad weather across the table like a plane from a fogged-in airport; he would have to wait and make a second approach. "You hope to be a singer?"

"I am a singer."

"Mint Secretti."

"Thank you."

"You just seem wasted here."

"Nothing's wasted here."

"But you could do very well—"

"I am doing very well."

She was stronger than he'd thought. "Don't you ever wish—"

"No. I like Checker's songs. The Derailleurs, this club—"

"If you're so all-fired happy, why do you look so hangdog all the time?"

Rachel pulled a thick strand of her hair directly in front of her face, but the nose of Eaton's plane was diving now, fog or no fog. "Checker says my nature—"

"I've heard plenty from Secretti, but not from you. You're a spectacular chick, beautiful, talented, and you walk around as if your pet just died. What's the problem?"

"Nothing," she said staunchly.

"All right." Eaton took a gulp of his Scotch, as if needing to fortify himself. "You know what Checker says your problem is, don't you? What he's told everybody, even me? And I don't even know the guy very well, I have no idea what he's telling me for."

"What," she said darkly, not a question but more a threat.

"That you're hung up on him, of course."

You do not name other people's secrets, even if they're not secrets—or especially then. Rachel stared back at Eaton, her pupils agape.

"That may not be true," Eaton added. "But that's his theory."

"I've never said such a thing."

"I don't know, Rachel," said Eaton, raking his fingers tortuously through his hair. "You seem like such a sweet girl, and however you feel about him, you're a real friend to that guy. It just wrecks me up to see it doesn't work the other direction. Because some of the stuff he told me—I shouldn't say this, I'm sorry. I should shut up."

Eaton waited a moment for her to say, "No, go on. What exactly did he tell you?" but Rachel DeBruin's world was up to this point still, barely, intact, and she aimed to keep it that way.

"I don't know, though," he followed up quickly. "Check said the other day, 'Honesty can be destructive,' and I said, 'But that gets you into a weird area awfully fast.' I guess I believe in people being straight with each other, Rache. I know I'm new here and all, but sometimes someone on the outside can see things people on the inside can't. There's something seriously ugly going on here, and it's at your expense. Really, you're a lovely girl, with a terrific singing career ahead of you, if you could get somebody to give you a hand instead of burying you here in this dingy Queens closet. Okay, that's your choice. But it hurts even more to watch you squander your loyalty than squander your talent. I don't know how you feel about that Secretti character, and I don't want to pry. But it's clear even from what you've said here tonight that you stick by him even behind his back, which is a damn sight better than he does for you. You gotta know who your friends are, Rachel, because misplaced trust can be dangerous. A friend doesn't go around bragging about how in love with them you are and how they don't give a shit—"

Rachel made a little sound. It was not "What?" but Eaton chose to interpret it as inquiry, anyway.

"Okay, he didn't say, 'I don't give a shit.' He's a songwriter, right? What was it? Something about fishing . . . Oh yeah. That picking you up would be like 'fishing a stocked pond,' he said. 'And catching the size you throw back.' He prefers 'deep sea,' whatever that means."

Eaton paused, letting his story sink in. "I'm sorry, but he just said all this stuff, and let me tell you, it made me pretty uncomfortable, too. You and I have hardly talked, but you've always seemed nice and you're good-looking and I guess I've felt a little shy. But when you know something you don't have the option on being an observer anymore. Even to keep quiet is to participate. I see you lately, I feel like I'm lying, you know? So I just wanted you to know how things stand, get it off my chest. There are some nasty games going on around this place, but I'm not playing."

The candle was now a fire hazard. It had lost its vertical integrity altogether and was spread in a pond over the table.

The wick squiggled over the top like a fishing line. The quote had done the trick, of course. Rachel had sung enough Check Secretti to recognize his lyrics.

Eaton blew out the candle; curls of smoke mingled with Rachel's hair like cassis in wine. Rachel kept staring at the candle as if waiting for the snuffed flame to relight, but instead, the surface curdled and stiffened; Rachel's face set with it, her expression glazing, the corners of her mouth firming up. The waitress turned on the neon top light, and all the romance of Plato's fled in its leaden blue glare.

"Listen, usually you kids can stay late as you want, but nobody's here and it's Check has the extra key to lock up. You're gonna have to call it a night."

Saying nothing, Rachel stood up, her blouse wilting in the humid summer air. As she walked away, the waitress set to scraping up the mess Rachel had left on the table. It would take considerably more work to clean up the mess that Eaton had made.

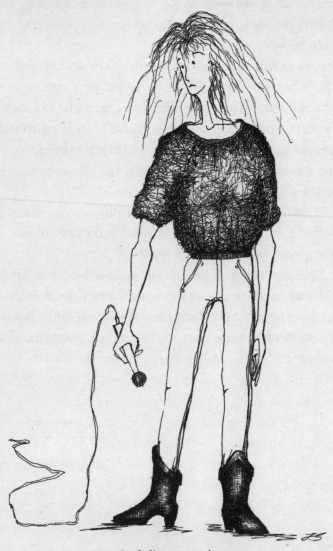

Rachel's voice is thin

14 / close to the edge

Checker had disappeared again. Each evening Rachel DeBruin sat at the same table, disemboweling new candles, lying in wait. Though she didn't usually drink, she made a point of ordering Scotch this week, straight up.

Regularly Eaton would stop by Plato's and note her presence with satisfaction, as if he'd planted a bomb and was pleased to find it still ticking. Sometimes he'd make conversation, though she was terse, and whenever he drew close, she hugged her big blue pocketbook; it rattled.

"What's your theory about Irving's disappearing acts?" asked Eaton one such evening.

"Everyone says it's a girl," she tossed off, hard.

When they performed that weekend, without Checker, Rachel's delivery was so vicious that more than one patron remarked on her shift in style. Eaton drummed her into that edge, like driving her toward a sheer drop.

Eaton himself was solicitous. He bought her more drinks, kirs and Tequila Sunrises with the reds oozing over the ice; Bloody Marys.

Yet finally, the next week, Eaton watched from the other side of the bar as in an instant all his painstaking hard work washed away. He was actually looking at her face when it happened—suddenly her expression went liquid; with a swing of that front door, all the thick black bitterness he had carefully distilled went pale and runny again. What a terrific waste of energy.

Checker's jeans were hanging lower on his hips than ever, and Eaton noted this latest weight loss was unattractive, though he doubted Rachel would notice. Rumpled and sweaty, Check looked as if he'd come back from a week of rowing crew. As he advanced into the club, Rachel's eyes thrashed wildly around the room, jouncing off stray furniture, grabbing on to candles and beer mugs as if trying to keep afloat in a rising tide.

Checker raised his head at a tilt, hearing the gurgle of something new. He went straight to Rachel. "How *are* you?"

An everyday question, but Rachel wouldn't get away with "Fine." She drew her legs tightly together. Checker put a hand on her shoulder, and she winced—not because it didn't feel good, but because it did—the strong calloused palm, the wonderful fingerprints. Her chin touched her chest; Checker wrapped his hand around the back of her neck and knelt before her chair. "What's the trouble, Jackless?" He put a hand on either side of her neck and turned her toward him, looking at her with a focus we could say was irresponsible.

So it was a long, cruel moment, Checker's big warm

hands, the eyes blue on brown, Checker the promising, handsome boy, never mind the weight, the one everyone liked, the fine drummer who'd been gone. She'd missed him. And Rachel, so white for the season, her skin like kid. Without the stocked pond this might have done her for weeks: Checker's hands around her neck.

He took them back. He held her fingertips instead, the plump of them between his, retreating as he always did, walking his favorite thin line. "Cannibals say that's the tenderest part of the human body," said Checker, pinching the inside of her thumb. "Like the oyster in the back of a chicken."

Rachel had tiny hands, and the nails were coated with pink polish that was flaking off. Her skin was moist and cold. She left her thumb with Checker. "Want a nibble?"

He folded it into her palm. "You have to save the best bites."

"Who for?"

Checker relinquished her fingers and sat across from her. She twisted in her seat, the string taut between them. It was dreadful to be hooked so soundly by a fisherman who only wanted you off his line.

Checker, on the other hand, saw not fish but something considerably more tender. It was like having responsibility for a tiny creature and being so careful, but also so big-boned and awkward, that no matter how gently you handled the animal, you were bound to mangle it in the very effort of keeping it alive.

"Toughen up!" Syria had mocked him when he'd appealed

for advice. "You don't have enough problems, is that it? You have to go out shopping for more?"

"Rache is my problem," he'd insisted.

"She is now. It's a cinch to grab problems; they're not so easy to give back. You ever play Old Maid? Nobody's going to stop you from taking the little lady into your hand. But try and get them to draw her back again."

"I don't think Rachel would appreciate being the Old Maid."

"Hearts, then. The Queen of Spades." True, Old Maid was a child's game, and nineteen may be precisely the age that games turn adult in a way no nineteen-year-old is prepared for; the Queen of Spades was an applicably more deadly choice of cards.

"So what's been happening?"

Rachel shrugged. "We played."

"How's Eat doing?" Check asked, having watched Eaton slip out the door as if deliberately leaving the two of them alone.

"Good"; but Rachel looked puzzled, since this was the wrong word. Because Rachel was not in Tibet but in Astoria, Queens, it wasn't possible for her to say, *But, Checker, he makes us think terrible, ugly things—you should keep him away from your drums, they're hurting, it's like turning your dogs over to a bad kennel. And, Checker, don't leave for so long, you don't understand the danger. He's a medicine man with a little black pouch, and he sets noxious powders into the air when you're not here—he drums messages to different powers.* Oh, who cared about Eaton Striker right now, anyway; who cared about anything? So she simply added, "We sound different when he plays," lamely.

"He's skillful. Better trained than I am. It's good for you to sing with different musicians."

"Don't act like your disappearing all the time is doing us a favor."

"I didn't mean that."

"I talked to him."

"Uh-huh."

"It was very interesting."

"He told me he thought you were pretty."

"Which is more than you've ever said."

Checker cocked his head, for it was dimly beginning to get through to him that something had happened. She knew very well that he couldn't tell her she was pretty, that was against the rules. "I think you're a knockout, Rache, you know that. But coming from Eaton—well, I'm not a girl, but isn't he pretty decent-looking himself?"

"Stop it."

"Stop what?"

"Trying to push me off on Eaton Striker."

"I'm not—"

"You are, too. Why do you think I want to hear you tell me how good-looking some other guy is? What's wrong with you?"

"Rachel . . . are you sure you want to do this?"

Rachel had that look of someone who has been perched on the high dive for a long enough time to have become a kind of pool fixture, but who has finally decided to jump in.

Checker's face shimmered before her, blue space and deep water. "I'm tired of this, Checker. I can't do it anymore. What's the point?"

"It's necessary." His heart was beating hard; he wondered what he was afraid of.

Rachel could as well have pointed her hands above her head and sprung. "I'm in love with you," she said. "I've been in love with you for two years. You know that."

"Yes."

"But you haven't done anything about it, have you? You've never even asked me to a movie."

Checker had the feeling that she'd never precisely made this observation to herself. "No," he said heavily.

"Maybe I'm growing on you. Maybe it's gradually moving from friendship to something more. Is that the way you see it?"

"Not exactly."

"Then how *do* you see it?"

Checker traced the romances engraved in the table: RC + MS. *Ricky forever.* "You're a great friend and vocalist, Rachel."

"And?"

"That's all."

"Look at me," she said, and that was definitely the meanest thing she did to herself that night, because he did and his eyes were both very beautiful and very honest. "Will you ever fall in love with me?"

"No, Rachel," said Checker softly. "It'll never happen. I'm sorry."

He'd thought that was what she wanted. Even Rachel

had thought that was what she wanted, or needed, to hear. They were both crazy. Nobody wants to hear that, ever.

"Excuse me," said Rachel, lost and astonished because she'd thought she was prepared for this. "I have to go to the john."

Blindly Rachel groped her way to the ladies' room, bumping into chairs, clutching the big blue pocketbook, trying to keep it from rattling so loudly on the way.

There was no danger of Checker finding *RDeB loves CS* anywhere on the table in front of him, for Rachel would never carve in plain view. In fact, she wasn't a graffiti type of person, and come to think of it, the tiny inscription on the bottom inside corner of the stall in Plato's ladies' room was the only thing Rachel DeBruin had ever written on a wall; each time she came in here, she moved the stack of toilet paper aside and checked that her initials were still there. Doubled over the toilet, Rachel traced her neat rounded printing behind the roll.

Back at the table, Checker sat numbly wondering what else he should have said. He felt sure he was about to be punished, though he wasn't sure for what. He had such a strong sense of what Syria would say to him now. *Melodrama!* Her arms would be akimbo. *You enjoy it, don't you? Court it, even. But of course, it's getting out of hand. This starts off as self-indulgent, idiot! You're an adult now. This is the big time. The stakes are high.* Syria faded with her warning, and he strained to hear more—more disgust, more slander and condescension, and though that seemed to be all for now, he was so pleased by the accuracy with which he could predict her, that in a moment of perfect bad timing he had to smile just as Rachel returned to the table.

She shot him a dirty look for the smile, though consoled herself that any bad behavior on his part now would make him feel worse later. She took her seat, oddly relaxed. She'd done the high dive, and here she was, head above water. "So isn't it a relief? Now you don't have to keep being nice and having little talks—"

"Rachel, I like talking to you—"

"You know, I said two years; even that was a lie. I think it's been five. I watched you all through high school. I nominated you for offices, anonymously. Campaigned to get your old band to play dances—"

"Big Sprocket," Checker ruminated, his mind beginning to wander, as if this scene were over; feeling the flaccid character of a bag whose cat was out, the terrible loss of tension between him and this girl.

"And even that first band—"

"God, Freewheel was terrible."

"Not to me. And I knew your locker number and your home room. I memorized your whole schedule every semester, and sometimes I'd ask to leave my own class to get a drink of water just to walk by your biology section and catch a glimpse of you in the front row. I'd go by your apartment building after school, and I'd figured out which windows were yours. There was always weird stuff in them—"

"Mobiles," said Check. "My mother."

"But everyone watched you—"

"Not really."

"No, they did. You'd walk down the hall and—there was just a feeling, 'like someone opened a window,' my friend Judy said once. Even teachers, Check. Didn't you know? Ms. Carlton—"

"All right!" Checker held up his hands. "We were friends." It was happening again, the queer accusation that people liked him. Checker stopped just short of saying "I'm sorry."

"Friends with your English teacher. You know there were rumors—"

"They weren't—"

"I don't care. The point is, everyone—well, they all liked your drumming, but you know very well that all you had to do was walk down the hall . . . Excuse me." In a feeble blur, she blundered back to the bathroom.

How long was this going to go on? Checker was exhausted. But the situation precluded cutting out, that would be uncool. So Checker just had to sit here, he supposed, and let her run out of steam. It was dreadful to actually be getting bored.

When she returned she told him, "My mother found my journal once and she said I'd better not get involved with a nigger, and I said you were only half black. She said that was even worse. Oh, we had a big fight over you. I did a regular Coretta King thing, you know? She said those black boys just want to get their girlfriends pregnant to prove they're real men, because that's the only way they know how. I said I'd love it if you proved you were a man with me, and she slapped me."

With this as with her other confessions, there was something disturbing about her delivery, an eerie breeziness, as if she had nothing to lose. As far as Checker could see, there was still a great deal to lose, and he finally intruded, "Rachel, you don't really have to tell me all this."

"I'm telling you how wonderful you are, why wouldn't you like listening to that? Besides, you won't have to do anything more for me after tonight."

It was the third time she returned from the bathroom, though, that Checker wasn't bored anymore. She weaved to the table, ricocheting back and forth between chairs. One of the few customers left in the club made a remark about her having had enough, but Checker knew that at least while he'd been there she hadn't been drinking. He stopped trying to inject his own comments, for she was no longer making much sense. She repeated herself a lot: "There's something I always wanted to tell you . . . I just wanted you to know . . . I always . . ."

"What?"

Her voice had softened; he had to lean forward to hear. Her consonants went thick in her mouth. Her lips were dry and puckered, her tongue plaqued. Her eyes were dilated and unfocused; her head would nod toward the table, then jerk up again. She lurched once more from her chair and wafted toward the bathroom.

"Rachel!" In a single furious swing Checker knocked her pocketbook out of her hands and sent its contents splaying over the nightclub floor. Amid the tampons and lipstick, white, pink, and red pills sprang over the brick, bouncing like hard rain. They leaped over the extent of Plato's, springing into cracks, where they'd be found years later, and sometimes taken by adventurous patrons who'd be disappointed when the tablets only made them feel tired. The pills were ecstatic, as if they'd narrowly missed a much darker fate, the very throat of disaster.

Checker grabbed Rachel's hair at the nape of her neck. "What are they?"

She smiled a sleepy grin and pulled ineffectually against Checker's grip. "Something to make me relax."

"How many?"

"Wassa problem?" she whined, finally feeling the painful tug at her hair.

Later, everyone left at Plato's that night had a slightly different story, but they all said they'd never seen Checker Secretti so angry. Checker being half black, it was hard to tell when his blood was high, but by all accounts his face was clearly red tonight, and the muscles in his jaw popped in and out as if he were cracking ice. He swooped down and scooped up a handful of the tablets, dragging Rachel down with him by the hair, and there was a look on his face as if he hoped he hurt her. Shoving the samples in his pocket, he shouted to the waitress to call an ambulance and herded Rachel into the ladies' room. "Out!" he shouted to the girl in the stall.

She still had her pants down when he pulled the door open, splintering the lock; she hurriedly tugged up her jeans, staring at the guy in the ladies' room holding this girl with her mouth hanging open, and frantically fastened the snap.

"Forget the belt," said Check, kicking open the outside door and pushing her out of the bathroom. He dragged Rachel over to the toilet; she could barely stand now. Holding her up with one arm, he squeezed her jaw to get her mouth open and shoved his fingers as far as he could down her throat. Her tongue lolled and flapped against his hand, more like a pet's than a woman's. It was weird how far back in there you could reach. Yet as the throat closed and sucked against his fingers, wet and dark and smaller in the back, all viscous and tight, she felt like a woman, all right. Vomit gorged over his hand.

Checker kept his fingers out of her throat just enough so she could breathe, but mucked back in there again as soon as her windpipe was clear. He got a little more out of her, but not much, for she was going under and her reflexes weren't working. Still, man, was it a mess—Check wondered why he'd bothered to kick the girl out of the toilet, since they'd managed to get so little of the stuff in the bowl. All over the porcelain, across the floor, and dribbling down his arm was a thin brown trail, all lumpy with tablets in various stages of dissolve. Noticing the overwhelming dominance of tablets over food, Checker was relieved when paramedics appeared at the door.

"Wait," he said as they strapped the girl on the stretcher and he rinsed his arms at the sink. "I'll go with you."

In the back of the ambulance Checker peeled off his T-shirt and tried to clean Rachel's face. It pained him to see that smoky black hair strung with bits of vomit, her white cheeks smeared with brown like fine china in the sink. It was crazy—she was already subsiding into a coma, and they'd surely just take off her clothes and make her throw up some more once she arrived, but still Check fixed her hair, swabbed her neck, and buttoned her blouse. These funereal reparations completed, she looked peaceful, if a little slack.

Pacing the hospital waiting room with no shirt on, Checker got looks, of varying sorts since he had a well-muscled torso, but Check himself was fully focused on the bank of pay phones staring him down on the opposite wall. It's hard enough to call any woman who you've just been told dislikes blacks and especially mulattoes when you're one of them, and who seems to believe you only want to impregnate her daughter. It's harder still to call this woman and confess that you've done far worse than seduce her daughter; you may have killed her.

"*What?*"

Checker closed his eyes and held the receiver away from his ear. "O.D.," he repeated evenly. "They say the pills are over-the-counter. She took a lot, but they're not very strong. They give her good odds, but we'll see."

"Dear God, why on earth?"

"Because of me," said Checker softly.

"You? I don't understand."

"I don't either, Mrs. DeBruin." Gently he hung up the phone.

"Checkie."

Checker started.

"What you doing in the waiting room?" asked a black orderly.

"A friend of mine tried to kill herself. I brought her in."

The orderly smiled. "Well, this is rich."

"It's not funny."

"I didn't say it was funny, Secretti. But after a while—well, we get tired of this shit, don't you figure? All the nineteen-year-olds wheeling in here, and meanwhile, these other chumps trying to stay alive, who'd do anything to be nineteen again, to have the strength left you people use to jump off buildings, to have the brains left you jokers use to buy bulk-rate discount barbs?"

"Stop it."

"How's it feel?"

"Like my fault."

"You can do better than that. You're a poet, aren't you, Secretti? I've heard you mouth-off. You're a whiz kid philosopher, isn't that right?"

"Leave me alone." Checker tried to shake the orderly off down the hall, but the man followed him with a squeaky rolling table piled with clean sheets. Checker ducked into the men's room, but the orderly stuck his head in and said to Checker's back, "Feel it, Secretti? Feel it deep down? Man, don't tell me in life there ain't no justice." And then, blessedly, he was gone.

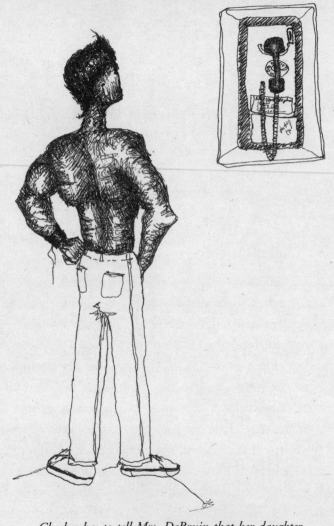

*Checker has to tell Mrs. DeBruin that her daughter
has tried to commit suicide*

15 / it's hard to be a saint in the city

Checker returned to the reception room to await Rachel's mother. He knew only a few things about her from Rachel: she was divorced, like everyone; she didn't come listen to her daughter sing because she thought rock music was bad for your hearing, just one of a whole quiver of opinions Ellen DeBruin kept slung over her shoulder to and from her job at an insurance company in Manhattan. She lived in a world of certainty, and it was somehow this characteristic that made her so recognizable when she swung into the hospital that night, the revolving doors flopping a full turn behind her. A trim, effective woman, she moved briskly and without hesitation. In a navy A-line skirt, a white V-neck blouse, low-heeled navy shoes with little perforations in the toes, she dressed for comfort and decency. As her eyes whisked over the contents of the waiting room, she didn't recognize Checker Secretti because he must not have looked the way she'd already decided he would look.

"Mrs. DeBruin, I'm Checker Secretti." Check shook her hand firmly and looked her in the eye.

She liked him. Instantly she liked him, feeling the queer energetic glow that had enveloped her as he approached, enjoying the dance in his eyes that was so inappropriate considering why they were both here. She had not planned on liking him; in fact, she'd screamed at him the whole way over in the car.

Ellen DeBruin's mouth twitched with annoyance. "Well, I've certainly heard my fill about you," she said, with the full brunt of her hostility. She may have liked him, but she didn't like liking him, not one bit.

"They poured Rachel full of ipecac. She's puked up most of the pills. She's still delirious, and we can't see her yet. But she's going to be okay."

Mrs. DeBruin took a breath; a wave hit her in the face, and passed. Her skin felt prickly, until the hairs over her arms fell gently back down again. She didn't have much time for Rachel, and often looked on motherhood as a second job; the strength of her feelings for the child, like her relief at this moment, always took her by surprise. Once more, as with her attraction to this boy here, she immediately felt a backwash of resentment. Rachel's mother experienced strong emotion as an attack. Ellen DeBruin was one of those inexplicable people whose lives are always getting in the way of their lives. She so valued efficiency that it rarely struck her to wonder: she was efficiently accomplishing what?

"Well," she said, wiping her clammy palms on her skirt, "you don't seem very upset about this."

"I'm not. She'll be okay. But I am pissed off."

"*Pissed off?*"

"Yeah. Aren't you?"

"I am—at a loss!" She threw up her hands. "What possessed her?"

"I did."

"You sound as if you want credit."

"Responsibility. She's in love with me, she says. I failed to return the compliment."

"She tried to kill herself over a crush?" Mrs. DeBruin ranged around the ugly plastic chairs. Of course, in some ways this wasn't a surprise. Rachel was such a quiet, dolorous girl. Where had she gotten that? Ellen had been energetic, popular—well, at least energetic . . . Anyway, her mother wasn't *sad*. "I suppose this wasn't a serious attempt, is that right?"

"If suicide isn't serious, I'm not sure what is."

"I mean, this is one of those cries for help, isn't it?"

Checker shrugged. "She botched it, if that's what you're getting at, and I guess you could say she wanted to. But suicide isn't exactly in the same category as whining at dinner or refusing to clean your room, even when it's bungled."

Mrs. DeBruin collapsed in a chair, the squalor and sterility of the hospital beginning to get to her. It was the middle of the night; she was exhausted, and this was awful. "Maybe I should have gone to some of those concerts."

Checker walked up behind her and put his hand on

her shoulder. The moment before, she would have bristled, but exactly now she enjoyed it; she was lonely. Briefly she understood, too, how her daughter might yearn for this big warm hand with such desperation. When Checker removed it, she felt a strange disappointed craving she hadn't felt since college.

Mrs. DeBruin turned to watch him, and saw something happen, though she'd never be able to describe it, since he didn't precisely do anything. Checker stood looking around the room, his weight on the balls of his feet, his chin raised, his fingers lifted lightly away from his jeans. The muscles in his chest subtly expanded, indenting here, there; his stomach sucked in. That was all, really, but there was a feeling—something rose in the room where he stood, and she, too, looked around, down the hospital halls, for a moment, she was sure, seeing them as he did: everything gleaming, the chrome railings, the instruments on trolleys, the wire rims of passing doctors; the pale greens and yellows suddenly mild, pretty; what was once sterile now simply clean. The idea that there was a place to bring sick people suddenly itself appealing, disgust at poor and expensive medical care in this country giving way to relief that even without money, if you were bleeding, these people would help you. Rather than be fatigued by the illness and injury stacked for floors above them, Checker and Mrs. DeBruin felt healthier than before, strong and resilient and full of spring; Mrs. DeBruin thought about taking up swimming again, and Checker thought of basketball, the bicycle. Turning to her, Checker said, "I think I have to go outside," but because she'd been watching and he'd taken her with him, she wasn't insulted when he turned on his tennis shoe with a squeak and loped out the door.

Checker started toward Twenty-first Street, feeling odd without Zefal, but those rare times a cyclist finds himself on foot can have an exhilaration of their own—to be relieved of the taxi and bus exhaust, no longer watching for drain grates and metal plates, free from the tyrannies of wind. Stray patches of grass were spongy, and the blades ticked rapidly against his rubber soles, loud in the wide quiet of five in the morning. On a whim Checker detoured to the Roosevelt Island tramway, feeling the jolt and sway of its lift-off and the tremor when its pulleys crossed their supports, listening to the wind sing over the top of the car. He was the only passenger on the tram, and there were few cars on the Fifty-ninth Street Bridge beside him; on the Manhattan shore a helicopter was landing, splaying the East River in a wide circular wake as it barely missed the water. Citicorp Center caught the red rising sun in its windows, and in the sway of the tram Checker felt the pleasant weavy lightheadedness of having stayed up all night.

On the other side, he surveyed Second Avenue from the platform. The air was unusually clean and cool, and all the lines of the buildings were crisp; in Astoria General, Rachel was still alive. The breeze felt good against his throat; breathing, breathing, he was glad to have had an adventure, too sleepy to feel guilty for enjoying this. He rehearsed the new word "ipecac" and meeting Rachel's mother. All right, there was a lot to come, a lot of shit. But just now it was a brassy early morning in New York City, and he would ride the tram back and stroll giddily up Twenty-first, watching people with puffy eyes grope into delicatessens for takeout coffee.

When he did make it back to Astoria, though, a small but insidious bereftness had worked its way into his elation, and Checker paused at the park, trying to decide which direction to go. He envied Rachel having a mother. His didn't count, not on mornings like this one. The only times his family had ever had breakfast, Checker had fixed it. She'd never tucked him in bed as a child, and now it was Checker who tiptoed into the room to pull a blanket to his mother's chin. And she still slept with a stuffed sheep. You did not go home to confide in a woman who slept with a sheep.

Resolutely he turned right and let himself into Vesuvius. The furnace breathed quietly on low; he felt a warm nostalgic rush of familiarity, the way it ought to feel when you come home. He noted Syria had cleaned up. She'd be angry he'd disappeared again, but Checker was getting good at riding through her fury, the way experienced seamen keep their balance through a storm. In fact, he looked forward to her tirade; with a smile he let himself down on a bench and fell instantly into that black dreamless oblivion which borders on death.

When he woke it was dark except for the furnace, and he was covered in a light sheet with a pillow under his head. His watch read 11:00; he'd slept for fifteen hours. Checker jerked upright.

"Relax," said Syria. "She's fine." Syria went back to marvering quietly, and Checker rubbed his eyes. He pulled on one of her musty green work shirts and fixed himself a cup of coffee. They didn't talk. Later, when he was more awake, she taught him to blow a bowl. The pipe was smooth and warm; her motions were liquid. Though with glass you had to move fast, she did so soundlessly and without abrupt changes of direction; when he failed to warm the piece or flash the punty she didn't shout, for once. At last someone who knew just what he needed—a hand to guide the roll back at the bench, support for his pipe when he expanded the bubble, simple admiration for his competence with a strange material: "You have a good sense of glass," the most generous thing she'd ever told him. It was a relief to concentrate on something physical, without feelings, for once an object that wouldn't misinterpret you or hold you accountable or demand that you love it with any particular devotion, though that was your choice. Just now he understood Syria's preference for form and color over people, if it came to that. The glass gave him heat and change and beauty, and he wondered whether in the end you needed more. He knew retreat to objects was a cheat, but he could see the seduction; the furnace called and churned so much like something live, you could put one over on yourself if you liked.

"Ordinarily I like the hot colors," said Syria. "But this will cool to ice blue. I think that's more your speed just now. I think you'll like it."

At about three she demanded, "When was the last time you ate?"

"I'm not sure."

"You're losing weight. That's like leaving good liquor open and letting it evaporate." She dragged him to Mike's Diner, where the late-night waiters knew her well, and ordered him steak and pancakes and apple pie with cheese.

He needed it. He'd burned up the meal at Mike's by late morning, so that by the time he showed up for visiting hours his stomach was yowling again. This time the hospital didn't exhilarate him with his own good health but made him feel pasty and tired. The ride up in the elevator, the lurch at her floor, made him a little sick.

Rachel was in a room with two other people, and at first he couldn't tell which bed, since the third seemed to contain a child. Looking again, he'd never realized how small she was. Her pallor blended with the sheets, so that all he saw at first was a tuft of black fur and two tiny eyes that shot open when they saw him. Kissing her on her cold forehead, he was amazed at the small circumference of her throat, the narrowness of her wrists under the taped IV. Her skin was translucent in the blue neon; her veins trickled in delicate tributaries over her arms. Smallest of all was her face itself, buried in the straggles of her hair. Checker was suspicious of comparing women with weak, helpless animals, but she was so bony and tremulous that the image of a kitten was unavoidable—the runt of the litter, undernourished and scared.

"I brought you a present," said Checker. As she tore away the tissue paper, having a hard time with the tape, as if even this much binding was too much to overcome, Checker felt a twinge; there was something a little warped about giving Rachel a goblet Syria had made. But his blue bowl was still in the annealer, and he knew very well he didn't want to give it to Rachel anyway. Couldn't he keep *something?* Besides, watching Rachel glow and shiver as she held the glass up to the ugly light, Checker decided giving her anything was probably warped. Whatever he brought her would unavoidably mean far too much. He wished he could have handed the goblet to her, saying, "Here, this is a gesture of guilt and obligation, nothing more." Maybe he could manage to break it on his way out.

"It's beautiful!" She clenched it over the sheet the whole time he was there.

"How are you feeling?"

"I've missed you! I've waited all morning. Caldwell was here, and Howard, and someone said Carl sat with me all afternoon yesterday, but I was delirious . . . I was waiting for you, though. I didn't care about anyone else."

"I'm sorry I couldn't come yesterday, Rache, but I had to sleep, I had to." Checker turned away. He was apologizing already, and for *sleeping.* "So what's it like, Rache, being delirious?"

"Like—having a nightmare, but you can talk."

"What did you say?"

"I don't remember everything. For a while I wanted to go to the bathroom." She played with the goblet, smearing pale fingerprints over the glass, embarrassed. "They wanted me to use a bedpan, and I think I was strapped in. I kept saying, Just let me go down the hall! Somehow I'd gotten the idea I knew where the ladies' room was and they wouldn't let me go . . . And I yelled for you. You weren't here, but I kept calling . . ." The goblet was now opaque with prints; the IV rattled on its hanger. "It's like watching a movie. You hear your own voice like someone else's far away. A little tiny buzzing sound, like David Hedison in *The Fly*."

"*Help me! Help me!*" Checker imitated sadly.

She laughed, for too long. Clearly he could do anything short of leave and she'd be happy as a clam.

"Is it fun? Is it like being high?"

"No," she shuddered. "It's awful."

"'Deliriously happy' is a strange phrase, then." Checker was running out of things to say.

"Checker—" Her hand reached out and clutched his shirt. "At Plato's—"

"Hey, you'd taken a whole drugstore, right? We can forget that entire conversation." Or try.

"No! I meant every word, and more!"

As she tugged at the material, Checker stared at his vocalist in horror. She was broken. She'd been fragile before, sensitive, the works, but never shattered. In the hospital bed before him was a woman with no pride, and it was like looking at a cripple or a vegetable or anyone else with something tragically missing. "You said, Checker," she went on, "you said you'd never fall in love with me." Her eyes were wide and blurry. "You said it would never happen, you said never. Checker, is it true? Did you mean it? Never?"

Checker looked down at the little white paw with its claws clutching the sleeve of Syria's work shirt. So what if you didn't want a pet? Someone leaves a basket case on your doorstep, what are you supposed to do, drown it?

"Oh, I don't know, Rache," he said slowly. "You're a wonderful girl. Sure, it's not out of the question."

Checker couldn't look her in the eye, and as she burbled, "I didn't think so!" tumbling on about how he should just tell her when he's "ready," Checker tried gently but firmly to release the green shirt from the grip of her nails. She wailed when he left, but Checker had to get out fast now, smoothing out the tight, bunchy wrinkles from his sleeve as he rushed down the hall. He was overwhelmed with a feeling he'd just done something terrible, though perhaps less to Rachel DeBruin than to himself.

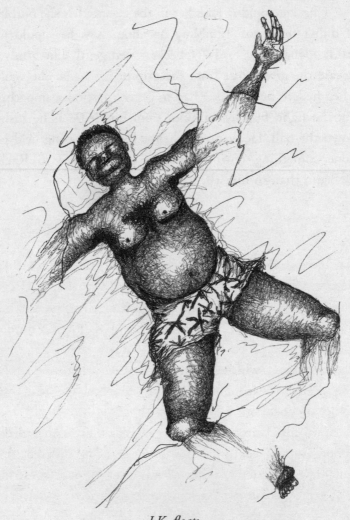

J.K. floats

16 / why we fought
world war II

Secretly, The Derailleurs were delighted Rachel had attempted suicide. An overdose was a damned sight more entertaining conversation than what suggestion to mail in this week for the *Late Show*'s Perfect Album Side; for once they sent Danno no card. And there was that stirring way Plato's patrons whispered in the corners when one of The Derailleurs walked in—thank you, Rachel DeBruin, who could ask for more?

For she'd introduced a charge, what they always tried to siphon from Checker: a sense of today being different from yesterday, a surety that Caldwell was right for once: these were the Old Days they would remember, even if no one had the nerve to name them Good outright. Kicking bottles by the river, scuffing up to the rail, staring wanly into the setting sun by the bridge; staying up late at Plato's even on week nights, a little disappointed that all the members left were boys and could not therefore burst into tears at slow moments to break up the evening—well, it was wonderful just to have something happen, and frankly, nine times out of ten when anything happens it's bad. Let's face it, graduations and award banquets don't make it. No, someone is usually dying or threatening you with a lead pipe; something you care about is at least at risk, if not swirling down the tubes altogether. Catastrophe is a queer route to feeling alive, but it nearly always works, as any VFW man could assure you. For most of us, the darker emotions are the richest of the palette: agony, rancor, *blame*.

Though accustomed to a certain notoriety, Checker noticed an unusual hush descend on the club when he walked in, a stony glare from the rest of the band.

"See Rache?" asked Caldwell tersely.

"Yeah."

"How's she doing?"

"She's a mess." Checker sighed, and might have gone on at length but caught himself just in time, as if starting to lean back in a broken chair. Only Rahim at the end of the table sent him a smile, the pretty, even teeth aligned like perfect soldiers at attention, troops on his side.

Side? There were no sides here, were there? This was the band, The Derailleurs, his people. So why did it seem they'd start talking again only when he left?

"Tonka."

The band rarely caught sight of this woman, and couldn't

help but stare. Her graying hair extended straight out from her ears and came to points over her shoulders, like small wings. Her eyes, too, were gray, perpetually mild. She floated into the room with a slight stoop, her gnarled hands balanced on either side. She looked older than she was, for Lena Secretti didn't "take care of herself." The only person who took care of her was Checker, and he was only nineteen.

Everything her eyes lighted on seemed to surprise her. She took her time, gazing at each of The Derailleurs in turn, smiling, though in a slightly feeble or disconnected way. She wasn't exactly crazy, but she didn't live at this address. She approached her son last of all and stroked his neck and told him why she was there, all with curiosity and confusion but no pain. As if it simply weren't her problem. "Romaine's been arrested, baby," she said in that airy voice of hers. "The police took him away. I don't know what to do."

Checker, whose feet had been up for only three minutes, took them wearily back down. Since it wasn't his mother's problem, it was obviously someone else's.

"See you guys," Checker sighed, and led his mother by the hand, feeling her exasperatingly light grip, preparing himself for the long ordeal of trying to find out from her where they'd taken his brother and what in God's name Romaine had done this time.

R o." Checker decided to stop there. It was critical to say as little as possible, since absolutely anything Check said would drive his brother into a frenzy.

Check left Romaine glowering on the station bench, hands shoved deep in his pockets, eyebrows low, lips pouting, pupils retracted into hard, resentful coals. There was paperwork his mother was not competent to see through, or at least that's what she pretended. Actually, Checker was beginning to figure out that his mother was a great deal smarter and more connected than she let on. He suspected she was perfectly capable of getting Romaine released into her custody, but the process didn't interest her and she wanted out of it. Little by little his sympathy was moving toward his father. She generated that mistiness of hers like a fog machine; it saved her all kinds of trouble. His mother sat next to Romaine with her hands quietly folded, looking just calculatedly sane enough that the police wouldn't think she was too weird and keep Romaine in jail. Of course, they weren't looking for an excuse to keep him—what did they want with another two-bit sixteen-year-old delinquent?

Checker showed his mother where to scrawl her looping imitation of a signature, glancing at Romaine, who was now slouched so low that he threatened to slide off the bench altogether. Romaine wouldn't meet his brother's eyes. No doubt about it, this was the world's most hopeless relationship.

Though Romaine Secretti was a mulatto like Check, he was more darkly complected. So Ro had decided to be black. He extruded his lips; he "talked street," though with the overly studied quality of an acquired tongue—his incessant "Yo!" got on his friends' nerves. He'd started using his father's old name, Jones—drab, but at least not Italian. He'd go to extravagant lengths to keep his friends from his mother, and not long ago, when he passed her on the street and she waved, he muttered, "Crazy white bitch," and kept on walking.

"Hey, ain't that yo mama?" asked one of his friends.

"That trash, bwa," Ro muttered.

"Don't razz me, sucker! That yo mama, I seen her wid you, three, fo time!"

"Bull, jive ass," Romaine insisted, and finally, rather than claim his mother, he ditched his friend.

Romaine loved to ride his older brother for having so many white friends; his latest nickname for Checker was "Clorox."

Romaine would inevitably hate his brother to precisely the degree Ro admired him, which was, unfortunately for both of them, very much. It was hell to be Checker's brother, and Check himself was aware of this, though sympathy only inflamed Romaine more. When, younger and stupider, Check had once made the mistake of addressing their problem directly, using words like "rivalry" and sheepishly naming some of his own successes, Ro never forgave him. "I guess I jus jealous a you bein so *popular*," he would quote viciously for years later.

Checker was their mother's favorite for largely practical reasons. While Check was self-sufficient from an early age, Romaine had expected to be a child, a real child, with a real mother. She resented scenes like this one, not because she was ashamed of Ro for getting into trouble, but because he forced her to confront a whole side of the world she preferred to neglect.

Yet Romaine's delinquency had the same too deliberate flavor of his lingo. He didn't have a flair for it, even his friends said so, and he too carefully got caught.

What with Rachel a few blocks away still clutching Syria's goblet like a promise she had wrested from him and would now never let go, and The Derailleurs up the way all, save Rahim, refusing him the time of day, Checker wasn't in the mood. Leading his motley family out the door with a date set for his brother's hearing, he muttered to Romaine, "I don't know what you're trying to pull off here, but it's not working." However, in that Romaine had added one more brick to a boat already riding low in the water, it was working, all right. It was working just fine.

T he following afternoon, returning from the recording studio, Caldwell was feeling expansive from Eaton's praise—his riffs were so sophisticated, his lyrics so subtle, this demo was going to blow Manhattan away. Thinking malignantly that Checker didn't go out of his way to compliment other musicians, Caldwell passed the laundromat on Eighteenth Street and caught sight of Himself.

As Caldwell stared in the door, Checker was standing before a top-loader with his eyes closed, fingertips resting gently on the machine, his chin raised, as if offering up a prayer to the God of Clean Clothes.

"You are whacked, man."

Checker smiled and sang "Good Vibrations."

The cycle spun its last verse; Checker unloaded the wet clothes into a cart. "I had that—effective feeling all day. Laundry was the ticket." He wheeled the clothes around a corner with a flourish and pushed; the cart careened down the aisle and stopped directly in front of a machine out of which a woman had just pulled her last sock—Checker got tail winds on the way to a *dryer*. He poked his head into the barrel and sang, "*You can't start a fire worrying about / Your little world falling apart / This gun's for hire / Even if we're just dancing in the dark.*" It echoed. He withdrew. "Better than a shower."

Check surveyed the bank of portholes with that proprietary air that distinguished his relationship to most objects. Checker bought little; he owned things simply by liking them so much. Shopping with Check drove Caldwell wild. Caldwell came back with a couple of albums full of disappointing cuts and a shirt he would stain with pizza sauce the first time he wore it; Checker's haul would include every outfit they'd looked at in windows, and all the good songs Tower had played while Check danced between Jazz and Rock and Caldwell frantically flipped through albums, wondering if he should really be buying CD's. Caldwell would blow his whole wad; Check would throw a bum a single quarter. Down at the strip, when Check admired a Corvette, its owner would grip the fender in a surge of jealousy when it was already his car.

"I love dryers," said Check, slapping his clothes with a *thwap* in the tube.

"Is there anything you don't *luv*?"

Checker looked up curiously and didn't answer.

"I mean," Caldwell fumbled, "don't you ever not feel like doing your laundry? Isn't it ever the last fucking thing on earth you want to do?"

"Sure. But I don't do it then."

"What if you never felt like it?"

"I guess I'd get pretty dirty."

Caldwell stuck out the load, trying unsuccessfully to remember Check was his friend, their good times together. Checker gestured to the window of the dryer. "It's like watching a *Star Trek* you've seen one too many times." Caldwell laughed, following the flashes of overfamiliar material up against the glass like watching TV. But there was something sad and lonesome about the weightless clothes, always falling, never reaching the bottom, like a bad dream. With winsome grace the arms of shirts reached toward one another but never quite met, legs wrestled and twisted and tore free. The dryer seemed tossed with agony and missed connections. When the load was dry, Caldwell helped Checker fold; he found himself stroking the shirts he recognized, smoothing out the wrinkles in heavy red cotton, overtaken with that particular Caldwell nostalgia for what should not yet be over. However much he reminded himself that nothing had changed, though, that wasn't quite true this time. As Checker cooed over the feel of fresh denim, the smell of clean sheets, the miraculous resurrection of laundry, Caldwell watched the scene like a memory: *Remember how Check washed clothes? Remember how he'd put his hands on the machine and hum like some kind of Zen crazy? Remember how he'd spend two dollars in quarters just so the towels fluffed out?* When Check buried his face in a thick magenta pile as in a woman's hair, Caldwell could have been looking at slides. He had to restrain himself from leaning over and whispering, while Checker played with the cart and its amazing castors, "I'll miss you, you son of a bitch," or even,

"I miss you now." Something horrible was happening, and his best friend in the world was beginning to annoy the living fuck out of him, and he couldn't stop it.

"Pick up a beer?" asked Check, slinging the sack over his back.

"No, thanks," said Caldwell formally, with the same twinge he felt when he turned twelve and for the first October in his life declined the offer to go trick-or-treating because this year he was too old.

T he Astoria Park pool closes at eight, but only technic-ally—it's nice that the lifeguards can call it a day, but the place is almost disappointingly permeable at night; though he often tore his clothes on the chain link, even Howard could scrabble over the fence.

That hot August night the band hadn't needed to make arrangements but naturally gravitated toward the pool, spilling in dribs and drabs over the fence, drawn by the expanse of water that on some level they all acknowledged, though they would not use this language, had mystical powers. The Astoria Park pool is the Stonehenge of Queens. Centered between the two bridges and twice Olympic-size, the huge blue rectangle is ringed with stairs like the Roman Colosseum. Three large inexplicable blue pyramids loom at regular intervals mid-pool. In hundreds of years archaeologists will unearth this place and assume it was holy ground.

Generously well lit, the water seemed to float above the park, reflecting the Triborough's entire string of lights. Though envious of Caldwell's beautiful flat racing dive, Howard disapproved—the whole pool was three and a half feet deep. As Howard eased onto his back, the lights of the bridge, the stars, and the Manhattan skyline swirled overhead. It was understandable why Checker had already been here an hour, tirelessly sidestroking across the far side, making only the faintest trickling sound as he passed by.

The crawl in the next lane may not have had the elegance or stamina of that seamless sidestroke, but Howard Williams was still a competent swimmer. While churning and gurgling with a suggestion of hysteria, Howard swashed a steady three laps to Checker's four.

Caldwell chopped a few rapid lengths and pulled out again. Dripping next to Eaton, who was reclining with his white Ban-Lon collar upturned, his neat blue running shorts crisp and pleated, Caldwell wasn't surprised that Eaton declined to jump in. Something about this guy was essentially dry.

Of course, it was happening again—it happened all the time now. The pool glimmered before Caldwell like a jewel in a window—something he couldn't have or something he'd pawned. It griped him that Checker didn't get tired. Just those few lengths and Caldwell was panting. There'd been no point in going on, though. With each stroke the water slipped away from him; cupping forward, his hands had desperately tried to collect the bright blue color, but it slithered through his fingers, the light shattering out of reach. *This is beautiful*, he'd thought. *Or I remember thinking this was beautiful before. I'll remember this as having been beautiful.* But however much he concentrated, it didn't seem beautiful as he looked at it, only after he looked away.

Eaton nodded at Check. "Seems our friend there's got some energy to work off. Guilty conscience?"

"Nah," said Caldwell. "That's just Check being Check. Mr. Rah-rah. Jacked on water. I've seen him swim three, four hours, nonstop."

"Discipline?"

"No, that's just what it isn't! That's how normal people would swim that long, Eat. But Check does it because he's *happy*."

"Even with his vocalist in the hospital?" Though she had been in three days, Astoria General was keeping Rachel a day or two more—her pulse remained uneven and eerily low. But then, any of The Derailleurs could have warned the doctors that Rachel's heart was not a resilient organ.

"Yeah, well." Caldwell twirled a strand of his white-blond hair until it frayed. "I wonder sometimes if that guy's got a conscience at all."

Eaton nodded; they watched the others. Rahim would shout and listen to the echo bounce over the water; "Sheck-air!" rang through the air like a toll. Quiet Carl slid along the bottom of the pool, holding his breath for minutes at a time. A floater, J.K. bobbed contentedly between pyramids like an unsinkable bathtub toy.

At last Checker hoisted out and stretched, the Triborough gleaming on his wide shoulders, condensing in his tiny waist, nestling in the hollows of his ass. He had cyclist's thighs but strangely slender knees. It may have been these extremes of breadth and narrowness that explained his impression of size. Actually, he was a small boy, but at this distance looked ample, intimidating.

Check splattered over to Caldwell. The rest had brought suits; Check was stark naked.

"You look pleased with yourself," said Caldwell.

Checker extended without embarrassment over the steps. "Just pleased."

Caldwell glanced slyly at Checker's prick, now withered into its testicles. It was hard to tell—the damned things kept changing size on you—but Caldwell decided his own was bigger.

"Do you consider yourself a hedonist?" Eaton asked.

"What's that?"

"Someone who lives for pleasure."

Checker considered. "Maybe," he said uneasily. Ordinarily Check loved new words—he could turn "vermilion," "flange," or "vise grips" around in his mouth with the savor of a good sour ball, but he got nervous when a word named not what you saw but what you were; it was a little like having the sour ball turn around and suck you. "This hedonist business. Is it supposed to be so great, or kind of crummy?"

"It's—problematic," said Eaton.

"Like other people," Check remembered. "Problematic" was one of Eaton's favorite words.

"Because of other people. It would be fine to live for pleasure if you were alone in the world. But as an ethic, hedonism falls a little short."

"Right over my head, Strike."

"I think," said Eaton carefully, "that something can feel good and be bad. Or feel bad and be good."

"Take Romaine," said Caldwell. "What'd he do yesterday, anyway?"

"He heaved a baseball bat through the window of the Victory Sweet Shop."

Caldwell laughed. "The usual."

"It's too bad," said Checker. "I liked the lettering on that place. Must have been fifty years old, gold, you know, and real ancient-looking."

"Did Romaine know you liked the lettering?" asked Eaton.

"Maybe, why?"

"Glass," said Eaton.

"What?"

"Well, what do you do for a living?"

Checker grunted. "So is Ro's vandalism my fault, too?"

"No, no," Eaton soothed. "I just mean it's lucky he didn't swing the bat at you."

"The point is," said Caldwell, "what if Ro gets jacked smashing windows, Check? What if that makes him the grinningest son of a bitch on earth?"

"But it doesn't," said Check readily.

"Come on, the swing, the crash, the tinkle-tinkle? Wouldn't it be gorgeous to land a bat in the Victory Sweet Shop window yourself?"

"No."

"Can't you at least admit it jacks your little brother?"

"No."

"Then why would he do it?" asked Caldwell in exasperation.

"Because it doesn't get him jacked. Which makes him angry. Which makes him smash more windows."

"So what would you recommend?"

"Stop smashing windows."

"How's that gonna get him jacked?"

"It won't. But it'd save a hell of a lot of plate glass." They were missing something: *When you love plate glass you don't want to smash it.* But Checker couldn't think of a way to say this that didn't sound dorky.

"Let's go at this from another angle," said Eaton. "When you do only what feels good, you rule out sacrifice. Do you think all those soldiers in World War II went overseas because they were in the mood for a European vacation?"

Checker slumped a little. He felt as if the two of them were heaving sandbags on his chest; it was harder to breathe.

"There's a whole other side of things, Secretti, that you like to ignore," Eaton continued. "Suffering. Doing things for other people—"

"I don't consider doing things for other people suffering," Check interjected.

"Sometimes it is. A lot of boys in World War II died, Secretti. And I don't think just because they felt like it."

Checker took a breath and sat up, unloading the sandbags methodically one at a time. "That's right. And *for what*?"

"Come again?"

"What did they die for, Striker?"

"Freedom—"

"To do what?"

"You lost me," said Eaton coldly.

"There's a monument down by the river, for the Astoria war dead. You know what it's for, really? Those guys died so I could do laps in the pool until two in the morning."

"They might have found that surprising in the trenches, Secretti."

"Bullshit they would," said Checker. "Any good soldier would know exactly what I mean. They fought World War II so you and I could order up home fries in Mike's Diner. So we could tune in The Cars live on NEW down by the river and drink beer."

"What are you talking about, Irv?" asked Eaton with disdain. Checker stood and stretched. "I'm talking about being alive, Striker. It has to count for something, or there's nothing to fight for. Now, how do home fries sound, boys? I'm starving to death."

If there was a monument to being alive in the park that night, it was not down by the river but stood in front of the two of them there at the pool, all its muscles rippling like the water beside them, reflecting the blue light and filling with lungful after lungful of thick summer air. Checker sighed often; Caldwell had remarked on this once and the drummer had explained, "I like to breathe." He was doing that now. Warmed up, Checker's prick fell long and voluptuous down his thighs, and Caldwell was no longer sure his was bigger, after all. In fact, though he was taller than Check by four inches or more, the boy before him, for whom all of World War II was fought, made him feel in every way considerably smaller.

Caldwell's best friend is inexplicably
beginning to annoy him

17 / the checkers speech

It's getting wider."

"I know."

"It can't get wider."

"It can."

"It better not."

"It has to, or this will have been pointless."

"It seems pointless now."

"Yes. So it has to get wider. So far apart that it comes together."

"That's crazy."

"This whole conversation is crazy." Syria shrugged and went back to work. "I'd just like to know," she shouted over the furnace, though they hadn't been talking about Rachel, "what are you going to do when something really is your fault?"

He didn't answer.

* * *

W e've been thinking of having a party for Rachel when she gets out tomorrow," said Eaton. "There's Plato's, of course, but it might have—"

"Associations."

"That's what we thought." Eaton's "we's" were funny. They didn't include the person he was talking to. "And none of us has our own place except J.K., and he's got the kid and all . . . What's the story on your apartment?"

An unpleasant scene loomed before Checker of about three in the morning, chips strewn around his living room, his mother already asleep, Romaine in the streets *window shopping*, the band one by one kicking out the door, clipping him on the shoulder, hugging Rachel good night; the last record clicking at the end, only a low light on, and once more Rachel having been drinking when she wasn't used to it; her sinking into the crumpled blue armchair and toying with his mother's stuffed sheep, it being only the two of them and Checker not able to leave because it was his apartment.

"That's Wilbur," Checker might inform her feebly.

Rachel would bend Wilbur's ears and smile (and not leave) and make expressions of entreaty on the animal's face. Checker had played with Wilbur before, so he knew that if you pressed its forehead down and folded the ears over its eyes, it could look incredibly pathetic.

"You want something to eat? A drink?"

She'd shake her head and still not say anything, since Rachel wasn't very talkative unless she was trying to kill herself.

So maybe in desperation he'd show her the pieces he'd blown at Vesuvius, holding that last bowl up to the light, its cool ice blue like the Astoria pool at night. Maybe he'd even suggest a swim just to get out of here, but she'd shake her head again and he'd run out of diversions and now it would be four and he'd be so tired and she'd get all soft, as if Rachel could get any softer, and—"No, Eat, no way, not in my apartment."

"We were wondering about Vesuvius, actually."

Checker winced. "Syr works at night, and she's been pretty clear about not having us hang out there."

"Just one night. For a good cause. Why not at least ask? Are you afraid of her?"

"You bet."

"What's she going to do, throw you in the oven of her gingerbread house? Been working for her a while now," Eaton prodded gently. "I'd think you'd be getting on friendlier terms."

"We are," said Check cautiously. "But Syr and her furnace have a lot in common. You don't get too close."

"Even if she's married to one of your best friends? I thought you went to dinner there and everything."

Checker grunted.

"You ask her and I'll stop by the studio tonight and see what the word is."

With a pat on the shoulder Eaton was gone, Checker staring after those miraculously immaculate tennis shoes flashing in the sun.

No clumps of potato salad where I work, no sale."

"Fine, I'll tell—"

"However." She pinged the big crystal snifter she was packing for SoHo. "You could have it at my apartment. After all, I have a caterer, don't I? His cacciatore is out of this world."

"I'd never have guessed you'd tame that Muslim spitfire into sautéing onions with a smile."

"Actually, I miss the old days. Once in a while I throw lasagna on the ceiling just out of nostalgia."

"Why, Syr? Why let us use your place?"

"Curiosity," she admitted. "All your little friends. To see what they're like."

"You'd be there?"

"You mean I'm not invited to my own apartment?"

"Just . . . Rachel, that's all, and you . . ."

"So?"

"Nothing," said Check hurriedly. "It'll be great." Checker swept viciously and thought, Oh, it'll be great, all right; it'll be priceless.

Though he'd never been inside before, Eaton sauntered into Vesuvius with cool lack of interest in the facilities. But then, Eaton tended to be bored by things, Checker had noticed.

"*You.*"

Eaton turned, feeling distinctly accused.

"You were the drummer at my reception. The second one."

"And you were the bride," said Eaton sardonically. "You do look different."

She stood with a punty, one end on the ground, bouncing it gamely from hand to hand. "Better or worse?"

"More like yourself, anyway," said Eaton with a smile.

"How do you know? You don't know myself."

"I often see more than people give me credit for."

"Cocky, your friend here," Syria told Checker, with a tinge of appreciation.

"How's the marriage of convenience going?"

"Conveniently."

"Irving here told me about your offer for tomorrow night. We're obliged."

"Girl returns from hospital still weak from overdose. Solicitous friends, awkwardness you can taste. Idiot bandleader. I couldn't find better at the Quad."

"I meant to ask you, Irv, are they definitely letting her out tomorrow?"

"Sure. It's a city hospital; nobody wants responsibility—"

"Except you," said Syria with annoyance.

"They'll just ask her, So are you going to do it again? and she'll say no and they'll say, Good, here are your clothes, we couldn't get all the puke stains out, sorry. They'll give her a pat on the ass and she'll be out the door."

"Incidentally, Irv, a few things she said to me yesterday struck me as queer. What all did you tell her, anyway?"

"You can go back to work, Syr, if you want."

"What'd you tell her, Checko?"

"Just that—she and I, that we weren't—out of the question . . ."

Syria let go of the punty; it fell on the cement with an incredulous clang.

"What was I supposed to do? She's in the hospital and asks me point-blank and—"

"And you *tell her*!" shouted Syria. "Where does this stop? Are you going to marry her because if you didn't she'd feel bad?"

"She's suicidal!"

"So, if she said she'd kill herself if you didn't, you'd marry her?"

"Is this your sacrifice, Irv? Rachel's your World War II?"

Checker looked at his watch and pulled off his apron. "I've got to get out of here. They say she freaks if it's too late in the visiting period and I haven't shown up yet." Not meeting either of their eyes, he washed up and put on a clean T-shirt.

"You're being blackmailed, darling," said Syria woefully as Check opened the door, and there was a seriousness to her voice, a tearing, that made Eaton watch her with sudden interest. Checker said, "I know"; as they looked at each other Eaton took mental snapshots, flash, flash. They were not pictures of employer-employee, that was certain.

"Well." Checker gone, Syria assessed Eaton, her arms akimbo.

"So you're an artist."

"I make things," she conceded.

"Could I see your work?"

"I won't stop you."

Syria stood in the doorway as he scanned the shelves of glass bones. "You bring out both the strength and fragility of the skeleton," he began. "Your work is an interesting commentary on both the resilience and frailty of human life—"

"Can it."

"I mean I'm impressed with these pieces—"

"I don't care."

"You had any shows? Have a gallery?"

"I don't care about that, either."

"You and Irving must get along great."

"What's with this 'Irving'?"

"Didn't you know? It's his real name."

"But it's a silly name and it doesn't suit him. Why do you persist in using it?"

"For fun."

"Whose?"

"Mine," he admitted.

"Don't use it around me. I don't like it."

"You and 'Check,' then. Must get along well."

"We do." Summarily she closed the storeroom door and led him back to the furnace. Syria sat and crossed her legs, folding her hands over her knee. "But you and Check, now. Isn't it sticky, being another drummer around Checker Secretti?"

"Hardly. I've learned a lot from him."

"So modest. That doesn't seem like you."

"How do you know what's like me?"

"I often see more than people give me credit for."

"Touché."

She leaned forward. "He's good at things, you must have noticed. Even at glass, he's a natural. Whatever he touches melts. Doesn't that grind a little bit? Doesn't that just tear you up?"

"No," said Eaton. "Why should it?"

"Oh, you tell me." She sat back again. "Admit you're jealous and you get my sympathy. Deny it and you don't. Your choice."

"If I'm so far gone I can't even admit it, why don't I deserve your sympathy all the more?"

Syria nodded. In some odd way, he pleased her.

"You seem awfully impressed with this kid."

"I am. That's surprising?"

"Not from his peers. But at your age, I'd expect you'd have more of a—perspective."

"My age?"

"Well, you must be, what, thirty-five?"

"Twenty-nine."

"Still, don't you get tired of hanging around young guys?"

"No."

"Well, I guess they are easier to . . ." He stopped.

"Go ahead."

"Control," said Eaton deftly. "Dominate, even."

Syria smiled. "Nothing in the world easier to dominate than an adult male who's losing his hair. The young ones still have some fight in them. Why, look at you! You're positively dangerous, aren't you?"

They met each other's eyes. Eaton was tremendously flattered. "So you want to control Checker Secretti?"

"I want to instruct him."

"Why bother? If he so all-fired wonderful already?"

A mistake. Syria sharpened. That trickle of loathing trailed like drool out of the corner of his mouth. There was no use wiping it away.

"I'm warning you," said Syria evenly. "Anything you do to him, I promise I'll do to you."

"I feel relatively safe, then," said Eaton, cleaning his nails. "Check and I are friends."

"Right. You and *Irving*." She saw him to the exit and said sweetly as they parted, "You're a worm," closing the door in his face.

C hecker prepared Rachel for the Carver Arms as he walked her from the hospital, but it seems his warnings were outdated. Disappointingly, there was no tomato sauce on the ceiling, no National Deesh on the floor. Nor did the rugs tinkle like the shores of the East River anymore—they weren't covered with glass but with the slashes of a vacuum cleaner. The window sashes shone from lemon oil. There were throw pillows and flowers; the volcanoes were framed, the igneous rocks by the lava lamp neatly arranged. Checker half expected Syria Pyramus herself to curtsy out of the kitchen scrubbed pink in a lacy white dress, a ribbon in her hair.

Of course, Syria strolled in to meet the guest of honor with dirt streaked across her neck, her hair uncombed, her shirt sleeves stuffed up her arms. He'd never seen her nails so black to the very tips, and though it hadn't rained in a week, her boots were mysteriously caked with mud, as if she'd delib-erately gone looking for the last remaining puddle in all of Astoria.

"Congratulations on fucking up," said Syria; when she shook Rachel's hand, it buckled. "Have a beer." With that she collapsed into a chair as if she expected the lights to go down and someone to run up the aisle for Jordan Almonds.

The rest of the band left their obscenely clean perches and hugged Rachel formally one at a time, never too hard.

"Syr, this apartment—"

"I *know*," she moaned, pulling a throw pillow out from under her and tossing it across the room—she looked wistful when nothing smashed. "I come home, I have to go to work throwing clothes, knocking something over. And have you noticed my jeans and shirts are always clean now?"

"Frankly—no."

She seemed relieved. "Well, that furnace in summer is a miracle cure. Unfortunately, apartments don't sweat.—I told him, *No doilies!*" Syria rose and tore a lacy antimacassar from behind Howard's head and threw it in the trash basket—which was, of course, completely empty. From there Syria ranged around the room, rumpling rugs, scattering rocks, pulling the bows on drape ties. "Makes me want to have a kid just to keep the place comfortable. What I really need here is a pile of shit-filled diapers and a three-year-old maniac with a Crayola 64."

"Nah," said Check. "This is a job for The Derailleurs!" Sure enough, after Syria's preliminary muss, the band unpacked instruments and papers and spread lyrics over the floor; cigarette and doobie ashes dusted the carpet.

Rahim swept out of the kitchen with tiny phyllo envelopes stuffed with feta cheese, followed by Baby Lamb Yuvetsi with avgolemono sauce, dilled cauliflower, and pilaf. Checker said the pine nuts reminded him of tiny rotting teeth. They were all grateful the food was so elaborate; it gave them something to talk about. After all, what were they to say to Rachel: Gee, are you glad you're alive? Do you really buy that Checker loves you—don't you think that's a sell? Uncomfortably, this was the first party The Derailleurs had ever thrown for Rachel DeBruin; it set an ugly precedent.

From a shortage of chairs they ate on the floor, and through dinner Rachel shuttled closer and closer to Check; he retreated as she advanced, until he ran smack up against Caldwell's shoulder. Caldwell shot him an odd look, and Checker duly edged back again, landing himself practically in Rachel's lap. Syria watched this dance from across the room with an indeterminate mixture of sympathy and disdain.

As Rahim collected the dishes, Eaton sidled over to Syria's extensive record collection and remarked with surprise, "Rock and roll!"

"Darling, I was 'Midnight Rambling' while you were nodding off to 'All the Pretty Little Horsies.'"

Eaton flipped methodically through her albums, searching for a weak point—a little flash of Carpenters, a limp Elton John or two. But so far, Adam and the Ants to Warren Zevon, it was a solid, even relentless collection—never a flicker of Carly Simon sentimentality, a falter of sappy Phil Collins. The rack was stacked with classics: Santana, Procol Harum, Iron Butterfly, shored up with a wide historical base that made Eaton feel unpleasantly young—all the Hendrix, Joplin, Cocker, and Creedence in their original issues, not the shiny new copies Eaton had. He might have pulled off a comment about her "opening an antique shop," and was working on the phrasing, until he'd come across too much Grace Jones, Prince, The Eurythmics, and Los Lobos to accuse her of being fusty. Come on, where was that peep of Peter, Paul & Mary, that brief moment of exhaustion in Tower when you bought the Janis Ian and Dan Fogelberg? Who your age escaped 1972 without getting saddled with at least one Cat Stevens? And while all the records here were hardcore, they were never silly, never all-out bad. She had the Airplane but not the Starship; the Smiths and The Psychedelic Furs, but never Iron Maiden or Twisted Sister. Neither was the selection hopelessly mainstream, but interestingly laced with Billy Cobham, Max Roach, Buddy Rich (drummers, Eaton noted), George Duke, even some foreign albums—Gianna Nannini, Bap, some Japanese he couldn't read. Eaton had never seen such a powerhouse collection in his life—right under a close-up of Mount Saint Helens, the records formed a solid flow of invulnerable sound. Impossible!

You bet. Scanning a second time, Eaton spied the unmistakable tufts of weakness. Eaton pulled them out as if finally having found a single wrong answer in an otherwise annoyingly perfect SAT. "Simon and Garfunkel!" he cried.

The whole room turned and stared. Eaton realized the scale of his elation was a little out of line.

"So?" asked Syria.

"They just don't seem to fit in here. A little—soft."

"Since those are all records that I like, they fit in fine."

"Garfunkel's pretty limp in the wrist if you ask me. And they date badly."

"I think they hold up," said Checker.

"Man, you can have 'em," said Caldwell, launching with J.K. into a satiric version of "Feelin' Groovy."

"I'll take them, then," said Check. "Great lyrics." He smiled at Syria. "Groovy."

Eaton stuck *Songs from the Big Chair* on the turntable, setting the needle down at "Everybody Wants to Rule the World." He returned to the circle to propose, "How about a party game?" since the last one hadn't worked out to his satisfaction.

"Pin the tail on the asshole," said Syria. "I'll go first."

"Something more adult," said Eaton. "A proposition: say, if you could be anyone in the world, who would you be?"

"Little much beer under the bridge for serious stuff, Eat," said J.K.

"Just idle speculation." Eaton leaned back languidly, curling the corner of his collar between his thumb and forefinger.

"And easy," said Caldwell. "Clapton."

"No way," said J.K. "Give me David Lee Roth any day."

Caldwell gagged. "Big J.! Clapton is to Roth as Wheaties is to Captain Crunch!"

"Musically, no argument. But we're talking life, right? And Captain Crunch got no problems and all the women in the world."

"And no little girl," said Checker quietly.

"He did say anybody." J.K. glared at Check, and turned to Howard. "How about Mr. Manager?"

Howard jumped. He was stoned. Howard liked the idea of getting stoned, but he always forgot what dope actually did to him, which was turn him into a total rabbit. Howard

Williams couldn't afford to turn into a rabbit. When Eaton posed his question, Howard had begun to sweat, groping for the names of rock performers; for some reason, the only group Howard could think of was Hall and Oates. Howard was not so stoned that he didn't know what a good laugh they'd all get out of that one—okay, a few nice tunes, but of all the people in the world?

"President," Howard stuttered.

Caldwell and J.K. guffawed. "Sit around listening to violins with your hands in your lap?"

"And married to Nancy?" asked J.K. "I rather be marooned on a desert island with a paper bag."

"Better start working on it, Howard," said Eaton. "'Manager of The Derailleurs' looks a little strange on campaign posters."

"What about you?" Howard accused.

"The Boss," said Eaton easily. Hard to top, but looking over at Checker, Eaton thought, *Then, I could have chosen anybody—anyone whose tickets you're lucky to scab up at double money. Anyone who looks down from the stage and sees your face as a blur in the cheap seats. In fact, let's play a different game: who would I like you to be? I wish for once you could step inside my shoes. Then you'd know what a drag it is to see you . . .*

Quiet Carl handed a penciled note to Rachel, and she read, "Danno on the *Late Show*."

"Me, next life, Craig Claiborne," said Rahim, passing around pistachio pastries. "Or maybe Sheckair, yes?" He picked the prettiest pastry for his wife. "Only Sheckair don have Syria."

"Don't be so sure," said Eaton.

Rahim's eyes narrowed and he opened his mouth, but Syria interfered, "No one has Syria, invertebrate."

"And who would you be?" Eaton asked her.

"Anyone who didn't ask that question."

"Not even Dale Chihuly?"

Syria looked at him sharply; Eaton smiled placidly back at her. "No," she said slowly. "He's in a rut, and he doesn't even do his own work anymore. He farms it out to grad students."

"But what if you could spread big red bones over two-page glossy layouts in *Art in America?* Or *American Craft*," he corrected apologetically. "Glass is considered craft, not art, isn't that right?"

Syria seemed about to close in for a returning barb, when she stopped and looked around as if realizing how old these people were. She laughed. "Well, you have done your homework. Congratulations."

"Rache," said Caldwell. "Joni Mitchell? Joan Armatrading? Or Rickie Lee Jones?"

"None of those, actually," said Rachel, glancing at Checker. "I saw a woman crossing Broadway once. She was sixty-five or seventy. She walked real slow, but she picked her feet up, she didn't shuffle. She was wearing a worn overcoat and stubby shoes. Her hair was short and straight and neat and very fine."

"So?" said Caldwell, looking worried.

"She had an expression on her face, a smile. It was—sublime. Is that the right word?" She turned to Checker for confirmation.

"Describe it," said Check uneasily.

"As if walking across the street were the most wonderful thing anyone ever did. She was alone, and old, and slow, and pretty soon the light changed and taxis honked at her, but her face glowed, you know? I wouldn't mind being her."

Once she'd finished reciting her piece, she beamed at Checker. He turned away, a little sick. The whole band shifted in their seats, looking out the window, though it was pitch dark. Caldwell lit a cigarette, and asked Syria for an ashtray. Rachel sat with her hands clasped, regularly cutting her eyes toward Check.

That was lovely, Rachel, what a fine thought. Checker got up quickly and ducked into the bathroom. So? What was wrong with wanting to be a sublime old lady? Oh, man. Checker rubbed his own neck. He took a leak, but there was only a dribble—had to drink more to hide out in the john.

Checker dreaded going back out there, feeling it was his fault and that everyone knew, everyone could hear it. *But I thought you'd be pleased.* Of course that's what you thought, dear. Boy, that's the second time in a week I've wanted to stick my fingers down your throat, little girl. Don't you *ever* do that again. *Do what?* Don't you EVER do that again! God, it'd been like listening to his own voice recorded at .33 and played back at .45—a mincing, chipmunk parody of his own convictions. Checker Secretti's parables from the hillside as read to you by Rachel "Magdalene" DeBruin and accompanied by The Derailleurs Tabernacle Choir. Checker shuddered. Truth turned tract was an ugly business, and he promised himself never, never to write a book or start a religion. She's trying so hard, he told himself. I know, he said back. But I'm embarrassed.

He splashed some water on his cheeks and glanced up, catching his own face with the same surprise of seeing a friend from childhood in a strange city. Surely looking in the mirror is among the most profound of everyday experiences, and tonight Check found solace there, the cheekbones high and round, the eyes meeting themselves squarely: Check, old buddy! He gushed with a wild affection for himself, the relief of his own company, feeling the simple comfort of staring into someone's eyes and for once knowing exactly what they were thinking. He liked his face. He liked his broad shoulders, all those veins down his arms, his girlishly small waist. Was this sick? Should he be looking for zits or finding his nose too upturned for an adult? Did Checker have a problem? Was not having a problem a problem?

Checker rubbed his face with a towel and braced himself to find out.

When he walked back in, they all stopped talking.

"You're the only one left," said Eaton.

"For what?" He was stalling.

"Party game, friend. Five billion on the menu. What's your pleasure?"

Checker felt the eyes of the whole room turn on him rather than to him—Howard's, stoned and resentful for having said "President," as if someone had made him; Rachel's cool because he hadn't said, *That was a lovely thought*; Caldwell and J.K. looking inexplicably preannoyed; Carl stewing blankly, perhaps newly aware how far he was from becoming a rock dj; Rahim in the kitchen, Check missing him as an ally and wondering why he should need one of those, all the while Eaton Striker fixing on him with something close to glee: *Generous of you to dig your own grave, Irving. I so hate to get my hands dirty.*

"Don't," warned Syria. "Don't play."

"Why not?" he asked slowly, and when he answered their question, the various expressions of his band members melded into homogeneous loathing.

"More than David Byrne?" Eaton pressed. "More than Bowie. Steve Gadd. Keith Moon."

"Keith Moon is dead," said Checker.

"Come on, Check," said Caldwell. "Even Howard did better than that."

"Maybe I just don't have a good imagination."

"Yeah," said Caldwell sourly. "Maybe not."

"But it's all in your control," Checker tried lamely to explain. "What your life is like. It really could be great to be an old lady crossing the street." He took the illustration away from Rachel, like removing an adult book from a child who couldn't understand it. "And it could be hell to be Eric Clapton. Don't you see?"

"I think Rache would be better off as Rickie Lee Jones," said Caldwell.

Checker sighed. Springsteen had been stuck on the turntable for some time: *Some all-hot half-shot was / headin' for the hot spot / Snap-nsome all-hot half-shot was headin for the hot spot / Snap-n . . .* They gathered their things to go home, making a show of saying goodbye to Rachel but only nodding at Check. He heard Eaton propose on the way out that they all go climbing on Hell Gate and cop a little graffiti, but no one invited Checker. Rachel remained behind, until Checker finally convinced her that he was staying to do the dishes and that since it was her party she wasn't to help. He sent her home with Carl.

Rahim insisted on doing the dishes himself, so Check and Syria debriefed in the living room. She put on Simon and Garfunkel. *Save the life of my child! cried the desperate mother. What's become of the children? people asking each other . . .*

"Why do you let them do that to you?"

"Do what?"

"Manipulate you so they can hate you better."

"They don't hate me. They're my friends."

"You keep telling yourself that."

Checker had been fingering a notebook in front of him and absently paging through. His own name caught his eye. "What the hell—" Checker bent over more intently, feeling intrusive, but this wasn't the kind of thing you put down just because you were respectful of other people's privacy unless you absolutely weren't a human being.

"What's that?"

"It's Howard's—and all about me!"

"What?"

"Just a second." It was the last pages Checker was interested in; he scanned: *irritating dumb cheer . . . likelihood of fraudulence . . . ecstasy as performance . . .* Right, left, right, to the jaw. "Here, take this away from me." He handed the notebook to Syria.

She appraised it quickly. "Very flattering," she said, and put it down.

"Not all of it. And not at all, really, Syr, I don't want this shit!"

She tsk-tsked and put her feet up. "Suicide! Disaffection! You kids do pack it in. God, watching the rise and fall of egos in here was making me seasick."

"You think because we're young it's all a joke?"

She picked up a piece of basalt and inspected it pensively. "Well, no, not a joke, not at nineteen, not at nine." She tossed the rock up and caught it. "I make fun of your soap operas because I'm jealous, you should know that. The way the intrigues, the dances, the individual Friday nights fill you people up. Your passions are so gaga. You can't all take it, but it's wild to watch."

"You don't honestly want to be nineteen again, do you?"

"No, I'm more useful as a grown-up. Still . . ." She set the rock down with a quiet rattle. "You know, that guttersnipe Striker implied I was such a failure. But actually I've been too successful with glass. It can take the heat; it's taken mine . . ." She looked up at Checker strangely. "You going to get out of here?"

"Sure." Check went to clap Rahim goodbye in the kitchen. He returned and picked up Howard's notebook, already dreading the scene of its return. Syria saw him wearily to the door. "Listen, you," she said, uncurling a kink of his hair, "don't let me patronize you. Your life's as real as mine, maybe more. But my world is a little small right now, and you have to figure that when I look around my living room and find it full of kids I feel a little crazy."

"Is that something to be ashamed of?"

"I hope not." As she kissed him on the forehead Checker was relieved he wasn't planning on clambering up Hell Gate with a can of spray paint, because God knows what he might have splayed over the rusty iron for the entirety of Astoria to read the next morning.

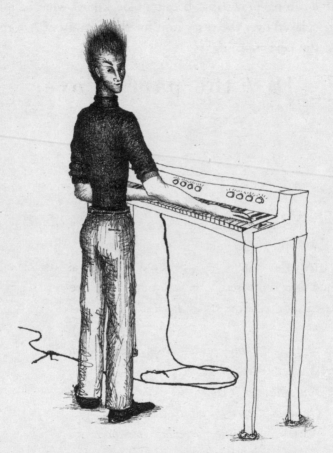

Carl doesn't talk

18 / the party's over

Checker began to write songs frenetically, as if harmony could by its marvelous mathematical properties force his friends in tune. Check believed in music as miracle elixir. When they rehearsed next, he brought in three new songs like bottled cure-alls, quart-sized:

The Checker Time-Buying Service

You squander it cheap
On dead sleep with no dreams,
Wheel of Fortune, *formulaic romances.*
We come round in the mornings,
Better Business warnings
Aside, aren't you willing to chance us?

Refrain:
It's the Checker Time-Buying Service—
No cause to feel nervous,
What we take is the waste you don't need.
You spend it over the sink,
Like money on drink;
Turn a profit on all that ennui!

Throw dull evenings in buckets;
Someone cancels, you chuck it—
Surprising how fast they collect.
Change that flat afternoon
From a burden to boon—
Our customers never regret.

    (Refrain)

Don't hold out for too long,
Thousands sell for a song—
Backers break down our doors to invest.
The market's flooded with surplus;
An hour is worthless;
The price of a month is depressed.

    (Refrain)

We get back to headquarters,
Put minutes in order,
Try out extra hours unseen.

Hey, we paid you in cash,
Good nickels for trash—
So you read one less bad magazine.

(Refrain)

How we use inventory's
A whole other story—
Don't think we'll leak this one out, Mac.
If you knew how we play
With years you throw away
You might try to haggle them back.

Hacking crudely at Caldwell's Roadstar, Checker felt the lack of accompaniment more keenly than usual.

While the others picked at this and that line, Howard kept staring over at Checker's Leedys, right at the bass, and finally Check twisted to see why; of course—lying under his gig bag, *An Inquiry into the Ecstatic State*. When Check turned back, Howard's face bricked over. Apologetically, Checker took the second song from his folder. It was slow and quiet:

Here Is the Party

Waiting for an invitation
All night.
Stay up late in irritation,
You might.
Moon rise.

Turn around,
Here is the party,
Howard.
Wake up,
Here is the party,
Wallflower.

Tooling down investigating,
Same park.
No one here is instigating;
It's dark.
Some lark.

Turn around,
Here is the party,
Howard.
Wake up,
Here is the party,
Wallflower.

For what are you procrastinating,
Coward?
What are you anticipating
These hours?
Soured.

Turn around,
Here is the party,
Howard.

Wake up,
Here is the party,
Wallflower.

"Did you have to use my name?" asked Howard tersely.

"Well, I could change it. But a lot of rhymes are built around it, and besides, I—"

"'Howard' is like a hundred million names," he observed coldly. "It should be easy to replace. I don't want my name in that song."

"Okay." Everyone was quiet. This was like a school talent show that wasn't going very well. Checker reluctantly presented his last song:

Hundred-Dollar Peanuts

My peanuts worth a hundred dollars,
Who needs your cashews.
My dreams in Technicolors,
Blow your VCR's fuse.

Don't want your Rockefeller's
Macadamia blues.
My goober's radicaler—
Rich nuts are bad news.

Tell you a story of
Boys of Astoria:
Don't make no money and

Don't eat chateaubriand.
Tell you the glory of
Ten-cent euphoria.
Our amps are secondhand,
But we're a macroband.

Don't want Italian leather,
Just worn tennis shoes.
Can't buy my bright blue weather,
Won't sell my good moods.

Lean out your yachts so wistful,
Lust for our rock-and-roll cruise.
But hundreds by the fistful,
And still we'd refuse.

Your yacht is snory, a
Andrea Doria.
Out here in wonderland
Boredom is contraband.
Our territory a
Phantasmagoria.
Our jokes are better brand;
Our scale is Baby Grand.

My peanuts worth a hundred dollars,
Who needs your cashews.
My dreams in Technicolors,
Blow your VCR's fuse . . .

In that same queer silence again, the band turned the orientation of their shoulders subtly toward Eaton Striker. He cleared his throat.

"You know, they want you to be satisfied with peanuts. You make an ideal proletarian."

"Who is they?" asked Checker.

"The elite, stuffing themselves every night with oysters on the half shell. Sure, on their yachts. They're laughing their heads off. They'd love your 'Hundred-Dollar Peanuts' song. Content yourself with the little things, right? Van Camp's pork and beans. Leave us the Jaguars and the Hamptons. There's nothing more convenient than a complacent underclass."

Checker sighed. "You've seen those tiny jars of macadamia nuts for, like, six dollars or something? You think they're worth that?"

"If you're Bruce Springsteen, the six dollars is nothing. You buy them if you like them."

"Bullshit, the Boss eats macadamias. Bullshit."

"You're naïve," said Eaton.

"It's a con, don't you see? People tell you what things are worth, but you don't have to believe them! There's a whole-wheat sourdough on First Avenue that I swear is worth twenty dollars, and it's a buck thirty-five. Why get bent out of shape you don't live in the Hamptons, when what's wrong with Astoria? And who really wants to eat raw oysters, Strike? I've seen those things, they're like live slugs."

Before Eaton could finish his assertion that oysters were an acquired taste, Checker's mind had already flown off on a

tangent, taken with the image of a family in rags seated in
the scullery, the little girl whining, "Not oysters again!" Her
father slumps at the head of the table picking with lackluster
at long strings of king crab. The kids are throwing pellets of
macadamias at each other, and the baby smears its Beluga
caviar all over its bib. Meanwhile, the little boy, Wattles, sneaks
up to the door behind which the masters are dining. "Oooh!"
he coos. Stacked in obscene opulence steam whole boiled
potatoes, the thin red skins beginning to flake off. A magnificent texture, they say, a little grainy but smooth and filling,
with an unusual earthy flavor, though of course Wattles has
never had one. None of that gnarled lobster his family has to
struggle with—

"Wattles, get away from there and eat your raspberries
and kiwi fruit with Chambord!"

Wattles sits dejected, mashing the raspberries with his
fork, pushing the scoop of ice cream around his plate until
it melts in a dissatisfied puddle. A spoiled little rich boy had
once given Wattles a taste of real Sealtest, and now, sickeningly rich and dense compared to the fluffy, lighter texture
of the real thing, Häagen-Dazs is worse than no ice cream
at all . . .

"Irving?" Eaton waved his hand in front of Checker's
face.

"Strike's right, bugger peanuts," said J.K., pulling out a
crumpled piece of paper. "I wrote this song, see." The litany
of the afternoon: *I wrote this song, see.*

"Take Me with You, David Lee" was strung with bikinis
and plastered with brand names: cars, stereo components,

top-shelf liquors. When it was over and the band cheered, Checker felt as if he'd just suffered ten minutes of ads waiting for the late-night movie.

"Yeah," said Check halfheartedly. "We can try that."

But there was more. Caldwell brought in "If You're Happy You're Stupid," an impassioned listing of the woes of the world, from toxic waste to nuclear war.

"Real artists should write about important stuff," Caldwell explained. "Not just beer by the river. Like you said the other day, Strike, remember?"

"Sure, Sweets. Though maybe we need to take on the issues one at a time . . ."

"You don't like it?"

"Sure I do! It's very—*dense*, that's all," Eaton assured him, walking a fine semantic line.

"And what about you, Check?"

"I—admire your intention."

"But do you like the song?"

Checker felt all his pores open like floodgates, but Caldwell was looking him square in the eye, so he said, "No."

"Yeah, well." Caldwell pulled the plug on his Roadstar with disgust, whipping the cord around his arm. "Somehow I'm not real surprised at that." Pressing his lips together so their edges went white, he took his seat beside Eaton and shot the other drummer a hard uh-huh look, before turning deferentially to Rachel and saying, "Rachel has a song, too. Maybe you'll like Rachel's song, Check." Again he turned to Eaton as if there was a theory behind this remark that Checker would soon confirm.

Rachel perched on the edge of the stool and clutched a big classical twelve-string to her chest. After a few wan strums, she began "Tell Me Why I Should Be Alive Tonight"; Check found himself studying the frayed extension cords curled at his feet, toeing the electrician's tape flapping off the wire. Anything but watch Rachel sing this song. With its explicit references to pills and IV's, the performance puzzled him— he'd often encouraged the band to open up to their audience, to be revealing. But there was a difference, say, between glimpsing a girl undressing through a window and watching her strip for money on stage. While awkward and unprofessional, this was definitely a strip job.

Damned if the whole band didn't turn to him as if to say, *See what you've done?*

"That's swell, Rache," said Check heavily. "Thanks a lot."

At the end of rehearsal Checker had an announcement: "Some official from the Parks Commission wants The Derailleurs to do a gig in Astoria Park, one of those outdoor concerts. Want to do it?"

The first enthusiasm of the afternoon. Check was afraid of that. While ordinarily the idea would have appealed to him—to play in Checker's park between Checker's pool and Checker's bridge, with (what used to be, anyway) Checker's band—for some reason the prospect of the concert filled him with dread.

He asked Howard to stay behind, and once the rest were gone silently handed back the notebook.

"I'm writing a novel," said Howard defiantly.

"No kidding."

"Did you look at it?" he asked, chin high.

"Just a little, Howard. I guess it could make an interesting book."

Howard shoved the notebook into his pack and was about to beat a rapid retreat when Checker called him back for a moment. "Howard," he said thickly, feeling a wave of inarticulation roll over him, "I'd like to explain, about this ecstasy shit—"

He stopped. He couldn't explain. "I don't know," said Checker, his shoulders slumping. "Maybe you think too much, huh?"

Howard, whose desire for an answer was every bit as intense as Checker's desire to give him one, looked equally disappointed, and sloughed out the door.

That evening Checker fled to the Triborough as if consulting an oracle. Rising over the ramp, he noticed one string of lights on her northeastern side was dark. The Triborough was a creature of balance; asymmetry seemed ominously out of character. Unsettled, Checker headed for Randalls Island, where a huge high-school marching band was practicing in the parking lot below the approach ramp. The bass drum pounded through the dark; brasses bounced in the underpass.

The whole trip was like that, filled with small fleeting phenomena that were somehow wonderful, as Checker careened on into Harlem past an evangelist forecasting the end of the world in exactly two weeks. Checker calculated

that this was the day of The Derailleurs' concert in Astoria
Park. On down 125th Street, record stores were open late and
generously broadcast blues and rap; smells wafted from Kansas
Fried Chicken of pepper and fresh fat.

Zefal was graceful tonight, swinging between grates,
shifting gears with a quiet *chock, chock* at miraculously low
speeds. Her tires tripped good-naturedly through passing
rubble. Stoplights synchronized so it was possible to pick up
speed, the freewheel clucking when he coasted, *Checker, let's
go faster—whistle warm air through my spokes; blur the reflectors
there to solid circles of white light. I love your feet in my stirrups,
shoved deep in the toe clips, your small ass high on the back of
my seat. Stroke my levers, warm my tape, whisper to my fork,
and don't touch the brakes. Just sock me into tenth gear and
push, hard—*

Checker laughed, turning Zefal around at Broadway,
though she resisted; she would have rolled all night if he'd let
her. His relationship with this machine was getting totally
sick. *It's been a while, you know.*

Janice. Checker didn't spend a lot of time remembering
things, but sometimes holograms would swoop down and
inhabit him, like the time he brought Janice home and learned
why they usually stayed on Plato's knotty-pine tables, carved
initials imprinting on his ass. At five in the morning his mother
flings open the bedroom door screeching, totally naked, her
tiny elongated breasts flapping against her arms. Janice leaps
instinctively on all fours from a dead sleep, nails clutching
the sheet, ribs protruding, lips drawn back from her teeth.
Checker quiet, in awe. *How dare you bring another woman*

into this house. Astride Zefal, Checker laughed aloud. *Another* woman. The deep-throated screaming, drapes in the wind, all that skin. He enjoyed the picture.

Of course, Plato's hadn't been foolproof, either; once Caldwell had walked in. Checker was half off the table, his chin stretched back; even upside down he would never forget Caldwell's expression as he opened the door to so much sweat and muscle and bushy black hair. Checker could as well have slashed a knife down the kid's gut, for he had that look of someone who's been ripped open but because of the shock hasn't yet felt the pain. Caldwell looked brutalized. His eyes grinding down on the floor, he grabbed his gig bag from the stage and slammed the door behind him.

Still, why the monastic denial lately? Checker could name five girls off the top of his head who'd jump on that table in a minute—not counting Rachel, since the idea of making it with Rache was about as appealing as mounting a nuclear warhead.

So Check had to remind himself how much he'd paid later for lying on that table and getting CS + LS semipermanently impressed on his ass. All those resentful looks from the audience. Suddenly someone to avoid. The explanations. Hey, these girls were very sweet, sure, but come on. And then having to stay up just as late but with a lot of weeping and no CS + LS on the ass, not by a long shot. It just wasn't worth it. Stick with the bike, Checko. At least the two-wheeler didn't want to brand you on the butt for the rest of your life. Zefal let you get off.

Crossing back over the bridge, Checker chuckled. All this

bullshit elation, it was just repressed fucking. "Howard!" he said out loud. "I've got the answer!"

And in a way, he had. He wanted *inside*. Checker Secretti wanted to fuck the living daylights out of the entire world.

R ehearsing for the Astoria Park concert was a nightmare. Everyone wanted to do his own song, getting through the others' numbers only to make it to his own. After days of this rock-and-roll Babel, Checker would hear all the new tunes playing at once when he tried to fall asleep, like down at the park on Saturday nights when the Trans Ams were stacked bumper to bumper, each blaring a different station. As he tossed and it got later, the songs would edge up in volume notch after notch until, all the dials on high, Checker would sit up in bed, the quilt of his favorite shirts rank with sweat.

Check might have been delighted with this renaissance of self-expression but for one little problem: the songs were rotten. They all knew it, too, which only made matters worse. Rahim was far too willing to express his distaste, but at least to one another's faces the rest kept quiet, and politeness is deadly between friends.

Checker spent a lot of time with Rahim, for while everyone else in the group seemed queered in some way, the Iraqi was loyal as ever, cleaning the mud off Zefal's rims, bringing Checker samples of his new recipe for apricot squares, and throwing himself so completely into Check's tunes in rehearsal that the bandleader's numbers were now less recognizable from their drive and wit than from the predominance of saxophone.

While Check had promised himself not to introduce any more new material of his own until all this was over (All what? And what would make it over? The concert? And what was that going to solve? Why was there anything to solve?), Rachel was constantly at his elbow wheedling: Couldn't he write her a song? Just one song? At last he capitulated and brought in "Too Much Trouble."

Too Much Trouble

I know I could outlast it.
I know I could get past it.
I know another year or two would do the job.
Crushes on my sixth-grade teachers

Now are through.
I don't remember their dresses,
Their addresses,
Their shoes down the hall.

So I could wait you out,
Rock,
Stare you down,
Tap my foot to the clock.
Hearts are muscles,
They tire.
I could burn down the fire.

> *But it's too much trouble,*
> *You bursting my bubble,*
> *The mornings,*
> *The afternoons.*
> *It's too much trouble,*
> *The year or two.*

> *So can I pass on your job?*
> *Can I punch in my clock?*
> *I know you and I won't do.*
> *So can I lie in your fire,*
> *Let the furnace shoot higher,*
> *No mornings,*
> *No afternoons?*
> *Because it's too much trouble,*
> *The year or two.*

While she was suitably ethereal as he began, by the end of his performance Rachel's forehead had rumpled. "Dresses?" she asked once the last chord had died.

"It's sort of the male version of your situation," Check explained.

"*I know you and I won't do?*" she remembered perfectly.

"I was just imagining your state of mind that night." Checker didn't look her in the eye.

"Can I see those lyrics?" asked Eaton.

"Sure." Checker handed him the sheaf.

"Sort of the male version," said Eaton with a faint smile.

*   *   *

Checker found himself appealing to Eaton more and more these days. There was an edge to Eaton, no doubt about it, but it could cut to the heart of a matter with a scalpel precision that was sometimes useful; so when the rest of the band dispersed that afternoon and Striker remained behind to watch Check face the wall with his forehead pressed against the paneling, his fingertips resting on the wood, Checker didn't say see you later, but waited and finally blurted, "It's Carl!"

Eaton took a seat and lit a cigarette. "Why, Carl is the one person in this band who couldn't have said a word against you. He can't talk."

Checker turned around. "He does to me."

Eaton raised his eyebrows. "You mean with words. And everything?"

"He's not deaf, for Christ's sake, he's a keyboardist. It's not that he can't talk—he won't. Except to me."

"But not anymore."

"Ever since Rache—I thought he and I just hadn't been alone. But before rehearsal today, we were the first ones here, and I said, How's it going, Q.C., and he didn't say anything, and I said, Listen, we've got to add a couple keyboard riffs after each refrain in 'Here Is the Party,' something high and minor, and he didn't say anything, and I said, Q.C., come on, it's me, what's with you, and *blank, nothing*, his face looked like set cement, Eat—flat and gray and about as talkative."

"Any theories?" asked Eaton, genteelly tapping an ash, watching Checker thrash around the room.

"Rachel. He has a thing for her, Strike, it's one of *those*."

As he said this last sentence with loathing, Checker was struck by an image of a long string of men and women encompassing the entire population of the world, all facing the same direction and chasing the person in front, one loving the next one in front, who loves the next one in front, who loves the next one in front . . . to finally connect back to the beginning and churn in a perpetual circle of despair and self-destruction, like a lizard nipping its own tail.

"He obviously blames me," Check went on, "and he probably should, since she's worse than ever and I don't know what to do . . . Eat, what's happening? Why is everything falling apart? *What's going wrong?*"

Eaton looked up at Checker with passing sympathy, wondering in a rare moment of self-examination whether he was simply hoping to win this boy over to himself so that no one else could have him—to cage this miraculous creature off away from the others like a nightingale with traps. Further, he even allowed himself to wonder if there were bands with two drummers, or if they could form the first one, snare to snare, bass to bass, each facing another set of drums like staring into a mirror. But the picture quickly faded. Who wanted to peer into a looking glass that only told you of someone far more fair?

"Nothing's falling apart, Irv," said Eaton smoothly. "Or nothing unusual is happening, anyway. Entropy is a universal principle. And I've been trying to alert you for a while now— when you insist on ignoring all the nastiness in the world and tiptoe through the tulips, it's bound to get the best of you eventually. Better to face up to it, use it. There's a lot of meanness and disappointment and pettiness out there. Just ignoring it doesn't make it go away. In fact, sometimes it does peachy keen when your back is turned, friend. Sometimes it positively thrives."

Eaton put out his cigarette on CS + LS and dusted his hands. The truth was harsh, but he'd delivered it quietly, almost kindly, he thought, though it was too late for warnings, as he very well knew.

19 / the last supper

He got up early and dressed with care, pulling out the charcoal slacks and sponging them damp where they'd folded over the hanger and wrinkled; he let them dry flat on the bed, patiently. He felt calm this morning, even serene. The salmon leather squeaked as he knotted his tie. Jutting his chin in the mirror, he decided not to shave. The three-day growth made him look older.

He chose his pink, blue, and gray argyles and laced the blue suede shoes. They scuffed so easily, he saved them for special occasions. Nestling his shoulders into the padding of the dove-gray jacket, he experimented with the effect of buttoned or open, standing with his hands in his pockets checking out the side view. He wet his comb and scooped the thick shock of black hair back from his forehead, feeling the floor through the thin soles of the expensive Italian leather. *Dazzling.*

For the final touch, he slipped five crisp twenties, cold

and unfolded, fresh from the bank, into his wallet. Eaton had decided to take taxis.

First stop: CBGB's. Eaton dipped in the dark doorway; his step faltered. He'd tipped that taxi driver thirty, forty percent. Way out of line. Probably seemed like an out-of-towner. Idiot.

His eyes had to dilate after the bright sun. The place seemed dingy during the day, the black paint chalky, posters tattered, and the smell of stale tobacco unpleasant even for a smoker. It was sickeningly quiet. When he bumped his foot on the passing table leg, he knew: first scrape on the blue suede shoes.

"Hey, slick, what you want?"

"I—left a demo here." Eaton's voice was unrecognizably high.

"Office." The man gestured.

Around the corner a girl with itinerant red curls perched on her desk, nattering with an attractive man as he cleaned his nails with a guitar pick.

"I'm Eaton Striker."

"Oh, *you're* Eaton Striker!" she exclaimed.

"That's right." His best smile.

"It was a joke, honey. Now'd you get the turkey with no mayo? A hundred calories a tablespoon, and you guys slathering that stuff on so it glops—"

"No," said Eaton.

"Then you cart it right back. This time I'm serious—"

"I mean I'm not here about sandwiches. I'm a bandleader. I left a demo here, and he said two weeks—"

"Harry!" she shouted to the next room. "Kid to pick up a demo! Whassa name of the band, honey?"

"Taxi."

"Back shelf!" someone shouted through the door.

The redhead fumbled among piles of paper and crusts of bread, rattling through cassettes, some without their jackets. "Oh, here." She held it out, not looking at him.

Eaton fingered the tape. Its lettering was smeared, and the tiny checks Eaton had penned on either side of the label seemed to have gotten wet and bled. Those silver tabs had been hard to find. "Um," said Eaton, who didn't usually say "um" and disapproved of people who did. "What's the word, then?"

"The word?" She seemed surprised he was still there.

"Did you like it? Are you interested?"

It still took her a minute to understand the question. Then she said, "No."

"Oh, okay," he said gratefully. "Thanks." He tried to keep from running, so he was still in the club when she called him back.

"Hey." She held out a couple of cards. "Passes for Wednesday night? Consolation prize." She smiled.

"Sure. Thanks, really. Thanks. Thanks a lot."

He did run this time. "Sort of sweet, huh?" he heard behind him, and laughter.

Eaton hurried up the Bowery as if avoiding an aggressive panhandler who smelled. His breath was shallow, his steps quick and small. He looked around as if he might be followed. He glanced down at his favorite shirt, checking for stains. Crazy, but that's the way he felt: stained.

By 14th Street Eaton had straightened his tie, combed his hair, and lengthened his stride. Galileo was considered a crank; Van Gogh lived off his brother. Oil shortages might come and go, but the planet's supply of ignorance was inexhaustible. So CB's didn't want Eaton Striker. That redhead would live to tell her girlfriends about the day Eaton Striker walked into her office like just anybody. They wrote articles about this sort of thing, you know. Huey Lewis had kicked around for years, scraping, and now look. Eaton hailed a taxi.

But by mid-afternoon, even with inspiration from Area and the Palladium, Eaton had run out of examples of genius unrecognized. Cassettes stacked in his pockets, ruining the line of his pleated pants, rattling against his thigh.

"That last track," a man at the Ritz said as Eaton was about to flee one more club. "The vicious little tune—"

"What about it?"

"Well, that one had—something. Kinda stuck in my head, you know? Maybe that's the right direction for you."

"Yeah, maybe," said Eaton, though somehow this admiration of "You Think You're So Great You're Not" didn't improve his mood.

At the Pyramid he inexplicably passed Howard Williams coming out the door. Both looked down, pretending they hadn't seen each other.

Eaton took the subway home. It got stuck under the East River for half an hour—typical—and he took the time to survey the wreckage: his tie had twisted oddly to the side, its knot turned to his collar; the shirt was half untucked, the pants creased. If his shoes had once been the color of a bright blue summer sky, they'd suffered a temperature inversion.

Back home, he peeled off the costume and stuffed it in his hamper, closing the lid tightly and walking away as if from the clothes of a homicide, for to Eaton the acrid sweat of failure marked them like blood.

A s The Derailleurs collected by the track, dragging amps from Caldwell's van and testing connections, Howard slumped on a nearby park bench and didn't help. Once the equipment was unloaded, he announced morosely that before Check and Rahim arrived they should talk. Everyone ignored him, as always. "*I said we have to talk.*"

They stopped. Howard whined, but never demanded. Something was up.

"Listen." He sighed. "I made a tape of you guys a while ago. Playing at Plato's. I made copies with my dual cassette deck. I didn't tell Check—he wouldn't like it—but I took them around to some clubs in Manhattan, and to a couple recording companies. I went around today and picked them back up."

"What happened?" asked Caldwell.

"None of the clubs is interested."

"You just did a pirate? With what machine?"

"My Walkman."

"Jesus, Howard! You do a demo, you record it at least on 8-track, if not 24! You go to a studio and—no wonder they turned us down—"

"Sweets," Howard interrupted, "I'm not finished."

Howard had a headache. In an effort to make the little rim of flab over his belt less repellent, he'd been taking off his shirt in the park the last few days to get some sun; he'd overdone it. Howard thought contemptuously to himself that he was just the sort of person who would sunburn. He didn't have any allergies yet, but he'd heard you could acquire them later in life; he was waiting. And where was the asthma? Anyway, he was beginning to peel, everywhere. They were all watching and this was important and he tried desperately to keep himself from picking at the little shreds of skin on his stomach between the buttons of his shirt.

"The tapes must have been good enough for them to hear something," Howard went on. "The Pyramid and the Limelight both said the drumming was 'rad.' Rad?"

"Radical," Caldwell explained.

"And that's good?"

"That's real good."

"And they said—" Howard didn't look at the others now. "The rest of the band was mediocre, but they liked the songs. This guy at SOB gave me the name of two 'rad' bands looking for new drummers. He said Check could take his pick."

They were all quiet. Finally Caldwell asked, "Whose songs were they?"

"I taped 'Gridlock,' 'Eaten by Salt,' and 'Pedestrians Are on Drugs.'"

"Checker's."

"Yeah."

"Well, you know, the bad recording," Caldwell roused, "it might not have done justice—"

"I'm not finished," said Howard heavily. "There's no problem with the recordings. I said I went to some companies. Warner Brothers, Atlantic—nix, the usual, they probably didn't even listen to it—"

"They don't," said Eaton.

"Some of them do," said Howard. "At CBS they took me inside. I said I was the manager. They got me a cup of coffee. We sat around a big round table—"

"Howard, *what?*"

"They don't want The Derailleurs, either! They love the songs! They say he's a good drummer and they want Check, Sweets, Check and only Check, and they want him to sign!"

It would be a lie to claim that no one knew what to say. They all knew very well: *I'm so happy for him.* But it isn't possible to be happy *for* someone else. It is necessary to feel happy oneself. No one said a word.

Finally Howard admitted with self-loathing, "And if I really am the manager, I get a cut."

"Too much, man," said J.K., "and you never so much as strung a guitar—"

"I wouldn't take it," Howard hurried to assure him, beginning to pick frantically at the skin peeling on his stomach.

"Howard, you sure know how to get a band in the mood for a concert," said J.K. "Great *management.*"

"You going to tell Check, Howard?" asked Caldwell.

"I have to, don't I? Besides, CBS will contact him eventually even if I keep quiet. But maybe not tonight?"

They all agreed to put off the upcoming powwow and try to enjoy the concert; this new turn of events had many "implications," as Eaton observed, which this was a poor time to address. Meanwhile, Eaton, Caldwell, and J.K. conferred quietly away from the others.

Check and Rahim showed up bustling with ice chests in which the rest showed little interest. *If you're happy you're stupid. Ecstasy as fraudulence. Blinded by the light. Why haven't you noticed that no one is talking to you? Who needs your idiot good humor if it means when none of your friends will look you in the eye you ratchet those drums and hum and make jokes we don't laugh at and it's all the same to you? You live in a fog like your mother. The whole world thrills you because yours isn't real. You're insane, you know that. We suffer, but at least we're intelligent. Our jacks are in the right holes. God, what do you need us for, really? We could be green trees, good weather. We keep our backs to you for half an hour and you see the other side of shapes. So go ahead, sign with a label, leave us. Don't think we care. Fine, fine. Don't think we care—*

T he Derailleurs had never performed quite like this before. It was like a free trip to Great Adventure. The music would climb up, up, until, *whoosh*, you were in free fall, your stomach lining ruined for life. For no sooner would the audience begin to sway or dance under the bridge, the runners step up their pace around the track, the early-evening tennis players pick up their games, than: *boom*, a stinker. Everyone dove for their coolers for more beer. What was going on here? A run of old favorites, the funny one about the peanuts, and then this bullshit about toxic waste? And that last one with the little girl and all that suicide, that was the final clinker—Downervista, man. Parties of picnickers moved their blankets farther from the band.

Though they had planned to finish with "Take Me with You, David Lee," J.K. himself suggested "Walkmans Make Creepy Squealy Sounds" instead, always a crowd pleaser. "Creepy Squealy" did arouse applause, but not strong enough for encores. The clapping petered out; The Derailleurs began to pack up. Unusually few fans lingered by the stage. The band caught passing phrases: "uneven" "sentimental" "played out" "Still, the drumming—" The drumming. The drumming. They'd heard that refrain before.

"Hey, skip breakdown and load-out for a while," Check proposed. "I picked up some shit for a picnic. Thought maybe we could hang out. Have some beers. What d'ya say?" Checker found he was actually frightened they would turn him down.

"Sure," said Eaton, for all of them. "Why not?"

Relieved, Check unbagged two jars of roasted peanuts and two jars of macadamia nuts. He unwrapped a loaf of First Avenue sourdough and opened a cooler with a flourish; inside, nestled in ice, three dozen oysters on the half shell. *Voilà:* a truce.

"And I got these dynamite little forks—"

"Check," said Rachel, "how could you afford—"

"Don't worry about it." He'd needed an advance from Syria, but when Checker threw a party he did better than play on lines from his songs—he unpacked cold cuts, fruit, cheese, Veniero's pastries, a gallon of the old reliable Carlo Rossi, since no one in the band knew good wine from drain cleaner, but they did know beer—Bass ale, Dos Equis, a few stouts. Check wasn't big on money, but when he spent it he enjoyed it, since there was no reason money should be different from anything else.

"All right, Eat, first oyster's yours."

If raw oysters are an acquired taste, one dinner out with your parents won't do the trick. Eaton buried the quivering gray creature with a gob of cocktail sauce and tossed it down like the stoic winners of "Gross Out" in junior high. He shot Checker an unsteady smile. "We'll work some class into you yet, Irv. Are these bluepoints?"

Checker himself examined and sniffed his for a minute or two before he speared the shellfish with the slender three-pronged fork and swallowed. He thought about it. He nodded. "It's like—the ocean. It's like eating the ocean. You got a point, Strike." He went enthusiastically for another and, with "ocean" rather than "slug" as the predominant metaphor, charmed both Caldwell and Carl into trying more than one. Rahim set about draining lemon over the lot, and spreading out cold cuts in decorative fans.

With a glass of wine in one hand and a chunk of Check's precious sourdough in the other, Eaton asked, "So when do you announce that we're eating your body and drinking your blood?"

"If this is the Last Supper and I cop the lead," asked Checker uneasily, "who does that make you, Strike?"

"Don't worry," said Eaton. "I'm not going to kiss you. I'm just one more fervent disciple, right? Among so many." Eaton took a pull on the Carlo. "You familiar with *Superstar*?"

"Yeah!" said Check. "Syria played it for me, and I brought it in for the band. We couldn't figure why it isn't still around, but nobody—"

"One of the things that's interesting about that opera, Irv"—Eaton cut Check off calmly—"is the job it does on the story. In *Superstar* Jesus is pretty much an asshole. Not very realistic; pompous. And Judas is the good guy. Judas just ends up doing what he's supposed to. Jesus is asking for it. He does a lot of stupid shit and he invites it, wants it, even, because martyrdom, that whole cross thing, it's the most pompous scene he could ever hope to pull off, right? Judas, well, he does the guy a favor. He's brave, even. In the end it turns out he's been suckered, of course, that he's the fall guy. But I always liked that opera, with Judas as the hero. And Murray Head, best vocals on the record."

"*What's the buzz?*" Caldwell crooned in the background, and pretty soon they were all singing album sides of *Superstar*, until they ran out of lyrics they remembered. Eaton made a good Caiaphas, and Rachel a fine Mary Magdalene, though her "I Don't Know How to Love Him" was, Checker thought, overly pointed.

As the rest tried to remember the Gethsemane scene, Caldwell stretched out on the quilt Check had brought and suddenly caught himself having a good time. But he didn't want one more memory to relive, to miss. It would suit him fine to remember the Last Supper as just awful. He would get his wish.

"Irving," said Eaton, curling the name around his tongue, "the band's been talking demos again."

Bip, a hammer on the knee. Reliably, Checker rose to the occasion. "Eat, not now."

"When, then?"

"Never. We've been over this a million times. And everything's been so screwed up lately. Let it ride."

"I thought the whole idea in not going for it was that playing in Plato's was so bloody fantastic, Irv. But the band being testy, why not move on?"

Checker was plagued by the feeling that they weren't talking about what they were talking about, and wanted out. "I pass," he said tersely.

"Why are you so entranced with failure?"

"I'm not!"

"Your insistence on being nothing. You bear down on it—"

"You fail when you set out to do something and you don't do it—"

"And you set out to be a musician—"

"I'm a drummer. I drum. I succeed in drumming."

"Then since you've already arrived, Secretti, if someone walked up to you tomorrow and asked you to sign with a record company, say, handed you the pen, would you turn them down?"

The entire band leaned forward a good fifteen degrees.

"Yes," said Checker, "I would," but he'd hesitated and felt funny and he wondered.

"All right, Secretti. You like Plato's so much, you can have it to yourself, then. J.K. and Sweets and I are forming our own band. It's called Taxi, and we aim to do some recording and hit some decent clubs. We want something *better.*"

Checker looked around the band, dazed. The park infused with lacking. He felt the tingle ebb from the air. The string of lights on the far side of the bridge was still dark. All the boys by the river looked bored and needed showers. One more night in Astoria Park. *We want something better.* It was heresy.

Checker later named the problem the Poison Carrot: whenever you define what you want as what you haven't got, you will never get what you want, since then you would have it and it would no longer be what you want, by definition. A "better" life is always an increment away. If you have decided your happiness will not really begin until you take, not the step you are taking, but the one after that, then you are set indefinitely on a treadmill from which only death, not love or money or fame, can save you.

"So," said Checker, feeling how completely he couldn't help them, "The Derailleurs are—derailed, then."

"But why should you need The Derailleurs, Irving? When you're so terrific by yourself?"

"I need you," Check whispered.

"Actually," said Eaton, "I believe that. Because you've got to surround yourself with people who will keep telling you how wonderful you are—"

"Because he is wonderful, slime mold," interrupted Rahim.

"But Mr. Wonderful won't try to record because it's a big bad world out there," Eaton barreled on. "There could possibly be a single recording company president who doesn't drop his flannels when he hears 'Walkmans Make Creepy Squealy Sounds' for the first time. No, you've got to play it safe and stay with your reliable groupies, who will be careful not to look too good beside you—"

"Hear how he say, Sheckair? I try tell you, now you see what he is—"

"For once you might see what *he* is," Eaton addressed Rahim. "Though I notice you're the one member of this band who's had the good sense not to challenge the poet laureate here. Maybe you know better than to ask for a little admiration yourself. The rest of us gave the guy too much credit." He turned back to Checker. "Everything's 'screwed up' now, is it? Well, it's about time. You use people, Secretti—"

"One word, Sheckair, I turn his face into pizza."

"No," Checker mumbled. "I want to hear this."

"When mad dog is in yard, you don open gate—!"

"Shut *up*," Checker told Rahim with surprising sharpness. "Let him finish."

As Rahim retreated from the quilt, hugging himself, Eaton proceeded uninterrupted. "See, that kid should be on the payroll! Know how much overtime each one of these guys clocks talking up your rep all over Astoria? And what do you do in return? Howard writes a song, you turn it into a joke. Sweets writes a song, it's too *serious*. Rachel asks you for a little encouragement *or* a little honesty, and gets neither. And tonight, you play their work, and they may not notice, but I can hear it, Secretti. I'm a drummer, too—I can spot sabotage in the back of the stage. Up against someone else's lyrics the rhythm just falls apart. Isn't that mysterious?

"Oh, but that's right. You're so chipper, that's what they get out of it. They get to watch you chirrup around the park and pitter-pat on drink glasses. Maybe if they stick around long enough, you'll toss them a tab of whatever you're on.

"Well, relax, Tinker Bell, you can let up now. We're closing down your run. It's quite a routine you've got going, but it's bogus, isn't it? Even worse, it's fucking boring, man. We don't even care if it's real anymore, that's your problem. But we're bored to death with watching the same show: Oh, this is so beautiful! This bread is so tasty! That little clinking sound by the river is so, so pretty to hear! A guy could suffocate from all that sweetness; we're too old for Mr. Rogers, understand?

"And most of all, can your loser philosophy. Just because you're a coward, don't keep these musicians from flexing their muscles in Manhattan. And spare us your diatribes about loyalty. Oh, I'm sure you believe in loyalty, all right—other people's loyalty to you. You're a petty tyrant, Secretti, one more fading neighborhood idol afraid to leave his adoring corner crowd because somewhere else he might not look like such a big man. Happens all the time in every high school in this country, and it's pathetic. Wake up and grow up. Have a real relationship with somebody for once, because right now you don't want friends, you want pets. Well, we're snipping the leash, Jack. We've got lives of our own."

Eaton was breathing hard. Howard had cleared his entire lower stomach of dead skin. Checker had been staring at the little section of bridge lights that wouldn't go on. Funny how disturbing that was. Funny.

Slowly Check turned his gaze back to the band. They were frozen, as if posing for a photograph; the picture stiffened and flattened before him. Is this what happens to you, Sweets? Is this nostalgia?

Checker reached for Zefal, nudging the kickstand, *bu-bong*, pushed off down the walkway, and was gone.

20 / into white

Y ou take it *back*."

Eaton sighed. "Why bother to say all that only to take it back again? I went to a certain amount of trouble."

"You take it back or I do things to your sister that in this country you don even have names for."

"Rescuing the hapless girl, I have no sister. I must say, I've found it ironic for a long time that you're Checkie's most faithful lapdog. It's hilarious when you think about it." Eaton leaned back, feeling pleasantly exercised.

"Why so funny, garbage scow?"

"*So can I lie in your fire, / Let the furnace shoot higher?* He's lain in his share of fire, you can bet. And with your wife."

Rahim made a lunge for Eaton, but J.K. and Caldwell caught him by each arm.

"You got any evidence, Strike?" asked J.K. "'Sides poetry?"

"Come on! She walks in the room and he melts!"

"Maybe," said Caldwell. "But even Check might have a hard time pulling in the Fire Queen. He thinks he's hot stuff with the high-school seniors at Plato's, but Pyro's the genuine article."

"Point is, man, here you don't go round sayin some dude bangin your wife without info you go to court on. You may got your problem with Check, but that where I draw the line."

"I'm the only one who has problems with Check, of course. The rest of you are all in love?"

"Check got his weak point, but I don't want to rip his guts out."

"Yeah," said Caldwell slowly. "Maybe you went too far, Eat. You really trashed the guy."

Eaton looked at the two of them in disgust. "You remember what you said yesterday, J.K.? 'Loser,' that was your word. Yours was 'guru,' Sweets, sorry I failed to get that in for you. And, Howard, that was your theory about how he's a fake, right? Man, that whole thing was just stringing together everything you've all said about Check for months now."

"Well," said Howard, squirming, "maybe it's different to say them to his face."

"It's braver," Eaton shot back. "Hell, I do you people a favor, and all I get is flak."

"I think we should go find him," said Rachel. "You, too, Eaton. You two should talk, try to straighten this out."

Eaton was about to mock her nicey-pudding optimism, but instead found himself shrugging in cool concession. He didn't want them to leave him behind.

"Where do you think he'd go?" asked Caldwell.

"Home? Plato's? The Triborough. Vesuvius."

Good guesses; wrong order.

C hecker propped Zefal in the alley and threw the Kryptonite around her wheel. He leaned his body fully against the hot metal door, his chest, his cheek, his instep.

Things happened and you went where it was warm. He stood in the doorway and watched the pendulum swing of her pipe, the red-orange glow of the bones, the furnace wide open, and Syria sober, quiet this time—there were no words in her face. The rib cage breathed in her hands.

She looked at him and wasn't startled and he was glad because he wanted everything smooth now. He couldn't see her eyes for the dark glasses, but something changed around her mouth and her face did have words; Checker found himself wondering what he looked like. He must have appeared different because she did. Seriousness-concern-anger. Always that last one.

She turned back to her work and he understood and was grateful she cared about things, yes, even things, enough to finish them and keep the heat even and gently, gently crack the amazing rib cage (blue, he remembered, the tank was ice blue) onto the kaolin blanket in the lehr. He appreciated care. He would like some.

This time she didn't smash the punty on the concrete to clean the end or send it hurtling with a clang to its barrel, but softly set it against the wall. She closed the furnace door, and though the roar was quieter, he was glad for the remaining sound, alto, like all the lullabies his mother had never sung him.

She walked forward and waited and then said, "What."

"They—" It was perfect to make rib cages out of glass, because that's what they were; his own was breaking.

He couldn't talk. Casually, Syria went and sat on the bench, leaned her back against the pole, put her feet up. She rested her arms on her knees, her hands patiently draped. She looked at him. He faced the furnace. He didn't want her to see him cry. He wasn't exactly ashamed, but felt disinclined to put any emotion (*quite a routine you've got going*) on parade.

Finding no tissues nearby, he wiped his nose on a forest-green work shirt. Finished, he held it with both hands. He loved that color. He loved that smell. He loved—*We're bored to death . . . A guy could suffocate from all that sweetness.*

Checker sat next to her feet, his own tucked under the bench, with the toes curled inside his tennis shoes. His spine curved and shoulders rounded, Checker bundled the work shirt to his stomach, wishing he weighed more. Those big people, he could see their point. Layers and layers and just a regular-sized person inside, laughing. *I've hidden in here and you can't get me. Just try.*

Syria nudged his thigh with her boot, once. Checker straightened up and looked at her. She couldn't help him if he didn't tell her what happened. So he told her everything, every word he could remember, which was every word. He delivered the story in a monotone, steady, reasonable: Cronkite.

"Well," said Syria calmly when he was finished, "you are pretty selfish, aren't you? You pursue your own pleasure more relentlessly than anyone I've ever met. Besides, you don't really deserve their admiration, do you? You're not what they think at all. On top of everything, you're a liar. A selfish liar."

She rose from the bench with a trace of weariness as if having just dispensed with one more job to do on an evening when she really could have called it quits an hour before. She rubbed the creases from her jeans and stood before him, with Checker completely curled over her shirt now and wanting to die.

"Now, how does that make you feel?" she inquired nicely.

Checker made a sound like *ungh*, his hands wrapped around his fragile chest, staring into his knees.

"*Ungh?* Like that?" She leaned down and took his T-shirt in her fist and twisted. "*Why doesn't it make you angry?*"

Checker was in the clutch of something beyond him, something that would take care of him all right, but not the way he expected.

"Get up! I said get up!" She pulled him from the bench by his T-shirt and slammed him up against the pole. "Listen. When Eaton Striker called you a 'petty tyrant,' when he called you 'Mr. Rogers' and 'Tinker Bell,' what did you do?"

"I—looked at the bridge."

"You *looked at the bridge*? My God, Checko, you didn't even have an argument!"

"What was I supposed to do?"

Syria hauled her hand back and slapped him full force across the face. His ears singing, he stared as she stood with knees slightly bent, her hands forward, waiting. "That," she growled. "That."

Checker eased away from the pole and stood with readiness, though he wasn't sure for what.

She hit him again. He was amazed at the wallop she could deliver for a woman. He took a step forward, she a step back. "Powder puff," she taunted. As Checker advanced she turned over an entire barrel of cullet in his way. "Tinker Bell?" She kicked over another barrel; its punties clanged on the cement. "More like Benji. Or those helpless decoupage doggies with the big brown eyes." He backed her up toward the furnace, the glass in his chest warming nearer the heat. His shoulders were broad. He felt a muscle in his stomach contract discreetly for each character she threw at him: Gentle Ben, Doris Day, the June Taylor Dancers. She seized a punty, keeping him at bay. "Because you'll believe anything. I could call you small or bossy or lazy and *poof*! that's what you'd be. Striker is right, you're a coward and a fraud. But he overestimates you. He thinks he's tumbled Goliath when he's really popped the Jolly Green Giant. King of the Vegetables. You just assume people say things like public-service messages, don't you? Here, this is something you should know. Think he was just being helpful? Because you need the short course in human motivation most people pass when they're three. Don't tell me—you were raised by Chinese—you had your brain bound."

The corners of her mouth were twitching. Checker's eyes glistened in the heat. He picked up a punty from the floor and knocked it lightly against hers, parrying. In the front of the furnace they dueled, two-handed. It began carefully, clang, pause, clang, another insult ("You carry spiders out and set them on the sidewalk instead of squishing them, don't you?"), but soon the fencing stepped up, until Syria threw so much of her weight into her attack that the vibration traveled to his shoulders and knocked him across the floor. While he was down she threw the furnace door open, stuck the end of her punty into the glass, and gathered. She sauntered over to Checker on the concrete, the molten bulb pointing toward him and trailing a bright string behind it, like the tail of a comet; quickly the tail darkened and cracked into lengths behind her, with small snaps and pings.

The glass glowed before him, a crystal ball. Over it sweat streaked her breastbone in olive runnels with muddy rims. Her hair was at a climax of peakedness, teased out, like Check himself. In the punty duel, the buttons of her shirt had come undone, and he could just see the sides of her breasts, heaving. It was the time in a swordfight where the hero has lost his weapon and things look bad. She put her foot on his chest; the boot was heavy. It was time for the hero to think of something. Checker could think of only one thing; he'd been thinking of it for six months or more.

As he reached up for the rod Syria shouted, "No!" and it was partly her horror that made it easy to wrest the punty away from her. Though he'd grabbed as far up as he could reach, by the time he flung it to the other side of the room his hand was seared. But it was worth it. He'd thrown her off balance, and before she regained it, he wrapped his arm around her waist, pulled her down, and rolled over on her stomach.

"You said never to play with the glass," Checker chided.

"I wasn't playing. This is serious."

"Yeah?" Checker studied her face, full of all kinds of expressions now, laughter, anxiety. It was an angular face, unusually long, almost Indian, already lined here and there, but not symmetrically—from years of sarcasm and lopsided cracks, the crease on the left side of her mouth was longer and deeper than the one on the right; the corner of her left eye was noticeably more crow's-footed than the other. He loved the lines in her face (*a guy could suffocate*) no, he *loved* the lines in her face. But what they told him flickered so quickly from invitation to mockery that whatever he might do now, he clearly ran the risk of her ridicule. He felt her midsection harden, supporting his weight. Though over her he could tell how amazingly narrow she was, Checker thought in a clear animal way: This is a creature of terrific resilience and resource, and you tangle with it on its own terms; *beware*.

Gripping her wrist, his right palm pulsed. "This"—he squeezed—"is a lot hotter than any punty. And a lot more dangerous."

"You're right," she said, and his only warning was an extra gathering underneath him; she flipped him over and with a twist held his wrists.

He wrapped his leg around hers, and rolled; to get her hands off his wrists he grabbed her hair. When he pulled hard enough she let go. That was fighting dirty, but this *was* dirty. The floor was littered with cullet; the sweat on their bodies picked up grit and bits of glass.

Yet with his hands in her hair he left them there. It was so thick, not just in quantity—each individual strand was strong, and even these, the thinnest extensions of her body, were disinclined to snap. When he tugged at single hairs they sprang back. He fingered into her scalp and involuntarily said, "Ah."

She whispered quietly, "And what about Rahim?"

Something gave way. A wave of anarchy broke over him, a release, a relief, a tide. Running over his own banks, Checker felt his waterline rise.

"*I don't care*" came from a place he didn't know very well.

So he kissed her, but with shrieking terror—not because of Rahim, who no longer existed, whom Checker had in the last three seconds deported to Iraq if not to another planet altogether, but because while he was a man who savored even the smallest moments he had never before done anything he could not lose a taste for; kissing this woman threatened to be the last thing he did in his life. In that recoil we all feel from the perfect drug to which we are perfectly susceptible, menacing us with a perfectly inextricable addiction, Checker had to pull out of her mouth for now and breathe. Any longer and she would have swallowed him whole, and he would have, gladly, let her.

He hid from the woman in her own hair, launching into the black forest where strands clung to his face in the dark like spiderwebs. He discovered her ear unexpectedly, and curled his way into the cave of it with his tongue. A salt mine. The shaft led him deeper in, pitch dark now and with that interesting flavor of ear wax, sharper than the salt, a little punishing, but he liked it. He tunneled out again and licked down her neck, lunging at the muscle strung at the top of her shoulder— good God, it was strong, and here the salt was even thicker. He laughed into the back of her neck. "This is like going through a whole bag of Doritos." He knew to get the jokes in now, since there might not be time later. She'd said this was serious. She'd promised this was serious. Syrious, he spelled to himself, and that was it. That was the last joke.

The two buttons still fastened on that green shirt both sprang off to ping in far corners like cane breaking. Getting it off her was another matter. She wasn't going to help, no, this wasn't a *here, let me* scene, so he had to force her on her stomach and pull the shirt off her back, wrenching her arms far enough behind her that it must have hurt; but he wasn't worried about her, not even when she flipped him off and he saw that one of her breasts was beginning to bleed; he met the red streaks with his tongue just before they dripped to the snap of her jeans. All the way up he licked toward the cut; this, too, salty, but more nutritious, until he sucked the wound itself, checking for glass.

She tried to tear his T-shirt in two. Though she pulled until the tendons stood out on her arms, she couldn't rip the collar; she laughed, leaving the tatters straggling around his neck.

He tugged off her boots and threw them into the dark; something crashed.

The jeans struck him first as an enemy, but that was before he started in with them. The sound the snap made was so promising that he tasted the copper riveting; the nap of his tongue stood on end like hair rising. As he pulled the zipper down he followed what it revealed with his mouth—a dark line on her abdomen of short V-shaped fur, as if there were another zipper under this one, with softer teeth.

He drew her across his lap and wrangled with the Levi's, the denim stiff and crackling with dirt. She was still fighting him, but Checker was finally the stronger of the two; in fact, he was much more powerful than he knew, for he was surprised to find how easily he could lift and twist her entire body with one hand while he worked the jeans down her legs, noting with a smile that she didn't bother with underwear.

They were in front of the furnace now, and as he lay on her stomach she worked his own jeans off with her thighs. Naked at last, they took a moment, panting, to look each other in the eye. They stopped fighting. She slicked her hands down his sides and perspiration whipped into the air, like stroking the body of a well-waxed sports car after a rain.

"You," she said. "I was beginning to wonder if you'd had a vasectomy and the knife slipped."

"You know how easy this is going to be? I could do this in my sleep. Because every night, I do."

"Do what? What do you think you're going to do?"

"This," said Checker, and he slid through the pool between their stomachs. When he raised up on his hands, their skins loudly sucked apart, the sweat having thickened, beginning to glue. He tangled through a smaller version of her hair, a thicket just as unmanageable and wild. Lodged between her thighs, he pushed back up again, his punty poised at the open furnace. Listening to the roar of the flame overhead, Checker looked up and inside, without dark glasses for once. The glass shifted uneasily; it was hard to focus, as always impossible to tell where the fire stopped and the liquid began. The only way to tell, he remembered, was to gently slide your pipe into the cavity, and at a certain point there was a tug; that meant you'd struck glass. If you were going to blow a big piece, like one of Syria's bones, you kept going, and the glass got thick and heavy and you rolled the pipe in the heaving red batch, collecting, pulling out, seeing how much you'd dragged, dipping back down, gathering again.

Checker stared at the furnace as it undulated; the image was so bright that it began to distort. The glass threatened to slosh out of its tank, the roar seemed to get louder, though he realized it was their own breathing instead, at so much the same pitch that the sounds blended into the breath of a single animal.

She eased him over on his back, but there was a chunk of cullet right underneath his spine; to avoid it, he had to rise from the concrete as he pushed into her. Between them their stomach muscles rolled like water, rippling in a yellow shimmer like the East River at sunset as a tanker ground by. Checker felt its wake roil up from his groin to his shoulders, where she dug between his muscles as if trying to get in.

Yet it was like doing hundreds of sit-ups, and he began to tire; while he didn't mind this being hard, he didn't want to think of it as work. With Syria still on top of him, then, Checker heaved to a stand, somehow managing not to leave her altogether. Her thighs around his waist, he pulled her ass tighter to him—a small muscular thing, about exactly a handful on each side—and carried her a few feet to the wall, where she could lean back on the cinder block.

They were right beside the furnace, where it was hotter than ever. Flames licked toward them and sweat ran down their bodies as if trying to put out the fire. The entire studio was pumped with gas now, a furnace; Checker imagined the cullet on the floor must be melting around him. In the other room Syria's life work was slumping, losing its detail. The window in the door was dripping from its frame. The scatter of their clothing burst spontaneously into flame. The coffee was boiling, ruined, and the pot would break. The doorknob glowed a dull red; punties and blowpipes drooped in their barrels. The thick iron slab of the marvering table bent toward the floor. The Sheetrock by the sink was ablaze. The air itself was on fire; steadily the whole studio glowed from scarlet to carmine to vermilion, then, losing red, to amber, brighter, saffron now, though even the yellows were going, weakening in the heat. It was too hot for color itself and the air went to cream. One by one objects disappeared, counters, benches, armchair. The whole picture overexposed until the walls themselves dissolved; Checker pulled Syria forward and assumed her weight, because there was no cinder block to lean back on anymore; he was afraid she would fall. The building bleached away, they were both outside now, on the beach. As the very last trace of color faded, the wide horizon went completely white. Suddenly there wasn't any heat left, either; the fire had consumed everything and had finally devoured itself, and Checker felt a delicious wash of cool like a breeze off the ocean. Despite the fact that the studio was ninety, maybe even a hundred degrees, he shivered.

21 / a cappella
in the underpass

Leaving Carl to watch the equipment, The Derailleurs trailed the pedestrian ramps, breaking into twos and threes, ranging the bridge like a posse. The ramps were deserted, and despite the luminous lights of the span and Manhattan behind her, the Triborough seemed desolate and forlorn. *What have you done? Where is the dark boy and his bicycle?* Their steps were secret; when Howard sent a bottle skittering, they started. The band spoke quietly, as if afraid of being overheard. *Where is the boy who laughs by himself and plays Steely Dan on my rail—?* With relief, they scuttled back down the stairs.

Plato's was a wasteland. No one had seen Checker. When they went by his apartment, his mother responded hazily that she didn't know if he was home, which seemed crazy, since it wasn't as if she lived in a mansion or something. She left them in the outside hall for five minutes or more; J.K. was sure that she'd forgotten what she was looking for. Finally J.K. knocked again and she said, "Oh," and then, "No," and with an aimlessly friendly smile shut the door.

So they headed for Vesuvius, Rahim claiming they should have gone there first, since Checker went to Syria for advice, Eaton agreeing readily and Rahim not liking that.

Rahim warned that Syria didn't like to be interrupted and stood on the same barrel he had climbed months ago to look in the window, checking if she was in the middle of a piece.

She was certainly in the middle of something.

"We find Sheckair," the Iraqi reported numbly, climbing down.

Caldwell reached for the door and Rahim grabbed his hand. "Don!"

"Why not?" As he started for the window, Rahim cried, "Don look there!" but Caldwell looked anyway, a casual glance at first, but then he cupped his hands over the pane and watched for as long as the band would let him.

"I don't think we need to make Check feel better, guys," said Caldwell as he stepped down. "The kid really knows how to console himself."

Once J.K. took his turn, he shook his head and whispered to Eaton, "Okay, Strike. You got my vote. Man, did you ever get Secretti's number."

"Jesus!" A virgin in need of helpful tips, Howard had to be dragged from the barrel to give Eaton a crack.

It took a moment for his eyes to focus, but gradually, amid

the wreckage of broken glass, splayed rods, and barrels on their sides, Eaton located the two bodies, upright beside the furnace, shimmering in gold sweat. *Here is the party?* Not in this alleyway, no way. The party's in there, Irv, and we weren't invited.

"What is it?" Rachel insisted.

"I don't think Rachel should look," said Eaton.

"Why not?"

"Cause Check fuckin her brains out, Jackless," said J.K. gently.

Rachel shoved past Eaton, anyway, and though no one would have predicted she'd have a taste for this spectator sport, Rachel watched longer than anyone.

Taxi collected in the street to confer.

"Man, this is the limit," said J.K.

"I'm beginning to get the creeps," said Caldwell bitterly. "Here the kid screws Hijack's wife to the wall—"

"Literally," said Eaton.

"—and treats us all like plant lice; meanwhile, he gets the woman and a contract and Manhattan gigs, while we're stuck in Astoria like a wad of used chewing gum at Plato's. Where does the punishment come in? Justice, like?"

Eaton looked down the alleyway for a minute. "The bicycle."

"What?"

They approached the familiar machine as she leaned against the wall, jealously eavesdropping. "Look," Eaton pointed out. "Its wheel is locked, but it's not secured to anything. We can't get through to Irv, that's obvious, but we might teach his bike a thing or two."

"I don't know . . ." said Caldwell.

"What going down in there he get shot for, Sweets. Rough up his bike, let him off light, you ask me."

So Caldwell hoisted the bike on his shoulder. "You coming, Hijack?"

"I wait for Sheckair."

"Lucky guy." Caldwell laughed. "Rache?"

"I think I want to be alone."

So the three of them carried Zefal off to the park, laughing in the dark, Howard dribbling after them, feeling very confused.

G radually the wide, white, undefined air filled in again with furniture, the lines draining into the room; there, a cullet barrel, a coffee cup, a shirt on the floor, like a Polaroid snapshot developing as they watched. Checker let the slippery body slide down his thighs. She was surprisingly light, and seemed smaller without the big green work shirt and heavy black boots. Soaked, her hair had relaxed down her shoulders. She was so much bluster—all that material, the aggressive strands, pushing you away. But look, a narrow, winsome woman, sinewy, but not so tough. He laughed, and she didn't ask him to explain. For a moment he felt victorious; he'd undressed her, called her bluff. Yet when she was standing in front of him only inches away, she suddenly seemed terrifyingly distant, and he pulled her back and held her. He didn't want this to be over. Much as he loved them, he didn't want the colors back yet, the shapes, the walls around him, the people and the neighborhood outside; he didn't want to find out not just all she might have meant by "This is serious" but what she might not have meant, not by a long shot; he didn't want to remember the leftover oysters spoiling in the park, the end of The Derailleurs, and all the accusations that might be true, and, most of all, he didn't want this small but sharp little worm beginning to tunnel into his middle, singing Checker's own little tune: *Maybe you see it now: / I am a garbage scow. / I'm not a hero, I'm a sleaze.*

"Water," said Syria.

Checker put on his tennis shoes and crunched through the cullet to the kitchenette to return with the gallon of water she kept there and a glass. She skipped the glass and emptied the commercial mayonnaise jar a full third before breathing. Taking his turn, Checker thought how fine eating and drinking were, to be able to take things in. Women were lucky. He finished the jar.

They weren't talking. Checker swabbed Syria's body with a wet towel, wiping the long back with the low-slung waist, the small hollow buttocks, the legs taut but surprisingly thin, with slender thighs. She stood patiently as he wet down her forehead and swept back her hair, stroked around her cordy neck and bony shoulders, and cupped each unexpectedly full breast with his towel. Her nipples hardened under the cool cloth. Her stomach was flat, but with tiny horizontal creases—an older woman. He wiped down the black triangle and was about to clean between her legs when she said, "No. Leave it."

A drip traced the inside of her thigh, thicker than sweat, just turning from milky to clear.

He brought her more water; she sloshed the jar in his face. She laughed. She splashed his back and threw him a towel. "You're daintier than I am," she said. It was true.

But they didn't say very much. Just small things, even trivial. Syria remarked about the mess, with no particular concern. She said he looked funny in only his tennis shoes. Wearing shoes was a studio rule, he recited, retrieving her own; and he'd never forget the picture of Syria Pyramus closing the furnace, completely naked except for those calf-high army-surplus boots.

Checker swept in front of the furnace and spread her sleeping bag on the floor. He laid Syria out just as neatly on top of it, smoothing her wrinkles, straightening her sides. He unlaced the boots, somehow surprised she let him; then, a rare wild animal will sometimes eat out of your hand. He liked taking care of her, a switch. Checker studied the artisan in the dim light. She looked like herself naked, and everyone didn't; but her corners were routered. Those eyes were wider than usual, all aperture, no iris—he'd found the door. At last her expression was symmetrical. He realized that for the first time he could remember she wasn't angry.

But as Check stretched beside her he thought: This is dangerous, sick because he didn't want to think that or to think anything; he didn't want consciousness or relationships or his future, and the best he could come up with now was sleep, though he didn't want dreams.

"Don't worry about it," Syria mumbled, and pulling his arm to nestle between her breasts, she pressed her back to his chest and went immediately to sleep.

Checker lay still, not daring to move his arm. The furnace purred while flames licked quietly around its door, as if cleaning its mouth, its paws. Yet the murmur kept hitting unsettling chords. Once or twice he began to fall asleep, but started awake again, catching himself: don't let it get light.

"Do you hear anything?" he whispered.

"Mm?" She turned over.

He heard it again—a scuffle, something. "There."

"Sometimes dogs try to get at the garbage," she muttered, reluctantly coherent. "Bitch them off if you want."

Checker extricated himself from her limbs, now grown around him like a tenacious plant. As he gritted across the floor in his All Stars, his prick bounced back and forth against his thighs. He wondered if he should throw something on, but modesty seemed silly for dogs. He opened the door.

The pack was gone, however, and the one that remained hunched on the doorstep playing with a piece of glass. The drummer didn't shoo this one away, because it wasn't a stray but a pet—Checker's own.

As the door creaked behind him, Rahim wheeled and stood up. They faced each other, Checker in only his shoes, his prick still lolling stupidly from thigh to thigh. When Rahim looked straight into Checker's eyes, he must have wanted to seem vengeful, but he only looked hurt. *I've done everything for you, and only asked for one thing, and you take it for yourself. How can you be so greedy? I would have given you anything but that. And you knew, too, I told you. It's true you found her for me, and I was grateful, don't think I wasn't. But all the worse, then, to take her back. You have a phrase for that in this country, though it's a joke, really—white-man giver would be so much more historically correct. Oh yes, I've picked up a lot here that I can't say yet—Americans think if you can't put it in English you don't know it at all, but—well, never mind that. I just mean, the more I get the feel for this place, the more I've been routing for the darker side of your blood. And as for darkness, I've always suspected—well, never mind that either, why should I care about that now? I just want you to know that I've defended you for months; the things they've said behind your back—you heard some of them tonight, but there's more, and I've never joined in, so now when I walk into Plato's the conversation stops as completely as if you'd walked in yourself, and that's made me proud. I'm Iraqi, and pride is important to us. You even said that about Rachel, how terrible it was to see her without pride in the hospital. Well, you might as well know that everyone saw you—they looked at my wife naked, doing that with my best friend, when I was the only one who kept saying how fine you were. They looked in the window like those booths in Times Square for a quarter. They're laughing at me now. Even I am laughing, and when you laugh at yourself it's all over. I'm only nineteen and I have no country and no family anymore. My brothers are dead and I will never see my mother. I like to splash in the pool and play sax in your band, but there's a lot of sorrow in my life and I never complain, do I? Eaton Striker talks about sacrifice, but he doesn't know what he's talking about; I do. I've sacrificed almost everything I've ever had. It's true that I'm resilient and I can keep moving. I ask for very little, but that doesn't mean I ask for nothing. My needs are simple but clear, and you've always known them: a*

*friend and my dignity and a woman. And in one night you
have taken every single one of them away.*

Rahim's lips trembled and he might have said some of
this, but all his English had fled. Instead, he spit, once, and
threw the cullet in his hand careening at a trash can. With
its single accusatory clang, he ran away, leaving Checker silent
and naked in the doorway, gazing down at his shoes. The
glob of saliva had landed on the toe of his famous Converse
All Stars, and Checker watched the spit drizzle down the
rubber, looking deceptively harmless. Just water. Just your
friend. Just his wife. Just disdain. What you are. Just your
life. Funny. It would make a good song.

Checker returned to the naked woman on the dirty
sleeping bag before the fire, surrounded by broken glass and
rumpled clothes. The scene suddenly seemed sordid, and his
desire for Syria lost its exaltation. So you scored again, didn't
you? You just have to have everything, don't you? You can't
let one woman go, let someone else have something you don't.
Syria says the others are jealous, but you're the worst of the
lot, aren't you? You not only want everything, you go out and
get it. You think you own the whole world—the bridges, the
dryers, the pools, the full length of 125th. You're a glutton;
you stuff down your neighborhood, you eat people whole. You
see this woman and she's wicked sharp and you have to fuck
her, don't you? No matter what the consequences, whose she
is, whom it hurts. You betray the one boy who was loyal to
you, and wasn't that part of the pleasure? Admit it: didn't you
like stealing her away?

Checker slipped on his jeans and the remains of his

T-shirt. He had to leave. With Syria still asleep and the night holding dark, he let himself out of Vesuvius, knowing full well that wanting to leave was a far cry from wanting to arrive somewhere else.

Maybe it was the bicycle that did it. Zefal was gone. Checker ran frantically up and down the alley, calling as if she would answer, until he remembered that in his haste he'd only locked her to herself, not to a pole, as he usually did—one more betrayal. He'd traded her for a woman who wasn't even his, for a fuck. How many times had he dreamed this at night, waking up sweating in the favorite shirts, Zefal lost or stolen or forgotten, the chases, the searches, the showdowns with vandals and thieves. She was innocent! He was suspect, he knew, an owner, a user, a taker, but Zefal did nothing but give and glide and accept punishment and wait patiently at parking signs for hours. He knew he didn't grease her or repack her bearings often enough, but she bore up, a laborer, heedlessly loyal—*Oh, you believe in loyalty, all right—other people's loyalty to you.*

It was a ludicrously beautiful early morning. Gray tinged one horizon; otherwise the sky was a searing midnight blue, with stars, no moon. As Checker fled toward the river, images reached at him like hands; the wind picked at his clothes. *Slow down. Stop, see, red.* Single colors found him, pretty gray concrete, patches of sky. Checker walked faster, almost running. Still, the pictures were clear and finished, round, perfect. Overhead, spotlights swept wanly in the distance, five of them, arcing apart, joining together, circling like ghostly night birds. There, in the window, a ten-year-old girl was up in her bedroom, five in the morning, why? She was dark and concentrated, picking out the tune to "Eleanor Rigby" on a toy xylophone. The notes came at him like arrows. She looked up and straight into his eyes; he smiled, she didn't, as if she knew something. She shook her head. Was he dreaming? She looked just the way he imagined Syria as a child—long, dark hair, underweight and overserious; easily hurt and quiet, except when you crossed her. Then she would bite and tear your hair. The girl went back to her xylophone, intent, making a mistake, trying the line again. She looked disappointed in him. *All the lonely people—where do they all come from? All the lonely people—where do—*Again.

On, under the accessway to the bridge, four young men sang the Beach Boys, barbershop. They were good, and the archway amplified their voices. Plaintive, serenading him, sirens, tempting him to stay and listen. *What is this?* Astoria was conspiring. Pulling out all the stops. Checker lunged up the stairs, but not without thinking, uselessly, that "A Cappella in the Underpass" was a great title for a song.

No good. It won't work. Sly, the colors, and the girl, she was genius, Syria in disguise—that woman follows me, she's a witch, I've known that from the beginning. She put something in that antiseptic the first night and uses it to track me. But I'm tired of magic, I won't be magic or know yours. Leave me alone. Still, that song title, that was a nice touch. Even now I can admire you for trying.

Up on the ramp the sound of traffic blotted out the Beach Boys, and Checker padded the slope softly. The bridge was asleep, her lights out, and he didn't want to wake her—the

Triborough was the worst, and she wouldn't like this, not one bit. She'd call him a heretic, she'd tell him it was a travesty, but then the Triborough was naïve, an optimist, a child of the New Deal, broken in with F.D.R. cutting her ribbon, a liberal Democrat for a father. She flew flags on the Fourth of July and strung lights over the river nights as if it were always Christmas. A little much. And, he thought more softly, maybe she was too bouncy, not that bright; but he didn't want to hurt her. Sssh. He didn't want her to see.

Mid-span her main cables draped graciously low, as if leaning down to give him a leg up—she'd be so furious later for having helped him. The cable was a full foot or so in circumference, easy to walk; holding the smaller cables on either side, he ascended the first length simply, as he'd seen painters and repairmen mount her before. The sound of traffic muted. It was windy up here. Farther up, the span steepened, and Checker had to stoop and grasp the cables more tightly; two-thirds of the way up, he slipped on the dewy blue-gray paint. He crouched for a moment, panting, clutching at the bridge like a small boy at his mother's skirt. Gosh, he almost fell! Checker shook his head and laughed, his eyes tearing in the wind. Man, whatever you may say of it, don't tell me that life isn't intrinsically ridiculous.

He stopped just shy of the top, which was too close to the shore of Wards Island; he was disappointed not to finish at her very tip, at the red light, somehow more climactic. But Checker had discarded magic and allowed this to mean nothing. *This is where the lights are out*. Checker refused to acknowledge the sign.

Still, he took a minute, standing as much as possible, breathing, because he liked to do that, certainly not because he needed to now. He'd never seen this view before. Manhattan's lights were out, too, also disappointing—he'd have preferred that Citicorp be shafting its triangular spot and the Chrysler scalloping behind it, maybe the Empire State lit a sedate blue and white, and a helicopter or two? *You are a trivial person, decorative. I don't think you should be thinking about helicopters.*

Still, Checker turned to the other horizon, where the sun was just beginning to rise over Con Edison. Forgetting where he was and what he was doing, Checker surveyed down the park fondly: the strip quiet for once, the ginkgoes leafy and wafting, the pool a brilliant baby blue. Surprisingly, he thought he could make out the tiny squares of amps and the circles of his drum set still on the hillside—why hadn't they taken the equipment to Plato's? It could be stolen, and dew was bad for the finish of the Leedys, the shells were wood and the varnish might bubble—

Your friends are objects.

Weaving as the wind whipped the tatters of his T-shirt, Checker felt suddenly tired. He crumbled into the familiar exhaustion. Too Much Trouble. Everything. Quickly the tiredness swallowed the sunrise, the ginkgoes, the tugging of the traps below. His body went limp. *And my bicycle is stolen. Well, that's it, I'm through. Being "jacked" all the time, do you know how much energy that takes? I've tried and it's too much. I'm not who you think at all. But that's a very fine part, and I do hope you find someone up to the role.*

The cable foreshortened and his stomach churned. The red bulb just up from his perch blinked hypnotically, the kind of light that sets off epileptic fits. Though the sky was getting brighter, to Checker the vista grew increasingly dim. His thoughts fragmented and strayed, as if themselves trying to get away from him, rats fleeing a sinking ship. As the birds began to chirp maniacally in the park, Checker could hear only his heart pounding in his inner ear. Colors darkened. The river below was flat and inky, motionless, like tar. Earlier, Vesuvius had bleached to white; now one by one the objects around him, the Leedys, the trucks on the bridge, also disappeared, but this time the world contracted. Walls rose and closed around him, until he was in a tiny closet by himself that was finally getting too small for his own wide shoulders; as its corners collapsed into themselves Checker dove blindly forward, thinking, *More greediness*, because if you had to have everything, you had to have nothing, too.

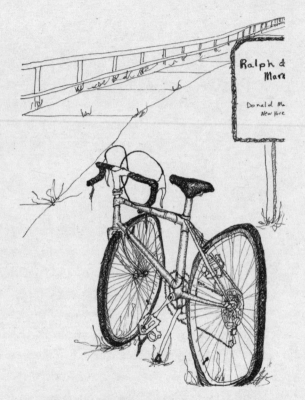

Zefal is actually one of the main characters

22 / a little help
from my friends

Propped by the river, Zefal squared her handlebars like shoulders, their tape palmed through from so many miles. Graying, with every reason to retire, she still put in a full day's work. She was losing her teeth, and her tires were bald. Her brake shoes were worn like the heels of old boots, her cables were stretched, her finish was peeling. She was losing her bearings. So why did she seem so intimidating? Why did Caldwell stand a respectful three feet away, wanting to apologize for the rough trip over? She didn't like being carried with the Kryptonite looped through her tire. It was like being handcuffed. And she wouldn't talk to these people. Where was Checker? Who was that lady in the studio? *Who are these boys?*

"It's a piece of junk, actually," said Caldwell, stalling. "I don't understand why he's so attached to it."

"But he is attached to it," Eaton observed. "That's all that matters."

"Right," said Caldwell without enthusiasm. "Well, what do we do? Slash the tires and shit?"

"*Slash the tires?* Why don't we just send it to its room?"

"It's metal, Eat. I can't twist it into pretzels with my bare hands."

"Come, boys," Eaton chided, "let's be a little resourceful." Eaton leaned over the rail and scanned the rocks by the river: a grocery cart, a muffler, an old TV . . . There. "Just what the doctor ordered," said Eaton, climbing down, to return dragging something behind him. "Give me a hand, J.K."

"A parking meter? What for?"

"For a piggy bank, what do you think?"

J.K. lifted the meter over the rail and hefted it up and down. It was heavy.

Again they approached the bicycle, until Howard, who had been keeping his distance perched on the rail, slipped off and walked none too steadily to stand between the three of them and the bike. "Guys," Howard quavered, "maybe this isn't a good idea."

"You got a better one?"

"Yeah, just—maybe we should take it back. I'll take it back. You can finish packing up and take the equipment to Plato's. And we could all get some sleep. I mean, let's not be hasty."

Howard hadn't quite understood what they were planning until he saw the meter. It was a big brutish thing, covered with mud. Its piping was four times as thick as Zefal's—no contest. Howard could sense the bicycle shiver behind him. Howard and Charlie had been together only for a few months, so he had the same sober awe for Checker and Zefal's relationship as for his grandparents' marriage. Nine years!

"You want to go beddy-bye, Howard, go ahead," said Eaton. "As for hasty, I'd say this is positively overdue."

"Well, maybe this thing with Check and Syria isn't the way it looks—"

J.K. guffawed. "Right, he wasn't really fucking her, it just seem that way."

"Well, Check may be guilty, but the bicycle never did anything!"

"Getting a little off the beam, Howard," said Caldwell. "Of course it's never done anything. It's a machine."

"It isn't," said Howard staunchly. "Check says—"

"Spare me—"

"—that anything you care about is alive."

"Better shut your eyes and put your hands over your ears, then," said Eaton. "Its little screams and big sad eyes might be hard for you to take."

Howard backed up and spread his arms over the bike. "Go home."

"How, you're overtired."

"You touch her over my dead body," said Howard.

Caldwell approached the manager and tentatively tried to pull him off the bike. Howard held fast. "The kid's cracked his nut, Big J. Give me a hand, would you?"

"Get away!" shouted Howard, but the two guitarists pried his fingers from the handlebars; J.K. held the frame and

Caldwell pinned Howard's arms behind his back, dragging him away from Zefal as he continued to struggle.

Handing the meter over to Eaton, J.K. was working furiously to concoct a version of this scene that kept it in the realm of happy-go-lucky pranksterism. "Nobody's put in a quarter, Eat," he said boisterously. "This bike impounded." They were just getting their kicks, boys being boys, sowing wild oats—J.K. slathered cliché on cliché like layers of plaster, trying desperately to shape this event into a practical joke. It was practical, all right; it just wasn't a joke.

With impressive exertion for someone so slim, Eaton lifted the meter over his head and brought its shank lunging toward the main crossbar of Zefal's frame.

Howard's scream echoed over the crunch of 5-3-1 tubing. Zefal crumpled to her knees, her crossbar V-shaped, the meter in its crotch. Copper paint flaked through the breeze.

In a way, it was merciful. Howard went limp. Caldwell let him go. With an ache in his throat, Caldwell stood over the crippled machine. His eyes heated and reddened, and he was so angry, so disgusted by his own sentimentality, over an object and over a friend who thought he was so hot and was really an asshole, that he picked the meter up himself and came down with a vengeance on the handlebars until they pointed the wrong way, like elbows breaking backward. He attacked the front wheel, though it took work—the alloy rim had survived years of New York potholes, and after two good blows remained staunchly true.

Finally he flipped the bike over to expose the derailleur, and brought the meter head down directly on the mechanism with unnecessary force. The derailleur is a delicate part of a bicycle, in need of very fine tuning, for even an eighth of an inch off and the derailleur will actually switch into the back spokes, to be mangled by the turning of the wheel. Yes, just a little out of adjustment a derailleur will self-destruct.

"That enough, Sweets," said J.K. quietly, not doing a good job at all of seeing this as boyish, as clichéd, as anything short of dreadful. Caldwell stood over the bike, panting. J.K. picked up Zefal's carcass and heaved her over the rail to the rocks below. She clattered, and lay still.

As J.K. picked up the stray nuts and bolts and the free-wheel on the sidewalk and tossed them after the bike, Eaton suggested they return to their equipment over the hill. Leaving Howard sniveling on the rail, the three hiked to where Carl was still patiently standing guard. Caldwell and J.K. had assumed Eaton was anxious to get the amps and guitars back to Plato's and away from dew, but it seems as far as Eaton Striker was concerned, the morning was new. If this was the time to stick it to the inanimates, a particular collection had it coming.

"What'd you bring the meter with you for, Eat? A souvenir?"

There they were, antiquated and ridiculously huge; creaking and bandaged with tape, wired and tied with bits of string.

So you miss the great master? Too bad. He's fucking the daylights out of a dried-up glassblower and left you to roll in the dew, that's how much he cares about you. His whole band thinks he's a slime bucket, even that hothead Iraqi now. And the old lady back at the furnace is sure to slip him his walking papers once she's got what she wanted. Older women are like that, they get these itches; it doesn't matter who scratches as long as he doesn't get inconveniently underfoot. So you've got no daddy, no hero, no big brother, nobody better. Those icons, they always disappoint. No matter how you exalt them, there will always be someone around like me to show you how small they are. And everyone else is grateful, I do them a favor. Who needs this larger-than-life shit? It's intimidating, it's discouraging, it's depressing as hell. You think you see giants walking around, but they're really just regular people on shaky stilts—a couple of good kicks will do it.

Had Eat the time to compose it, he might have sung Checker's Leedys a familiar little song:

Junky-clunky, you Derailleurs,
Now defuncty.
You're no morey, poor Derailleurs,
That's the story.
Sunk in funky, lead Derailleur,
Now debunked-y.
Your bouncy bunk's half-baked,
Your exaltation's faked,
Don't tell me you own rock and roll.

Get off that bandstand,
This is a reprimand—
We need a harder, stronger, smarter leader.
Your coddled tubs will shred,
No more pats on the head—

These rattletraps deserve a better beater.
Your skins are pampered, Irv;
Strike throws a sterner curve—
You'll find my rhythm's parking meter.

Eaton had decimated the bass by the time J.K. and Caldwell understood what he planned to do. They both might have entertained notions of throwing themselves in front of Eaton à la Howard Williams—because that was no bicycle, *those were Check's drums*—if instinct for self-preservation hadn't interfered. You did not plant yourself in front of a maniac swinging a wild parking meter, period. So in dull horror the guitarists from the fledgling band Taxi watched their new leader descend on the traps, wood splintering, rims crumpling, heads buzzing, ticking, and flapping in the wind. The Zildjian-K's clanged a less-than-clarion call across the hills of the park, their bells inverting into the dirt. Eaton slew the high hat to the grass, now more of a beret. The snare swallowed the head of the meter whole and rose with it over Eaton's head, but Eaton dislodged it with redoubled fury and took his vengeance for the delay. Felled early, the crash shimmered in the wreckage with each new blow, its rivets tingling like raw nerves, though this was a show of liveliness not unlike a snake continuing to writhe and rattle after you've cut off its head. As Eaton dealt his final blow to the throne, the first gray light of sunrise hit the red flag in the weapon's window: EXPIRED.

Caldwell and J.K. looked at each other. "Hey, J.—"

"Tomorrow," J.K. whispered fiercely.

They moved very smoothly and very carefully and very quietly. "Some solo, Eat," J.K. muttered in passing; that was all.

The guitarists loaded the rest of the equipment into the van; Caldwell hid his Roadstar under the back seat. They worked stealthily but fast, moving the amps away from Eaton Striker like making points in Pick-up Sticks. They did not want him to move.

He didn't. Eaton stood with his hands in his pockets staring off toward Hell Gate, his collar high.

The equipment loaded, J.K. and Caldwell collected the remnants of the Last Supper. The ice in the chest had melted, and the remaining oysters had sunk to the bottom. The water was gray with a pink tinge from the cocktail sauce; lemon slices floated nicely on top, amid bits of horseradish. J.K. closed the lid with funereal care.

Peanuts and macadamias scattered underfoot. The cold cuts and cheese were curling, the pastries crusted. Caldwell dunked the sourdoughs in a can like basketballs.

"This tuna isn't opened," said Caldwell softly. "Want to save it?"

"Sweets, you joking."

So Caldwell piled the rest of the spread on the cloth Check had brought for the picnic—a funny sort of quilt, with patches of suede, velour, corduroy. It was pretty mangy, so Caldwell rolled it all in a bundle and shoved the quilt in a can, the way they used to discard the toys and clothes of children with scarlet fever. Having touched the old food, the tiny forks, the squares of cloth with pockets and buttons,

Caldwell felt tainted and wiped his hands on his jeans. As he poured out the rest of the Carlo Rossi, it stained the grass red, and its rising acrid smell turned his stomach.

"You coming, Eat?"

Eaton didn't even shake his head. Nothing. Just his back. Caldwell and J.K. left their new bandleader with palpable relief.

Only when the van had churned away did Eaton stir. Listlessly he shuffled through the remains of Checker's drum set, kicking at stray rims, turning over cymbals as if sifting through the ashes of a fire looking for something that had survived—a piece of the family silver, a gem, a charm. Finally he picked up a metal plate and worked the splinters off its rivets: *Leedy*. Although he slipped the plate into his pocket before roaming off between the concrete pillars of Hell Gate, Eaton didn't seem to have found what he was looking for.

23 / the ghost
in the machine

Howard leaned over the rail by the river, listening to the birds begin to twitter, the water lap against its glass shoreline. There was a strange Eastern peacefulness to this rock garden, with the breeze, the near-dark, the contortion of the metal below like an abstract sculpture—it *suggested* a bicycle.

Howard climbed over the rail and balanced down to the frame, to stroke her bedraggled tape and work the brakes, now flaccid from broken cables. While Checker admired slow change by habit—the sharpening of sprocket teeth, the toeclip indentations in his All Stars, laugh lines—watching the dead decay was another matter. Howard couldn't imagine Checker would want to study Zefal as she dropped her bolts one by one into the East River while he leaned over the rail with a beer. Howard reached down to heave the bike off the rocks. As he did so, a small dark shape in the sky caught the corner of his eye.

He thought it was a bird, and later, when he saw something bobbing in the river, he didn't pay much attention to it, either. He was tired and had a job to do. Howard dislodged Zefal's pedals and threw her toward the river, but she landed short and still cut that stark figure on shore. He clambered farther down, getting his shoes wet. The blac¹ thing floated closer by. He threw her again, and though she landed in the water this time, she was still sticking out, more pathetic than ever. Howard slogged out knee-deep, finding the current quick and his balance unsteady, even at this depth. Still, he wrestled the bike once more and pitched her with all his might; blessedly, she sank from view. Howard was about to go home, already thinking of a long hot shower and his favorite flannel sheets, when the black blob bobbed past and Howard looked it in the eye.

Howard leaped from rock to rock, frantically keeping pace with the flotsam, until he found himself square in front of the monument to the Astoria war dead. He glanced up from the shore and read: *No greater sacrifice has he than a man lay down his life for his friends*. The quote had always given him chills; this morning it actually made him shudder.

You say personal loyalty is one thing. I don't think so. I think it's everything. It's the beginning of everything, anyway, Striker. It's the bottom line.

Sure, Howard realized it was an inadequate ethic, finally. It didn't cover everything, not nearly—it occurred to him that sometimes you were loyal to two different people, and in order to stay loyal to both of them, you had to do absolutely opposite things. And when one of those people was yourself, well, that was an especially sticky wicket. But it was a nice ethic all the same, both reliable and a little stupid, like the people Checker had been loyal to, and the person he must have, until tonight, considered himself to be. It helped, and Howard wasn't about to let it gurgle down one of those whirlpools under Hell Gate like the last cup of water down a bathtub drain.

R achel had been wandering the streets of Astoria, but she couldn't remain forlorn. The view in the window of Vesuvius hadn't really surprised her. She'd noticed the electricity between those two before. It was the sort of picture that should have shot her into an all-night drugstore; instead, it threw her onto the unbelievably steady bedrock of herself. Checker was making love with someone else, and she didn't even cry. She felt a little like the first time she looked into a mirror and realized she was pretty, only this time she realized she was strong. Rachel walked the streets with an unreasonable calm, embraced by what Checker called the Great Okayness that can so surprisingly follow romantic disappointment. The row houses beside her had thick walls and full basements; their healthy rosebushes sported large stalks. Fences were in good repair and flagstone uncracked. Hardy grass sprang between squares of sidewalk. At six in the morning tenacious old ladies waddled out to prune with well-made shears.

She got hungry as the sun rose, and stopped in a bagelry for a sesame, hot off the tray. She remembered, Checker always asked for "hot and light," for which he could get burned-out all-night clerks pawing through the bin. Checker loved bread. Checker loved—

Well, Checker. She sighed. She wondered if he knew how handsome he was. Maybe not. Or maybe he did this morning. Syria was pretty old for him, but that somehow made sense. She still had a good body, anyway. And noshing down Ditmars, Rachel felt sadly pleased that Checker had found someone to hold him after Eaton Striker said those dreadful things and he had to go.

Sunrise was lush, and Rachel's steps were generous. Her hair fluffed out and rose in the humid air of late summer. The old ladies gargled good morning, and Rachel waved. When on a lark she tripped down the steps to Plato's, she was humming The Police, one of her favorites.

Caldwell and J.K. were there, looking a little the worse for wear. They stopped talking when she skimmed in.

"Hello, boys."

"Morning, Rache," said Caldwell gently. "Up early?"

"Late." She smiled.

"Yeah, us too." Caldwell stretched, and exposed his long, flat stomach with a "Ho-oh!" Rachel slapped him playfully under his raised T-shirt. He shot her a quizzical look.

"So are you guys really going to start a new band?" Hands on her hips, she stood between them.

"That a matter of discussion, Jackless," said J.K.

"Yeah, we're—concerned," said Caldwell uneasily.

"About what?"

"That Eat—uh—"

"That Strike ain't playin with both sticks."

"You mean because of what he told Checker?"

The two guitarists eyed each other. "Yeah . . ." said Caldwell. "Say, listen, we're sorry about Vesuvius—"

"On my account?" Her voice had acquired a clarity to its consonants. Full and pretty, it wasn't *thin*. They looked at her differently.

"Yeah."

"Checker and I are friends. That's all." Slowly both their heads tilted at this oddly self-assured woman standing between them. She shrugged. "I know. Sure. I've had a thing for him. But it's not going to fly, right? So the guy's—spilt milk. Why cry." She looked between the two of them, her mother's daughter. Insurance. A-line.

"This time," said J.K., "she take tranquillizers."

"By the way," said Rachel, looking at the stage, "where are Check's drums? You didn't leave them in the park?"

"As a matter of fact—we did."

"You spiteful assholes! Sweets, give me the kcy to the van and I'll go get them myself. I mean, just because he doesn't like your songs—"

"Rache," said Caldwell, "you don't want to get Check's drums," in much the tone of voice the husband must have warned his wife from the door after the second wish in "The Monkey's Paw."

"Why not?"

"Strike play some boffo tunes, see—"

"With his usual delicate touch—"

"Cut it short." This was unlike her, but Caldwell was actually glad to be spared the song-and-dance.

"Striker pulverized them with a parking meter."

"WHAT?"

Caldwell rubbed his face. "Have you noticed how weird everything's gotten lately, guys?"

"*I wish I never / woke up this morning*," Rachel sang. "*Life was easy / when it was boring.*"

"You said it," said Caldwell. "Man, I could use some real dull shit just about now. Check makes fun of 'em, but, boy, I could go for a game show. *Let's Make a Deal . . .*"

"Nope, too exciting," said J.K. "Clapping and screaming and big money. I more like in the mood to watch bathwater evaporate."

"But only if it's not too hot a day. So it doesn't dry too fast and make our heads spin."

"Yeah, maybe evaporation too wild. Erosion?"

"Photosynthesis."

"Too funky, Sweet. Howard right, them little green leaves outta thin air, that weird shit, man. I need *ordinary life*, buddy. I wanta walk to the corner and buy a banana. You got your nice day and sun and shit, and then you got your nighttime when you sack out, and that the end of the story. Don't even need no rock and roll."

"Paint peeling."

"That the ticket."

But ordinary life would have to wait for another morning.

"Where is Checker Secretti?" It was an accusation.

J.K. and Caldwell prepared their expressions before they turned to the door. It would be difficult to marshal real disdain from scratch once they'd faced her.

"Well," Caldwell drawled, "last time we saw him he was with you."

"And when was that?" She didn't seem nervous, but factual and in a hurry.

"Like, two in the morning? Seemed you didn't want to be disturbed." Caldwell tried a salacious grin.

It didn't work very well. None of the disdain, in fact, worked at all. She wasn't embarrassed, or even very angry; more inconvenienced—the taunting took time. "Where is he now?"

"What's wrong?" asked Caldwell bravely. "Like it in the morning?"

She towered over him; Caldwell froze. "You kids don't know what you're playing with. Checker disappeared from my studio, and I don't trust him. So you tell me if you've seen him and where. Now."

Caldwell took his feet off the table and fumbled with a guitar pick, clicking it against his thumbnail. "No, really," he said, looking up. "I'm sorry, I—haven't seen him."

"What about you two?"

They shook their heads.

Syria sighed and slumped against a post, sliding her palms down her thighs. "I woke his mother up, the park—"

"How come you don look for husband? He gone all night, you don care?"

Syria knocked her head gently against the post. She didn't turn around, and the level of her voice didn't vary. "Because, Chick-pea, you don't worry me. You've been through a lot of crap, you can take a little more."

Rahim strode into Plato's with as much of a Western bar swagger as he could manage, but he hadn't expected to find her here, and the sudden sight of her back through the door had set him shaking; he immediately had to sit down.

"In my country, you know what we do to you?"

"The whole point is to make this your country, Chick-pea. And here, we do jackshit."

"We cut off your head!"

"You're the worst of the lot." She pointed a finger at Rahim's chest. "Mr. Middle Eastern Melodrama. Well, spare us the spurned and betrayed number. Okay, so you want something and you can't have it. Ask your friend Rachel there, that's a hard nut to crack. But don't dump your disappointment on me, and whatever you do, don't dump it on Checker."

Rahim sulked at his lap. "I already dump on Sheckair."

"When?" she asked sharply.

"Not long ago."

"So he knows you saw us?"

"Everyone see you," he said, with eyes like awls. "*Gahba*." It was Arabic, but Syria had heard the word for "whore" before.

The charge seemed to bore her; she turned from Rahim and surveyed the room. "At least my husband stuck up for him. But when that viper lit into your friend in the park, what did the rest of you do? Any of you?"

J.K. ground a cigarette butt into the floor that had been out for days. Caldwell broke his pick in half. Rachel's hair frayed into her face.

"Right. With friends like you, who needs cardboard?" Syria turned and was about to go when one last Derailleur burst in the door. He leaned on the doorknob catching his breath.

"Ch—" he said. "Chuh—Chuh—Chuh—"

"Checker?" asked Caldwell.

"Tuh—tuh—tuh—" He shook his head wildly, as if rattling a radio with a bad connection. "Tried! To duh-duh-duh-drown himself!"

For a moment it was hard to decide which to find more incredible: the information or the fact Carl had delivered it.

Syria made an unusually small sound for a woman of such efficacy. She pressed her thumb between her eyes; air whistled through her nostrils. That was all. Slowly she let the thumb down and moved calmly toward Carl. She took his face between her hands. "Is he all right?" Her voice was music, keyboard, the lower middle notes, even tones.

"I duh-duh—"

"Take your time." Still, she held his face and looked at him and smiled; Carl did talk to his mother and he used to talk to Checker, and this was an interesting combination of both of them.

"I don't know."

"And where can we find him?"

"The r-river."

"In the river, or out?"

"Out."

"And where along the river?"

"In R-r-rah—Rah—"

She stroked over his forehead and crown and set a subtle

low vibration into the air that only Carl could hear, the very bottom end of the octave now, the pedal depressed.

"Ralph DeMarco, north of Hell Gate," he told Syria with perfect fluidity.

"And has anyone called an ambulance?"

"I—I did," said Carl, and the shy pride with which he told her this was quickly overtaken by the memory itself, dialing and stuttering horribly to strangers, listening to their exasperation, the way they kept trying to finish his sentences for him wrong and he'd have to say, "N-n-n-n-*no*" trying to give them the right address until he had to put in a second quarter; but that memory was swallowed by still another, the reason for the call, and Carl began to cry. Syria held him and hugged him hard and kissed him on the forehead and then said, "Bye."

The crusty Levi's crackled down Ditmars and vaulted the plum-colored railings of Ralph DeMarco, to the knoll where Checker Secretti was laid out on the grass like a piece of kelp.

Leaning over him, Howard was soaked and barefoot, his shirt plastered to his sunburn; his expression was of an intensity rare for Howard the worrier, the analyzer, the imitator. But then, Howard was in a flow state. Howard had little endorphins wriggling all through his body.

Howard was busy dredging up his Red Cross training, realizing that he'd never quite understood what the instruction "Clear the throat of foreign material" was referring to. It is a desperate experience to try to remember what you were taught two years ago while most of the class joked about artificially respirating some girls on the other side of the pool. Howard had already earned his Lifesaving certificate, and it was hardly fair to have to retake the test two years after the course was over.

Yet the human mind retains everything somewhere, and coughs up what it has to when the test is for more than convincing your mother you did something productive with your summer vacation; Checker was getting oxygen somehow. When Syria pulled him away, Howard resisted at first, not realizing she simply wanted to relieve him.

It wasn't a relief, actually; it's a lot easier to act in these situations than to watch, as the others also discovered when they screeched up in Caldwell's van, hurrying to—stand there. They could only pace and memorize the bizarre picture in front of them—Syria stooped over their friend with her hair spidering everywhere, and Checker Secretti sprawled as the heretic exemplar of his own religion, everything he despised: inert, stoic, humorless. Looming overhead, Hell Gate was only metal now, and mute; Ralph DeMarco belonged to the Park Commission—Checker himself didn't even own a laundromat. Color had fled its greatest fan; his fingers splayed fat and bleached over the grass like plump veal sausages. His lips showed more hue than the rest of him, but ice blue. The All Stars burbled in dingy brown water:

> It's the Checker time-chucking venture,
> The end of adventure;
> Striker's right, you're a dumb SOB.
> You spend your life in the drink
> Like time at the sink—
> You don't even get the ennui.

There was a moment as the ambulance screamed around the corner that Syria leaned over him and didn't rise again to take her own breath; the shade of his lips beneath hers warmed subtly from ice to cobalt, a richer, livelier blue. She let go of his nose, and instead put her hands behind his neck. Howard thought there was something wrong and started forward, but Caldwell restrained him.

"She's kissing him, stupid," muttered Caldwell. "He's breathing."

Checker's pudgy white arm reached up and clung to Syria's shoulder. Even the paramedics waited a respectful moment or so before lifting him onto a stretcher and slipping him in the back of the ambulance.

24 / comfortably numb

When Rachel rang the doorbell Eaton had been practicing in his living room, though he was grateful for the interruption. His own drums had turned against him. The bass was flat. The cymbals waffled and glared in the speckled sun, hitting weird harmonics that hurt his ears. He'd been playing along with *Wheels of Fire*, which usually gave him satisfaction, since he considered himself so much better than Ginger Baker, but this afternoon he couldn't seem to get through a whole song.

Eaton's drum set was clear Lucite. It was expensive and stylish, but in his nightmares the shells would disappear. The hardware would float over the floor. When he struck the heads, his sticks would pass through the rims and make no sound at all.

His mother ushered Rachel in and shot Eaton a hopeful, complicitous smile before padding away. It was about time.

Her son had been popular with girls since he was fourteen, yet despite his pervasive distractedness and secrecy, not a single female had phoned this whole last year.

Rachel advanced cautiously onto the ivory carpet, worrying about dirt on her shoes. The whole living room should have been wrapped in plastic. Except for the brown pressboard that protected the feet of Eaton's drum set from making indentations in the rug, every appointment was white or chrome. The wallpaper was expensive woven bamboo, the kind that looks delightful in a decorator's sample book and crushingly bland on the wall. Amid the glass and alabaster, sumi prints and kokeshi dolls gave the apartment an arbitrarily Oriental air.

"Has your mother been to the Far East?" Rachel asked.

"Sure," said Eaton. "Bloomingdale's. Way over on Lexington."

Rachel perched on the couch piping. "I've never been here before."

"I've never invited you." Eaton stayed behind his traps. Rachel was surely here on a mission of reconciliation. She was one of those women who have to have everything pink. She couldn't conceive of two people simply not liking each other.

He was right in guessing she was nicer than the rest of the band. "The others," she began, "didn't think I should bother. But you were a Derailleur, for a little while. Besides, you'd hear it soon enough. I thought it was better if one of us told you."

Eaton looked at her hard. He had always preferred keeping his own secrets to being let in on other people's. And he suddenly felt nervous. Rachel looked as if she desperately wanted to leave.

"Checker—" she went on, but paused, for she could as well have rolled a land mine onto the thick white carpet. They both stared stupidly at a spot in the middle of the room, as if the name had settled there and was so heavy that it would make a dent in the rug and Eaton would get in trouble. It was no longer possible to say this word simply. No wonder Eaton had started using "Irving." He couldn't say "Checker" out loud anymore.

Rachel proceeded carefully, not wanting to trip the mine, for while Eaton felt fear, Rachel saw only fury. "After we left Vesuvius," she said breathily, "he jumped off the bridge."

Into this perfectly inopportune moment Eaton's mother chose to intrude herself. She was a thin and tremulous woman, though not, as the decor might suggest, cold. The room was so immaculate because she was not daring or aggressive enough to believe she had a right to affect her environment in any way. Her own apartment cowed her; you could see by the way she tiptoed over the carpet and laid a mat under the tray, which itself was coated with a doily and piled with napkins and coasters. Even so, she glanced apologetically around the glass table, as if it could refuse her pimiento triangles, which might leave crumbs. And clearly she was terrified of her own son. "Eaton honey, I brought—"

"Mother," Eaton interrupted. "One of my friends has just committed suicide."

"My," she said faintly, now humiliated by these silly sandwiches, attentively manicured without an edge of crust, by having remembered both regular and diet soda, since girls always appreciate that, all in the midst of this—oh dear. "I'm so sorry."

"No, Mother. You're not sorry. You've never even met him. You're just saying that."

"For any young man, it's tragic—"

"How can you be all broken up when I don't give a shit?"

"Sweetheart, you can't say that—"

"I just did."

Rachel had been about to explain that Eaton had misunderstood, but was so fascinated and appalled that for now she kept quiet.

"Women," Eaton continued, looking at both of them. "You people have to have everything sanitized, don't you? All pretty. It's boring. Suicide? I'm not even surprised. He was weak. I tried to tell you that. Weak," Eaton repeated, convinced his voice was not making enough noise. In fact, it had grown rather thin. So had the Cream record, still playing; not only did it sound quieter, but as if someone had turned the bass to zero and the tenor to MAX—*White Room* whined like a faraway tree saw. And the whole apartment now seemed temporary somehow. Like a set. The walls looked hastily propped up, and Eaton was no longer convinced there was a larger building outside them. Everything seemed fake. The couch looked slipcovered, though he knew it was upholstered; the chrome looked like paint. Worst of all, when he stared down at his drum set the hardware began to float in its pool of Lucite, just as in his dreams. He reached out surreptitiously and touched the snare, finding it was there, but still not relieved. Oily sweat poured from his fingertips. Sunlight blotched his hands like liver spots.

So no more pavid solos from the calf skins. Eaton had

Astoria to himself now. He could play Plato's every weekend. Now he could—

He didn't care.

Eaton began to tremble. He held the drumstick before him and watched it shake. Dizzying apathy washed over him in waves, so that he could no longer sit up straight; his drumstick drooped to the invisible snare. In a panic he ran through topic after topic, groping for a hook. He didn't care about Cream, The Who, Steely Dan. Rachel: he didn't care about girls. Sandwiches: he didn't care about food. His mother, his room. Why were they looking at him so strangely?

"You never did understand, Rachel," Eaton went on. "Your friend bugged me. Bugged the hell out of me. I didn't like him." Eaton felt the way he sometimes did in the middle of a riff when no matter how much harder he struck the head, it was never loud or climactic enough. He kept trying. *"I'm glad he's dead."*

Rachel rose from the couch, now white as the decor. His mother looked down in apology. "Then I'm sorry to inform you that Howard pulled him out. He's in the hospital, a little beaten up, but he's going to be all right."

With a style of which Eaton would never have considered her capable, Rachel coolly picked up a pimiento sandwich and let herself out. When the door closed behind her, his mother approached Eaton on his throne, her hand gently extended in one of those moments of astonishing parental insight. She pressed his head to her breast as he pulled at her linen blouse and wept with relief.

*   *   *

S een Check today?"

"Yeah. Still *Night of the Living Dead*, man. Coulda been talking to the bedpan."

"When are they letting him out?"

"Out? Sweets, they talking Bellevue."

"They can't do that!"

"Can. He booked as suicide."

"They don't *book* you in a hospital."

"Might as well. Our man strapped in, you notice?"

"How'd they know Check did it on purpose?"

"Damnedest thing. Howard said they took one look at the kid and wrote S U I C I D E down on the form."

"I can't figure the whole thing, Big J. If somebody asked you the one guy in your whole life who'd never jump off a bridge, who would it be?"

So Checker had finally done the one thing that proved Check was not Check, after all. He had called his own fraud.

I f they took any satisfaction in their friend's not being who they thought he was, they would get more.

Howard's afternoon with Check had been as exciting as a visit with a bowl of stewed prunes. The patient refused to eat; the regular drip of a glucose IV had begun to make Howard sleepy, and as he left the room an orderly walked beside him.

"So Checkie made it one more time, huh? How many lives that cat got left? Three or four tops, I say."

"Yeah?" asked Howard warily.

"Now, this bridge number had class. Shoulda gone out on that one."

"Uh-huh," said Howard. "Excuse me, I forgot something." Howard turned on his heel and marched back into the room of the boy whose life he had saved—one more time, it seems.

"Check, let me see your wrist."

Checker obediently held out his hand.

"No, the other one." Looking Checker in the eye, meeting the glaucous whites head on, Howard unlaced the famous leather bracelet, angry for ever having admired it. The thong was sticky and kinked. Slipping the cuff off, Howard turned Checker's wrist in his hands. Long white worms squirmed two and three inches up and down the veins, with a dreadful neatness, laid out carefully parallel. Up and down, not across—a deliberate and well-researched job. It was like discovering an infestation of maggots.

Howard laced the leather back up hastily, with embarrassment, though Checker himself seemed placid enough and didn't even watch. He was staring dully out the window.

"So this is what you do on your days off," said Howard hotly.

"Not always," said Checker, in B flat.

"What else do you do?"

He shrugged, barely. "Stuff. Walk around."

"But not so *jacked*."

The same shrug, like a twitch.

"How many times have you tried this stunt?"

Checker waggled several fingers.

Howard kicked the hospital bed so that it wheeled a foot away. "Maybe that doctor's right, they should put you away."

Howard stalked out of the room and headed for Plato's.

W*alks around?* Walks around and tries to kill himself."
They sat at the table with their feet up, muttering "Huh" and "Son of a bitch." They were almost disappointed. They *were* disappointed.

"I like the idea of a female one hell of a lot better," said J.K.

"Or Check playing with a little red wagon off in the park. That's more—"

"Check."

Howard toyed with his pen clinically. "He's a manic-depressive," he announced, with that common terminological victory, as if to name something was to have it roped and tied.

Since the incident by the river Howard had commanded more respect, but Caldwell couldn't resist some of the old scorn. "Is that right?"

"You know what that is, don't you?"

"I guess. He gets happy. He gets sad. So?"

"In simple layman's terms, that's pretty much . . ." Howard enjoyed the new way they treated him, and didn't like this familiar glare. "Well, I thought you might like to know what he is."

"I know what he is, thank you, and you could as well call him Georgie Porgie—"

"Just like I know what *you* are?"

"What's that supposed to mean?"

"You know. J.K. knows. They don't know."

"Hey, How," J.K. intruded. "We all pretty worked up the other night—"

"Some of us more than others."

"I'm sorry," said Caldwell softly.

"What are you talking about?" asked Rachel.

"Please," said Caldwell. Rachel's opinion of him had been growing oddly important.

"*What?*" Rachel insisted.

Howard sighed. "We played that *prank*, taking Check's bike? Well, it was—stolen."

"Oh no!"

While they conferred on what to do about it, Caldwell tried to think of how he could properly thank Howard later.

"Soon Check may not be riding anything but an elevator between wards," said Howard. "Dr. Spritzer says if Check doesn't pull out of this autistic thing, that's it."

"Hey, Hijack," said Caldwell carefully, "been to see Check yet?"

"No."

"Why don't you, you know. Tell him it's okay or something. Try to snap him out of it."

But the boy slumped at the end of the table like bitter grounds in the bottom of a cup, and didn't look like the kind of present you sent to the bedridden to cheer them up.

* * *

You take my woman, you pay."

Checker looked down to the knife at his throat and back up again. His expression was flat and pasty, like unrisen pizza dough.

Rahim pressed the knife tighter, letting Checker feel its edge but still not breaking any skin. Checker raised his eyebrows and looked into the Iraqi's eyes with the indiscriminate friendliness of the mentally retarded.

"You don realize I come here to kill you?" In his frustration, Rahim removed the knife from Checker's throat.

He wiped the fingerprints off the blade with his sleeve. "Syria act like nothing wrong, you know that? . . . She come here often, yes?"

Nothing.

"And we have no rehearsal, no band. Everything fall apart because of you." He walked over to the chrysanthemums on the bedstand and pruned some wilting blossoms with his knife. "This better. Old flower is depressing." Rahim threw the blossoms away and brushed the petals littering the table into his hand with the blunt side of the blade. "You like food here?"

Checker shrugged and nodded at the IV.

"I find new recipe for bran muffin, with banana and yellow raisin? Vedy moist. You like bran muffin?"

Rahim opened the drapes, filled the pitcher, and poured some water in the vase. He straightened the blanket at the bottom of the bed, and neatly piled the newspapers and magazines Check hadn't been reading. All the while the Iraqi kept glancing down at his knife as if to remind himself why he'd come here, like checking a grocery list.

The area completely straightened, Rahim turned the knife shyly in his hands. "I buy just for you. Pretty, yes? You see handle?" He showed Checker the inlaid mother-of-pearl. "I shop vedy careful. Just like you say, no such thing as ordinary day. Ordinary knife. Special knife for Sheckair. You like?"

Checker nodded, and reached out to touch the edge.

"Careful! Is vedy sharp."

Rahim pulled Check forward and plumped his pillow. "You want you die so much, maybe I revenge, I don kill you. How you like that?"

Meanwhile, Checker's expression had gone from unleavened dough to congealed salad, and looked headed for a slightly runny blancmange. None of these did Rahim count among his favorite foods. "You know, Hijack don have such good fun since last time he clean toilet bowl."

Finally Rahim began to feel as angry as he'd planned to be when he first stalked in here. His best friend had turned from a dessert soufflé, a swirling zabaglione, a wild floating island, to this—tomato aspic, this—cornmeal mush, this—noodle casserole. Checker Secretti was an egg white at soft peak, a stiff whipped cream, yolks at lemon yellow, pound cake rising in the pan and splitting at the top. Checker Secretti was active yeast and a brand-new box of baking soda. He was the powdered sugar you sifted six times before folding it into the angel-food batter, so light that when you sneeze it flies all over the kitchen and you have to start again. Checker Secretti was burbling buttermilk biscuits and sugar syrup boiling over on the stove; a teakettle at high whistle, steam in the air. For two years Checker Secretti had been the icing on his cupcakes, the head on his beer. But now Rahim was looking at anything he'd ever made that disappointed—glutinous white sauce, lumpy curdled custard, fallen confections with dense layers of sad.

Rahim ground his sneaker in a semicircle on the linoleum. The rubber squeaked shrilly on the wax. "This is act, yes? When I leave here you play Danno on *Late Show* so loud and everyone dance and all the nurses fall in love with boy in 207?" His sneaker grabbed the tile, snarling. This time he leaned down and held the knife to Checker's throat in earnest. "I see you with Syria, I so angry, but I don hate you. I want to so much and I try, but I still remember swimming pool and hundred-dollar peanut. But when Quiet Carl come in door of Plato and say—when he say you try drown yourself, Sheckair, I hate you so hard I can't see. You hurt, well so? Think only you hurt? Think I don see my own brother cut in front of my eyes? Think Syria don hurt from her father, every, every day? This is good. You eat your pain. It is like cake, it is like butter. It is life as much as good times by river. You go bed with your pain like woman. You laugh with your pain like old friend. You think we feel sorry now? We don, we hate you. And we hate look at dumpling in hospital bed. So you don laugh, right this minute, I cut your throat in half."

Checker stared at Rahim, down at the knife and back again. "Let me get this straight," he croaked slowly, his voice dry from so little use. "You'll spare me if I fuck your wife, but you'll slit my throat if I won't laugh?"

Well, yes, that was pretty much the size of it; Rahim pushed the blade tighter against Checker's esophagus.

"Now that," Check squeaked, "is funny."

Rahim felt the sound rise under his knife. Nurses looked in the door. Rubber wheels squirreled to a halt. Checker's comatose roommate sat up in bed, looking wide awake and even professorily cogent, though he was still sleeping off anesthesia. He scrutinized Checker, his eyes bright. "What is that?" he asked. "Is he laughing or crying?"

Rahim lifted the knife off his victim and stroked the drummer's hair, the way Check had so often consoled him. "Is same," Rahim told the other patient. "We say, No dark, no day. Your roommate here, I wait for he will understand. This drummer boy, he can be pretty stupid." The Iraqi tugged his shirttail from Checker's fingers. While so much wider and more scarred, in this weak light and fastened to another man, those hands weren't so different from Rachel's. Rahim pulled up a chair. "You save your life," said the Iraqi softly, wiping the tears from Checker's cheeks. "Now, for jump off bridge, I not so sure. But for what you do with Syria: I forgive you."

Check sighed and collapsed back into his fluffed pillow. "Okay, Hijack. That's the best revenge in the end, anyway. Cause let me tell you, being forgiven is a totally disgusting experience."

"If I'd known suicide was such a good time, I would have tried it."

"Nah," said Checker. "Try it at your age, everyone figures you're embezzling funds."

The man who walked in the room was handsome and well, even sedately dressed, but with touches—a rebellious gleam in his black skin, a slyness to his pinstripe, a tie that only close up revealed a pattern of tiny red trumpets, a glint of diamond studs at his wrists—that showed something well covered but irrepressible. It shone through in the excessive, self-satisfied shine of his cordovans, the overly flashy design of his watch, and especially in the way he walked to Checker's bed, as if he'd been training for years to walk that slowly, that close to the ground; as if even this short distance took discipline not to run. He had learned to walk the way he was supposed to, and to a casual observer he pulled it off. But Checker knew better, because Checker was his son.

Tyrone Secretti was a man who'd learned everything over again—to talk without getting off the subject, to sit at dinner and not play tunes on the tines of his fork. No, he went to four-star D.C. restaurants and muttered that the fish was overdone. He had learned to look bored; he had trained himself not to draw pictures on his *Congressional Record*. Strolling down the common of the Smithsonian, he did not take his shoes off, or balance on the rim of the reflecting pool. He stayed on walkways with his shiny cordovans and his careful imitation of a middle-aged man rushing somewhere important.

"I wanted to bring you a present. So I wondered, are you still friends with that Iraqi illegal?"

"Ask him. Hijack, this is my father."

They shook hands.

"Well, it was a little difficult because your *mother*"—he rolled his eyes—"got the name wrong, but once I sorted that out—"

"I thought they were doing an investigation."

"Investigation! The INS—" Tyrone laughed. "The computer was down, as always. But I managed to find one of those antiquities who could still work a typewriter." He reached into his wallet and handed Rahim a card. "Technically you have to stay with your wife for two years to apply for citizenship. If you'd prefer not to do that, I can slip a bill through Congress that would naturalize you right away. That usually costs two or three thou, but those characters owe me a few favors."

Rahim looked from the card to Tyrone as if his fairy godfather had just floated down from the sky. Then he looked at Checker. "Why—?"

Checker shrugged. "He wouldn't do it before."

"Don't think jumping off a bridge is how to get your way with me," said Tyrone severely. "But I decided I'd been too harsh."

"I like the congressional idea," said Checker. "It's got style."

"Listen, it's gratifying to be *effective*, Check. I'm telling you, there's a whole other level out there you haven't touched—"

"So you've enrolled me in Yale and you've already marked the good poli sci profs in the catalogue."

"I didn't come here to argue—"

"You came here to lecture instead. Which is just an argument where I don't get to talk."

His father sighed. "Forget it."

"You got Hijack his green card to impress me, didn't you?"

"Sure."

"Well, good. I am impressed."

They smiled. Truce. "So am I. I met a woman in the hall—"

"Syria. Did you like her?"

"She's terrifying! And not too pleased with you at the moment."

"Nobody is."

"I sensed a—storm on the horizon. Man to man, I felt I should warn you."

Rahim had been examining the card in his hand, its eerie waves of beige rippling through the photo like alien weapons on *Star Trek*, the long rows of inexplicable numbers, his own beloved fingerprint on the back. He realized he might be looking not only at entry into a new world but at his divorce papers. For such a thing he couldn't bring himself to say thank you, so, twisting it in his hand half hoping it would break, he took leave of Checker and his father, saying, "Is not green!" and rushing out the door.

Alone, the two were uncomfortably silent. At last Tyrone mentioned, "It runs in the family, you know."

"You make it sound like a disease."

"An affliction, anyway."

"This happens to you?"

"I've got a milder case—"

Checker gestured at the suit. "So I see."

Tyrone paused. "I've never understood why you're so angry at me."

"Neither have I."

"This problem—you can turn it to your advantage."

"So far it hasn't exactly been a lucky penny."

"Your glassblower friend knew precisely what I meant. There are engines fueled by garbage, did you know that? You can even get energy out of manure."

"I should run off my own shit?"

Tyrone shrugged. "Power is power."

"I have a feeling we're not talking about the same experience."

"Why is it so important to you that we're totally different? That I couldn't possibly understand you?"

Checker smiled. "I'm nineteen."

His father reached out and touched his leg. "See that you turn twenty, then." Averting his face, he said goodbye hastily and bounded from the room.

He heard her talking to the cigarette man, the boots clomping on the resonant linoleum. He could sense when she leaned on the other side of the wall, smoking, though she'd quit years ago. The smoke would spiral past his open door. The longer she waited, the worse it would be.

She had something to tell him and was putting it off. Of course Checker could have predicted it. She was twenty-nine; she ran her own business. Though wearing thin in places, she still turned more than heads; he'd seen men stop and wheel in the street. And he was a kid. They'd flirted for months, and that builds up a certain tension. Right, she found him attractive. Finally they'd screwed; now it was awkward. And he'd gone and done this *thing*, which made it harder to blow him off. She'd have to be sensitive about it. That wasn't her style.

At last she turned resolutely into the room, marching to his bed, looking at him with—he couldn't even say. He realized he didn't know her very well. What was that? Disdain? Compassion? Like an umpire: decision. He wanted desperately to influence her in some way, but the play was made. In perceiving how little he could do now, Checker reclined farther into his pillow. Helplessness can be curiously relaxing.

He asked for a cigarette. She neglected to point out he didn't smoke, and flicked the lighter for him. Experimenting with his new prop, Checker felt as if he were in a movie. *We are so cool*, he thought. *I'll pay for this in a minute, but this is a riot.*

Syria sat down and crossed her legs. She folded her hands in her lap and leaned her head back, closing her eyes. Checker looked down at his formless hospital gown with its unflattering square neckline and no longer felt cool. He would have paid a nurse hundreds of dollars at that moment just to retrieve his favorite red shirt.

"They say you're talking again. I heard you laugh. It was nice."

Now he just wanted her to get this over with. He said nothing.

"You always a zombie afterward?"

"Sometimes."

"You snapped out just in time. This afternoon they're deciding whether to release you to a shrink or throw you in a rubber room. Looks about fifty-fifty. And they want to see you with your mother. Seems they'd meet with the whole jolly family, but Tyrone's headed back to D.C."

"It's sixty-forty for the rubber room, then. Unless they decide to cart her away instead."

"Or me. When I checked you in, I said I was your mother."

"Why?"

"So I could hang around overnight," she confessed with gruff embarrassment.

"Well, no danger of running into Lena here," he said sourly.

"Actually, she stopped by yesterday while you were asleep. I confused her at first, but she perked right up when I explained. All but handed over your baby pictures and bronzed booties. Told your roommate here she was your aunt. Ate it up, being your aunt. Frankly, kiddo, that's no hundred-dollar bill you've got there. She's retarded."

Checker took a pull on his cigarette and concentrated on not coughing. "Now Hijack has his green card, you getting a divorce?"

She poured herself some water and tossed it down like a shot of Scotch. "You bet. Time to call an end to this whole shebang, Checko. Too fucked up."

"Yeah . . . Hey, pour me some water, too?"

They each kept having to touch something.

"You remember jumping, Checko? The fall?"

"Sure. But I don't know if I could describe it."

"Try."

"Now?"

"Why not?"

"It took a long time," he began. "There was a lot of wind, shooting up my nose and down my throat, cold—but otherwise it was like in an airplane. The air was big and stuffed, like a First Class recliner. I half expected a stewardess to come along midway to the river and offer me a complimentary cocktail."

"What would you order?"

"Something special." Checker leaned back. "A *mimosa*. I like the word . . .

"I looked around. Everything seemed, I don't know, *neat*. The sun was rising. My eyes watered from the wind, but the tears cleared over my temples fast enough so I could still see. The park got all crisp, see, with the pool, and I thought, It's *so* blue.

"Well, I thought about practically everything. Even you, a little . . . Till toward the last it was like the end of your flight, when you get restless and look at your watch and you've read all the magazines. Except I don't get bored flying much. I fly to D.C. to see my dad, and I love taking off, pressing back in the seat; I love landing . . ." Checker's voice died off. "Do you get sick of me saying how much I like stuff?"

Syria considered. "Not that I've noticed. But I guess if I had to listen to how great every goddamned thing was for the next fifty years I could get pretty sick of it."

"But we're not talking about the next fifty years, are we?"

"No," she said casually. "We're talking about jumping off a bridge. Go on. I'm interested."

"Well, right as I hit the water I felt—" Checker squirmed. He wanted to get this right. "In Vesuvius," he continued slowly, "when we—"

"Fucked."

"The studio went all white. And on the cable, everything went black. But right when I hit the river everything went black and white at the same time."

"Checkered."

"Yeah! I was—bummed out of my mind and—jacked to the hilt. I've never felt anything like it. Sometimes I feel so good it hurts, you know that feeling? So it was like there was a knife in my back that was this sadness, and the other, the good pain, like a knife under my ribs, and the very tips of the blades met and clicked in the center of my body. Does that sound crazy?"

"Yep."

Checker slumped. End of swan song. Weak applause. "Well, I tried."

"I think you should work on some metaphors that don't involve lethal weapons."

Syria got up and paced around the small room, picking things up and then tossing them down again as if they'd done something to annoy her. "Listen," she said, clawing into her hair, "we have to talk."

"I guess I thought that's what we were doing."

"Yeah, well." She stood with her hands in her pockets, her back to him. *There will be a lot of disappointments. Toughen up.* Checker looked over at Syria because he could swear she said that, but she was only looking out the window.

"You remember you went to see your friend Rachel here, and you were afraid to set her off again, so you told her something was possible that wasn't? What did I say you should've done?"

"Told the truth."

"Because you can't treat people like porcelain. They have to live in the world the way it really is, right?"

"Uh-huh," said Checker dully.

"If they can't take the way things are, they should go ahead and kill themselves, because you can't make a whole other world for them, you can't protect them, it's too big a job, isn't that right?"

"Uh-huh."

"So I'm not likely to come in here, believing that, and tell you something you'd like to hear just because I don't want you to do something crazy."

"Sure," said Check, his voice cracking a little. He cleared his throat. *Relax, just keep your legs parallel, rest your palms sticky side down on the sheet. Let this go by. Listen and nod and take it, and wait very, very patiently for this to be over. She has to leave this room eventually, she'll even want to.*

"But I do want you to tell me," she said, turning to look him straight in the eye. "If I say that you and I are a lousy idea and I'm not interested, what are you going to do?"

"I'm not going to kill myself, Syr," he croaked, "if that's what you mean."

She sat down again. "Why did you jump off that bridge, Checko?"

"Hijack . . . Because Eat was right . . ."

"Yeah?" she said skeptically. "But without Chick-pea you'd have jumped because you burned your dinner or your geraniums died." She leaned in closer. "It's only that chickenshit crumpling of yours, isn't it? And if you think I can save you, forget it. I have my own life and my own work and I expect you to take care of yourself. If you want to hang out in hospitals, I'm sorry—visiting hours are during my classes, got it?

I need a man who can really fuck and really play drums and really wake up in the morning. If you're not up to that, forget it."

Checker looked a little dazed. "Forget what?"

Syria rolled her eyes with that huge, powerful irritation with which she felled benches and smashed glass off punties and poured barrels of cullet into the furnace mouth. "Forget marrying me, asshole."

There was a long and awkward silence, during which Checker rehearsed back to himself her entire speech, and then farther back to everything before that, and only when he had run through this sequence three or four times did he allow himself a shy little smile. He flipped the sheet off and put his feet up on the railing, clasping his hands behind his head. "Maybe I don't want anything more to do with you. Maybe I just wanted into your filthy jeans and that's the end of it."

She faltered. "And maybe I'm the man in the moon," Syria returned, but a little late.

He smiled again. "Maybe."

"You're getting uppity."

"Yeah. Yeah, that's kinda the idea. You think that's what you want, but you'll be surprised. I don't think you'll like it much at all. You loved pushing Hijack around. You can't do that with me. I'm an American."

"Is that so?"

"Yeah. And stop condescending. It's not my fault I'm nineteen."

"All right," said Syria, rolling up her sleeves. "I won't humor you. This is middle-class adolescent histrionic crap.

Why be a glutton for suffering? It arrives in the mail! Murder, diseases, nuclear war. Plenty guys would throw you off that cable, for ten dollars or for kicks."

"One thing I like about you is your cheerful perspective, Syr."

"No, but I like yours. Clearly I can use it." She looked at her watch. "Listen, we've got to get down the hall and convince those doctors you're ponderously sane."

"Am I?"

"Maybe you should forgo sanity for charm. It's actually a more attractive quality."

She helped him loop the feeding tube around its stand, and together they walked down the hall wheeling the IV behind them, like a pet. She held his arm, and the IV went squeegy-squeegy.

"One of my students is a diver, and I told him about your adventure on the bridge. He asked me when the funeral was. I told him you made it without even a broken bone. He said that was incredible. He said even for a skilled diver that was high. I laughed. I told him you were good at things. Because you did it *right*, didn't you? You couldn't help yourself, you wanker, you do everything well. And you had a wonderful time on the way down, isn't that what you were trying to tell me? I think you survived because you *enjoyed* it."

"Does it ever occur to you I'm only nineteen? What I'll be like in a few years? Ever make you nervous?"

"Sure. I like being nervous. But you haven't seen me yet at forty-five."

Now that was a threat.

Howard has a nickname

25 / spirits in the
material world

As Drs. Finding and Spritzer paged despairingly through Checker's voluminous file, Checker remarked, "Kind of like *Friday the 13th*, huh? Too many sequels."

Spritzer shot him a grim smile, determined to get to serious business, but Checker was learning he could play people like drums, and this was a pretty solo. He mocked his past failures in a comic refrain, threw in a few incisive accents of self-perception, a riff of elegant irony, even a beat or two of silent emotional reflection. He colored the performance with a careful balance of regret and onward-ho. He led Finding into a long cadenza about how hard it must be for a psychiatrist to help a patient he dislikes. Spritzer followed progressive rock, and wondered what Checker thought of *The Queen Is Dead*. They moved their chairs closer to the drummer. Checker smoked another cigarette.

Syria kept putting her hand over on Checker's thigh and remembering she was his mother and taking it back again. They asked her about Checker's childhood, and Syria expounded fluently. He'd had depressive episodes as a kid, she said. But the rest of the time he was amazing. He'd set up pots and pans all over the kitchen and play them with serving spoons and spatulas. Cookie canisters with paper clips for a snare . . .

The doctors canceled their next appointments. Still, they ran overtime. Finally they looked at their watches with evident regret and closed Checker's chart.

"I don't think we have to—" said Finding.

"No, you really do seem pretty—" said Spritzer.

"If we could see you once a week, I think—"

"Twice," said the younger man. "Considering the severity—"

"Twice, then," Finding agreed. "In fact, I personally would be happy to—"

"Oh no," said Spritzer. "Your caseload is so heavy, Dr. Finding, I really should take Mr. Secretti's—"

"We'll discuss this later," said Finding severely.

"I'm doing a study that Secretti would fit so—"

As the foursome lingered in the hall, Howard Williams stormed toward them in his new dark glasses. He paced beside the group, clicking his mechanical pencil against the clasp of his clipboard, making a note or two, humming, tapping his new pointy leather shoes, a luminous fuchsia.

"You spring the kid?" Howard asked Syria tersely once the doctors had pumped Checker's hand and argued off down the hall.

"Looks like it," said Syria.

"Address that matter we discussed?"

"Not yet, so go ahead."

"I've been talking myself blue in the face for two years and he doesn't listen to me. You said you would—" Howard stamped his foot. "You said—"

"Could I please get my jeans on?" Check intervened. "My ass is hanging out of this gown."

Checker stood outside Astoria General smoothing down the nap of his jeans, now purged of river water and exuding the severe, punitive smell of hospital laundry. They'd thrown out his T-shirt; Checker rolled up the sleeves of the new red flannel Syria had maternally brought him, thinking if he wanted a wife instead of a parent it was going to be a fight. Probably the easiest way to get her off his back would be to get her pregnant.

"Why are you smiling?" asked Syria.

"Nothing. It just—feels good here."

It was Labor Day. Traffic was light. The first wisps of cooler fall air trailed through his breath. Late afternoon, sixish—he didn't know, since he'd ruined his watch in the dive. Checker twisted the big leather cuff. Howard had laced it up too loose, and now it hung down on his hand so that the tops of the scars showed.

"So how about a little dinner action?" Howard proposed, taking charge.

"The Neptune?"

"No, somewhere decent. I say the Charcoal Grill."

"That isn't hamburgers, Howard. I've heard it's like twenty plus, no frills."

"On me," Howard dismissed. "*Tax deductible*."

Unprepossessing as it might sound, the Charcoal Grill is Astoria's poshest restaurant—Italian, a little garish with the fountain in front, but the waiters pad between tables hush-hush—taking orders in whispers with little bows—more of the neighborhood's characteristic innocent pretension. Howard fit right in—demanding lobsters all around, and a Beaujolais Villages that he pronounced like the name of a condominium development. He kept his sunglasses on, and slipped his mechanical pencil behind his ear.

"Howard, this is going to cost—"

"Ah, listen," said Howard, taking the pencil back out and chewing on the eraser with deliberation. "Since that incident the other day? We're canning the 'Howard.'"

"How, we've been through this name thing—"

"Uh-uh. No 'How,' even."

"So what is it this time?"

"Sidestroke," Howard muttered shyly.

"Did you come up with that—?"

"No," Howard whispered. "Sweets did."

"No kidding."

"No kidding."

"Pretty decent of the guy."

"Well, it just sort of—came about, you know. And it's sticking. I know it's your stroke, though, if that bothers you I—"

"No, take it. Howard!" Checker exclaimed proudly. "Sh-sh!"

"I mean, Sidestroke, you sly dog, you got a nickname."

"Yeah." Howard glanced away, readjusting his glasses and clearing his throat. "Anyway," he tried to continue, through Checker's laughing and beaming. "We've got a proposition."

Officiously Howard laid out the record company's offer while they slurped down their oysters on the half shell and Checker went through three baskets of Italian bread. (He was starving. Glucose just didn't cut it after a while.) "They've been trying to get you all week," he explained. "I decided it wasn't in our best interests to say, Well, guys, do they have twenty-four track at Bellevue? So they think you're holding out, that you've got other offers. I've gotten them to triple their original bid, but I don't think they'll go much higher. I think we should take it."

"You've got a knack for this, *Sidestroke*," said Syria.

Checker kneaded his forehead. "I've told you over and over—"

"All right, Pyramus," said Howard. "Hit it."

Checker turned with a groan to Syria, who shot him a sweet warning smile.

"I'm happy in Plato's—"

"Don't make me laugh."

He made himself laugh. "You can't do the right things for the wrong reasons—"

"I'm confused," said Syria flat out.

"I don't want to please a bunch of midtown executives."

"Too late, you already have. Besides . . ." she added slyly, twirling a feeler.

"What?"

"It would be fun."

Checker looked as if someone had hit him in the head.

"There's a big world out there," she went on. "Play with it."

Something clicked. It was as if someone had opened the gate by the swing set and let down the fences around the kickball field and suddenly, instead of the playground dissolving, it took over everything outside. Checker felt the presence of Manhattan behind this restaurant tingle up the back of his neck. The skyline teased him. *Here, look, it said. You've learned to like oysters? I am your oyster. Both shiny World Trade Towers baubles for your amusement. And plate glass? I'll show you plate glass. You are the protector of the fragile and the beautiful, so I will trust you with miles of tinted windows and dozens of quaint corner bars with proprietors who will stand you drinks when they recognize your face from videos. Did you know in the lobby of IBM there are whole bamboo trees? Climb them. Ride my elevators up and down. Take my helicopters and land on the roofs of buildings. Don't be afraid. I take only what you offer, but I want what you have. There are grown-ups in penthouses here who could use a good laugh. Sit them down and play your latest riffs with well-weighted silverware on the shining obsidian of the bright bar, and I will order you a mimosa. Feel the plush salmon pile of the upholstery tickle your fingertips hair by hair.*

Hello, Checker kept thinking. Hello, hello. We've never talked before. We have a lot to discuss. Checker felt as if he were making an appointment. How does Friday sound to you? So he let Syria and Howard continue, and enjoyed their convincing him. "Go on," he said, cracking a lobster claw and dipping it in the drawn butter. "Do it."

"You said recording was the best thing that's happened in a hundred years," said Howard. "Better than the airplane, you said. And radio? You can't believe it's free, you said. You'd pay, you said. You sent Danno a dollar once, remember?"

Syria asked him as if reading an oath, swearing him in, "Do you love rock and roll?"

"Yes."

"Do you love your own songs?"

"Yes."

"Are you glad that musicians you admire are widely available for $5.99?"

"$6.99," said Howard.

"$7.99," said Checker. "But a bargain."

"I rest my case."

"You rest jackshit," said Check. "Do you love glass?"

She didn't respond.

"Do you love your own work? Because that room in the back of Vesuvius is beginning to look like a crystal concentration camp. Are you planning to teach people to 'center their piece' and 'flash the punty' and do production goblets for the rest of your life?"

Syria worked the meat from a lobster leg meditatively with her teeth. "Howard, we've created a monster."

"You get yourself a gallery or I stay in Plato's until my arteries harden into lead pipes."

"I don't care what anyone thinks of my bones," said Syria. "They're none of your business."

"They are now."

It was something between an agreement and an impasse. That's the way it would always be with them, too: perfect loggerheads. They would take turns being irresistible force and immovable object.

Howard was not clear on what had just happened, but it was time to get to Plato's for The Derailleurs' private party, and he desperately needed rescuing from this lobster. The crustacean lay in a crumple of meat and shell, less like an animal he'd eaten than one he'd run over.

Outside the Charcoal Grill, Checker was suddenly reminded that he had no bicycle. A strange feeling—bad, of course. Yet it's a relief to be delivered of anything. He didn't have to worry about grease, or if someone had stolen her seat. One of the horrors of all deaths is how nice they are, really. No more responsibility—for your plants, your dog, your mother.

As they approached Plato's, Checker had to remind himself he'd been here last week, for he felt like a visitor years later; he half expected a different paint job and new management. Maybe they'd finally put in a row of blinking lights along the perimeter of the bar and veneered over CS + LS with plastic laminate. The waitress would be courteous but inattentive. They'd look around Plato's (Chumpy's now? Barky's. Socrates'), quietly sipping the new brand on draft, paler and cheaper than the old Bass ale. There'd be a poster on the door advertising a new band, The Eviscerators, though no one would be playing yet; the three of them were all so very much older that they came to nightclubs at eight o'clock and went to bed before the band began. Checker, he upbraided himself, you sound like Caldwell. Whatever happened to him?

Yet when Checker walked in and the knotty-pine paneling remained, the initials still polyurethaned into his favorite table, and the familiar band members around it not noticeably older than one week, this quality of visitation did nothing but increase. And it was not Caldwell's nostalgia, either, for he did not feel a harking backward. Checker walked to his friends with a steady finality that was neither happy nor sad. It was one of the most interesting moments of his life.

The band, too, felt the amount of time that had passed, for calendars lie; real time is not mathematical at all. While we can leap decades like brooks, some of us will spend the rest of eternity slogging our way through a particular five minutes. That they had only been rehearsing for the Astoria Park concert ten days before was an uninteresting technicality, and they had to resist reminding each other, Remember, we used to play together, back then.

Checker stepped into the candlelight, his face flickering like the image of someone whose likeness you cannot quite recall. He kept looking familiar, then not, distorting and fading as the flame bent from the draft of the door. The circle tensed. They gripped each other's hands as if in a séance where they had inadvertently conjured a spirit when no one really believed in ghosts.

Caldwell deliberately broke the spell by leaving for the men's room, to return, coasting, braking at the toe of Checker's sneaker. "It's your suicide present."

As Checker stroked the frame it shimmered and twitched like the withers of a horse. The finish tingled, a quick metallic blue. He lifted the entire machine with one forefinger. Light.

"Campagnolo, top to bottom," said Caldwell.

Checker spun the pedals, and their bearings sang like a well-rehearsed choir. The brakes grabbed at a touch and leaped back at release. The bike seemed to have a hard time standing still. It didn't like being inside. A racer. High-strung, nervous, recklessly wild for speed. Something you went places on.

But it was young and new, and they were strangers. Without history, it would stream down the street because it hadn't learned yet what happened when you hit a metal plate at thirty-five. A kind of stupidity, actually. Blankly cooperative, it would sweep underneath him, but it would do that for anyone. It had not learned loyalty, or its price. A few accidents down the road and they'd understand each other better, he supposed.

"What's wrong?" asked Caldwell.

"Sorry," said Checker. "I mean, thanks. It's not Zefal, that's all."

"Yeah, well," said Caldwell. "You can't have Zefal, right? So you just tool up to the next one. Who knows, maybe tomorrow you'll take this blue sucker and roll it under a fat M-5. Then you get a black one or a red one or a motorcycle, right? You just keep the program moving."

Somewhere in there Checker recognized his own philosophy; what he didn't recognize was Caldwell saying it. Or Rachel confirming it. Or the two of them holding hands.

"Exacta," said Checker.

"What say?"

"His name. Exacta."

Everyone was relieved. For Checker to name something was to accept it. "*He* this time?" asked Caldwell.

"Zefal always made my girlfriends jealous." Checker smiled. "If they had any sense. But I've got better ways to keep a wife on her toes."

"Sheckair," asked Rahim heavily, "make wife?"

"That's right," said Checker. "You can keep the country, Hijack. But I don't think you get the girl."

Checker wheeled around the nightclub, the click of the freewheel sharp, Exacta tugging underneath, Checker sternly keeping him from careening into chairs. When he rode past the stage, Check came up so short he was thrown off the seat. He dismounted and put down the kickstand. "Where are my drums?"

"It's got a cyclometer, too—" Caldwell pointed at the handlebars. "Digital. Four different functions—"

"Sweets. The drums."

Caldwell pressed the "mode" button on the cyclometer—one, two, three, four—and breathed. "They're gone."

"Uh-huh," said Checker, without any noticeable horror. "Where?"

"Eat sent them to the cornfield."

"Seems they got a parking ticket," said J.K., and explained with merciful brevity. "But, Check, we looked into it. We want to replace the traps, but they hundreds—"

"Don't worry about it."

Slowly Caldwell and J.K. looked directly in Checker's

eyes for the first time since he'd said the word "drums." They were a serene blue. His hands were in his pockets. He sprang gently on the balls of his feet. He kept looking around at the band and smiling.

"Why aren't you upset?" asked Caldwell.

"Like you said, keep the program moving."

There was an art to losing things, as Zefal's disappearance had trained him. You just—let go. Like dropping a leaf in the river and watching it float downstream.

"I thought they were your best buddies. That you talked to them. Celebrated their birthday."

"Syr pointed something out the other day," said Check, gesturing to the glassblower. "She said she's the same way with glass. Talks to it. Names it. But when it breaks or slumps too much in the annealer it doesn't touch her. She says—" He stopped, and looked back to Syria; she nodded for him to continue. "She says the bike, the drums, the bridges—it's not them, they're things. See, when you're very big, she says, you take up a lot of space. Your body doesn't begin to cover it. So you—infest stuff. Inhabit, she said. She said that's why I need bridges, because they're so big. She said I'll need even more space soon, that I can live in the Manhattan skyline now. And later I may need horizons, she said. That she'd take me to volcanoes. Syr says they're about the right size for her; right, Syr? She says she's real comfortable on Krakatoa."

"Yeah, well, we think you're big, too, Check," said Caldwell, swallowing. "You tell him the deal, Sidestroke?"

Howard tapped his mechanical pencil as if flicking an ash. "We're negotiating."

"Cause we have one more present, Check," he went on haltingly, having rehearsed this too many times. "We want you to go to CBS. Don't worry about us. We don't want to hold you back. We want to say we knew Checker Secretti when he was a kid. We all like to play, and we're not gonna quit. But you've got a chance to be more than any of us could ever be, and we think you should take it. We're proud of you, Check. We're giving you a ticke˙ out of here."

"And what if I don't want to go?"

"We're telling you, we won't play with you. We refuse. And not because of Taxi, that's not going to fly—"

"Don't you think you should tell me that first?"

The Derailleurs froze.

"We was gonna tell you, Strike," said J.K.

"How considerate," said Eaton, closing the door coolly behind him. "But it's just as well. I'm working on a couple of backers who are interested in putting together a top-flight commercial band. Going out and buying the best of everything. And we certainly don't need to bail out low-self-esteem cases in Queens." Eaton turned from Caldwell and J.K. and didn't address them again. "Well," he said to Checker. "Resurrection and all."

"They skipped that in the opera, did you notice?"

"Maybe for good reason. I've always thought the ending of the New Testament was a cheat. Like stories that end: *And then he woke up and it was all a dream.*"

"Disappointed I rose again from the East River?"

Eaton shrugged. "Suicide *attempts* are kind of faggy, don't you think?"

"But a successful suicide isn't?"

"There's no such thing," Syria intruded.

"Stay out of this," said Checker sharply.

"How can you stand there being so civil? That kid chewed you up and spit you over the rail—"

"I *am* civil," Checker overrode. "You and I are different. Don't interfere or I'll kick you out. It's my party."

Syria glared and flounced into a chair, putting her boots on the table with a clomp of protest.

"So I threw you off the bridge, did I?"

"No, you don't get credit for that one."

"You mean blame."

Checker's smile twitched. "Whatever."

"You sure managed to dish out a good case of the guilties," said Eaton. "A regular plague."

"Did you really feel guilty?"

Eaton considered. "I was more disappointed. I'd figured you for better. It required so little to take you down. An easy victory's a bore."

"Victory?"

"Well."

Checker rested his fingertips on the table beside him. Only the exact top ridge of every whorl touched the wood. He was sure he was capable of resting his fingers this delicately only because he was so strong. Total power; perfect restraint.

"In some ways I admired it," said Eaton.

"Why?"

"You needed to make a big move. The dive was clever.

Really pumped the sympathy around here. Big tearjerker stuff. So, yeah. I was impressed."

Checker's eyes were neutral. In his mind he sealed Eaton in a plastic bubble, so that everything the boy said simply bounced back to Eaton himself. Eaton would be all right in there—it was big enough to breathe—but he had better be careful or he'd hurt himself. Eaton seemed aware of his encasement, acting newly guarded. He would have to keep his projectiles small, for he couldn't afford to throw anything he couldn't take bounding back in his own face.

"Well, I'm not impressed," said Check. "I think it was stupid."

"Of course you have to say that," said Eaton blackly, but a moment later every drip of that acid splattered Eaton's way, and he rubbed his arms, stinging, and he thought, *Where did this come from? I hate you, you're hurting me.*

Check said nothing, still standing with his fingertips on the table, looking horribly mild.

I totaled you, and you're smiling? Don't you want to get in a few licks? Come on, tell me I'm a lousy musician. Tell me I'm a slimy two-timer who seduced your whole band away from you. Tell me I'll never amount to anything, and then I'll tell you, I'll show you, I'll—

"I can't take the suspense," Eaton hastily interrupted himself. "You going to sign with CBS or not?"

"Sure," said Check.

Eaton snorted. "No big surprise, I guess. A lot of talk, but when it comes down to—"

"That's right. No big surprise."

"You're pretty ambitious, aren't you?"

"Yes. Though for something in particular."

"Madison Square Garden."

"No. Just a good life."

"Such a humble guy."

"That's not humble. It's arrogant."

"Still churning out the old cult philosophy. I expect to see you any day now on the subway collecting quarters for Happiology."

"I meant it. I'm arrogant. You were right, Strike, I think I'm hot stuff; it's like, disgusting. And I've got you partly to thank for that."

"Lost me, partner."

"I heard you played some heavy metal on my traps."

"Yeah, well." Eaton shifted uneasily on his feet.

"I just wanted to say thanks."

"What."

"I was flattered. You've studied down at the Collective and all. You know your stuff, so your opinion means a lot to me. You've given me confidence. I figure if you're right, I can go to midtown and knock 'em dead."

"What," said Eaton.

"Well, Strike. You've got standards. You wouldn't smash to bits just *anybody's* traps, now, would you?"

Eaton's and Checker's eyes met and flashed. "Nah," said Eaton. "I'm a picky guy. But I had it in for those drums from the beginning, Check. As you would say: they didn't like me."

"Those heads didn't dislike you, Strike. They didn't understand you. They never figured out what they did to deserve all that punishment. They tried to cooperate, but you were never satisfied. They could see how you'd play and then how unhappy you'd get, and it made them blue, Striker. They wanted so badly to please you and they couldn't and you broke their hearts."

"Spare me the projection, and please spare me the sympathy."

"No, sympathy is my revenge. We've all got a petty streak, I guess. Let's face it, Eat, you deserve it. Take your pity like a man."

"You think I'm total plant lice, don't you?"

"Actually—no. I think you're a good drummer, and you love rock and roll as much as I do. We've got the same tastes. You've got a crack brain—"

"Cracked brain," said Caldwell, but Checker ignored him.

"I mean you're sharp. And you're pretty goddamned funny. You've got a bite, I like it. See, the hysterical thing is, I probably like you better than anyone else here does. I think a lot of you, Striker. I figure I like you better than *you* do."

"This holier-than-thou-turn-the-other-cheek routine is making me gag, Secretti," said Eaton, but he turned away from Checker as he said it, because he couldn't believe what he was hearing or that he wanted it so badly to be true.

"Eaton," said Checker softly, "why did you come here tonight?"

Eaton laughed bleakly, raising his hand to his face as if to shield himself from the glow of righteousness a few feet away. "You're not going to believe this."

"Try me."

Eaton attempted a snicker, but it came out plaintive, and though he tried to sound sarcastic, this came out completely straight: "I was hoping we could be friends." He turned all the way to the door now, his back to Checker. "Isn't that a laugh?"

"Yeah," said Checker quietly. "I said you were a funny guy."

As Eaton reached for the doorknob out, Checker raised his voice for the first time that night. "You know, you make me *sick*, Striker!"

Eaton paused, waiting with relief to hear a little parting vituperation to soothe him later in the park as he listened to the water slap against the rocks over the carcass of Checker's bicycle.

"I needed a friend, you asshole," Check went on. "I'm lonely. I could've used you."

Forcing one more shot, Eaton said, "Yeah, I'm sure you could've *used* me," and hating himself, he left the club.

"Lonely, huh?" said Caldwell, twisting his long blond hair.

Checker rolled a discrete grain of sand on the floor with the toe of his sneaker. "Thanks for the ticket to midtown, guys. But I would have gone anyway. The Derailleurs are out of gear, aren't they? I'm not leaving anything behind, am I?"

There was a glancing away on so many people's parts that there was no inch of the room that someone was not looking at.

"But were you serious about refusing to play with me? Even one last time?"

"You mean tonight?" asked Caldwell.

"Why not?"

"No drums—"

"I used to play on pots, cookie cans—"

"I made that up!" said Syria.

"Let's open the club. Round up some locals in the park. Carl. How about going down by the river and spreading the word we're going to play?"

Carl looked back at Check in stony panic.

"Q.C.," said Check, walking an interesting line between patience and anger, "I'm not in the mood for bullshit, you know? In fact, I may never be in the mood for bullshit again in my whole life. So yes or no?"

"Y-y-y—"

"No bullshit."

"Yes."

"Thank you." From then on "No bullshit, Q.C." was a miraculously effective phrase in tuning Carl's station.

They brought in the trash cans from outside and set them bottom up on the dais. Checker tapped down the line of bar stools until he found two at the proper pitch. He pinged over the liquor bottles and pulled the Wild Turkey, the Absolut, and the Glenlivet Plato's had stocked expressly for Eaton Striker, and lined them on a bench. Rachel found some resonant pan lids in the kitchen, which she hung on either side of a music stand. Checker stood on the stage itself and brought his foot down on the hollow wooden platform, *boom*. Everyone started.

"I found the bass."

Advertisement from a renowned mute proved an effective hook; a full house began milling into the club. Word was out Check's drums were impromptu; filing past the stage, patrons brought Checker beer bottles, a discarded tailpipe, a rusty muffler, and the side of a grocery cart that went *ching!* One of the last donors delivered the actual head and rim of a tom-tom, and Checker took a minute to realize it was a scalp from his own set.

They played all night, from "Fresh Batteries" and "Frozen Towels" to "I Bared My Breast to the INS," after which Gary Kaypro hooted wildly. When they played "Walkmans Make Creepy Squealy Sounds" (*Hunky-dory we Derailleurs, / more-and-morey*), they fought back nostalgia and turned it to something else: Checker with his trash cans, thumping the dais with his All Stars, hitting the Wild Turkey and hundred-proof vodka, *ting-a-ting*, chips of rust from the muffler raining on the crowd, beer bottles breaking on the beat, the pan lids falling off the music stand, *pang!*—this would happen only once and then tomorrow everything would be different, but that was the deal, wasn't it? Every goddamned minute happened only once, and this was one more evening that would occur, precisely, with a certain rhythm as Checker wore holes in the galvanized garbage cans and his hands began to bleed. It was an evening precious exactly as every evening was precious, and when they thought, *We will never play like this again*, they also knew that had always been true—that each time The Derailleurs had ever assembled had been the only time they would play that way that night. It was a sensation of both infinite possibility and infinite limitation, for however precious it might be, the very singularity of each moment condemned it to something imperfect and concrete—each minute ticked by exactly as it actually happened, with the stuttering in Carl's announcement by the river, the high note in "Too Much Trouble" Rachel hit off key, the one drink too many that sent Caldwell off to the men's room for all of "Perpendicular Grates." There was no waiting, only this endless arrival, with its relentless demand that you compose this moment, and the next, that you do something with it besides *spend it over the sink, / Like money on drink*, a responsibility and an opportunity that so burdened Checker Secretti some nights that he carved his initials into his own wrist or flew into the sunrise toward nothing rather than have to make something one more time. It was hard and tiring and the clock was always running, but some nights you were up to it, and this was one of them.

epilogue / oh, you mean that checker secretti

Caldwell and Rachel lasted for two years, until she left him—which was wonderful for Rachel, though someone else usually suffers for that kind of self-improvement. Actually, Caldwell went through something of a bad period. It took work to put together another band, and members turned over lickety-split; nothing clicked.

As a bandleader, too, he began to sympathize with Checker's old woes, for taming wild egos was harder than tigers—he was tempted to show up at rehearsals with a whip and a chair. Yet all in all, moving on from The Derailleurs wasn't as awful as Caldwell had always feared. As long as you don't just sit in the corner and sob, most losses come with their compensatory gains. There was no replacing Check exactly, and there was no going back to the Old Days exactly, but there were other drummers, other days. Caldwell's latest percussionist has stuck around now for over a year. A young cowlicky kid with a crazy American eagerness, Randy is goofy and a little sloppy, but a lot of fun. And Randy's uncontemplative good cheer compares interestingly to Checker's elation. It's simple and responds to beer; Randy never disappears. Checker's euphoria is of a different order—richer and thicker; without source, and therefore a little frightening.

Caldwell is a karate instructor; his sensation of pure physical competence helps make up for his limitations on the guitar. Feeling proud and protective, tall and dangerous, Caldwell often hustles Checker into his limo from the back entrance of Radio City. Or the Beacon Theater. The Meadowlands . . .

What do you mean, "Oh, you've been talking about *that* Checker Secretti"? How many Checker Secrettis are there?

Caldwell tells himself so often: Lucky me. Guess who I grew up with. But it's never easy to watch your friend from the old neighborhood suddenly become the world's friend while you're still back in Astoria. You press your fingers to your temples when your friend gets *one more* phone call while you're trying to discuss your limping love life, and he has a long argument over whether the dust jacket should be graphics or lyrics, and you wonder: What's the difference between him and me, anyway? How did this happen? You meet his wife's eyes, whose career isn't going so hot and heavy either, and you think she's still a knockout and you remember she's said you're cute, so that for a moment when the two of you roll your eyes at each other you consider flirting with her; in fact, that's what you're doing. This is okay, just this, but then you deliberately break the gaze and militantly quash the twinges that keep coming at you, zinging into your gut like sharpened boomerangs, when you'd love to have an argument over dust-jacket design and even lose the argument, as long as there was a slim black disk, digital, soon out in CD, with your name on it inside. You remember the guy is good and he deserves it; you rehearse to yourself the songs you like, *Can't buy my bright blue weather, / Won't sell my good moods* . . . Of course, he has sold them, and for plenty . . . Quash! Even if the boomerangs are still coming at you, they aren't as frequent now, and you flick the crumbs around the kitchen table, refusing to look at his wife like that again.

Though you don't know it, your friend, who's seemed so engrossed in his phone call, actually doesn't care that much about the dust jacket and has been watching you the whole time; he saw that look at his wife, and he saw you break it off. He remembers the dozens of tiny difficult concessions you've had to make, the autographs you've been asked to secure, the conversations you've had with girls you were trying to pick up that they spent asking about your friend's personal life and whether he fools around on the side. He thinks about all the moments of generosity you take for granted, like the times down by the river when someone casually observes what an obnoxious big shot he's become and you stick up for him even routinely, though it must be tempting to agree.

Caldwell can go on record, then, as Checker's friend and fan from the vantage point of obscurity, and loyalty in someone's shadow sheds a certain soft gray light of its own.

* * *

J.K.'s lot was easier, for he took a fortunate turn right about the Ten-Year Week: *J.K. has decided his life is ordinary, and that's the way he likes it.* Checker doesn't approve of the word "ordinary," but Checker is now in little danger of using it. J.K. doesn't have any problem with the term at all. J.K. finds his life relaxing. He wouldn't actually want to be a professional rock musician, so often on the road and keeping long, odd hours. He likes to sleep in. He likes sitting on the stoop and tossing a ball with his daughter, making her chase it when he misses. He doesn't mind schlepping mail sacks for the post office as long as he gets to quit at 4:30; he looks forward to his pension. He loves leaning over the rail in the park and listening to NEW on his box, shooting the breeze with Caldwell and making plans to go on exotic vacations they will neither of them take, thank God. Those excursions pass the time under Hell Gate great, but to get on a plane sounds exhausting. Why go to Hawaii when the best corned beef is up the street?

For J.K. is actually better suited to the small-town Astoria life, with its slight passivity and complacency, than Check. He likes to eat and sit and stroke heavy, luxurious chords on his bass. He likes being an amateur musician, for he savors smallness for its real size, evenings that rest in his hand. Checker always had to expand Astoria into something huge and incomprehensible—he made the colors gorge and the bridges talk and, Jesus, the place couldn't have taken much more pumping up. This is *Queens*, for Christ's sake. Much more of Check's effusion and the whole neighborhood would explode.

* * *

Once he could ask for a three-pack of TDK's at Uncle Steve's instead of just pointing at the shelf, Carl's mother decided he wasn't hopeless, after all, and sent him to a speech therapist. Checker has promised that when Carl is ready he can arrange for Carl to interview him on Danno's *Late Show*. Q.C. is still so determined to be a disc jockey that in preparation for his debut he will talk to anyone, at length, so that everyone agrees that if there's a problem now it's that Quiet Carl never shuts up.

Of course, the only way to find an identity is to realize you have one already—"identity crises" resemble those frantic searches for keys when the ring has been in your back pocket the whole time. So Howard has decided not to fight but to join himself. He wears clashing plaids and fey pastels, Bermuda shorts and dark glasses with bright yellow frames. And as Checker Secretti's most fervid admirer, Howard has turned idolizing into a full-time job.

One that pays handsomely. Howard is a good manager. He makes CBS cough up the kind of money that he himself would shell out for Checker, pulling off historically unprecedented contracts. When Sidestroke flaps into CBS offices in his ungainly plaids, executives groan and clutch their wallets, wishing they'd taken a longer lunch.

Now that Rachel's greeting-card business is off the ground, she has less time for music, but her children brush their teeth quickly if she promises to sing them Checker's still unrecorded "In the Pocket" before they go to sleep. Rachel sings at weddings, around the piano at Christmas, and at Fourth of July picnics in Astoria Park; she's sometimes done guest appearances at Plato's with Caldwell and J.K.'s latest band. She sings over the dishes and in laundromats, and belts out "Too Much Trouble" walking down Ditmars past Checker's house. Music itself requires no contract, and all the former Derailleurs have appropriated it for their own purposes, whether for selling out Madison Square Garden or vacuuming the carpet on the stairs.

Most of all, she likes to tune in WNEW while making dinner with her husband, Lyndon, and between the Shadow Traffic reports from the "Blaupunkt R-E System" she'll point out, "That's your Uncle Check, boys." She sings along, Lyndon bruising garlic cloves with such simmering jealousy that he crushes them to pulp with the flat of his knife. Rachel will always have a thing for Checker, but she enjoys that now, even if Lyndon doesn't. She does sometimes think of Check when making love to Lyndon, and that bothered her when she was first married, but not anymore. She figures that when you marry someone, you embrace every man you've ever loved. It makes sense that the others visit from time to time.

Sometimes Check comes to dinner when he's in town and plays with the kids. She loves to watch him on the floor, because he doesn't humor the boys—he really enjoys rolling the trucks along the carpet, constructing a city with skyscrapers like the one he's just come from. They are the same for him, the big maple rectangles in Rachel's living room and the long, tinted windows at CBS; he gets every bit as involved in blocks as in buildings and doesn't come to the table until the food is cold. His attention never wanders but instead gets too acute, so that the kids' only complaint later is that Uncle Check always takes over.

Rachel has heard he's the same way with his own children, only worse; they've got three now. He obviously gets a lot of song ideas from them, like the last album, *Die, Daddy, Die.* It's still a little hard for her to see those kids, and Syria—but, boy, he pays for that woman, so they must have something. Everyone is waiting for her to mellow out, but Checker claims (rather proudly) that she's more likely to burn up than burn out. Rachel wonders where they get all that energy.

There was a time, too, when it looked as if they were really going to split, and sometimes Rachel secretly hoped it would happen. But Check was so wrecked then, sleeping on her couch or staying up all night in the studio in Manhattan or sacking out at Caldwell's, that she ended up rooting for them with a surprising sincerity. It seemed like such an impasse—Syria wouldn't take care of the kids while Check was on tour, but Check, who'd been raised, or not raised, dawdling by himself on the floor and ordering take-out Chinese at the age of four, wanted his kids to have a real mother. Furthermore, Syria still had no interest in ordinary domesticity, and though he'd warned her he wouldn't, Checker ended up doing most of the cooking and cleaning just to avoid a life of wall-to-wall sweaty green work shirts and crusts of pizza; besides, she was so *pissed off* all the time, and the whole business was about to crack until Rahim Abdul showed up last year.

He'd gone to cooking school and had been through the restaurant scene in several cities, and wanted to start his own catering business. He needed time to build a clientele and space to work. Everyone said the setup was insane, with their history, but the kids adored Rahim, and his cooking had only improved. Since Check and Syria now owned a whole brownstone, they installed a larger kitchen for Rahim and gave him a room on the top floor. They're happy as clams, say the neighbors, who should know, since they've only called the police twice this year, and claim that not a single window has been smashed all summer.

It must be nice, Rachel imagines, with a caterer around, always big salads and cakes left over, so that Check can easily invite his band over without Syria shattering her last year's work over the distance of two floors.

Evidently Rahim has become quite a ladies' man, with no sign of settling down. Every weekend it's a different dark little dancer skittering up the stairs, trying not to wake the kids. Little wonder, too; he's turned into a real jewel, that pearly smile matured with a tiny sinister glimmer—all style, of course, he's a complete sweetheart. He always was, and people "don't change," says Checker, "they just get more and more the same."

Frankly, there are evenings when her business has been edging toward the red and the kids take forever getting ready for bed that Rachel is actually relieved she didn't marry Checker Secretti. She doesn't have the constitution for it. Sometimes all she wants is to lie in front of the TV and watch something stupid, munching greasy popcorn. Lyndon is good for that, for around him she never feels, as she always has with Checker, the compunction to be spectacular, even if in the old days all she could muster was being spectacularly morose.

And she definitely couldn't have taken the "B Side," as Checker calls it. Check says his "siestas" are milder now, but his stories from the Derailleur days are harrowing—like the time he lay down on a Central Park bench and didn't move for five days, with wind, rain, and no food. When he and Syria were first married, she actually locked him in the apartment until it was over. Rachel will never forget last year, knocking on a door that usually led to a living room, which suddenly journeyed to the center of the earth. She'd looked in Checker's eyes and seen nothing but lurching magma, black rock, the shifting of continental plates, Checker's bright mantle from the underside. Screeching, she'd run down the stairs, like a little girl afraid of the dark.

Furthermore, as a professional, Check can't disappear right before a gig at the Omni in Atlanta, and he sometimes gives a concert of a different hue—encores of "A Cappella in the Underpass," midnight blues. Besides, "Power is power," as Tyrone told him long ago, and Check has begun to discover that he is less Jekyll and Hyde than a coin with its flip side, heads or tails, hard currency. More and more at his best, too, Checker brings his knives together, blades meeting and clicking, pleasure and pain finally, somehow, the same emotion. For while Checker watches undulating crowds at the Omni, Lena is developing inoperable cataracts, living in a fog no longer of her own choosing, as one generation's vision literally gives over to another's—increasingly one that melds the glee of careening forward with the sorrow of looking back, a bittersweetness less a result of getting older than of getting more intelligent.

Every once in a while, someone in Plato's wonders out loud, "Whatever happened to Eaton Striker?" No one seems to know for sure. Maybe Eaton's found a band his speed to do small clubs and weddings, resolutely settling down to a less elaborate success than he might once have hoped for. Maybe he's a drum instructor. Or maybe he went to law school, realizing he wouldn't make his mark in rock and roll, and finding a better use for his talents. Maybe he's found a girl who admires him and makes him feel so important that he no longer needs the approbation of several million fans. Maybe he's quietly disappointed about the drumming, but sees it as what he did when he was young and remembers his nights in Plato's warmly, recalling the parking meter incident with distress. Maybe he's followed Checker's career, giving the albums to his friends as Christmas presents. Maybe he has his own little boy now, who comes down to the basement in Eaton's suburban split-level to watch his father knock around on the old set, Eaton playing along with the radio, smiling when "Hundred-Dollar Peanuts" comes on, noting he still can't keep up with the guy. What amazing subtlety. What playfulness—

"You know, Checker Secretti was a friend of mine," he might confide to his son, whose jaw would drop.

"Bull," says the little boy.

"No bull. In fact, I discovered him," says Eaton shyly.

"Bull," says the little boy.

B ull," says Caldwell.
"Bullshit," says J.K.

Pretty much everyone says, "Bull." Pretty much everyone thinks that's not what happened to Eaton Striker.

T here have been times, though, that Check's been reminded of his old friend, like when he talked to a musician who recorded in the studio next door. The man had used a new session man once or twice, though the drummer hadn't meshed and they found someone else. "But the guy went blooey, Check. Like a neutron bomb. Took down the whole band, no human life remained. No joke, like, only the mics were still standing. This is gonna cost thousands in therapy. My people are *mangled*, man. Guitars, shit, they can't even pick their *noses* without bursting into tears—"

"What's his name?"

"Man, I don't even remember. Wish I did, actually. Cause there should be warnings on that package. Somebody should hang a bell around his neck."

Later, there was a reviewer in *Rolling Stone* who gave Check the most scathing criticism of his career. *Die, Daddy, Die* was "treacly with mindless positivism. Gushy and gaga with a child-ishness we are explicitly instructed to admire, Secretti once more oozes self-congratulation and star-struck awe at finding himself on stage. Appalled by Secretti's paucity of sophistication, this reviewer is just as incredulous." The byline read "Wylie Powers," and he's never appeared in the magazine again.

Likewise, there are countless trails of kicked cats and censured children and waitresses who had to take back turkey sandwiches because the customer had asked for Russian on the *side*. But very likely, none of these people has been Eaton Striker.

There was one morning not long ago, about five—Check had been rehearsing all night and asked his driver to let him out a few blocks from home. It was an interesting time of day, with that eerie indeterminate light, grainy like photographs blown up too many times. The sun hadn't risen yet, but the neighborhood was newly visible anyway, as if the brownstones and rose gardens glowed of their own accord. Check turned into the all-night bagelry that had so cheered Rachel years before at about this time of morning, when suddenly Checker's chest stabbed and vaulted; swallowing, he pivoted on his heel and kept on walking, fast, until, safely at the corner, he broke into a run. He didn't pick up any breakfast but went straight home, closing the door behind him with both hands and panting with his back against the door, his palms flat on its wood as if to continually confirm that it was closed. Syria had recently come home; she walked into the hall still in her drenched work shirt and stopped. "You look green. What happened?"

Checker's heart was still pounding, and he didn't reply right away because he was so puzzled. "Why should I be afraid of him?"

"Who?"

"At the bagelry, I thought—I thought I saw Eaton Striker."

Syria slipped her long, scarred fingers around his neck. "And he frightened you?"

"I don't know if it was him. But he gave me a terrible look. Whoever it was, he recognized me. And on his face, there was this flat—blank—hatred. His eyes were black, but dead, you know? It was dead hatred, I don't know how else to describe it." He shivered, and Syria took him to bed.

Dead hatred. There comes a point when even dissatisfaction is dissatisfying. Maybe that wasn't Eaton Striker, but no matter—there are a lot of Eaton Strikers walking around, stopping at all-night bagelries at five in the morning. They are dangerous, and they should frighten you. Actually, they're insane. But there are varieties of dementia we have to permit on the street, because we can't lock up half the country.

Dead hatred. When Eaton was nineteen he had bite, as Check said; his eyes glittered; he loved rock and roll. He was young and still sustained by his own resentments. Close enough to a few bright moments in high school, he could still maintain a version of himself as a member of the ascendancy—being young is like that, you can do anything because you've done nothing, and it's wonderful; pure potential is a beautiful thing. So at nineteen Eaton had energy and he was naïve. But over time there's no fun left in scorning songs on the radio, and the joylessness of envy feeds it. Wherever Eaton is, he is likely still sealed in Checker's plastic bag; its sides are streaked like the walls of subway bathrooms; the air is fetid now, and dark.

*   *   *

S o the Fire Queen is living with a rock star. Journalists ask only about her husband. Lately she's decided: I tested him; now he tests me. It's fair.

For after she married Checker, Syria's bones grew more attenuated and translucent; many of them shattered. Their suggestion of mortality didn't cheer the glass market, with a taste for pretty things. Exquisite but gruesome, her slides came back from galleries overnight by return mail.

Anyway, that whole showdown over taking care of the kids and cooking—that's what they told their friends it was about. But the real problem was believing what other people said. Check started acting put-upon when she asked him to pick up some boxes for goblets, as if that was too trivial for Mr. MTV . . . And then she'd get another rejection from a glass show, in Portland, of all places . . . Well, it's true, both acceptance and rejection are traps, and Syria is now amazed that Checker sensed this as young as nineteen. But together with Rahim they once more built a separate kingdom, where even such an absurd threesome is possible, and there is only music and color and glass; talk and baklava and children.

If you haven't heard of Syria Pyramus, that's all right. She still loves the late nights when Checker is through with a gig and, exhausted, drops by the studio while she's just finishing a piece. Then she shows him the one from the night before, now out of the annealer, and he sits on the bench and turns it in his hands, holding it up to the light of the furnace with his eyes glistening, running his finger down the curved crimson femur. He sets it down on the bench with care, and kisses her. Along with the loyal roar of the gas, the shine of fire in her own sweat, the languid droop of melted sand, their regular vacations to volcanoes, and the spectacular arguments she sometimes stages just to keep her edges honed, Syria is happy.

F or gradually they will all stop making fun of happiness. The Derailleurs' disbandment, the Triborough—only the first pebbles in an avalanche of disappointment and despair. One by one their parents will die, their uncles, their sisters, their best friends from high school they'll have been meaning to write to for ages and now cannot. J.K.'s daughter will come down with leukemia at fourteen. Caldwell will develop a drinking problem. Howard, later managing a whole stable of musicians, will finally get in over his head, and Checker will have to manufacture an album in six weeks, like Dostoyevsky writing *The Gambler* just to get his friend out of hock. The United States will be suddenly and dangerously at war in an obscure corner of the world before anyone outside Princeton can spell the place correctly and newscasters are still stressing the wrong syllable of the word.

So they will learn to take good luck with gratitude, finding in the midst of this mire occasional examples, as Checker Secretti will always remain, of delight, no longer a suspect quality, no longer to be revealed as empty. Single evenings with the radio on and their feet propped on the kitchen table will arrive like checks in the mail.

And they will learn about satisfaction, that Eaton Striker didn't understand it. That while admitting Rachel's voice is "thin" provides a kind of blue-black pleasure, a special crooked smile, Howard will never forget that the richest moment of his life was underwater, holding on to Checker Secretti's hand in the middle of a whirlpool under Hell Gate and feeling the drummer pull him lower, and lower, and still not letting go.

index of song titles

about the book

Writing *Checker and The Derailleurs*

Every once in a while I meet someone who's read *Checker and The Derailleurs*, a book that seems to inspire a distinctly collusive passion. Previous to the HarperCollins reissue, I was abashed to learn that apparently *Checker* had become a "cult novel," its furry, rifled Penguin paperbacks passed hand-to-hand; considering the modest sales record of its initial printing, that would be a very small cult indeed. Since I have a particularly tender relationship to this novel, I'm grateful to HarperCollins for giving it a second life.

As a rule, I don't let working titles out of the house; they're commonly so ghastly. Yet while my editor wisely dissuaded me from using the manuscript's original title—it has kooky religious connotations—*The Ecstatic* did aptly capture its protagonist. I wanted to write about a character who lived his life to the fullest and was able to savor small, simple pleasures to a degree that made him irresistibly attractive to other people.

While writing the novel, I was living alone in Astoria, Queens, a block from the roiling East River and across the street from the charming Astoria Park. I loved the neighborhood, then still retaining the vestiges of Italian and Greek immigration (much of Astoria has since gone Hispanic): delis with halva and feta, bakeries with big sesame-encrusted breadsticks, tiny manicured front gardens with Virgin Mary statuettes. It was one of those rare New York niches where not many novels had been set.

I stayed up late in those days, playing Joni Mitchell and Kate Bush loudly enough that neighbors would thump on my floor. Often restless after midnight, I'd escape my tiny rent-stabilized apartment to run headlong beside the river and up and down the hillocks of the park. Some summer nights I'd slip a swimming suit under my cutoffs and sneak over the fence to glide through the park's huge blue night-lit public pool. During the day, when I wasn't cycling between my freshman composition classes in three different New York boroughs, I thought I was writing about a fictional drummer. Looking back, I get it: I was writing about myself. Rather, about the best of myself.

That is a self, I am sad to say, who no longer streaks out after midnight for the sheer thrill of the breeze through her hair or leaps in midair lunges down the steep hill beside the baseball field. Oh, I still run, but only as a discipline, a dreaded trudge that I'm always glad to see the back of when I return. I no longer sneak into municipal pools after they've closed. Thing is, I was once capable of the ebullience that Checker Secretti exudes in spades. If I paid for those manic phases with equally extreme funks, the even keel of middle age is terribly dreary in comparison.

In *Checker*, I wanted to write about not only joy but goodness, although goodness, as opposed to virtue, may be joy by another name. It's difficult to do justice to goodness, a quality that can be surprisingly off-putting; it's often confused with prissy rectitude, mere obedience, or posey, self-aggrandizing righteousness. Using Fyodor Dostoyevsky's *The Idiot* as a model, I gathered that goodness was best made appealing by putting it in danger. Thus Eaton Striker was born—Checker's envious nemesis, a Salieri-like creature who would become Checker if he could but, lacking Checker's savoir faire, would opt for second-best: to destroy him.

Hilariously, given that my parents were both professional Presbyterians, only when a deprecating review slagged off *Checker* as a painfully obvious retelling of the Christ story did it ever occur to me that my plot might have been influenced by the New Testament. I'm an atheist in theory, but I guess there's really no getting away from your roots.

A word about the illustrations: One of my early memories is of being quizzed by a friend of my father's about what I wanted to do when I grew up. I was eight or nine years old, and my enthusiasms were then equally divided between storytelling and crayons. So I told this adult that I wanted to write and illustrate my own books. He treated me to a patronizing chuckle. "But won't you want to write books for grown-ups?" I said, I guess; I hadn't thought about it. "Because grown-up books don't *have* pictures." Bam, a hole in my balloon. It took me more than twenty years to prove this family friend wrong, but finally inserting my rapidograph drawings of my characters in *Checker* was satisfying payback.

Also, a word about drumming: I like it. I have a curious

habit of falling in love with drummers, and have now—knock on wood—settled down for keeps with a drummer who has a long, distinguished career in jazz. (Indeed, my husband read and loved *Checker* before we met, which helped to grease the romantic skids in advance.) I don't know of any instrument that's sexier, that requires more astonishing independence of all four limbs, or that looks, from the outside, like more fun. Delightfully, the drums retain a conspicuous connection to their primitive, child-like antecedents: bashing pots and pans with serving spoons and beating logs with sticks.

As for the song lyrics, I had an absolute blast writing them, and if anyone is ever inspired to set them to music, they're welcome to give it a try. Indeed, the stylish London singer-songwriter Marsha Swanson has done just that. The demo she sent me of all the lyrics in the novel set to music was delightful, and she hopes to produce an even more finished recording in the near future.

Among my novels, *Checker* remains one of my favorites, if only because I fear that I'll never be able to write a book of this nature again. Innocent, upbeat, bursting with appetite for being alive, and—dare I say it—*sweet*, this rock-and-roll fairy tale is a rare Shriver novel with a straight-up happy ending. At the time, I imagined that I was writing about "young people" from the perspective of my hoary old age. Only now do I realize that, at not even thirty, I was still a baby myself. That must be a signature of being young: that you think you're not.

Lionel Shriver
2015